LOVE'S DWELLING

LOVE'S DWELLING

AMISH BLESSINGS

Kelly Irvin

ZONDERVAN

Love's Dwelling

Copyright © 2021 by Kelly Irvin

Requests for information should be addressed to:
Zondervan, *3900 Sparks Dr. SE, Grand Rapids, Michigan 49546*

ISBN 978-0-310-36448-1 (softcover)
ISBN 978-0-310-36449-8 (ebook)
ISBN 978-0-310-36451-1 (downloadable audio)
ISBN 978-0-8407-1223-3 (mass market)

Library of Congress Cataloging-in-Publication Data
CIP data available upon request.

Printed in the United States of America

23 24 25 26 27 CWM 10 9 8 7 6 5 4 3 2 1

To my Kansas family,
love always.

My Father's house has many rooms; if that were not so, would I have told you that I am going there to prepare a place for you? And if I go and prepare a place for you, I will come back and take you to be with me that you also may be where I am. You know the way to the place where I am going.

JOHN 14:2–4

Glossary of Deutsch*

Ausbund: hymnal used by the Amish for church services
beheef dich: behave yourself
bobblemoul: blabbermouth
bopli, boplin: baby, babies
bruder: brother
bu: boy
daadi: grandpa
daed: father
danki: thank you
Das Loblied: "The Praise Song"
dawdy haus: attached home for grandparents when they retire
dochder: daughter
dumkupp: dummy
Englischer: English or non-Amish
eck: the corner table where the bride and groom sit at the wedding reception
fraa: wife
Gelassenheit: submission to the will of God; attitude of tranquil humility
gern gschehme: you're welcome
Gmay: church district
Gott: God
guder mariye: good morning
guder nammidaag: good afternoon

gut: good

gut nacht: good night

hund: dog

Ich bin gut: I am good

Ich bin schlescht: I am bad

Ich bin zimmlich gut: I am pretty good

Ich bin zimmlich schlescht: I am pretty bad

jah: yes

kaffi: coffee

kapp: prayer cap or head covering worn by Amish women

kind: child

kinner: children

kinnskind, kinnskinner: grandchild, grandchildren

maedel: girl

mammi: grandma

mann: husband

meidung: shunned, excommunicated from the Amish church

mudder: mother

nee: no

onkel: uncle

Ordnung: written and unwritten rules in an Amish district

rumspringa: period of "running around" for Amish youth
   before they decide whether they want to be baptized into
   the Amish faith

schmeir: a sandwich spread made of peanut butter, corn syrup,
   and marshmallow cream

schnee: snow

schul: school

schweschder: sister

sei so gut: please (be so kind)

suh: son

Wie bischt du: How are you?
wunderbarr: wonderful

*The German dialect spoken by the Amish is not a written language and varies depending on the location and origin of the settlement. These spellings are approximations. Most Amish children learn English after they start school. They also learn high German, which is used in their Sunday services.

Featured Haven Families

Delbert (minister) and Loretta Byler

Emily   Carrie   Nicholas   Chrissie   John   Robert

Job and Dinah Keim

Perry   Georgia
(deceased)

Georgia Keim-Carter and Clayton Carter

Mason
Keim

Bobby
Caldwell

Kevin
Caldwell

Kathy
Spencer

Donny
Spencer

Jennie
Spencer

Caleb and Elizabeth Mast

Rachel   Joel   Elinor   Melissa   David   Micah   Anna

Bryan (bishop) and Esther Miller

Michael   Nadine   Serena   Micah

Leroy and Connie Weaver

Cassie

Samuel (deacon) and Anita Zimmerman

Adam   Jana   Seth

CHAPTER 1

A robin perched on top of the empty bird feeder outside the kitchen window. Cassie Weaver paused, a package of pork chops in her hand, to study it. Didn't the dandy with his red-breasted plumage know he was early? Spring wouldn't show its face in southern Kansas for another month. February was an in-between month when Mother Nature couldn't seem to make up her mind. Five inches of snow had fallen since dawn, and the fluffy wet stuff continued to accumulate.

Working for Dinah Keim, who was fast losing her eyesight, made Cassie acutely aware of the blessing of sight. Not to be able to see a ruby-throated hummingbird clothed in delicate, shimmering greens and blues, sipping nectar from purple, pink, and red pansies, would diminish her world. Having seen it and now to be bereft of it only made matters worse. Cassie stopped to count her blessings. She could see, which meant every day was a beautiful day, beginning with a brilliant sunrise and ending with her sister sunset.

Life was good.

"Cassie? Are you there?"

Dinah's arrival signaled that the time for gathering wool had ended. Cassie forked the pork chops into a cast-iron skillet on the stove and turned. "I'm here. I'm making pork chops and fried potatoes for lunch. Did you check your blood sugar?"

Her wooden walking stick making a *thunk, thunk* on the oak floor, Dinah trotted to the kitchen table with a sure step. Every piece of furniture in the house remained in the same resting spot it had occupied for years, so she never had to worry about colliding with a misplaced chair or table. "I feel light-headed."

"The potatoes are done. The slaw is on the table. All I have to do is fry the pork chops. Check your blood sugar while I finish." Cassie turned up the gas flame under the skillet and strode to the propane-powered refrigerator. The never-ending balancing act between too high and too low blood sugar had become more difficult as Dinah's frail body failed her. "I'll get your shot ready."

When she started working for Dinah and Job Keim six years ago, Cassie had been squeamish and then timid about the shots. Not anymore. Were she not Plain, she might have been a nurse or even a doctor. Snorting under her breath at the fanciful thought, she took a tiny bottle of insulin from the box on the refrigerator shelf, placed it on a saucer, and added a syringe. The cotton balls and alcohol were already on the table.

"Something smells *gut.*" Job barged through the back door and stamped snow from his enormous work boots on the rug. Her employer had the biggest feet Cassie had ever seen. But then, he stood well over six feet tall. The feet matched the man. "I shoveled off the walk, which makes no sense, I know, fed the animals, fixed that hole in the fence, and chopped wood. Now I could eat an elephant."

"No elephants on the menu today." Cassie smiled as she set the saucer in front of Dinah. "But I can see if the meat market offers it next time I go into Yoder. It's probably more tender than the last chuck roast I bought from them."

Job's belly laugh always made Cassie laugh with him. His smile wide over a long black beard shot through with silver, he slapped his broad chest and let one rip. "You tickle my innards, girl."

"Someone's coming." Her head cocked, forehead furrowed, Dinah leaned forward in her chair. Her thick-lensed black glasses magnified her blue eyes. Failing eyesight had amplified her hearing. "Sounds like a van or an SUV coming up the drive."

"Somebody has gut timing, *fraa*." Job squeezed his wife's shoulder as he walked past her. "They managed to arrive just in time for lunch. I'll meet them at the front door."

If they wanted lunch, Cassie was in trouble. Six thin pork chops wouldn't go far—especially with Job's insatiable appetite. The man didn't have an ounce of fat on his sixty-seven-year-old frame, even though he inhaled all the food Cassie put in front of him.

"I wonder who it could be." Dinah took care of her finger poke, used the test strip, and handed it to Cassie to read. "How am I doing?"

"Time for the shot and then some food. Guests or no, you need to eat." Cassie administered the shot with an ease that her sixteen-year-old younger self would not have thought possible. "There you go. I have some sugar-free banana pudding with vanilla wafers and banana slices for dessert."

That drew a delighted whoop from Dinah, who barely seemed to register the injection anymore. The dessert was a favorite. Her sweet tooth seemed to grow in direct proportion to her disease. She preferred chocolate-frosted brownies or apple pie with ice cream, but even those made with sugar substitutes had to be saved for special occasions. Her thin body was just what the doctor had ordered.

"Fraa, come out here." Job no longer sounded jovial. "Now."

"She just had her shot," Cassie called back. She shook her finger at Dinah. "I'll go. Start with a roll. They're in the basket on the table, along with the butter."

She turned off the stove and moved the skillet to a back burner.

"Dinah, you need to get out here."

Something akin to bewilderment mixed with panic reverberated in Job's deep voice. He didn't rattle easily or at all. Cassie raced down the hallway to the living room. Job stood in the foyer. He'd taken off his black wool hat. He kept running his big hand through curls more silver than black so they stood up all over his head.

Lined up in front of the fireplace stood five English children in stair-step fashion. The oldest one, a boy, held the youngest one, a girl whose red cheeks and wet face told the story of recent tears. A gray-haired lady in a green pantsuit, a worn leather satchel in one hand, joined them.

In the doorway loomed one more visitor. A tall, muscle-laden man with charcoal-black hair and blue eyes who methodically wiped his muddy work boots on the rug. He wore faded jeans with holey knees, an untucked red plaid flannel shirt, a fleece-lined jean jacket two sizes too big, and a Kansas City Royals baseball cap. Everything about his stance said he'd rather be sitting on a doctor's exam table than standing in the Keims' living room.

"I only have six pork chops." The words came out of Cassie's mouth of their own accord. Embarrassment flooded her. "I mean, I can heat up the leftover roast from last night's supper—"

"They're not here for lunch." Job settled his wide-brimmed

hat back on his head. His cheeks were damp and his face ashen. "They're—"

"Perry? *Suh*?" One wrinkled hand outstretched, Dinah tottered past Cassie, heading for the man standing on the welcome mat. "Is that you, Suh? Where have you been? I've missed you so much. Where's Georgia? Is she with you?"

"I'm not Perry. He's my uncle. I'm Mason. Mason Keim." The man's big hand sought the doorknob. He took two steps back. "I'm Georgia's son."

"Georgia? Our *dochder*'s suh? *Gott* has answered our prayers." Dinah's face brightened as if a lamp's oil had been replenished and light restored. "Where is she? Where's my dochder?"

Mason Keim's jaw worked. His gaze went to the children who stood oddly silent, too still for kids. The girl with a tangled dark-brown ponytail that reached her waist grabbed the smaller boy's hand. Finally, Mason spoke. "She died."

Confusion clouded Dinah's face, extinguishing the light. "Died?"

The smallest girl buried her head in the boy's shoulder and sobbed.

The walking stick clattered to the floor. Dinah crumpled in a heap beside it.

CHAPTER 2

The girl dressed in an old-fashioned dress and apron directed a troubled frown at Mason. That said it all. He'd messed this up big-time. Just like he did when he told his half brothers and sisters. At twenty-two he had no experience delivering death news. The police officer who'd told him about his mom and Clayton's deaths had been kind but quick. *"Better not to beat around the bush,"* he'd said, with a quick man-pat on Mason's hunched shoulders. Apparently that didn't work with everyone.

Mason dropped to his knees next to the prostrate woman—his grandmother, Dinah Keim, according to the caseworker. Dinah and Job Keim were his grandparents. He'd never had grandparents before and he'd practically killed one of them already. He dug his cell phone from his pocket. "Is she all right? Should I call 911?"

The girl in the dress and apron shook her head. "She fainted, that's all. It was a terrible shock. You should've waited until she sat down to give her such grievous news."

"Let me at her." Job scooped up Dinah—Mason's brain couldn't cope with calling them Grandpa and Grandma—like she weighed no more than a baby. He carried her to the couch and sat down beside her. "It's okay. You're fine."

The naked love on his grizzled, whiskered face was too much to bear. It only existed in cheesy movies, didn't it? His mom and her one-after-the-other husbands sure never stared at each other like that. Leastways not where others could see. Mason stood.

The girl brushed past him. "I'll get her some orange juice, Job. She already took her shot. Her sugar is bound to be low."

Dinah stirred and moaned. "My *bopli*, my bopli."

What was a bopli?

"I know." Job wiped tears from her face with the back of his hand. His thin cheeks seemed to crater under high cheekbones, and his blue eyes shone with unshed tears. Those brilliant blue eyes had been passed down to Mason's mother and to all of his siblings. "But she was gone long ago for us. Dead to us."

Such harsh words. Did he really mean that?

"I'm sorry. I didn't mean to upset her—"

"When?" Dinah strangled the single syllable. "When did she die?"

"Three weeks ago." Mason cleared his throat. "January nineteenth. Just before midnight."

"Where is she now?" Job's arm slid around his wife. She leaned into him. He stared at Mason with despair in his eyes. "When was the funeral?"

A dark, cold, snowy landscape and the images of kids standing around two holes in the ground haunted Mason's dreams. Jennie was so heavy in his arms. Her screams visited him at night. How did a person explain to a four-year-old that Mommy's body had to be put in the ground?

"She's not in her body anymore. She's in heaven with Jesus," he'd whispered over and over again as he stroked the little girl's silky dark-brown hair and tried not to lose his mind.

Bobby's doubtful scowl almost undid Mason. *Yeah, right,* it said. Mason's knowledge of heaven and a guy called Jesus was garnered from the occasional excursion to the closest church with a candlelight service on Christmas Eve.

A white lie to comfort a child. Surely God understood that. "She's in a cemetery in Wichita, close to where we live. Her and Clayton both."

The bills kept coming—ambulances, ER, doctors, two burials. Every effort had been made to save his mother and Clayton. For which Mason was deeply grateful. But they had no insurance and had made no arrangements in event of their deaths.

"We would've liked to have been there." Job's arms hung slack at his side. Bleak sadness made his face ancient. "She was our daughter."

"We didn't know about you then." They hadn't even known the Keims existed until Mason found a safe-deposit box key in Mom's jewelry box. That led to the living will. But that was another story. "We thought Uncle Perry was our only family."

He might be their only family, but Perry hadn't let that influence his decision not to take them into his home. His reasons had been plentiful—not enough money, not enough room, not enough experience with children. *"You can handle it, Mason. You've been taking care of them for years."*

He'd actually been able to say that sentence with a straight face.

"Maybe I should take it from here." Delores Blanchard, the caseworker assigned to his half siblings by the Kansas Department of Child and Family Services, made a *tsk-tsk* sound. Her doughy double chin shook like it always did when she was stressed. Which was most of the time. "Mrs. Keim isn't the only one who's upset. Why don't you calm down your brothers and sisters?"

Mrs. Blanchard was right. The kids huddled together in a

tight cluster, faces worried, full of fear and uncertainty. They'd lost their parents. Now they were being forced from the only home they'd ever known to live with strangers. They were perfectly capable of taking care of themselves. As Uncle Perry had pointed out, they'd been doing it for years.

Mason trudged over to them. Bobby, the oldest at sixteen, shushed Jennie, the youngest at four. Even though they were the product of two different fathers, his siblings had a strong family resemblance—blue eyes and various shades of dark-brown to black hair. Like their mother, when she didn't treat herself to one of a rainbow of hair colors.

"There's nothing to be afraid of, Jennie. You didn't do nothing wrong." Bobby rubbed his sister's back with a practiced hand. Like Mason, Bobby had a lot of experience parenting. He scowled at Mason. "Can we go home now?"

"This is what Mom wanted." Mason took Jennie from him. She immediately wiped her runny nose on his coat and wrapped her arms around his neck in a stranglehold. He smoothed her tangled brown curls. "It's okay, sweetie. She'll be okay. She was just surprised to see all of us. Like a really big surprise birthday party."

"I want to go home too. I promise to be good. " Donny, who was six, tugged at Mason's arm. "I'll remember to put my dirty clothes in the basket, and I'll wash all the dishes every night. I'll be good, I promise."

"You're not being punished. These folks are family. Mommy wanted you to get to know them." Mason sucked in a breath. Why hadn't she introduced them to the Keims years ago? It would've been nice to have family. To have grandparents. Finding that living will had been the sucker punch that kept on giving. "You'll be better off here."

A six-year-old couldn't begin to understand the logistics of single parenting five younger kids. The cost of day care, food, clothing, medical bills, utilities, and rent. Mrs. Blanchard and the advocate appointed by the judge to make sure the kids' best interests were safeguarded had helped him fill out mountains of paperwork to get government assistance. Otherwise he'd still be drowning in red tape. Until he found the will, he'd had everything under control. Almost.

"Mason's right. We need to honor your mother's wishes." Mrs. Blanchard's head bobbed in agreement, which meant her double chin bobbed too. She'd made it clear from the get-go that the will gave the Keims legal standing with the children—whether he liked it or not. "You'll love it here out in the country with all this fresh air and farm animals."

As an adult, he could sue for custody. If he could afford to hire a lawyer, which he couldn't. The bigger question—the one he'd wrestled with every day since he'd discovered the will—revolved around what was best for them. He hadn't wanted to show it to Mrs. Blanchard, but it didn't seem right to hide it or destroy it. To deny them the chance to have grandparents would be wrong. "That's right. I saw horses when we pulled into the yard, and chickens and a cat."

Mrs. Blanchard edged closer to the couch. She settled in a straight-back chair on the other side of a thick, homemade coffee table. "Mr. Keim—"

"It's Job."

"Mr. and Mrs. Keim, I'm sorry we had to come to you in such unfortunate circumstances. Your daughter left a document that specifically stated that she wanted you to have custody of her children should anything happen to her."

The girl was back with a glass of orange juice. She turned

and smiled for the first time. She had dimples. She didn't dress like any girl Mason had ever known. No makeup, no bling. Every bit of her arms and legs was covered by her long dress. Yet this girl was far prettier than most. "Welcome, Georgia's children, welcome."

Her face still lit up like she'd just received a new car for her sixteenth birthday, the girl helped Dinah with the glass of juice. "Drink it all up, Dinah. You'll need your strength. You have five new grandchildren to get to know." Her smile tentative, she glanced at Mason. "Or is it six? Dinah thought you were her son, Perry."

Stop staring. She wasn't much bigger than a kid herself. She had dark-cocoa-brown eyes and fair skin. The little bit of hair showing outside the white covering on her head was a shiny brown. She didn't resemble his mother at all. Besides, she was too young to be one of the Keims' kids. A grandkid maybe. His uncle Perry had never married, and his mother said he was her only sibling.

"Mason? The young lady asked you a question." Mrs. Blanchard's thin eyebrows rose. "Don't be rude."

"Sorry . . . I was . . . Yeah, Georgia was my mother. Who are you?"

"I'm Cassie Weaver. I keep house for Job and Dinah. I'm sorry for your loss. Both your parents in one fell swoop. That's so sad."

"Clayton wasn't my father." Mason couldn't let it go, even though it might be easier. "He wasn't father to any of us. He was Mom's third husband."

Their sudden frowns said it all. He might as well have said she was a polygamist or a prostitute. Did they know she had never married Mason's father? Probably not. That might induce a stroke for the two older folks. Cassie's smile melted into sad disbelief.

"Jake Caldwell is Bobby and Kevin's dad. They don't remember him, but I do." Enough to know he was an okay guy who sold used cars and mostly held down a job. But he drank too much. "Mom ran him off after she caught him kissing a sales associate behind the counter at Buck Doolittle's Used Cars." Why had he shared all that?

Mason gritted his teeth, sucked in air, and forced himself to keep going. "Deacon Spencer is Kathy, Donny, and Jennie's dad. He's in the army. He's stationed in Germany now."

"He's nice," Kathy volunteered. She slung her waist-length dark-brown hair over her thin shoulders, dug around in a ratty backpack, and produced three tattered paperbacks. *Little House on the Prairie*, a Nancy Drew mystery, and an Amelia Bedelia book. All of which she'd read to Jennie and Donny at least twenty times. "He brought me these. He knows I like to read."

"Reading is good." Dinah's smile looked determined. "He sounds like a good father."

"He is." Kathy sighed and rubbed her small hand over the covers. "I miss him."

Mom had married Deacon after knowing him for two months. Kathy came along eight months later. By that time Deacon was doing a two-year tour in Afghanistan. When he was around, he was a stand-up guy who bought presents for all the kids—not just his. After he returned to the States, Donny made an appearance, followed by Jennie two years later. Deacon's request that Mom follow him overseas for a six-year stint in Germany had resulted in a sudden divorce. Jennie was two when Clayton entered the scene.

Not to think ill of the dead, but no one would miss Clayton. He was a mean drunk with a foul mouth and a wandering eye. The two did nothing but fight and make up from day one.

"So now you know all the parties involved." Mrs. Blanchard pulled a folder from her satchel and opened it. "We've been unable to find Mr. Caldwell thus far, but we'll continue to search for him. Mr. Spencer has been notified of your daughter's death. We haven't received a response from him. Either or both could contest your daughter's will and seek custody of their children."

"They're not coming forward." Mason fought to hide his bitterness. "They've never been real parents."

Mrs. Blanchard gave a long-suffering sigh. "We'll cross that bridge when we come to it, Mason."

Mason waited. Surely one of them would ask. There was a hole in the story. Or maybe they knew and didn't want to talk about their daughter having a baby out of wedlock. Did anyone even use that phrase anymore? Not in the real world. In the Amish world, it was probably the ultimate sin. Maybe it didn't matter anymore. He was an adult and no man had ever come forward to claim his role as father.

He certainly wouldn't do it now that the one person who could confirm his story was six feet under.

"In the meantime, Job and Dinah always wanted a house full of children." Cassie clapped her hands and smiled so big her face had to hurt. "What a gift from God that they have this big house with plenty of bedrooms for their grandchildren. There's a big yard and a pond for swimming and fishing. You would like that, wouldn't you?"

That last part was directed to the kids. Donny nodded and grinned. Kathy chewed her lip, her hands clasped as if in prayer.

"I don't know."

Job and Mrs. Blanchard spoke at the same time.

They stared at each other. "Go ahead." Job gestured at the caseworker. "You first."

"It seems like Mrs. Keim is in poor health. If that's the case, she may not be in a position to care for five young, rambunctious children. Cook meals, buy clothes and other provisions, supervise bathtime, bedtime, make sure they go to school . . ." Forehead wrinkled, Mrs. Blanchard studied Job and Dinah as if seeing them clearly for the first time. "You folks do send your children to school, don't you?"

"Yes, we do." Job didn't seem affronted by the question. He leaned forward, hands on his knees. "Through eighth grade—"

"I won't go to school?" Bobby's incredulous shout filled the small living room. "I have to graduate high school to go to the police academy. I'm not staying here. This sucks."

"Language, Bobby." Mrs. Blanchard swiveled to shoot a frown at him. "I know you're having a rough time, but that's never an excuse for being rude."

Maybe this was an out. Maybe the family court judge would see this as a valid reason to set aside the will. Mason kept that thought to himself. "Chill out, Bobby. Let the man finish."

"We share a grade school with English families in Yoder. Our kids attend first through eighth. After that our teenagers receive what the state likes to call vocational training. They learn to farm, raise food, take care of livestock. Some learn carpentry, dairy farming, or other skills."

Job propped his elbows on his knees and steepled his long fingers. "We can give these children, our grandchildren, everything they need as far as clothes, food, and such, but my wife's health does worry me a bit. It's a hard thing you're asking. I can see our daughter's face in every one of these precious children. We prayed for years to have children. God gave us two and they both chose to leave the faith. Now to have grandchildren . . ."

Bobby clamped his mouth shut and wiped at his face with both hands.

No one spoke for a second. Kathy released Donny's hand. She trotted past Mason, scooted around Mrs. Blanchard's chair, and stopped in front of Job. "Don't be sad, Grandpa. We'll stay if you want us to." She patted his knee. "When I'm sad I sing songs. That's what Mommy told me to do. Do you want me to sing you a song?"

"Maybe another time." Job took her hand and squeezed. "What's your name?"

"I'm Kathy. It's really Katherine, but nobody calls me that unless I'm in trouble. I never get in trouble. I'm eight." She pointed at the others. "Should I introduce you to the rest of my brothers and sisters?"

"Give us a minute, Kathy," Mrs. Blanchard intervened. "Please, honey. Go sit with Mason, why don't you? The grown-ups need to work some things out before you get too comfortable."

Kathy appeared puzzled, but she did as she was told. She was like that. Mason put his arm around her and hugged her. "You did good."

She smiled up at him. "That's our grandpa. We never had a grandpa before."

"I know."

Whether Job Keim would claim the title still remained to be seen. He might simply be another in a long line of disappointments for Kathy and the rest of Georgia Keim-Carter's kids.

"Maybe they could come visit, you know, like grandchildren

do." Job rubbed already-red eyes. "If they could be placed in a home nearby—"

Dinah set her juice glass on the coffee table with a bang. Her hands flailing, she jabbered a string of words in a language Mason had heard on his construction jobs in Wichita that included Amish workers. Once he'd heard Mom singing a song in that language while planting flowers in their front yard. When he asked her about it, she shrugged and said it was made up. *"My own special language from when I was a kid."*

At least part of it was true. "What's she saying?"

"She wants the children here. She insists that they be allowed to stay." Cassie sounded as if she approved of her employer's stance. "She says she'll block the door if someone tries to take them away. I believe she would too."

Dinah still had plenty of get-up-and-go in her skinny body. She wanted the kids. That was a nice change.

Job's gruff response came more slowly. His hands reached for his wife's. She accepted his offering, but her words came faster, seeming to fall over each other in an effort to be heard.

A person didn't have to know the language to understand what was happening. Two people who'd been married forever were pouring their hearts out to each other over something important, something that would change everything. They were in it together.

Mason had never seen such a sight in his life, but he still recognized it. He still wanted it. If the Keims took the kids, he might be able to have it, if the right girl came along at the right time.

No, that was selfish. Stupid and selfish. The kids needed him. "It's okay. If they don't think they can do it, the kids can stay with me. I'll become their guardian. I can take care of them."

"Mason, we've been over this. Your mom's wishes were

specific. And you can't support six people on what you make in construction."

"I'll get a second job."

"And who'll supervise the children?"

"Me." Bobby's bellowing didn't help Mason's case. "Just like always. Nothing will have changed."

Bobby was a shorter version of Mason. His hair was lighter, more of a burnt-wheat-toast color, but his eyes were just as blue. His shoulders were broad, which was good because he served as Mason's second in command. He was the master of the microwave. Corn dogs, fish sticks, bagel bites, frozen pizzas, mac 'n' cheese. His arsenal of easy-to-fix meals was almost as good as Mason's.

"No sixteen-year-old high school boy should be responsible for four younger brothers and sisters if there's another option. In this case there is and it's one the court recognizes." Mrs. Blanchard's no-nonsense approach to the world was born of much experience—or so she'd told Mason a dozen times. "Dinah, you thought Mason was your son. Were you confused? Cassie mentioned a shot. Are you on medication?"

Dinah straightened and withdrew her hand from Job's. "I've had diabetes since I turned twenty-six. My mother and my great-aunt both had it. It runs in the family. I take insulin shots, sometimes twice a day." She adjusted her glasses and smiled firmly. "It has taken its toll. My eyesight is affected and my kidneys, and I have numb hands and feet, but I'm not a doddering old fool. I know Perry is much older now. It was a shock, that's all."

Mrs. Blanchard didn't seem convinced.

"I can help Job and Dinah take care of the children." Cassie ran the words together in her obvious excitement. "I'll move in.

I'll do the cooking. I do it now. It's just a matter of cooking a lot more." Her cheeks turned pink as she picked up speed. "Kathy can help. The other kids will help with the cleaning and the laundry and the garden. That's how Plain families work. Most of them have more children than this. We can do it. That is, if you want to have them stay here at the house, Job."

Breathless, she stopped, her hands clasped as if in prayer.

Job's frown deepened. He shook his head. "There's no money to pay you more than we do now, Cassie."

"No need. I'll receive free room and board in exchange for my services. My pay remains the same. It's a perfectly good arrangement for all of us."

Mason swallowed the retort that rose in his throat. He didn't want to do anything to jinx the offer, but the girl was crazy. Cassie obviously had no experience taking care of children. Stay-at-home moms, childcare workers, teachers, and nannies should be paid more than pro basketball players and celebrity actors combined. Anybody who'd spent any amount of time taking care of kids deserved a fat paycheck, a vacation in Aruba, and a presidential medal of honor.

Job squinted as if trying to see the future. He scratched his forehead and studied his boots. Dinah's hand crept back into his. He studied their hands for a while. Finally, he took a long breath. "I reckon if it's what Georgia wanted and it's what my wife wants and with Cassie's willingness to help, we should give it a try. We'll see if we can do it. If that is okay with you, Mrs. Blanchard?"

All nine pairs of eyes in the room turned to stare at Mrs. Blanchard. She nibbled on her lower lip. Her fingernails, painted a pearly white, tapped on the file folder in her lap. "I agree with Job that this is a challenging situation. Let me ask this. You say you can provide for them. You are probably in your sixties, Job, retirement age. How do you plan to pay for the needs of five children? It's a chunk of change. What exactly do you do for a living?"

"The Amish don't exactly retire. Usually the children take over the farm or business and the grandparents move into the *dawdy haus*—a little house attached to the main house. We don't have that option, obviously. I still build furniture to be sold on consignment in a Yoder store. With the snow, you probably didn't notice our big stand out at the road, but when the weather's good we sell vegetables, jams, canned goods, baked goods, and some of my wooden toys. Some get sold in stores in town. Tourists love Yoder. We make our clothes and grow much of our food. Our district will help with whatever we need. Including paying for medical care."

"You no longer farm, as such."

"No. It's not possible to make a living from farming here on such a small piece of property. I plant alfalfa, milo, corn, and such for my needs and to sell to some of the other farms around here, but that's all."

"Understood. This information helps." Her lips pressed together in a thin line, Mrs. Blanchard furiously took notes. Everyone seemed to hold their breath, watching her. Finally, she lifted the pen and used it to shove her glasses up her nose. "Given your daughter's wishes, I have no choice but to agree to this placement. I'll let the children's advocate know. She'll want to visit as well. We'll both want to keep an eye on the situation. Expect visits."

"Yay!" Kathy clapped. "It'll be fun."

Jennie mimicked her big sister. So did Donny and Kevin. Only Bobby seemed gloomy.

Mrs. Blanchard held up her hand. "We had a preliminary hearing in Sedgwick County since that's where the children lived. You live in Reno County. Every Kansas county has different procedures for handling placements in these situations. I'll get back to you on next steps. There will be another hearing at some point for permanent custody. Regardless, it's usually a formality where the parent's wishes are known, the children aren't at risk or in danger, and there are no special needs."

"We don't go to court." The lack of emotion in Job's words matched his stony profile. "It's not our way."

"You'll want legal standing to make decisions about your grandchildren's medical care, and what if the fathers do enter the picture? You'll want to be able to defend your custody. That requires a court hearing."

Job didn't seem convinced, but he nodded. "I'll talk to the bishop about it."

"I have a question." Bobby crossed his arms over his chest. "Does that mean I have to be Amish? No way I'm wearing those clothes."

A good question. Bobby might only be thinking of the clothes, but Mason knew more about it than his little brother did. Amish was a way of life, but it was also a religion. Mom had taken him to church a few times in the early years, mostly at Easter and Christmas. For all her craziness with booze and men, she still seemed to find comfort in it.

If the kids didn't want to convert to the Amish religion, maybe they would still end up with Mason.

It might be what he wanted, but the same question remained: What was best for them?

CHAPTER 3

I t's a gut question."

Ignoring Tater's mournful whine, Cassie pulled her ancient hand-me-down suitcase from under her bed and plopped it on top of the Sunshine and Shadow quilt. The doubt in her mother's words didn't surprise her. Nor did the dog's quick understanding that the suitcase meant Cassie was leaving. Tater was smarter than many people, and Mother had a practical, commonsense approach to life that often didn't leave room for small miracles. The answer to Bobby's question remained to be seen. "The littlest one is four and the oldest one is sixteen. Plus the grown-up one, Mason." Mason with the stormy blue eyes, black hair, and wary stare that said he didn't know who to trust. "They've never been around Plain folks. With time, they might learn to love it here. They might learn to love our life."

"That won't make them Plain." Mother folded a dress and laid it in the suitcase. Her thin fingers caressed the faded cotton. "Job and Dinah will be in for more heartbreak if the *kinner* decide to leave like their *dochder* and *suh* did. Like us, they wanted more *kinner*, but Gott had other plans. I hate to see them go through that again."

If anyone could relate to the Keims' heartbreak, Mother could. Cassie leaned over to scratch behind Tater's ears. His tail thumped. The brown-and-black German shepherd plopped on the piecemeal rug and lowered his graying muzzle until it lay on his big paws. "You would settle right in the way, wouldn't you?"

Still mulling over her mother's view of the situation, Cassie stepped around him and took another dress from the hook on her bedroom wall. "They can't not try because they're afraid of getting hurt again, can they? Wouldn't it be a special gift if these little ones decided to embrace our faith? Wouldn't it be *wunderbarr* to see them grow up and start families here in our *Gmay*?"

"Spoken like the true optimist that you are." Mother chuckled. The crow's-feet around her gray eyes crinkled and her pale cheeks dimpled in the same place that Cassie's did. "Also spoken like someone who hasn't been tested by the fire yet. I am thankful to Gott that you haven't had to know pain yet, but Scripture says there will be trouble in this world. You've never mothered one child, let alone five."

Her smile faded, replaced by a troubled frown. "These aren't puppies or kittens you can feed and give an old blanket to sleep on next to the fireplace. They're not kittens abandoned by their mother that can be bottle-fed until they're able to fend for themselves." Mother knew Cassie too well. Her penchant for mothering every animal on the farm was among Father's favorite stories told to her aunts and uncles. Every animal had a name. When it came time to slaughter a chicken or a pig, she fell into a funk for days and refused to eat the meat. "Don't fall in love with these kinner, Dochder. Remember they aren't yours and they aren't Plain. It's likely they'll leave as quickly as they came into your life."

Don't be softhearted, Cassie. In other words, don't be yourself. Mother had an uncanny way of knowing things that never failed to amaze Cassie. She shrugged and did her best imitation of nonchalance. "Dinah will be there. She may be sickly in body, but she has a sturdy, even fierce, spirit. She'll show me what to do."

Mother was too late. Cassie's heart had a mind of its own. Jennie with her tears. Donny and his pledge to be good. Kathy's determined attempt to cheer up her grandpa. Kevin who said nothing but wiped at his face when he thought no one would see. Bobby was all bluster.

And what about Mason? A feeling, like butterfly wings fluttering against her skin, came and went before she could capture it. Her heart squeezed in painful acknowledgment of the hurt that he wore like armor. Mason had seen more than his share of the world's trouble, and it showed.

"You need to tell your *daed*." Sadness draped itself across Mother's skinny shoulders. "If you're really sure you want to do this."

"*Mudder*, it's a chance to help Dinah and Job have the family they've always wanted. Their hearts were broken when their dochder and suh left."

Cassie had no younger brothers and sisters. This was her chance to practice being a mother. God willing, she would have her own children one day. Lots of them. True, not every couple was blessed with a big family. Not every woman found that one true love. So far no special someone had driven his buggy up to the house to take her for a ride on a crisp spring night. Not yet. She was twenty-two. Most of her friends were married or had beaus. That didn't mean it was too late for her. Whatever God had in store for Cassie, she would embrace it. Starting with these five sweet youngsters.

"Cross that bridge when you come to it, Dochder."

"What bridge?"

"Marriage and motherhood."

Mother saw too much. In order for there to be a marriage, there had to be a man, a suitor. Cassie added nightgowns to her suitcase. Tater raised his head, sighed, and let it fall to his crossed paws. Animals loved without limits. People should do the same. "I'm content. I truly am."

"For now." Mother swooped in and hugged Cassie, quick and hard. Her body, even though it had grown wirier in recent years, offered the same comfort it always had. "What you're doing for the Keims is kind and good-hearted. The right thing to do. Just don't lose yourself there. These jobs aren't meant to be a substitute for becoming a fraa and having your own family."

Cassie drew away. She shut the suitcase and zipped it up. How could she explain to Mother the feeling that had sprouted in the vicinity of her heart earlier in the day? A feeling of breathless anticipation that grew and blossomed. Like she'd been waiting for this moment her entire life only to have it arrive suddenly and in circumstances she could never have imagined. "Don't worry, I won't."

"Worrying is a sin. I'm . . . concerned . . . about what your daed will say."

Mother didn't give Cassie time to respond. She marched from the bedroom, one of five in the house where Cassie had grown up. Tater close on her heels, Cassie followed. Over the years one room had been turned into a sewing room. One served as a guest bedroom, and a third provided storage. As a child Cassie often wondered why no brothers and sisters slept in those rooms. Mother had patiently answered her questions and turned away—but not before Cassie saw the tears in her eyes. Better not to ask.

Mother led the way to the kitchen where a pot of venison chili simmered on the stove. The spicy scent, mingled with the aroma of freshly baked cinnamon rolls, made Cassie's mouth water. She poured food in Tater's bowl and refreshed his water. The dog had made it clear he should eat when they did. Tonight he turned up his nose and plopped down next to the wood-burning stove.

"Fine, be that way." Cassie went to the cabinet and pulled out three bowls and three saucers. "I'll tell Daed over supper."

"You'll give him indigestion."

"Daed will understand—"

The door swung open, bringing with it a rush of frigid evening air. His breath white puffs of steam, Father strolled in. He had the collar of his black woolen coat turned up and his black hat pulled down. "What's for supper, Fraa? Something warm, I hope."

"Chili, hot and spicy, just the way you like it." Mother hustled to the stove. "Wash up. It'll be ready in two shakes."

Five minutes later they were seated at the table, the praying done, and Daed had a serving bowl–sized portion of chili in front of him. He picked up his spoon and stuck it in the soup. He paused. "What is it I'll understand?"

Taking her time to gather her wits, Cassie stirred her chili, dunked her spoon, and blew on a chunk of venison. "What do you mean?"

"I may be old, but my hearing hasn't gone yet. When I came inside, you two were talking about me. I could tell by the guilty expression on your mudder's face." Father grinned at Mother. "Did you know it's impossible for her to lie? Or keep a secret? At least from me."

"It's true." Mother's chagrined look faded after a second, replaced by a demure smile. "But that is a gut thing, isn't it?"

"It works for me." Father swiped an oversized roll from the basket and picked up a butter knife. "So what is it you're afraid to tell me?"

"I'm not afraid." In a way it was fear. Fear of making her father sad. She never wanted to hurt either of her parents. Their lives had been hard enough already. "It's nothing bad."

"So spit it out, Dochder. My hair is turning white while I sit here."

It was an old joke. Father's head held not a single hair. He'd been bald since his early twenties. Mother said it only made him more her "cup of tea."

Cassie tried not to think too much about what that meant.

"I'm moving in with the Keims." Best to spit it out all at once. Of course Father knew Cassie would leave home sooner or later, but in the continued dearth of beaus, he surely expected it to be later. "They need me to help take care of their grandchildren—five of them."

A frown replaced Father's smile. He laid his spoon on the table and wiped his mouth with his napkin. "That seems like a decision we should've talked about first."

"It all happened so fast and it seemed like the only solution to their dilemma." Cassie rushed to explain, outlining the day's events. "After much back-and-forth, Mrs. Blanchard approved of leaving the kinner with Job and Dinah. The oldest son, Mason, will bring the rest of their belongings later in the week. All they brought was enough clothes for a few days. I think Mason was hoping Job would say no and he could take them home again."

Even if he brought their clothes, she would need to make clothes more suited to living in an Amish district. Which brought Cassie back to Bobby's question. How would the boys feel about homemade denim pants with no zippers and long-sleeved blue cotton shirts? What would Kathy think of wearing dresses instead of the flowered leggings, red sweater, and red sneakers she'd worn today?

So many questions. No need to dwell on them. Food, a roof over their heads, and lots of love—those came first. Others would figure out the rest. Cassie's fingers itched to get to the sewing machine.

"It's a hard row to hoe for those kinner, no doubt." Father picked up his spoon, then laid it down again. "When would you go, then?"

"Tonight. I put a casserole in the oven for supper and helped them make up their beds so they'll be ready for bedtime." Cassie's appetite vanished. She shredded her roll into small pieces. "But Dinah needs my help. I need to be there to cook breakfast in the morning—"

"You're needed. I understand. Finish eating. I'll hitch up the buggy." Father dropped his napkin on the table and scooted back his chair. "You take the cinnamon rolls to the kinner. Your mudder and I shouldn't be eating them anyway. Knowing your mudder, she made way more than two people can eat."

"Daed—"

"Dress warm. It's colder than Alaska out there and we'll probably get more *schnee*."

He stalked over to the rack by the back door, grabbed his coat, and left in the same blustery wind that had ushered him into the kitchen.

Mother gathered up her dishes and headed for the sink.

"I'm sorry."

"It's fine. He just needs time to adjust. We knew you would leave home. All kinner do. It just didn't seem like it would be soon, with you not . . ."

"Not courting."

"It's selfish of us, but we like having you around."

Cassie stared at the mess she'd made with her roll. "I like it too."

Evenings spent putting together jigsaw puzzles or playing checkers. Eating popcorn and drinking hot chocolate by the fireplace in the winter and watermelon and lemonade on the front porch in the summer. Her father reading tidbits to them from *The Budget* newspaper while she and Mother sewed. Father's bad jokes and Mother's long-winded stories from her childhood. Life at the Weaver house had an even, peaceful keel that could be counted on.

That didn't mean she didn't long for the day when she would share a home with a husband and her own children.

It didn't mean this new, unexpected chapter with the Keim grandchildren didn't leave her feeling almost dizzy with anticipation. As if she'd been waiting, simply waiting for something to happen in the two years since her baptism.

God wouldn't have put her smack-dab in the middle of the Keims' lives for no reason. Or maybe this was her consolation prize. A lovely prize, to be sure. He knew what her future held. Husband. Children. One or both or none.

"Just because it happened to your daed and me doesn't mean it will happen to you."

Cassie dropped her spoon. It clattered on the oak floor. Tater raised his head, a soft growl in his throat. He got up and stalked from the kitchen. Cassie rolled her eyes. The dog had far too much attitude. "You have to stop doing that."

"Doing what?" Mother ladled chili into a plastic storage bowl. "I didn't do a thing."

"Reading my mind."

"It doesn't take a mind reader to know you worry about having boplin. Any woman in your shoes would." Mother stuck the plastic container in the refrigerator and returned to the counter. "Don't let it keep you from opening yourself up to the possibilities."

The possibilities. Joseph Hostetler had approached her once after a singing. Cassie pleaded a headache. He never asked again.

Other lost opportunities paraded past her mind's eye in slow motion.

"I'm not afraid."

Not much. Maybe those weren't lost opportunities. Maybe she was supposed to wait. *"For such a time as this."*

God had a plan. She couldn't wait for it to unfold.

CHAPTER 4

Father barely gave Cassie time to say good-bye. "It's not like you won't see us every other day," he admonished as he tromped ahead of her through the back door with her suitcase clutched in one hand. "The horse is freezing his tail off."

True, but it wouldn't be the same. She wouldn't be living with them. Cassie waved to her mother who stood in the doorway, her thick woolen sweater wrapped around her middle. After a second, Tater joined her. He woofed softly, then more loudly.

Father dumped the suitcase in the back of the buggy. He chuckled. "That *hund* won't be happy here without you. It's bad enough that you're gone every day. He won't sleep. He'll pace the floor. You'd best take him."

Job and Dinah wouldn't mind. As long as Tater didn't mess with the cats that made their barn home. "Come on, Tater, hurry up. We haven't got all night."

Tater shot forward in a lope worthy of a younger dog. He leaped into the back of the buggy. No second invitation needed.

His happy panting in her ears, Cassie settled into the seat next to her father and waited. Her father wasn't happy. Sooner or later, he would have his say. Still, the ride to the Keims' place passed without conversation. The only sounds were the horse's occasional snorts and the crunch of gravel under the squeaking buggy wheels on the road that followed her parents' property line until it gave way to the Keims' farm. Snow began to fall again, slowly at first and then in a thin blanket of fluffy wet flakes that threatened to cover the road. Still, Father had nothing to say. Other than a gruff "Are you warm enough?" after he retucked a thick fleece robe around her knees, he kept his thoughts to himself.

"Are you mad at me?" Cassie couldn't hold it in any longer. "Don't be mad."

"I'm not mad." Father snorted and shook his head. "Why would I be mad? You're a grown woman doing a kind thing for friends of ours. It won't be easy, but you're willing to work hard and sacrifice. This is a gut Christian thing to do. It's what we taught you to do. If anything, I'm mad at myself for being selfish."

"I'll miss you too."

"It's not like we won't see you."

But it won't be the same. Cassie finished the thought in her head. Like the Keims, Mother and Father surely prayed for their only daughter to be yoked to a loving husband and to have children—their grandchildren.

"There's still time." It took a moment for her to realize she'd spoken the words aloud.

"For what?" Father's breaths came in quick white puffs. "Time for what?"

"For me to marry and have kinner."

"The will of Gott be done." Daed knew how to close a subject.

They pulled in front of Job and Dinah's house. A lamp cast shadows through the living room window. Lights glowed in several windows upstairs. Those rooms had been dark at night for years. The change had already begun. *For the better, right, Gott?*

Father made no move to get out of the buggy. "We'll see you Sunday at church."

"You don't want to come in for a hot drink before you go back? You could meet the kinner."

"I want to get home before the road gets worse."

Cassie slid from under the robe and hopped to the ground. Tater joined her. She pulled her suitcase from the backseat. Why did this feel like good-bye? Her parents lived eight miles down the road. In a buggy she could be home in half an hour. *Stop being silly.* She smiled up at her father. "Be gut."

"That's my line." Then his smile faded. "This isn't on your shoulders. Your mudder and me will help. So will the rest of the Gmay. I'll speak to Job tomorrow to see what he needs. I'll go with him to talk to the bishop."

"That would be wunderbarr. Job had doubts about doing this." Unlike Dinah, who'd sprung up from the couch with the vigor of a much younger, healthier woman. "He'll want your support with Bryan."

Bryan Miller had a year under his belt as bishop. Sometimes he tended to be overzealous in his new duties.

"You'd better get inside before your nose freezes and falls off." Another old joke. Father gathered up the reins. "You be gut."

He took off at a steady clip. Despite his admonition, Cassie remained where she stood, watching him go. Snowflakes collected on her coat and gloves. They tickled her nose and eyes.

Tater woofed softly.

"I know. It just feels like a big change." Like she wasn't a young girl living with her parents anymore. She was a woman with a full-time job. "It's gut. This is really gut. *Danki*, Gott."

Cassie stretched her arms up high, lifted her head, and whirled around, once, twice, three times.

Grinning, his tongue hanging out, Tater pranced around her like an awkward dance partner who didn't know the steps.

Breathless, laughing, she jolted to a stop. The buggy's taillights disappeared into the darkness. Cassie inhaled air so cold her lungs burned and picked up her suitcase.

A car engine started, a sputtering, halfhearted rumble that carried on the northern wind that cut right through Cassie's coat. The sound came from somewhere behind the house. Why would a visitor pull around back? An English visitor. Had the caseworker returned so soon? Was she "monitoring the situation," as she had put it? Cassie contemplated the thick, black night. Bother Job or investigate first? Job had his hands full.

The heavy suitcase banging against her leg, she trudged through the thickening snowflakes to the graveled drive that led to the backyard, corral, and barn. His head up, his snout sniffing, Tater trotted at her side. The solar-powered light mounted to the back-porch roof flicked on at their approach.

A gray SUV idled, puffs of gray smoke fluttering from the tailpipe, where the gravel drive met the dirt road that continued to the corral and barn. The headlights were off and the interior dark.

Why sit there? Why not knock on the door? Cassie marched toward the SUV. The headlights came on, blinding her. She slowed and put her hand up to shield her eyes. Irritation ran through her. "Who is it? What are you doing out here?"

The headlights switched off, leaving her disoriented for a few seconds. The driver's-side window lowered. Mason Keim stared at her, his expression a mixture of shame and belligerence. "Sorry. I didn't know it was you."

"What are you doing out here?"

"Taking care of my family the only way I can."

. . .

Mason winced. His response probably sounded as stupid to Cassie as it did to him. No way she could understand his compulsion to get in the Blazer after Mrs. Blanchard dropped him off and drive back to Haven to sit outside the Keims' house, eating a Quarter Pounder with cheese, drinking a large coffee, listening to Lee Brice on the radio, and freezing his tail end off. The Trailblazer's twelve-year-old heater was on its last leg.

Turned out the coffee was also a big mistake.

The irritation faded from her face, replaced by a question mark. "Why out here? I heard you start the engine. Have you been sitting out here with the car off? Aren't you freezing? Wouldn't you be more comfortable if you came inside?"

The blitz of questions matched her style from this morning. The girl had a rapid-fire approach to conversation, which didn't give a guy much chance to think. He'd turned off the SUV so he could get out and find a place to relieve himself. Talk about freezing. He couldn't tell her that.

"I'm an adult. I don't need them to take care of me."

Cassie edged closer. The big German shepherd stuck to her side. The dog was massive with a noble graying face and alert black ears. He had *protector* written all over him. "Who's your buddy?"

"This is Tater. He's my friend."

"I can see that. Hey, Tater."

The dog woofed, but his alert stance didn't change. Cassie's fingers wound themselves around his collar. "You're their grandson. They were so excited to meet you. Job offered you a place to stay for the night—for as long as you want. Dinah wanted you to stay."

They had offered. The disappointment on his grandmother's face when he declined had almost been too much. He couldn't stay. He had to be at work at eight in the morning. He had a job and rent to pay on a house that was now too big for a lone single guy. "I have to work in the morning."

The cold had turned her cheeks red. Snow clung to her black bonnet and coat. A few flakes landed on her eyelashes and sparkled like sequins in the light from the back porch of the sturdy wood-frame house painted white that stood firm against the dark night. "We get up before dawn. You could leave here early. What kind of work do you do?"

More questions. She and Kathy would be good friends. His sister never stopped with the questions. "I'm a carpenter. I work construction."

"In the winter?"

"My boss flips houses as well as builds them. We're rehabbing the inside of an old house in Wichita right now."

"Is that where you live—Wichita?"

"Yes. You must be freezing. Go inside. I'll leave, I promise."

"I know you're worried. I can see why you would be." She enunciated with that stilted cadence of a person who'd learned English as a second language. She brushed the snow from her face with mittens small enough to belong to a child. Everything about her was compact and lean, like she'd never quite hit that last growth spurt in adolescence.

"I like the cold. Why not come inside and spend this one night? Your grandparents are kind, decent people. They've waited years for this moment, never knowing if it would come to pass. You'll see. I'll feed the children wholesome food. I'll make them clothes. Dinah and Job will love them."

"Is Dinah dying?"

"No. Don't say that." Cassie wrapped her arms around her thin middle and shook her head. "The older she gets, the harder the diabetes is on her body. It's harder to control. But she's much stronger than she appears."

"Good to know. You said you'll make them clothes?"

"That's what we do."

"They're not Amish. They'll never be Amish."

"Your mother was Amish."

His father might have been as well. His mother never wanted to talk about it, so Mason would never know for sure. How much did Job and Dinah know about his parentage? Anything at all? Maybe he could finally find out. Maybe the guy was still around.

"I know." He rubbed the wheel with both icy hands. The air from the Trailblazer's unreliable heater barely reached them. "Sometimes, when she'd been drinking more than usual, she talked about it. She said it wasn't bad when she was a kid, but later she had to leave because she couldn't breathe. That's how she put it. Smothered by all the rules. If we're going to talk like this, get in. It's a little warmer in here than out there. Sort of. Tater can come too."

Shaking her head again, she took two steps back and nearly tripped over her suitcase. "I couldn't do that. I shouldn't even be standing out here talking to you. Come inside instead."

She seemed genuinely horrified at the idea of getting into the Blazer. Mason spent a good part of his free time keeping the twelve-year-old SUV running. With two hundred thousand miles on it, the Blazer often tried to slide off into a car graveyard. Maybe she was repulsed by a non-Amish guy. Maybe he scared her. "Don't be scared. I wouldn't hurt you."

Cassie's arms dropped. She drew herself up taller—maybe five-five, if that. "I'm not scared of anything."

Her bluster made him want to smile—almost. This girl-woman was a bundle of contradictions. So different from the girls he'd dated in those rare times when he wasn't working or dealing with the latest fiasco with the kids. The amount of makeup and jewelry the girls wore increased in direct proportion to the scantiness of their clothes.

Cassie just might give the kids a run for their money. Kathy would love her. That would be dangerous. She'd get attached and the Keims would decide they couldn't make it work and send them back home. "I should go."

"Don't—"

He rolled up the window. In his haste to leave her behind along with all the ways this situation could go wrong, he mashed down on the gas pedal too hard. The Trailblazer plunged forward and its bald tires slid in a zigzag. Breathing hard, he let up and the SUV's path smoothed. He glanced in the rear-view mirror. Cassie raised one gloved hand and waved. An Amish housekeeper—probably still a teenager—had no fear. He couldn't let her outdo him.

On the other hand, he had much more to lose.

CHAPTER 5

Who thought up counting sheep to fall asleep? And why sheep? Why not cows or horses? Cassie wiggled on her side and stuck her clasped hands under her cheek. A woman who worked as hard as she did never suffered from insomnia. If anybody were to ask now, she would claim her inability to sleep had to do with sleeping in an unfamiliar bed in a room not her own. The pillows were too soft and the blanket itchy, and her toes were cold. It had to do with the space Tater took up at the foot of the bed. Job hadn't batted an eye at his new guest. The children were already asleep, but they would love Tater. Everyone did.

No, her insomnia had nothing to do with Mason Keim and their conversation earlier in the evening in the middle of a steady snowfall.

Nothing at all.

Cassie rolled over to her back and stared into the darkness. Tater shifted and whined in his sleep. "Hush, hund, everything's fine."

Fine and dandy.

The image of Mason's tense face with those blue eyes, high cheekbones, and square jaw filled her head. *Taking care of my family the only way I can.* Cassie didn't have brothers and sisters, but if she did, she wouldn't want to be separated from them. She wouldn't want them left with strangers, even if they were blood relatives.

She wouldn't even do that to her animals.

A muffled scream broke the silence. Cassie sat up. Growling deep in his throat, Tater joined her. Sobs echoed down the hallway. Cassie threw back her covers and grabbed her robe. "Stay, Tater, stay."

His indignant *woof* summed up his thoughts, but Tater did as he was told. "Gut hund."

She rushed into the hallway. The sobbing stopped. She stood still, listening.

Words whispered. She couldn't make them out. They were coming from the room Kathy and Jennie shared. Cassie tapped on the door, then opened it. After a minute her eyes adjusted to the dark. The girls huddled in the middle of the bed. Kathy had her hand over her little sister's mouth. Tears streaked Jennie's face and her nose needed wiping.

"We're sorry. Jennie had a bad dream. We didn't mean to wake you up." Kathy shrank against the pile of pillows. Her hand dropped from Jennie's mouth. "Did we, Jennie? We'll be quiet, won't we?"

Jennie nodded, but she hiccupped another sob. "Josie spanked me. Mommy never spanked me. I want my mommy. Where's my mommy?"

"You know where she is." Kathy hugged her sister. "Mason told you. She's in heaven."

"When is she coming back?"

"She's not."

"Can I visit her?"

Kathy's sigh suggested this wasn't a new conversation.

Mason believed in heaven. That was good to know. Cassie

turned on the gas-powered lamp. Their faces fearful, both girls shrank back against the blankets. Cassie tried out her best smile. "It's okay. You're not in trouble. I promise." She moved to the bed and sat on the edge. "Who is Josie?"

"It was just a dream," Kathy answered for Jennie. "A bad dream."

"The lady next door. She took care of me." Her face pinched and wary, Jennie shook her head. "She spanked me. I wet the bed. She said I was too old to wet the bed."

"Josie took care of Jennie when we were in school and Mom was at work," Kathy rushed to explain. "It was cheaper than day care, I guess. Mom told her no spanking, but I guess she was pretty mad about the bed."

"I'm sorry that happened to you, Jennie. You don't have to worry about that here. We don't spank children for accidents. You didn't wet the bed on purpose, did you?"

She shook her head.

"Then you have nothing to worry about. I promise."

Jennie crawled from under the covers and into Cassie's lap. "You're nice. I like you."

"I like you too." Cassie slid her arms around the little girl and inhaled her sweet scent of soap and toothpaste. "I'm so happy we're going to get to know each other. We can bake cookies and bread and plant vegetables, and I can teach you how to sew. We have horses and cows and pigs and chickens. You could learn to ride a horse too. Does that sound like fun?"

"Yeah. It does." Kathy tugged a pillow from the pile and held it like a baby in her arms. "Is Dinah your grandma too?"

"No. I work for her and Job, but she's also my friend."

"What's going on in here?" A kerosene lantern in one hand and her walking stick in the other, Dinah padded barefoot into the room. Her thick white hair flowing down her back, she wore only her nightgown. "I heard talking. Are you girls all right?"

"Everyone is fine now." Cassie kissed Jennie's soft brown curls and helped her return to the warmth of the covers. "Jennie had a bad dream, but I think she can go back to sleep now. You shouldn't be traipsing around without a robe or slippers. You don't even have socks on. You'll catch a cold."

Nor should Dinah be carrying a lantern. She might fall and start a fire. Cassie went to Dinah and tugged the handle from her. "Let me carry this. Say good night to your *mammi*, girls."

"Mammi?" Kathy giggled. "Is that like nana?"

"I guess so. It's from the language Plain folks—Amish—speak to each other. It's the first language we learn, before English."

"Will you teach it to us?"

"*Jah*. That means yes. But right now, go to bed."

"Can I kiss you good night again?" Dinah took a small step forward. "Would you mind?"

"I like kisses," Jennie offered. "If they're not too slobbery."

"Me too." Dinah smiled as she stepped forward. "I don't like slobber either."

She planted kisses on each girl's cheek, and they returned the favor. Her smile grew so big it surely must hurt her face.

Cassie took her arm and they headed for the door.

"Could you leave the light on?" Jennie pulled the blanket up to her chin. "Please."

"She's afraid of the dark." Kathy adopted the role of a long-suffering big sister. "She's used to a night-light. I told her she didn't need one with me here, but she's still scared."

Kerosene, a flame, and small children combined for a recipe

for disaster. Were there battery-operated night-lights? "I'll tell you what, Jennie. I'll leave the door open. I'm two doors down. I'll leave my door open too. If you need anything, call my name and I'll come running."

"You promise?"

"I'm a light sleeper. I promise."

Jennie relaxed against the pillows. She snuggled closer to Kathy and closed her eyes.

"*Gut nacht.*"

"Gut nacht." Kathy's rendition of her first words in Pennsylvania Dutch seemed to come naturally. "Gut nacht, Mammi and Cassie."

Still smiling, Cassie guided Dinah back to her bedroom. The other woman hummed as they walked. "What's that you're humming?"

"'How Great Thou Art.'"

The hymn fit the moment perfectly. Cassie hummed with her until they reached the door to her bedroom. It stood open. "I can't believe Job slept through all this racket. He must've been tired."

The humming died away. "He has trouble sleeping. He has for years. Ever since Georgia and Perry left. He sleeps on the couch a lot. At first I think he wanted to be right there to open the door when they returned. To welcome them home. Then I think it became a habit."

"It must've been very hard . . . for both of you."

"It was, but we weathered it." Dinah shuffled into the room and climbed into bed. The bedsheets and blankets were a twisted mess. "He was my rock then, and he's my rock now."

Cassie set the lantern on the cedar chest at the foot of the cherrywood bed. "Let me fix your covers for you."

Together they straightened the pile of blankets and quilts. Dinah was always cold. Cassie tugged them back. "Hop in and I'll tuck you in. Do you want a hot water bottle for your feet?"

Dinah shook her head. "They sounded so happy tonight. When they were getting ready for bed. I was worried when they were so quiet at the supper table. They barely made a peep."

"Maybe they were busy eating. They could use some meat on their bones."

"There's nothing wrong with their appetites, praise the Lord. They ate the taco casserole, rice, and beans, plus the oatmeal-raisin cookies Job brought out from his stash. They thought it was funny that he hides the cookies from me."

Dinah had been known to ferret out the location of Job's sweets and help herself—though she knew it was a big no-no. Just a bite or two wouldn't hurt, she insisted.

Words that couldn't be further from the truth.

"My mom says kids have hollow legs. They're growing so fast."

"Kevin kept one hand on his plate while he ate like he was afraid we'd take his plate before he was finished."

"They've had a hard life."

Dinah patted a spot next to her on the bed. "Sit with me for a bit?"

How could Cassie say no to such a woebegone face? She eased onto the bed and leaned against the headboard.

"Our dochder died in January, and we didn't even know it. I thought I'd feel it if something happened to one of them. My heart would stop beating for a minute. My body would turn cold too."

"I'm so sorry, Dinah." Words were inadequate. Dinah's loss was made even greater because she hadn't seen Georgia in twenty-three years. No doubt Dinah and Job had prayed every day for Georgia's homecoming and for her redemption. Instead, she'd died without returning to her faith. No words existed to assuage that pain. "Gott have mercy on her soul."

"We should've tried harder to find them."

"I'm sure you did everything you could."

"The bishop then didn't want to go to the sheriff or the police. He said it was a community matter. They weren't missing. They were adults and they chose to leave."

"A hard word."

"Unbearable. Do you think Gott forgave her for her sins?" The deep wrinkles on Dinah's forehead creased. "Do you think she's in heaven?"

"I don't know." If a wise woman like Dinah couldn't figure out these things, how could someone so young and silly do it? Cassie longed for her mother's presence. Mother had suffered so much, and she had a deep well of wisdom because of her trials. "Mudder would say His ways are not ours. We can hope she asked for His forgiveness. He is gut. He is faithful. He is merciful."

"She's right. She is a wise woman. I don't want the same thing to happen to Perry. Surely he knows that the kinner are here. Surely he'll want to come home, too, at least for a visit." Dinah pulled the quilt up around her chin. Without her glasses she seemed vulnerable and younger than her sixty-three years. "Mason will know where he is."

So much time had passed. "He might be afraid of how you'll receive him."

"Maybe Mason can give him a message for me."

"That's a gut idea. A very gut idea. Job can talk to him."

"I don't know if he'll do it. Their leaving is a wound that has never healed. He won't want to open it up again."

"Even if Perry's salvation is at stake?"

"You're right. One way or another the conversation must be had. We'll figure it out." Dinah threw back the quilt and enveloped Cassie in a hug. "You're such a gut girl. We're blessed by your willingness to live and work here full-time. I know it's a sacrifice—"

"*Nee.* It's not."

"It is. You're at the age when you should be courting, marrying, and starting your own family. Job and I expected to hear your banns published in church one of these days. We still do."

Cassie slid from the bed and stretched. "From your lips to Gott's ears."

CHAPTER 6

The rich aroma of coffee brewing reached Cassie as she trotted down the stairs in the quiet predawn darkness. She let Tater out and went to the kitchen. Her first morning as a live-in housekeeper and someone had risen before her and brewed the coffee. Her determinedly optimistic plan to greet everyone as they filtered into the kitchen where Job and Dinah had eaten alone all these years already had a big wrinkle in it. In the midst of her tossing and turning, she'd created an image of the children crowded around the table—Job would need to build a bigger table for the dining room as soon as possible— smiling and eating a wholesome breakfast of oatmeal, toast with strawberry jam, milk, and juice.

Truth be told, a large pot of oatmeal was easy to make, would fill many hungry tummies, and was cheap. Job would also need to go to town for groceries this morning. The mental list of meat, milk, cheese, vegetables, fruits, and baking supplies multiplied in Cassie's head. The necessary budget for food at the Keims' house had exploded overnight. She picked up her pace and entered the kitchen, ready to work.

Job stood at the counter with a cup of coffee in his hand. He seemed to be staring out the window at the darkness. Cassie cleared her throat. He didn't turn.

"Guder mariye."

He jolted. Coffee slopped over the side of his oversized mug. *"Ach."* He grabbed the washrag from the sink and sopped up his mess. "Guder mariye."

"I'm sorry. I didn't mean to startle you." Cassie rushed to his side. "Did it burn your fingers? I'll get the B&W Ointment."

"Nee. It's fine." He dabbed at reddened skin on his thumb. "That's what I get for daydreaming."

"It's hardly day yet." Cassie backed away. "I figured I'd be the first one up. I'll try to do better tomorrow. Your *kaffi* will be waiting for you."

"Don't worry about that. I can make my own kaffi. I like having a cup by myself before the day starts."

"I know you can. I just want to be as helpful as possible. Especially now that we'll have to get the kinner up and ready for *schul* each day."

"I'm just a grumpy old man this morning." Job held up his mug in a silent toast to his admission. "I didn't sleep much last night, thinking of Georgia's death and the kinner living here. So much has changed from one day to the next."

"It's enough to take a person's breath away, I reckon." Cassie busied herself heating milk, water, rolled oats, cinnamon, vanilla, and a pinch of salt in a large pot. Nothing like cooking for a crowd. What a great way to start her new job. She would add raisins, banana slices, and honey when she served it. "I guess the kinner aren't going to schul today?"

"It's Friday. I figure it's better to let them get used to us today and over the weekend. They can get a fresh start in their new schul on Monday."

"That seems like a good plan. I know Dinah will want time to get to know them better. Do you think you can take me into Yoder this morning? We'll need to stock up on groceries. Plus

I'll need a mountain of material and sewing goods to start making their clothes."

"Jah, we could stop at the thrift store in the meantime for pajamas, shoes, socks. The Mennonite committee always makes sure their used clothes are in good shape. Mason will bring the rest of their clothes from the house, but if what they were wearing is any indication, we'll still need to buy them a few things." Job leaned against the counter and took another sip of coffee. Still, he held his body stiff as if he were filled with tension. "It makes me wonder what Georgia and that *mann* of hers did with their money. Or what they did to earn money."

"Raising six kinner is expensive in the *Englisch* world." Cassie kept an eye on the oatmeal concoction, waiting for it to come to a boil so she could turn the heat down and let it simmer. No one liked burnt oatmeal. "We have lots of canned fruits and vegetables in the basement we can use. But meat—"

"I'll slaughter a pig. We have plenty of eggs from the chickens. The Masts will sell me one of their sides of beef. We still have canned beef, pork, and venison in the basement."

Cassie couldn't stop the shudder. She hated deer-hunting season. They were such beautiful animals. Everyone in her family hunted, not just deer but rabbit, quail, dove, geese. She sighed. "I suppose it's necessary."

Job smiled, but he didn't make fun of her. "We raise livestock for this purpose. And I never waste any part of the animal when I hunt. You know that."

That didn't mean she liked it. "I can make most of their clothes."

"I've been noodling Bobby's question from yesterday. Do we make them dress as we do? Is that fair to them? Do we give them time to adjust to our way of doing things? Those are hard questions."

"My daed—"

"Cassie, Cassie, I slept all night!" Still dressed in a stained, faded flannel nightgown, Jennie shot into the kitchen. In one hand she clutched a ragged, half-naked Barbie with a shock of blonde hair. "I didn't have to yell for you."

Cassie had just enough time to lean over and hold out her arms. Jennie ran straight at her. One thin arm tightened around Cassie's leg. Cassie hugged her tight. "That's good. I knew you could do it."

"I can still have a night-light, can't I?"

"I'll ask your *daadi* about it, okay? We have to see if we can find one that doesn't need electricity."

Job's shaggy eyebrows rose, but after a second he nodded. "Cassie and I will see what we can find when we go into town this morning."

Jennie let go of Cassie and skipped across the kitchen to Job. "Can I go with you? I like to shop. What is a daadi? When are we leaving? Can I have breakfast first? I'm starving. Do you have Cap'n Crunch? Peanut Butter, not Crunch Berries—"

"Whoa, whoa, little girl." Job picked her up and stuck her on his hip. Whatever reservations he had about taking in this horde of children melted before Cassie's eyes. "One question at a time. It's very cold outside, so it's probably better for you to stay here where it's warm. The buggy isn't like a car. *Daadi* means 'grandpa.' Cassie is fixing breakfast. What is on the menu today, Cassie?"

"I thought oatmeal. It's hot and it sticks to your ribs."

"Food doesn't touch your ribs." That announcement came from Kathy, who stood in the doorway still in her cotton nightgown so faded it was hard to know what color it had once been. She smoothed back dark-brown hair as wild and woolly as her sister's. "It goes down your esophagus to your stomach. We learned about digestion and nutrition in school. The boys won't eat oatmeal. They'll want cold cereal and milk. That's what we always ate because it was fast. Me and Bobby had to make sack lunches for school. Mason didn't like us to cook when he wasn't there."

"You ate cold food at every meal?"

Job set Jennie down at the table. Kathy plopped on the bench next to her. She yawned so widely her jaw cracked. "No, Bobby used the microwave to make stuff. Like corn dogs and bagel bites when we were home during the summer. He could make mac 'n' cheese too. Mason would bring us pizza or hamburgers or whatever takeout he felt like for supper when he got off work, so that was hot—depending on how long it sat in his Blazer."

"Around here, I do the cooking and we eat a lot of vegetables we grew in the garden and fruit that Dinah and I canned in the summer."

"Good luck getting the kids to eat those." Kathy shook her head and tut-tutted, like she was the grandmother in this conversation. "I don't think anything green has ever passed through their lips."

One short bark sounded at the door. Tater. Cassie had forgotten about him. She let him in. Tail swishing, he trotted into the kitchen like he owned the place.

Jennie shrieked and hid behind Kathy, who backed away, both hands to her chest as if Tater might eat them.

"This is Tater. He's my friend."

"He's big. His mouth is really big." Jennie still behind her,

Kathy edged toward the hallway. "He has big teeth like the big bad wolf."

From *Little Red Riding Hood*? "He's very sweet. He would never hurt anyone. He likes everyone."

"We've never had a dog or a cat. Not even a hamster." Kathy stopped moving. Jennie peeked around her big sister. Her eyes were huge. "I told Mom we would take care of it, but she said we couldn't take care of buying food or vet bills or replacing carpet if it peed on the floor. Does he pee on the floor?"

"Never. He has very good manners. And he never bites little boys and girls. In fact, he takes care of them."

Job knelt next to Tater and put an arm around the dog. "Tater, this is Kathy and Jennie. Kathy and Jennie, meet Tater."

The girls tiptoed forward. Literally. As if a noise might scare Tater into suddenly devouring them. His tail whipped back and forth. Jennie got up the nerve first. She petted his back, careful to stay away from his face and those big teeth. Kathy joined in.

Tater grinned. He was in heaven.

"Now that everyone has been properly introduced, it's time to get dressed. We sit down to breakfast dressed, hair brushed, and faces washed." Cassie made a swishing motion with both hands. "Both of you, go get cleaned up so you're ready to start the day after we eat."

Job nudged Jennie. "That includes socks and shoes. Your feet must be ice cubes."

"He's soft." Kathy edged closer and put her arm around Tater's neck. He licked her cheek. She yelped. Her hand flew to her face. "Dog slobber."

"He kissed you. That means he likes you."

"Oh, I like him too. I think."

"Good. From now on when you get up in the morning, you can feed him. I'll show you how much food to put in his bowl."

Tater would love Kathy even more if Cassie put her in charge of his food.

"In the meantime, you two need to get dressed. We don't eat in pajamas around here."

"Okay, Grandpa. I mean Daadi." Jennie danced toward the door. She stopped and turned in a complete circle, her eyes traveling around the room. Horror replaced delight. "There's no TV. Where's the TV?"

"No electricity, no TV, doofus," Kathy answered first. "No iPad. No computers. No internet. Remember when Grandma explained about electricity last night? They like living off the grid so they don't get contaminated by the bad, sinful world."

For an eight-year-old, she had quite the vocabulary. It had to be all the books she read. She was smart, no doubt. She understood and remembered Dinah's lesson. She would absorb new information at school quickly.

"We also don't call names." Job intervened before Cassie could speak. "That's right, though. We don't watch TV."

"No TV!"

Donny, Kevin, and Bobby traipsed into the kitchen like one unit. They howled in perfect unison.

Tater barked. The howling stopped. The boys froze.

"Dude, he's a monster." Kevin forged ahead of the others. "Is this your dog, Grandpa? I always wanted a dog. Can I pet him?"

Kevin might turn out to be Cassie's soul mate. She stood back and let Jennie make the introductions this time. Tater rolled over onto his back and let his tongue loll out the side of his mouth. He was ecstatic. The boys seemed as excited at the prospect of having a dog as the girls had been. Maybe they would forget about the TV.

"I want *Peppa Pig*." Jennie rubbed her eyes and wailed. "And *Arthur*. I like *Arthur*."

Peppa Pig? And who was this Arthur? A friend?

"*Peppa Pig* is for girls." Kevin nudged Jennie aside and made for the table. "Let's watch the new *Power Rangers*. They're legit." He chopped with his hands like he was attacking Kathy.

Legit? Cassie exchanged glances with Job. He shrugged.

Scowling, Bobby gave Tater a last pet and slunk across the room to the door. He crossed his arms and stood erect as if standing guard.

"We also don't fight or pretend to fight." Job moved to the table where he loomed over his new brood. "Cassie told you girls to get dressed, so go. You boys need to do the same. Everyone needs to be back at the table in ten minutes, ready to eat. Go on, go."

"Hurry!" Cassie held up the ladle. "Oatmeal's ready. I have bananas, raisins, honey, and walnuts to add. Does that sound good?"

Bobby shook his head. "I'll pass. I'm not a big fan of breakfast anyway."

"Around here everyone sits down at meals together. Whether you eat is up to you, but you'll be mighty hungry before noon rolls around." Job didn't blink. "Go get dressed."

Bobby wavered for a second, then employed an exaggerated swagger to follow his siblings from the room.

"That wasn't so bad." Cassie managed a smile as soon as Bobby disappeared through the door. "We can do this."

"Everything is so different here from anything they've ever

known." Job tugged at his unruly beard. "I don't know if we have the right to impose—"

A muffled thump emanated from the second floor above them. A shout immediately followed.

"Grandma fell. She fell!"

Job beat Cassie to the stairs—just barely. They both took them two at a time. Gasping for breath, they arrived at the same time at the spot where Dinah balanced on her hands and knees. Her face was chalky white. "I tripped." She leaned back on her haunches and held up a plastic toy that looked like it was half man, half car. "Somebody left this in the hallway."

"That's my Transformer." Donny took her offering and immediately burst into tears. "I didn't mean to. I'm sorry. I won't do it again."

Bobby grabbed his brother and stepped in front of him. "It was an accident."

"Are you hurt?" Job squeezed past the children and knelt next to Dinah. He patted her arms and legs. "Does anything hurt?"

She pushed his hands away. "Stop, I'm fine, I'm fine. My ankle hurts a little, but I'll live. Help me up. Donny, look, see? I'm fine."

With Job's help, she struggled to her feet and took a wobbly step. She winced but kept going. "See, no harm done."

"Your ankle is hurt." Job slid his arm around her. "We need to ice it down. She's right, it was an accident. But you all have to understand this: Your mammi can't see well. Her balance isn't good because her toes are numb. So you have to be careful. Don't leave anything on the floor. Put chairs and other furniture back exactly where you found them. Does everyone understand this?"

The children nodded.

"Around here we say jah."

"Jah," they repeated.

All of them except Donny. He was still hidden behind his big brother.

"Donny?" Dinah tilted her head and leaned forward. "Can you come out?"

Donny edged from behind Bobby. Tears streaked his thin white face with its smattering of freckles.

"What exactly is a Transformer?"

"It's a robot that turns into a car." Animation replaced the sorrowful, wary frown. "You've never seen the Transformer movies? They're awesome."

"Can you show me how to transform him?"

Cassie hid her grin. It had been years, but it didn't seem as if Dinah was out of practice. She knew how to talk to a child.

Job eased back and Donny rushed forward, toy in hand, and demonstrated. "He fights evil."

"What kind of evil?"

"The bad guys."

Dinah enveloped the boy in a hug. "We don't need robots to fight evil. We have God."

Donny's nose wrinkled. "Mom said God shows up when He feels like it."

Job's feet shuffled. Dinah shook her head at him. "We'll talk more about that later. Right now, I'm starving. I could eat a horse. How about you?"

Donny's eyes widened. "Do you eat horses?"

Dinah chortled. "Nee. That means 'no.' If we did, how would we drive our buggies?"

"Breakfast!" With a jolt Cassie lurched toward the staircase. The singed smell drifted up the stairs. "My oatmeal."

Everyone scattered.

"No rush. I'll be starting over," she called after them. "Be sure to comb your hair."

Job and Dinah followed her down the stairs.

Dinah fell, breakfast got burned, and the kids wanted TV. They were off to a bumpy start.

Things could only get better from here. *Right, Gott?*

CHAPTER 7

Like the guy said on the HGTV show, demo day was the best. On these cold, snowy winter days, Mason served as muscle instead of a carpenter. Which meant he got to swing a sledgehammer and take out half a dozen walls in a 1980s ranch-style house with dingy lighting, nineties décor, and the smell of cat pee in the filthy carpet. He could blow off steam and sweat out his stress without taking it out on his coworkers.

All the while, still arguing with himself.

Were the kids better off with Dinah and Job?

Mason grunted and swung the sledgehammer like his favorite baseball bat. It rewarded him with a gaping hole in the drywall. Home run. Dust, dirt, and nasty dead bug stuff floated in the air. The sound of men gabbing like old ladies in Spanish and German mixed with a radio blaring Mexican music. A crashing sound, cussing, and then laughter. Electric drills and saws added to a cacophony that was a familiar, soothing boon.

Back to his dilemma. A quiet, clean, peaceful, healthy existence in a two-story A-frame house nestled among wheat fields and cornfields. Good food that didn't come out of the frozen section of the grocery store. No exposure to the sewage in big-city schools. No gang violence, mass shootings, drugs, alcohol, teenage sex behind the bleachers at a football game.

The Keims could give them what Mason couldn't. Attention. Supervision. Safety. Values. Faith.

The Keims could give his siblings something to cling to in hard times. Hope. They offered hope.

Hope would be nice.

Two more swats and a fierce kick with his steel-toed boot and the wall tumbled down. Mason's job also had another advantage. His boss utilized a crew of Amish workers who handled flooring, brickwork, and finishings. The crew leader, Virgil Hostetler, was a good guy. He and Mason had talked shop on several occasions, as well as hunting and fishing—pastimes they both liked. He would be the perfect source of information on this new topic. The Amish.

Mason found him seated on a red cooler, his large metal lunch box next to him. His crew members had taken up spots around what would be the master bedroom. Virgil looked up from his sandwich and smiled. "Young Mason, how goes it?"

Mason squatted next to the cooler and considered where to begin. "I need some . . . advice, I guess."

"From me?" Virgil's thick brown eyebrows rose. He smiled, laid the sandwich on a piece of wax paper, and wiped his hands on a napkin. "Are you wanting to put in some hardwood floors?"

If only it were that simple. "It turns out, I'm Amish. Or at least half Amish. So are my brothers and sisters. On my mother's side."

Clear as mud.

Virgil's forehead wrinkled, but his smile broadened. His chuckle held kindness mixed with skepticism. "It doesn't generally work that way. Your clothes and your . . . vocabulary beg to differ."

Mason did tend toward cussing binges. He learned them from the best. If Clayton had to finish a sentence without an obscenity, he wouldn't be able to speak. On the other hand, come to think of it, Mom didn't partake of filthy language, even on a bad day, and she had a lot of those.

So how did it work? Mason hunkered down cross-legged on the dusty cement that lay exposed for the first time in years. He explained the situation as best he could. Virgil nodded a few times, tsking now and again. His eyebrows drew together in unison with his somber frown. "Uh-huh, uh-huh."

"So that's the deal. Job and Dinah Keim are our grand-parents. My mom was Amish. I guess that makes us Amish."

His lips pursed, Virgil shook his head, but he didn't speak. He fished around in his lunch box and brought out another sandwich. He held it out to Mason. "Eat this while I try to digest your story and explain some things."

The Dunkin' breakfast sandwiches were ancient history. Mason accepted the offering. He took a bite of ham and cheddar cheese with spicy mustard on the best bread he'd ever eaten. Virgil finished half a sandwich in two bites, chewed, and wiped his mouth.

"I live up by Partridge, south of Hutchinson. It's only a few miles from Haven. I've run into Job many times. He's a good man. Your half brothers and sisters are in good hands."

"So now they're Amish, just like that? Bobby's sixteen. He wants to be a police officer. He can't be Amish and go to the police academy, can he?"

"Having Amish relatives doesn't make you Amish. Technically a person becomes Amish when he's baptized into the faith. Amish isn't just how you live; it's what you believe. Was your mother baptized before she left?"

"I don't know."

"Did your grandparents have any contact with her after she left?"

"Job said she was dead to them."

"She was shunned then. She left her faith after baptism. They weren't allowed to have contact with her."

"That seems awfully harsh."

"We don't have time for a discussion of *meidung* or shunning right now, but it's our version of tough love." Virgil extracted a handful of enormous cookies from the lunch box and offered Mason his choice of chocolate chip or oatmeal raisin. Mason chose chocolate chip, having an aversion to fruit in his cookies. Virgil smiled as if he approved of the choice. "Bobby will have to decide for himself if he wants to embrace the faith, just as all of you will. He'll have *rumspringa* at sixteen—that translates roughly to running around—and then decide if he wants to be baptized. If he does, he'll take classes and join the church."

"I can't imagine my brother doing any of that."

"Or he could come back to live with you. He's old enough to make that decision for himself, I reckon."

If a person got past the bowl haircut, long beard, straw hat, suspenders, and homemade pants with no pockets, he found himself talking to a man with his fair share of common sense and wisdom.

"CFS and the courts are involved. My mom left a document, a living will, that gave the kids to the Keims. I'm an adult, so I get to choose, obviously." Mason ducked his head. He flicked crumbs from his faded, stained jeans. The hitch in his voice made it hard to continue. "I'm not sure what to do next."

"I reckon that depends on you. The Keims and their community will take care of your brothers and sisters. They will want for nothing they truly need. The question is, where do you fit now? You need to pray for God's will to be done for them and for you."

God had plenty to do, given the state of the world. He obviously didn't have time for a dysfunctional family like Mason's or He would've stepped in a long time ago. "I wasn't brought up to pray much."

"If you want to know what's best for those youngsters, you need to find out who you are first. Is your heart open to the possibility that God is calling you to a different life? He has a plan for your brothers and sisters. He has a plan for Dinah and Job." Smiling, Virgil closed his lunch box and unfurled his long, skinny legs. "He has a plan for you. You may not be talking to Him, but He hasn't forgotten about you. In fact, it seems like He's trying real hard to get your attention."

With that out-of-left-field statement, Virgil stood. He dusted crumbs from his beard, shirt, and pants with calloused hands big enough to palm a basketball. Mason didn't even know where to begin to respond. No one had ever talked to him about God like that before. Like God took a personal interest in Mason. Where had He been all this time? Hanging out, waiting for the perfect moment to jump out and say, "Tag, you're it?"

"Thanks for the advice." The words sounded lame in Mason's ears. "And your time."

"If you have questions about our faith, you know where to find me. If I can't answer, I can ask my bishop. You're in a strange pickle, I reckon, and it's one that will take some getting used to. For all of you. For Job and Dinah too. They're probably talking to their bishop right now."

"Thanks."

"No thanks needed." Virgil moved the cooler and his lunch box into a corner. He brushed his hands together and smiled.

"If you decide you want to be closer to your family, let me know. I'll have a word with my brother, Obie. He works out of Yoder. His crew is rehabbing a house south of Hutchinson. I'll be helping him once this job is finished."

"Thanks."

"No need for thanks."

Virgil squatted next to another crew member. Together they ripped up a chunk of matted, once-tan carpet. The smell of cat pee wafted through the air, accompanied by dust and dirt. Mason threw his forearm over his face and backed away. Cat pee was the worst. He whirled and hotfooted back to the kitchen.

After a half day with the kids, Job and Dinah were probably hiding behind bales of hay in their barn. Or calling Mrs. Blanchard to come get the kids. Mason had no way of knowing. They didn't even have a phone. Mason had asked for their number before leaving the first time, and Cassie had given him the number to the phone shed at her parents' house. Job and Dinah didn't feel the need for a phone.

Who didn't feel the need for a phone?

That left Mason disconnected from his siblings. Not a situation he relished. And one he planned to rectify.

No matter what one Amish guy said, God had been missing in action for too long for Mason to believe He'd show up and turn this world right side up.

Life didn't work that way.

CHAPTER 8

Buying English clothes proved to be a head-scratching ordeal. It was for the best that Job went to the hardware store to search for a night-light while Cassie flipped through hanger after hanger of shirts, dresses, pants, and blouses, in five different sizes, at the thrift store. He would have lost patience long ago. Mason would bring more clothes, even if they weren't suitable for the children's new Plain life.

Dinah's and Job's instructions had been long-sleeved dresses, tights or leggings to wear under them, black or white tennis shoes, snow boots, and long-sleeved flannel nightgowns for the girls. For the boys, they agreed to jeans, long-sleeved nonpatterned shirts, and black sneakers. They would need black pants for church. They might be English clothes, but at least they would be modest and in accordance with the *Ordnung* in terms of colors.

For now. The conversations about faith were only just beginning. Mrs. Blanchard had made it clear that CFS would not allow heavy-handed conversion tactics—those were her words. The Amish didn't do conversion, Job assured her. They allowed young folks to make up their own minds after having been presented with all the necessary information. At some point in their rumspringa, they chose whether and when to attend baptism classes. Those who never chose the classes eventually left the community. But that didn't happen often. Georgia and Perry were the exceptions.

Choosing to join the faith hadn't been a struggle for Cassie. She never considered doing otherwise, but these children came to the Keims from another world, loaded down with material things they'd been taught were impossible to live without. Like TVs, cars, computers, and cell phones. Bobby was sixteen, the age at which rumspringa normally began. He knew nothing about their faith. How could he even begin to make a choice? Was it too late to offer him one?

Those questions were better left to Job and the bishop. Cassie returned a Strawberry Shortcake shirt to the rack and dug around until she found a solid dark-blue blouse in Kathy's size and added it to the growing mound in her basket.

"Cassie! I thought that was you." A stack of small pants under one arm, Nadine Miller squeezed through the aisles. Her plain, freckled face lit up with a delighted smile. "I feel like it's been forever since we've seen each other. I sure didn't expect to see you here."

"Things have been so busy since church two weeks ago. I meant to stop by and never had the chance." Cassie tucked a dark-maroon dress into the basket. Kathy would need a long-sleeved white shirt to wear under it. "I didn't expect to be shopping here either, but I imagine you've heard why."

The efficiency of the grapevine that sprawled across Partridge to Haven to Yoder to Garnett and beyond made sure of that. Her friend grinned. "Five *kinnskinner*. Job and Dinah must be so happy." The grin faded. Nadine's long fingers went to her skinny chest in the vicinity of her heart. "Of course, it is sad that Georgia passed away without returning to the faith. That would break any parent's heart. Do the kinner know where Perry is?"

Nadine kept up her running commentary while straightening stacks of children's pants on the table that separated them.

She had learned the fine art of chatting and working simultaneously in her four years at the Mennonite store.

"They are sad and happy at the same time. Job reminds us that Gott's ways are mysterious and He has a plan for us even when we can't see it." Cassie returned to her search. Job would be back soon and ready to go to the grocery store. "I don't know where Perry is now, but the oldest *kind* is in touch with him, so we hope Perry will hear about the kinnskinner coming home and decide to join them."

"What a blessing to be able to shepherd these kinner and bring them back into the fold. Everyone in the district will help. Everyone is just waiting to step in." Her face shining with excitement, Nadine smoothed a stack of little boys' jeans. "They'll be in church on Sunday? We're excited to meet them and make them feel welcome. My daed especially."

That was Nadine. She always made a point to try to make people feel at home. Her father was also the bishop. If all went well, one day he would teach the baptism classes to these children. "Danki. They've had a hard time. They're such sweet kinner. They need lots of loving."

"So why are you buying them clothes here? Aren't you and Dinah making them . . . ach, I suppose Dinah can't see well enough to sew anymore, but still—"

"I will make clothes, but there are five of them. It will take time. I can't make them fast enough."

"I'd be happy to help. So would my mudder and the other women."

"That would be wunderbarr." Cassie started toward the counter at the front of the store. Nadine was an excellent seamstress, as were most of the women in the district. It would be good for Kathy and Jennie to see how the women and girls worked together for the good of the community and had fun at the same time. "It's just that we're not sure yet what clothes they'll wear."

"What do you mean?" Nadine trailed behind her. "It's not like we have a huge number of choices."

Cassie grinned. As teenagers, she and Nadine had tried on English clothes in a Hutchinson discount store. Seeing each other in a full-length mirror in the dressing room had been a startling revelation. Cassie chose a lime-green tank top with skinny jeans while Nadine struck a pose in a hot-pink sleeveless blouse and black shorts. Neither of them had the courage to leave the dressing room. They giggled about it all the way home. "They're not Plain. Not yet, anyway. They're Englisch. The older ones are old enough to have a say in what they wear and what they believe. This will be a long haul, not something that happens overnight."

"Jah, jah, of course, I understand." Nadine grinned. "Don't worry about it. We'll have a frolic next week. I'll organize it."

Nadine was a great organizer. She loved telling people what to do, and most of the time no one minded because she was so exuberant in her delight for whatever fun event came next.

Cassie dug into her bag for the money Job had given her. It had been far too long since she spoke with Nadine. "How is Simon? Has he popped the question?"

A subject sure to turn the conversation on its head. Courting was private, but Nadine had confessed she might burst if she didn't confide in someone. Cassie didn't mind. It allowed her to live vicariously. Plus she was tickled to see Nadine so happy.

"He's sweet as chocolate fudge." Nadine scurried alongside Cassie. She smacked her lips and giggled. "Last night he kis—"

"Cassie, are you ready?" Job stood at the front door, one

hand on the bar. "I got what I needed at the hardware store. Time's a-wastin'. It's past noon. I don't want Dinah trying to cook lunch for the kinner. You know she will."

She would indeed. "I'm paying right now."

Nadine waved at Job, patted Cassie's arm, and hurried back to work. "I'll get back to you with details for the frolic," she called over her shoulder. "We can do it at Job's or at my house, whichever works for you."

Cassie smiled as she transferred the clothes from the basket to the counter. Nadine had a good heart—no one could deny that. Cassie quickly paid and followed Job out to the street where the buggy was parked. They deposited their parcels and headed for the grocery store.

Halfway to their destination, Bryan Miller stepped from the coffee shop, followed by Cassie's father. They were deep in conversation and didn't see Job and Cassie immediately. Job cleared his throat and offered a gruff salutation.

Bryan stopped in his tracks. "Job! Your ears must've been burning. Leroy and I were just talking about you and the painful news you received yesterday regarding Georgia, wrapped in the blessing of six kinnskinner you never knew you had. Gott's ways are not our ways, to be certain. But joy does, indeed, come in the morning."

Job simply nodded, but the grim lines around his mouth and eyes spoke of his supreme effort not to respond in a torrent of words. What could Bryan, with his four children and another on the way, know of the trials Job and Dinah had faced and still faced? Cassie longed to comfort him, but it wasn't her place. She studied her snow boots, slushy from the water puddled on sidewalks that had been shoveled and salted before the stores opened.

Her assessment of Bryan was unfair. She hadn't walked a mile in his shoes. He surely had his own trials. Everyone did. *Sorry, Gott. I'll try to do better.*

"We should get together to discuss the way forward with these youngsters. They've been brought up English, that's indisputable." Bryan rested one hand on a horse hitching post and pulled on his dark-brown beard with his other hand. "It won't be an easy adjustment for them, or for you. The Gmay will help. I'd like to get Samuel and Delbert with me and come out to the house to meet them. How about tonight?"

Job's grimace was so fleeting the men couldn't have seen it. Cassie chewed on her bottom lip to keep from responding. She had no business speaking. She was a young girl in their eyes, of no standing. Father wouldn't be happy if she crossed the line.

"They are still settling in. So is Dinah. This has been a shock to her system—both good and bad. We know that Gott has a plan for us. Dinah is grieving, but she's also filled with joy for the kinner." Job spoke as if that same mixture of emotions hadn't also inundated him.

He jerked his thumb toward the grocery store. "We're stocking up to feed them. We need to get back before Dinah feels like she needs to fix lunch. Could we hold off on throwing more strangers and questions at them for a few days?"

"Understandable. Uh-huh." Bryan's head bobbed in agreement. "In the meantime, I'll talk to Samuel and Delbert about how to best approach this in regard to their dress, church, and schooling."

"The social worker says we'll have to go see a judge about permanent custody when the time comes. I told her I would talk to you about it." Job smoothed his hands on his pants and rocked back on his heels. No Plain person wanted to think about dealing with the English court system. "I could stop by your house later so we can talk about it more."

"That's fine. We'll talk more about it this afternoon. We need to move quickly. They should be in school on Monday. We can't have them falling behind."

"I'm also here to help." Father's words were steeped in kindness. "However you need. The other men and I can help build an addition to the house if needed. Anything I can do in the way of just listening, I'm happy to do that too."

"We're gut with bedrooms, but the offer is much appreciated. I'll keep the other thing in mind." Job stepped from the sidewalk as if to cross the street. "We'd better get going."

That didn't give them much time to make the children feel at home. Or sew some clothes and explain the role the bishop, deacon, and minister played in the district. Cassie hadn't asked if they'd ever been to church. They knew about heaven, though, because they thought their mother had gone there.

So much to learn, so much to teach, and so little time.

"We'd better hurry," she called to Job as she tried to keep up with his long strides. "Like you said, time's a-wastin'."

CHAPTER 9

Graven images were wrong according to Scripture. That didn't keep Cassie from peering over Dinah's shoulder at the color photograph Kathy had handed to her grandmother. Cassie should be putting away the groceries and washing the clothes they'd bought in town. So much to do. Instead she was lollygagging over a cup of coffee. Seeing Dinah so happy with her grandchildren was a treat after the late-night talk of Georgia's defection and then her death.

Kathy used the faded photo as a bookmark, but she'd been eager to share it with Dinah after they started talking about their memories of Georgia—mostly good ones, as if Kathy feared upsetting her new grandma. Or maybe she didn't want to remember the bad. What purpose did it serve? Dinah's gnarled fingers touched the edge of the photo. She sighed.

"You'll have to describe your mother for Mammi," Cassie prompted Kathy. "She can't see the details of the picture."

"She's smiling. She's blowing out the candles on a chocolate two-layer cake with pink frosting." Kathy leaned closer to Dinah as if to help her see. "She just had her hair cut and colored. She favored auburn—that's what she called it—but this time she went for strawberry blonde. It's long and curly. She always said she was gonna wash that gray right out of her hair. Jennie's sitting in her lap. And Donny's on one side and I'm on the other."

Dinah sighed again, this time as if she was remembering, celebrating that birthday with her daughter. "Where're Mason, Kevin, and Bobby?"

"I think they were outside cranking the ice cream maker. Mommy liked homemade vanilla ice cream."

"With caramel syrup."

"That's right. How'd you know?" Kathy giggled. The sound made Cassie want to giggle. Some might say it was undignified for a grown woman to giggle, but life needed more laughter. Kathy had the right idea. "Oh yeah, you knew her first. You know she liked her french fries skinny and her salsa spicy."

The boys had taken Tater outside with them after the sun warmed up the winter day. They were exploring the barn and the corral. Donny wanted to make a snowman. Or have a snowball fight. Jennie had crawled onto the couch, curled up in a ball, and gone to sleep after regaling Dinah and Cassie with stories of food fights and bubble gun wars and eating barbecue-flavored potato chips until she threw up—all of which occurred when Georgia wasn't home.

"It's nice that you have a picture to remember her by." Dinah wiped her nose. She'd been teary-eyed all morning. Georgia and Perry had been gone more years than they'd lived in this house, but no doubt she'd always harbored hope that they would return one day. Georgia's death had to be like a fresh, jagged wound. "Was she still skinny?"

"She was always on a diet. She said she had to watch her girlish figure." Kathy sounded so full of longing. How she must miss her mother. Kathy was so young to experience such loss. "I thought she was the prettiest mom in town. I'm never going on a diet. I'm going to eat all I want. If we're going to die anyway, why not?"

"Because Gott gave us these bodies. They belong to Him and He expects us to be good stewards of them." Dinah held out the photo to Kathy "Thank you for sharing it with me. I always wondered if she changed much."

Kathy didn't take it. "You can keep it. I saw her my whole life. You're her mom."

"I can't see it, but even if I could, I wouldn't be able to keep it." Dinah laid the photo on the table. She rose and grabbed her walking stick. "I'm going to check on Jennie. If she doesn't wake up soon, she won't sleep tonight."

Her shoulders bent, she shuffled from the room.

"Is Grandma mad at me?" Kathy's face held hurt and bewilderment. "It's mine to give her, I promise. Mason gave one to each of us kids, except Jennie, on account of she's too young. He thought it would help us not miss her so much. Now I'm here with you, so I don't need it. You probably have lots of pictures. I'd like to know what she looked like when she was a kid like me."

Cassie sat on the bench next to Kathy and put an arm around the little girl. This would be one of her first lessons about what it meant to be Amish. "Your grandma's not mad. She's sad. She wishes she could see your mom again. She can't keep the photo because we don't believe in taking photos. Exodus 20:4 in the Bible says we shall not make any graven images of ourselves."

When a Plain child died, parents were allowed to keep a lock of hair and an outfit. All their clothes were given to others who could make good use of them. Their images were engraved on the heart. "I've never had my picture taken. Neither has Dinah or Job. Until she left home, I reckon your mother hadn't either."

"I don't know what *graven* means." Kathy sounded dubious. "Does the Bible say you shouldn't use electricity either?"

"Not exactly. It tells us not to conform to the ways of the world. To hold ourselves apart so we don't get caught up in wicked ways. To do that we find it's best not to make it easy for ourselves to always be connected, like with TV, radio, computers, and the internet. Do you see what I mean?"

"I guess so." Kathy leaned her head against Cassie's shoulder. "I don't see how having regular lights hurts, especially when you have trouble seeing. I can't imagine not being able to read. Is it okay if I use my flashlight to read at night after Jennie goes to sleep? I have one in my backpack. I used it to read after Mommy kissed me good night. She said it was okay."

"I don't think Dinah and Job will mind as long as you get enough sleep. Reading is a gut thing. It stretches your brain. But little boys and girls need their sleep, too, so they can grow big and strong."

"I'm already big and strong. I can't wait for you to teach me to bake and cook so I can help."

Kathy was a smart girl and thoughtful. Optimism bloomed in Cassie. She'd given her first lesson in the Amish faith to Dinah and Job's granddaughter. It wasn't hard and it was born out of a conversation, a question from Kathy, not a thrusting of belief on her when she wasn't ready.

"I'm hungry." Jennie trotted into the kitchen, one hand rubbing her eyes while the other clutched her Barbie doll by the hair so the doll swung behind her. "I want corn dogs and tater tots and pink lemonade Kool-Aid."

She grabbed a chair and pulled it toward the refrigerator before Cassie could respond.

"What are you doing?"

"I can make food. Can't I, Kathy?" The chair squeaked on the wooden floor and Jennie huffed. "You turn on the oven. I'll see what's in the freezer."

"Whoa, Nelly." Cassie caught the little girl's arm. "Somebody got up in a bad mood. Little girls don't decide what's to be served at a meal. Secondly, we don't have tater tots. And in the third place, no one turns on the stove unless an adult says so."

Jennie's face crumpled. She wailed, tugged free, lost her balance, and tumbled to the floor. The wail turned into an outraged scream. "Owie, owie." She crawled toward Kathy. "I want corn dogs. I want corn dogs. With catsup. And mustard."

"Are you hurt, Jennie?" Walking stick tapping in front of her, Dinah trotted into the room. "Did you break something? Are you bleeding?"

"She's fine. That's her fake cry." Kathy knelt on the floor and pulled Jennie into her lap. "Cassie says no. Grandma will fix us something yummy. You'll see. Right, Grandma?"

"I'm making beef stew with lots of potatoes and corn and tomatoes and carrots and peas." Cassie stepped around the girls and went to the stove to stir the beef that would simmer in stock until it was tender and she could add the vegetables.

"There's no reason they can't have a snack in the meantime, is there?" Dinah sounded like her eight-year-old granddaughter. "Hot chocolate would be good on a day like today."

"Yuck. I hate stew." Jennie threw her body on the floor and writhed. "It has peas in it. I hate peas."

"Why does Cassie get to decide?" Kathy ignored her sister's full-fledged fit. She scrambled to her feet and went to Dinah. "We could drink hot chocolate while she makes supper."

"We decide together." Tapping with her stick, Dinah cleared the two shapes huddled on the floor in front of her and went to the stove. Kathy trailed after her like a shadow. The two were teaming up against Cassie. "Can you get me a big saucepan from the shelf on the wall?"

"Cocoa it is," Cassie acquiesced. After all, this was Dinah's house, her kitchen, and her grandchildren. After dropping Cassie and the groceries off, Job had gone on to Bryan's house to talk to the bishop some more about the children. Bryan's wife would probably feed him supper. The routine could be a little topsy-turvy this one time. "Let me make it for you."

"I'm not totally useless." Dinah took the saucepan from Cassie. "It's simple as can be. Kathy will help me."

Jennie, who had stopped wailing, scrambled to her feet. "I want to help too. I want marshmallows."

The next few moments passed in the teaching of an age-old tradition—how to make hot cocoa from scratch. Kathy knew her way around the kitchen nearly as well as a Plain girl would. She also knew how to measure out the ingredients. Cassie chopped vegetables while standing by to jump in if things went south. This would be fine. More than fine. Dinah was cooking with her granddaughters. She knew where everything was. The girls could be her eyes and hands. Cassie could be the backup.

Dinah leaned close to the saucepan and smiled. "Smells gut, doesn't it?"

Back up, back up. Cassie gritted her teeth. Nobody liked a backseat cook.

"Gut is good, right? Yum. Like chocolate." Kathy bounced along the counter in her excitement. "Is it ready? Can I pour it?"

"Nee, the pan is too heavy." Dinah grabbed a pot holder and lifted the pan off the burner. Her arm smacked against Kathy's.

"Ach."

Hot liquid splattered as the pan fell to the floor.

"Ouch, ouch!" Kathy shrieked. "It burns, it burns. Mammi, are you burnt too?"

Cassie tossed aside her washrag and ran to assist. "Let me see. Both of you."

"I'm fine." Dinah clutched her arm to her chest. The cocoa had splattered on her hand, wrist, and forearm. "It's nothing."

"It's not nothing. You burned your arm."

Kathy had almost exactly the same red blotches on her much smaller arm.

Cassie marched them both around the mess to the table. "Sit while I get the first-aid kit. I have B&W Ointment. Jennie, you sit on the chair against the wall and don't move. The floor's a sticky mess. I don't want you to walk in it and track it around."

"I want cocoa," Jennie wailed. "I want marshmallows."

"You're a spoiled brat." Sounding like an irritated mother, Kathy shook her finger at her sister. "Stop boo-hooing."

At that order, Jennie cried louder.

Tater chose that moment to rise from his spot by the stove and bark insistently.

The sound of the back door banging against the wall joined the dismal chorus. Job walked in with Mason. "What is all this racket?"

His frown growing, Mason stalked toward his sisters. "What did you do to Kathy?"

CHAPTER 10

Social workers were like cops. There was never one around when you needed them. Mason stalked past Job who had hushed Tater and ushered him out the door. Mason immediately stepped in something wet and sticky. A brown liquid spread under his feet. Too late to avoid it now. He kept going. He dropped two large garbage bags full of clothes, shoes, coats, underwear, and socks on the floor in the corner.

He scooped up Jennie and hugged her to his chest. Her hiccupping sobs abated. The kitchen smelled of scorched milk, chocolate, and simmering beef. Cassie bent over Kathy, smearing some sort of ointment on his half sister's wrist and arm. Dinah sat next to the girl, clutching her hand to her chest.

"What happened here? What are you putting on her arm?"

"There was an accident. They were making cocoa—"

"No, let Kathy tell me."

Something he'd learned from Mrs. Blanchard. Children should be allowed to explain these things in case the adults decided to lie to protect themselves. Was it an accident? Probably, or Dinah wouldn't be burned too. But he was far too cynical to take anything for granted. "Go on, Kathy—tell me what happened. How did you get those burns on your hand? Why is Jennie crying?"

Jennie raised her head and jumped in before Kathy could.

"'Cause I want corn dogs and cocoa and Cassie said no corn dogs and Mammi spilled the cocoa. Cassie says we have to eat vegetables. I hate peas."

"Why was Dinah cooking?" Job folded his arms over his chest and glowered. "You know better, Cassie."

"Could everyone just shut up for a minute and let Kathy talk?" Heat rushed Mason. "Sorry, no disrespect intended."

Job's frown said he found that hard to believe.

"Dinah was teaching me how to make cocoa." Kathy shook her fingers as if it would help soothe the burn's sting. "We bumped elbows and the cocoa slopped over the sides and the pan fell on the floor. I'm sorry, Daadi. It was my fault. You can punish me."

"No one's being punished." Job's glare subsided. "Don't you agree, Mason? It sounds like an accident to me."

"I suppose so." They were Amish. Pacifists according to Virgil. Did they believe in corporal punishment? Mason had neglected to ask him that question. "When Cassie gets you fixed up, you need to clean the floor, Kathy. You can help her, Jennie."

"Cassie, you know better than to let Dinah near the stove." Job shook his finger at Cassie like she was a small, naughty child. "What were you thinking?"

"Making hot chocolate is not cooking." Dinah spoke for the first time. "Don't go blaming Cassie. I'm a grown woman, even if you like to treat me like a child."

So much for Amish women being meek and mild.

"Splitting hairs."

"I want corn dogs with catsup and mustard. Will you make us some?" Jennie patted Mason's cheeks. Her hands were sticky. "And pink lemonade."

Pink lemonade? Where did she come up with this stuff?

"You're way too old to be throwing a fit. What do I always tell you?"

Jennie's lower lip protruded. "You get what you get and you don't throw a fit."

Mason set her on her feet. "You need to go to the bathroom and wipe your nose. You have snot on your lip."

Jennie giggled.

"And get back here to help clean up."

Her smile disappeared. "I want to help Cassie make supper."

"You'll be in the way—"

"Of course you can help. In fact, you should. You and Kathy both." Cassie handed a mop to Kathy and smiled at Jennie. "Wash your hands first, okay? And Mason's right, your face is a mess."

Her injury apparently forgotten, Kathy mopped with more vigor than accuracy while Jennie skipped from the room, singing the *Bubble Guppies* song.

They needed a woman in their lives who could teach them stuff Mason couldn't. But they also needed a man who could teach them to change a flat tire, unplug a toilet, and fix a leaky faucet. Mason telegraphed his silent thanks to Cassie.

She smiled back. "Stay for supper?"

After the way he'd acted over spilled milk—albeit scalding-hot milk—he should stay and try to make a better impression. On Job and Dinah, not Cassie. "I would like that. Thank you."

A mere forty-five minutes later they were seated around the table. The stew smelled delicious. Eating Virgil's sandwich seemed like hours ago. Mason reached for the basket of rolls the size of softballs. Bobby elbowed him. Mason surveyed the table. Everyone had their heads down. Jennie had her hands clasped together.

Okay. Growing up, Mason had eaten dinner at houses where his friends' parents said grace before meals. He closed his eyes and waited.

Nothing. He opened one eye and peeked. Job's head was still down.

He squeezed his eyes shut.

"Amen."

All five kids started talking at the same time. Cassie passed the basket to Mason. She grinned. "Now you can eat."

"Thank you."

"You're a gut *bruder.*"

"Gut bruder." He tried the words on for size. They didn't sound the same coming from his mouth. "I hope that's a compliment."

"It is. You're a good brother. Dinah and I plan to teach the kinner—the children—Pennsylvania Dutch. That's what we speak among ourselves. They'll do great at school because they already know English. They also need to learn German."

"Only if they decide to stay here when they get older."

"Jah. Yes." Her dimples deepened. "We hope they do. We hope you do."

She turned away to help Donny clean up the stew he dripped on the table. Then Jennie needed help with the butter. Cassie was a natural. Why wasn't she married? He didn't know much, but Mason knew Amish women mostly married young and had lots of kids.

The stew was thick and savory. When was the last time he'd eaten a home-cooked meal? He couldn't remember. The bread melted in his mouth. He helped himself to seconds.

"This is really good stew, Cassie." Bobby offered up his opinion before Mason could. "You're a really good cook."

Mason studied his brother's face. Bobby hated vegetables. Mason couldn't remember the last time he willingly ate something healthy. He was really making an effort. This was good. Really good.

"Thank you, but it's just stew." Cassie's cheeks turned pink. "Any cook around here worth her salt can make stew."

"You're blushing." Bobby ducked his head and grinned. "You can't take a compliment. I'm surprised. You must get them all the time."

Mason peeked at Cassie, who seemed engrossed in buttering her roll, then back at his brother. What was going on here?

"We don't need compliments for doing what needs to be done." Job patted his lips with his napkin and threw it on the table. "It's expected."

Bobby shrugged and helped himself to more stew. "Doesn't hurt to be grateful, though."

In all his years Bobby had never expressed thanks for Mason's efforts to feed him. Of course, that usually involved food that came in a paper sack.

Still, it was good to see him show some manners. Even if it did seem sort of like flirting. Bobby was sixteen. If he had a girlfriend back in Wichita, he'd kept it to himself. The age difference was just enough that Mason and his half brother never hung out or played around together. They shared a room for years, but Mason was either at work or at school most of the time. Bobby was into skateboarding and hip-hop while Mason liked baseball and country music.

The chance to be close seemed to have passed them by.

The first notes of a Miranda Lambert tune played from the vicinity of Mason's hip pocket. Sudden heat toasted his face. "Sorry about that. It's work." Tugging at the phone, he slid from the bench and headed for the back door. "I always answer when the boss calls."

"That's a good policy." Job waved away the apology with his fork. "Don't mind us."

Mason ducked outside and answered. His boss sounded harried, which made perfect sense somehow since his name was Harry. "Can you come in tomorrow?"

"Tomorrow is Saturday. I'm beat."

"I know, but it's OT. I'll pay you double time. We're running behind schedule and the owners are getting antsy. Their lease will be up at the end of the month. They don't want to have to move into a month-to-month rental."

Harry had the upper hand. He knew Mason always needed the money. "Sure, I'm game."

"See you around six then."

Mason groaned. One of two days when he allowed himself to turn off the alarm. "Make it eight."

"Seven and we'll call it even."

"You know how to hurt a guy."

Mason returned to the kitchen. "I hate to eat and run, but I have to get home. It turns out I'm working an early shift tomorrow. I need to do a load of laundry. My work pants are so dirty I could stand them in the corner."

"Don't go, Sonny." Jennie used the nickname Mom had preferred for Mason. "Don't go."

"Yeah, don't go," the others chorused.

"It's OT, guys. I don't have the luxury of turning down good money."

Jennie slid from the bench and trotted to his side. She tugged on his sleeve. "When will you be back?"

Honestly, he didn't know. "Soon."

"Promise." The protruding lower lip was back.

"We'll see." He slipped through the back door and made it to the Trailblazer without tearing up. *Cowboy up, dude.*

"You didn't get dessert."

He started and turned. Cassie stood behind him. She held out a stack of peanut butter cookies wrapped in a napkin. Her nose wrinkled. "Even I know 'we'll see' means no."

"It'll be easier if I stay away."

"For you, maybe. Not for them. Sunday will be their first visit to church. Monday they'll start school. It's a scary time for them. They need their big brother." Her compassion for his children, whom she'd just met, told him so much about her. "The bishop is coming for supper Monday night. Come, too, so they can tell you all about their first day at school. You can talk to the bishop about any questions you have about us—who we are. It's a good opportunity to learn more about how we live."

When she put it that way, Mason had no choice. He ducked his head and sighed. She had him right where she wanted him. "Fine. I'll be here."

"We'll eat about five thirty. I'll make chili and cornbread. Do you like venison chili?"

He had no idea. His chili usually came from Wendy's. "I like anything I don't have to cook."

"Gut. Gut." She paused. Cassie should never play poker. Every emotion showed on her face, and right now she wanted to say something but wasn't sure how to do it.

"Say whatever it is you need to say."

She took a long breath and let it out. "Dinah wants Perry to come home. Can you tell him?"

"She shouldn't want him to come home." Mason cursed inwardly. Being mean didn't help. Still, if Dinah knew her grown-up son, she wouldn't be so eager to have him in her life. "I mean, I know he's her son and her only child now, but he's never been one of my favorite people."

"Why's that?" Disappointment shrouded her words. "Did he do something bad?"

"For one thing, he took off after the funeral and never even said good-bye. He didn't offer to help me with the kids. He's their uncle—my uncle—but he wanted nothing to do with raising them. I guess Mom knew he wouldn't. That's why she left instructions for how to find Job and Dinah."

"He's not married? He doesn't have kids of his own?"

"No. I think he might have been at one time, but not now. He was always making cracks about Mom being a baby-making machine. Once he said something about it being in her genes."

At the time Mason hadn't understood. Now he did.

"Dinah wants to see him." Cassie's shoulders hunched. "He's her son, like you said, and he might not be perfect, but he deserves forgiveness. And Dinah deserves another chance to know him. Surely by now, he must want that too."

"If he did, he'd be here. And I don't know about forgiving him for abandoning the kids when they had just lost their mother."

"There's nothing that can't be forgiven." Cassie pulled her coat tighter and shivered. "Do you have a way to reach him?"

"I have a telephone number. I tried to call him after he did his disappearing routine. I wanted to give him . . . to let him know how wrong it was to abandon the kids. They needed him. I got voice mail. He never called me back."

"Will you try again? For Dinah's sake?"

How could he say no to such a kind soul, such a sweet face?

Mason had known very few truly nice people in his life. "I'll think about it."

"Good. You are a good man, Mason. Better than Perry. My mother always says take the high road. Thank you for taking it. I'd better get in there before a food fight breaks out."

"I said I'd think about it."

She whirled and scampered toward the house. Her laughter rang in his ears long after he shoved the Blazer in gear and drove toward the highway. That and her teasing words.

Something inside him stirred for the first time in a long time. It felt like anticipation. Or possibility. That something better might be possible.

All from a girl's laugh.

"You're losing it, dude." He turned up the radio and sang along with Blake Shelton. He still couldn't drown out the sound of her sweet, sweet laughter.

CHAPTER 11

The arrival of Georgia's five children would definitely assure that no one fell asleep during the church service at the Millers' house on a bright, sunny Sunday morning. With the heat from the fireplace and sixty or more bodies stuffed into the living and dining rooms, naps would normally be expected. Keeping her smile to herself, Cassie nodded at the Masts and waved at her mother, who sat with Cassie's aunts and her grandmother. Mother smiled and mouthed, *Talk to you after*.

Cassie guided Kathy, Donny, and Jennie to a backless wooden bench midway back from where the ministers—meaning the bishop, deacon, and minister—would take turns speaking. Every person in the district—even ones who'd been missing recently because of illness—had made it to church this morning. Despite the icy rain and furious north wind. No malice or ill will intended. Plain old human curiosity. Everyone knew the story of how Georgia and Perry had disappeared one day without a trace.

Now they wanted the rest of the story.

"Have a seat, kinner." It had been decided that Bobby and Kevin would sit with Job, even though the teenagers typically sat farther back than the older men. Job would explain the service, which would alternate between Pennsylvania Dutch and German throughout. "The service will start in a few minutes."

"I want to go back out and pet the horse." Jennie tugged at Cassie's hand. "Won't he be sad and cold outside by himself?"

Every time Jennie said something like this, Cassie wanted to laugh and hug her. Was it possible to hug a child too much? She had so much wonder at everything new in her world. "He's wearing a coat. He won't be cold and he's out there with all the other horses. They're probably gossiping about us right now."

Jennie giggled. "Do you speak horse?"

"I don't."

"Me either. I wish I did." Kathy picked up the *Ausbund* and flipped through a few pages. "What is this?"

"It's our hymnal. It's called the Ausbund."

"There's no notes."

"We don't use music."

Her brow wrinkled, Kathy studied the room. "There's no piano."

"We don't use musical instruments either."

"Mommy liked to sing." Kathy smoothed her small hand over the book. "She liked to dance too. She and Clayton would turn up the music and dance all over the living room on Saturday nights."

"You'll learn these songs with time. We sing them over and over. You'll see."

Kathy didn't seem convinced, but she settled onto the bench and folded her hands over the book.

Bryan announced the first song. The song leader stretched out the first note and the congregation began to sing. Cassie quickly found the page in the hymnal and pointed to the words for Kathy. It might help to hear and see at the same time. This was the best part of the service, though Cassie knew better than to say so aloud. Hearing her family and friends singing as one, holding each syllable for several notes, filled her with peace. All was right in her small world. It took thirty minutes to sing one song, but in that half hour they melded together as one in praise of their God and Savior.

Kathy tried to join in, but she kept shaking her head and frowning.

"What is this?" Jennie clapped her hands over her ears and shouted at Cassie, even though she was sitting on her lap. "I don't like it."

Cassie dug a small doll from her bag and handed it to the girl. "Play with this." She put her finger to her lips. "No talking, okay?"

Jennie took the doll. "What happened to her face?"

Nadine, who was seated in front of them, turned and offered a compassionate smile. *It's okay*, she mouthed.

Cassie shrugged and mouthed, *Sorry.*

Finally the second song began. Cassie's favorite because she had sat on her mother's lap as a child and sung it with her. Every service included it.

"*Das Loblied*. There." She pointed to the page for Kathy. "'The Praise Song.'"

"What does it say?"

"It's thanking God for His goodness and His mercy."

"I know a song. *Haters gonna hate . . . I'm just gonna shake*," Jennie sang at the top of her lungs.

Her cheeks hot, Cassie sought a glimpse of Job. His big ears were red and his mouth set in a thin line. She put her hand over the girl's mouth and bent close to her ear. "Hush, child. That's not a song we sing in church."

"She doesn't know. She's never been to church." Dinah held out her arms. "Give her to me."

With a soulful glare at Cassie, Jennie went willingly. She crawled into Dinah's lap, leaned against her chest, and closed her eyes.

Well, she *was* the grandma. Not Cassie.

Ten minutes later the first sermon began. Bryan preached about yielding to God's will in times of trial. It was a familiar theme, illustrated by stories from the *Martyrs Mirror* and the lives of folks in the district. Everyone could relate.

"I'm bored." Donny slid from the bench and settled on his back on the floor, one knee crossed over the other. "And I'm hungry."

Only the older folks who'd gone deaf with age didn't hear his pronouncement.

"Donny, get up," Cassie whispered. She tugged on his arm. "I have crackers."

"I want a Dairy Queen hamburger with cheese and an Oreo Blizzard. Can we go out to eat?"

Dinah reached down, grabbed his ear, and tugged the boy into a sitting position. "Nee."

"Oww!" The boy covered his ear and began to cry. "I don't like church."

"Me either." Bobby stood in the midst of the men's section. "This is bull."

Bull? Embarrassment turned Cassie's vision fuzzy. *Lord, have mercy!*

"Why isn't the service in English?" Kevin didn't bother to speak quietly either. "This is America, for crying out loud."

Some of the women gasped. Nadine clasped her hand to her mouth. Dinah simply rocked Jennie and shook her head.

"Quiet. Quiet." Bryan held up his hand. Silence descended once again. "We have some visitors in our midst today. This might not be the best time to introduce them, but it seems that they have our attention. We should extend the same mercy and grace to them that God does to us. We have with us Job and Dinah's kinnskinner: Bobby, Kevin, Kathy, Donny, and Jennie. This is their first time in a Plain church. They'll gain understanding as time goes on. For now, let's do our best to make them feel wanted, loved, and accepted."

A murmur swept the room.

God knew what He was doing when He made Bryan bishop. "After the service, please make it a point to introduce yourself to the kinner. This is a hard time for them. They've lost their mudder and her mann. They don't know us. And they're kinner. Jah, they should be seen and not heard. They will learn. They have much to learn. Our job is to help them."

With a sigh Bobby plopped onto the bench and propped his chin on his palm. Kevin dropped down next to Job. Dinah patted Jennie's back and smiled. "Gott is gut," she whispered. "He is wise."

Jennie and Donny slept through the remaining two hours of the service. Kathy's eyelids drooped, but every time she started to list to one side, she straightened. Cassie gave her a pencil and a piece of paper to draw on. That seemed to help. No more outbursts occurred on the men's side.

Danki, Gott.

Halfway through the second sermon—this one on Moses and the Ten Commandments—Jennie pushed away from Dinah. Fear emerged on her elfin face. "I have to potty. I have to potty now."

A titter of laughter ran through the women's side. Dinah set her on her feet. "Remember, no talking."

Her eyes wide with concern, Jennie took Cassie's hand and trotted from the room into the hallway. "Are you mad at me?"

"Nee, I'm not mad. This is all new to you. You have to learn."

"I don't like church. It's no fun."

"It's not supposed to be fun. We're here to worship God."

"Why does it take so long? Isn't God hungry?"

Cassie couldn't help it. She chuckled. "Maybe He is. Either way, He won't mind if I give you a snack in the meantime. Wash your hands. And next time, go potty before the service starts."

The rest of the service passed without incident. Afterward Cassie took Jennie from Dinah's arms and together they made their way to Job. He took charge of Donny, who hummed a tune and skipped between the benches, chipper after his long nap. The girls headed to the kitchen where the women crowded every inch of floor, getting the food ready while the men rearranged furniture in the other rooms.

"That was quite a spectacle." Nadine squeezed between Dinah and Cassie, holding a platter of sandwiches. "I thought Peter Raber was going to pass out. His face turned purple."

"Like Bryan said, grace and mercy, grace and mercy. My kinnskinner have a lot to learn, but they'll be fine if everyone treats them like family." Dinah placed cookies on a platter without missing a beat. Cassie could never figure out how she did it. "It would be nice if you'd ask your bruders to make friends with the boys."

"I will." Nadine snatched a snickerdoodle from the plate and took a bite. "Maybe they can help them get settled at schul tomorrow too."

"That would be so helpful."

"Consider it done." Nadine winked at Cassie. "My mudder says Saturday is a gut day for a sewing frolic. She says it would be easier for you if we come to your house. Is that okay with you?"

"Perfect." Cassie had already shared Nadine's idea with Dinah. She was all for it. "I have everything ready."

"Gut. I'll go check on the boys." Nadine patted Jennie's head. "You have your mammi's eyes."

"She's a gut friend." Dinah watched Nadine slip into the dining room. She wiped at her face with the back of her sleeve and cleared her throat. Then she held out the cookie platter to Kathy. "Would you like to help Cassie serve?"

"Jah." Kathy grinned at her grandma. "That means 'yes.'"

"Can I help too?"

Jennie's hand went to the plate. Dinah brushed it away. "You can help, but let Kathy carry the platter. You can have a cookie after we've served the others and you eat your sandwich."

Jennie's exaggerated sigh coupled with an eye roll made all of them laugh.

Cassie let the girls go first and then Dinah, who leaned harder on her walking stick than usual. Dark circles ringed her faded eyes. "Are you all right? You seem tired."

"My kinnskinner are with me in church today. It's the hand of Gott moving in Job's and my life." Her smile lit up her face. "I'm wunderbarr." At the door she paused. "Gott didn't say it would be easy. Only that He would be with us during hard times. Don't you feel Him moving here today?"

Cassie nodded. Then she remembered Dinah's dim eyesight. "I do. My hope is that the kinner feel Him too."

"Don't you worry. He's working on them. Our big mistake is thinking it's our job to fix them. I think He laughs at the thought. Us, with our puny ways, thinking we're in charge."

Her chuckle soothed Cassie as they waded into the crowded living room with platters of sandwiches. She wasn't in charge.

"Mammi, Mammi." Jennie ran willy-nilly through the crowd. "Bobby called a boy a bad name."

Cassie caught the little girl before she hit Dinah full force. Job's face was crimson. Nadine had bright-red spots in the middle of her white cheeks. Her brother Micah had his hands over his nose.

God needed to speed up His plan.

CHAPTER 12

Too many firsts too fast. If it were up to Cassie—and it wasn't—she would've let these children have a few more days to adjust to their new home before sending them to school. Job had rejected Dinah's suggestion along the same vein. *"No time like the present"* was the bishop's directive. Then he marched Bobby out to the barn where the boy would get his first lesson in mucking stalls and feeding livestock, followed by chopping firewood. Neither of them was smiling.

Cassie glanced at Kevin sitting on the buggy seat next to her. It was obvious he took his cues from his brother. She'd tried talking to Kevin, but so far his glum responses had consisted of grunts and an occasional "nope." His teeth chattered despite his down jacket, thick woolen stocking cap, and gloves. He clutched the lap robe up around his shoulders. The ride to the school took more than thirty minutes. A northern wind over-rode any attempt by the sun to warm the early morning air.

"Are we there yet?" Donny called from the backseat. "I'm freezing. How come you don't have a car? Or a heater? I don't want to go to school. I won't know anyone."

"You'll get to know them. It'll be fun meeting new kids," Kathy piped up. Ever the positive ray of sunshine. How did she do it? "Some of the girls I met at church yesterday will be there. Rachel and Sarah and Kimberly. They're all eight years old too."

"I won't know anyone. I want to stay home with Jennie. How come Jennie gets to stay home?"

"Because she's a baby. You're not. You just act like one. A big baby."

"Be nice." Cassie took a breath of ice-cold air and let it out slowly. Kids were kids, no matter their background. She didn't have brothers and sisters to bicker or whine with growing up, but she'd seen it in the families of her friends. She longed for it, though she knew her longing might fall in the category of "be careful what you wish for." "Bartholomew and Christopher are your age, Donny. You met them at church yesterday. Besides there will be English—non-Amish—kids in the school too. You won't be the only ones who aren't Amish. It's a good mix."

They wouldn't be expected to know Pennsylvania Dutch or wear certain clothes. Or recite Scripture. They would fit in. On the other hand, going to a public school wouldn't help them assimilate into their new lives either.

Kevin snorted and turned so he faced the side of the road.

Most Plain communities had their own private one- or two-room schools taught by Plain teachers with no more than an eighth-grade education. Not Haven. Cassie didn't know why. They just didn't. Her English friend Phoebe Meade taught fourth grade and would have Kevin in her class. *Gott, give her strength.*

Outside the school Cassie parked the buggy between two tractors. Fathers dropping off kids. Some people might find the sight odd, but not around here. The newer, fancy tractors had cabs with AC and heat. Job didn't own such a machine.

Kevin climbed down, and Kathy followed. Donny didn't move. His face was white and peaked. "My stomach doesn't feel so good." He scooted back on the seat. "I think I have a bug."

"A bug?"

"Yeah, Mason said sometimes you get tummy bugs that make you throw up. I think I have some of those."

"It's just first-day jitters." Cassie climbed into the backseat and put her arm around him. "What if I promise to stay for a while? Just until those bugs decide to leave you alone?"

His bottom lip trembled, but he nodded. "You promise?"

"I promise."

They walked into the school hand in hand. Even Kevin took Donny's hand without complaint. Their woebegone faces made Cassie want to let them turn around and race back to the buggy. She'd never been the new kid. She attended the same school with the same kids from first through eighth grade. What did it feel like to move from home to their grandparents' home and get thrown into a new school?

Scary. It had to be scary. Cassie stopped at the double glass doors and gathered her charges close. The wind whistled through the branches of a nearby oak tree. She shivered and they huddled closer, their faces full of expectation for her words. They thought she knew what she was doing. That she had words of wisdom to impart.

Gott, help me help them. "Today will be your only first day as a new kid. Tomorrow will be better. Soon you'll know everyone, and they'll know you. No matter what happens, remember that your grandma and grandpa love you. And I love you."

"Aww." Kathy swooped in for a hug. "I love you too."

Donny joined in, his mittened hands patting Cassie's face. Kevin held back, but he straightened his shoulders and jutted out his chest.

"Come on. Let's go do this." Cassie pulled the door open and held it for them. "We don't want to be late on your first day. Job will come get you this afternoon, but I'll be waiting for you at home with snacks and hot cocoa. I can't wait to hear about what you learn today."

As it turned out, registering new kids took some time. For some reason it hadn't occurred to Cassie that she would have to fill out a pile of paperwork. Like a parent would. Only what she knew about these three would fit in a thimble. She chewed her lower lip and stared at the paper. Parents' names. The kids even had different surnames. Address, date of birth, place of birth, last school attended, immunizations, doctor, food allergies, and so on.

She tried asking the kids, which worked for some things, like birthdays and last school attended. She could figure out the birth year by simple subtraction. Kevin knew his dad's name but not where he lived. Kathy could name their dad but only knew his address as Germany. They couldn't remember the last time they went to a doctor. Hopefully that meant they were healthy instead of neglected.

Cassie tapped the pen on the form. A bell rang. The start of class. First day and they were late.

"Having trouble?" Principal Patterson sat next to Cassie. The principal had been a fixture in the school for as long as Cassie could remember. She surely had a first name, but every child who came through her school thought it was Principal, including Cassie. Her once-chestnut hair was a shimmering white now, but it still touched the shoulders of her trademark turtleneck sweater. She still smelled like roses and wore pretty pink lipstick. Her tortoiseshell glasses made her violet eyes appear huge. "Cassie! It's been forever since I've seen you. How is your mother—still making those gorgeous quilts? Who do these little ones belong to? Surely not you."

Cassie explained the situation, and the principal nodded and tut-tutted in all the right places. "Why don't we do this? You take the forms home and let Mr. and Mrs. Keim fill out what they can. They can get the rest of the information from the children's caseworker the next time she visits."

"That would be wonderful."

The principal patted Donny's cheek and winked at Kathy. "You kiddos will love it here. We have so much fun. Today is Valentine's Day. We're making valentines for our parents . . . or other people we love. How does that sound?"

"My mommy died. Mason says she's in heaven." His thin shoulders drooping, Donny wiped at his nose with his sleeve. "But they put her in a box and put her in the ground, so I don't know. We could send the valentine to the cemetery."

"I'm sorry about your mom. You must be sad."

Donny nodded. "I'm sad, but I don't cry. I'm a boy. Bobby says boys don't cry."

Bobby was wrong, but that was a conversation for another time. "Your mom doesn't need a valentine to know you still love her." Cassie stifled the urge to hug Donny. It might embarrass him in front of the principal. "You know who would like a valentine? Your grandma Dinah and your grandpa Job."

The picture of a much older child, Kathy patted her brother's arm. "Cassie's right. And you'll get to use scissors and glue. You like that."

That sounded good to Cassie until she caught the mortified look on Kevin's face. Boys probably weren't as excited about making valentines.

"Glue and scissors. We aim to please." Her smile resurfacing,

Principal Patterson held open the door. "Off we go. I'll show you to your rooms. Here at Haven Elementary, the sky is the limit and every day is an adventure."

The comical horror on Kevin's freckled face sustained Cassie as she followed the principal to Phoebe Meade's fourth-grade classroom. The sound of applause greeted them before they made it through the door. "I guess they're excited for a new student." Principal Patterson's eyebrows rose. "Students, this is Kevin. Be sure to make him feel welcome."

"Hello, hello, welcome." Grinning, Phoebe pointed out an empty desk in the second row between two boys who might have been twins. "Take a seat. We're having a spelling bee today. Nicole correctly spelled *caterpillar*. She's leading the pack right now."

Nicole was a cute redhead with a blanket of freckles on her fair face. She curtsied and fist-bumped the girl next to her.

"How's your spelling?" Cassie nudged Kevin forward. "It seems like the boys could use some support."

"Not bad." His cheeks ruddy, Kevin ducked his head. "I won the spelling bee at Carson Elementary two years in a row."

"Girls, the gauntlet has been thrown down." Phoebe gave Cassie a thumbs-up and cocked her head toward the door. Time for Cassie to bow out. "Show us what you've got, Kevin."

Kathy made leaving her easy. She simply walked into the room, introduced herself to her new teacher, and commandeered an open desk in the front row.

"She's a trouper," Principal Patterson murmured as they walked away. "I would keep an eye on her, though."

"Why's that?" Cassie matched her stride to Donny's shorter one. He seemed to slow more and more as they approached the first-grade classroom. "She's like a little mama bird to the others."

"Exactly. That's a big burden for such small, young shoulders, don't you think?" Principal Patterson halted in front of a door decorated with a wreath of pink, red, and white heart-shaped valentines. "She's holding it all in. Don't be surprised if one day it all pours out at once in a major meltdown. Be ready."

Good advice. The principal opened the door. Veronica Haag waved from the dry-erase board where she stood writing a list of words. "We have visitors. Yay! We love visitors."

"Not a visitor. A new student." Principal Patterson introduced Donny, who immediately whirled and hid his face in Cassie's apron. "He's feeling a little shy today."

Veronica laid her marker on the desk and bustled to the door, where she knelt next to Donny. "I'm Miss Haag. I'm so excited to meet you, Donny. I have some special animal friends I'd like you to meet. New students get first dibs on taking care of them. Do you want to meet them?"

Donny's death grip on Cassie's apron eased. He nodded.

Veronica took his hand and led him to a long, low shelf filled with picture books. On top, in front of a set of double windows, sat a cage that contained two gerbils. One ran with great agility in a spinning wheel. The other stared out at them with a curious glint in its tiny eyes. "Clyde's the one getting his exercise and Beatrice is watching us."

Donny let go of Cassie's hand and moved closer. "They're cute. Do they bite?"

"Yes, they are. No, they don't bite when they feel safe. It's time for their morning snack. Would you like to give it to them?"

"Can I?" He sounded breathless with delight. "What do they eat?"

"For snacks we like to give them carrots because they're good for their teeth."

She handed Donny a plastic bag that held small chunks of fresh carrots. "Just a few. They have tiny tummies."

Veronica winked at Cassie and smiled. "I think you can go now."

Cassie waved at Donny. Grinning, he waved hard and held up the bag. "I'm feeding the gerbils!"

Smiling, Principal Patterson closed the door behind them. "You've known these children, what, three days, four? They already trust you. They like you. They want to please you. That's amazing. Mr. and Mrs. Keim are blessed to have you."

"They're so easy to love. I can't imagine anyone not loving them."

"All children need unconditional love." Mrs. Patterson shoved open one of the glass double doors that led to the outside and held it for Cassie. "These particular little ones need to know you're in it for the long haul. You work for Mr. and Mrs. Keim, but right now the children aren't making a distinction. They think you're part of their new family."

She was. In a way.

Principal Patterson walked with Cassie out to the buggy and watched her climb in. She still had something to say, it was obvious, so Cassie waited. Mrs. Patterson rubbed her hands together. She must be freezing. "I've lived around Yoder and Haven my entire life. I have many Amish friends. I know how it works. You're helping out Mr. and Mrs. Keim now, but you're biding your time. You can't wait to get married and have children of your own. Mrs. Keim is in poor health . . . What does that mean for these children?"

No one could foresee the future. Only God knew the plan. Cassie shivered and pulled the buggy robe up over her lap. The children had Job and Dinah for now. And then there was

Mason. He was young like she was. He surely wanted to marry and have his own children, but these kids were his flesh and blood. "They have two older half brothers and a little sister who is four. Bobby is sixteen. Mason probably in his early twenties. He wants all five of them with him."

"Good to know. Tell him to come by the school. We'd love to meet him. He can attend their programs and be involved by helping with their homework." She wrapped her arms around her middle. "If he's any kind of man, he'll always be their brother who cares for them, even when he marries and has his own children. They need to know that."

"I've only talked to him a few times, but that seems to sum Mason up well. He will never abandon them. In any case, neither will I."

"I know that's what you think now, but priorities change. Life happens. All three of them are desperate for love. Their hearts are precious, tender. Be careful with those hearts."

"I will." Cassie clucked and snapped the reins. Mamie took off through packed snow and mud on the asphalt road.

Be careful with those hearts. So many hearts were involved. And they didn't all belong to children.

CHAPTER 13

If Mason had to choose one word to describe supper with Bishop Bryan Miller at the Keims' house, he would choose *awkward*. How much had Job told the man about his daughter's life after she'd left home? Did Bryan know her six kids had three different fathers? An examination of their faces might cause him to suspect, but if he did, it didn't show. He seemed nice enough. He didn't flinch at Jennie's method of eating spaghetti with her fingers, which was probably preferable to Bobby's slurping up two or three noodles at a time with puckered lips, or Donny spilling his water not once but twice.

So far the conversation had centered around the kids' first day of school and Jennie's obsession with the wringer washing machine. Kevin finished third in a spelling bee and some kid in his class threw up. Kathy liked her teacher. Donny fed the gerbils. All in all, a satisfactory start.

His brown beard full of crumbs, Bryan buttered another piece of toasted garlic bread. He turned to Kathy. "What church did you attend in Wichita?"

Here we go.

Kathy wrinkled her nose. "You mean at Christmas or at Easter?"

"Is that the only time you went to church?"

"Once I went with my friend Samantha and her parents

when we had a sleepover. It was just a regular church, I guess. Jesus was hanging on a cross. He had blood on His forehead. Samantha said it was from the crown. It had thorns in it. I'd rather have a tiara made of silver. Like a princess."

Bobby snorted. Kevin laughed. Mason telegraphed a stink-eye *Stop it* at them. They shut up.

"Your mom never talked to you about Jesus or God?" Bryan's eyebrows rose, but his words held no challenge. "Did she read to you from the Bible or pray with you?"

"We went to church a few times at Christmas and Easter, like Kathy said." Mason spoke up to save Kathy from further cross-examination. "Mom wasn't one to talk about her religion."

If she had any.

"She never talked to you about the Amish faith?"

Sometimes she'd run across a preacher on TV when she was recovering from a hangover on Sunday morning. Then she would pick apart his sermon while she lay on the couch with an ice pack on her forehead and a Bloody Mary she called "hair of the dog" on the coffee table. "Not really."

"Maybe you and I could talk about it more after supper."

Mason nodded. Cassie was right. He needed to understand the Amish faith before he ruled it out for the kids. Or for himself, for that matter.

After pecan pie and coffee, he and Bryan settled into rocking chairs in the living room while the women cleaned up and the boys followed Job outside to do the final chores of the day.

"I didn't know your mother. She left long before I became the bishop." Bryan studied the flames leaping in the fireplace. "It pains me to know she died without coming back to her faith. Or passing it on to you and your brothers and sisters."

"We've done all right."

"Job believes you are concerned about them being introduced to the Amish faith. That we might brainwash them or something like that."

"The thought crossed my mind."

"That's the last thing you have to worry about with us." Bryan leaned back in his rocking chair and began to rock. It squeaked under his weight. "We follow the teachings of Jesus. That means everyone has a choice. They choose whether to join the faith. That's why we have adult baptism."

That was a new one. "I thought people were baptized as babies."

"In most Christian denominations. Not us. We believe a person has to understand what it means. It was a heretical idea back in the day when the Anabaptists broke away from the church in Europe. They were persecuted for their beliefs, burned at the stake. Eventually many of them came to the United States so they could worship freely."

"I don't know why my mom left after she was baptized. She never talked about it."

"I don't expect you to know. I'm only asking you to keep an open mind. You're the son of a Plain woman. So are your brothers and sisters. We would like to have the chance to introduce you to our beliefs and our way of life."

No mention of Mason's father. Obviously that topic hadn't been broached by Job. "It's hard to imagine giving up my car and electricity and the internet and dressing . . ." Mason stopped, not wanting to offend Bryan. "I mean—"

"It's all right. You're bound to feel that way. You've been brought up in a different world, a world where material things are valued above all else." Bryan leaned forward. "Normally we wouldn't suggest a person brought up English even consider joining the faith, but in your case, you have strong ties to the community. You have Job and Dinah. Your brothers and sisters are still young."

"I don't want them pressured into converting."

"We don't pressure." Unsmiling, Bryan gripped his hands in front of him. "Be assured of that, Mason. We share our faith by our actions. We witness by the way we live. We don't proselytize."

Mason wasn't even sure what that meant. "What exactly do you believe?"

"That Jesus Christ is our Lord and Savior. He is the Son of God. We put our faith first, family second, and community third. We hold ourselves apart from the world so that we don't conform to its sinful ways. That's it, in a nutshell, but there's so much more to it. More than I can possibly share with you on a single night like this."

"I don't know. I just remember the baby in the manger at Christmas and people being so happy about this baby being born."

"He who knew no sin was born of the Virgin Mary in order to save us from our sin."

Mason nodded. He didn't know what else to do.

"Take a gander around you. Tell me what you see."

Mason followed Bryan's gaze. "It's a room. A living room. A sofa with a quilt on the back. Four rocking chairs. There's a basket of sewing sitting on the floor. Some newspapers and seed catalogs next to one of the rocking chairs. A propane lamp. A desk with a bunch of papers on it. A fireplace. A table with two chairs that has some boxes on it that look like board games. That's about it."

"Look again. Look hard."

Mason tried to see the scene through Bryan's eyes. "It's Job's house—"

"It's a home." Bryan grinned and clapped. "He and Dinah have made a home here. A home built on their faith and love of God and love of each other. They want to share that love with their grandchildren—all of them. They're asking you to give them a chance."

A love like nothing Mason had ever experienced in the house he grew up in. Sudden tears choked him. Embarrassed, he cleared his throat and stood. "I have to go. It's been a long day and I have to work tomorrow."

Bryan stood as well. "I hope I didn't dump too much on you at once. We don't often talk with outsiders about our faith. I don't have much practice."

"You'd never know it."

"I told Job I would try. I did my best."

"I appreciate that." Mason backpedaled toward the door. Turning his back on the bishop seemed like a bad idea for some reason. "Thanks for taking the time."

"Leaving so soon?" Cassie trotted into the room with Kathy and Jennie on her heels. "The girls want to say good night. They need to go to bed. They've had a big day."

"So do I. I have work tomorrow." Mason knelt to give Jennie and Kathy hugs. "I think we're all tired."

Hands on her hips, Cassie planted herself next to Mason, but her gaze ping-ponged between Bryan and him. "Did you two have a good talk?"

"We did, we did." Bryan edged closer to the fire. He put his hands behind his back as if to warm them. "At least, I think we did."

Mason rose and grabbed his coat from the hook by the door. "It's a lot to take in, that's all."

"'Seek and ye shall find.'" His smile gentle, Bryan offered a quick wave. "Come talk to me when you're ready to know more. The invitation is always open."

"Good to know."

Cassie followed him to the door. "Drive safe."

Her expression was hard to read. Her dark-brown eyes were somber, but she smiled. He couldn't help but smile back. "I will."

"Hurry back." Her face flushed. "The children miss you. They need to know you're coming back."

"I'm coming back."

"Good. That's good."

Everything about her was so inviting. Mason lingered in the doorway. The house waiting for him in Wichita would be cold, dark, and empty. This house held warmth, light, and people who actually wanted him around. Like family. He might've grown up in a house full of people, but it never felt like this.

Luck of the draw, bud. "I'd better go."

"Are you sure? You're always welcome to spend the night here." What would Bryan think of that plan? Cassie peeked over her shoulder at the bishop. He seemed caught in deep reflection in front of the fireplace. "It's a long drive home."

"Work tomorrow. But thank you for the invitation. I appreciate it."

She nodded. "Drive safely."

"I will."

"Good."

Still, he lingered. "I'd better go."

"You should. It's late."

In the Blazer Mason sucked in air and let it out. He gritted his teeth and put the SUV in gear. *Get a grip, dude, get a grip.*

He might not have a clear picture of the religion thing, but Mason understood the home part. It sounded so good. It felt good. Especially with a pretty girl standing in the doorway, her tiny figure silhouetted in the light and warmth of her home.

The road away from both stretched long and dark.

CHAPTER 14

Saturday brought dark clouds and rain—much to the dismay of the children chomping at the bit to play outside after their first week of school. They didn't buy Cassie's suggestion that it was perfect weather for a sewing frolic. She didn't blame them. After a long winter, playing outdoors sounded nice to her too. Instead she enticed the girls to help her bake banana, cranberry, and zucchini bread for the frolic. Their faces perked up when she mentioned the other women would bring cookies and maybe even pie. Sweets could win over even the most accomplished whiner.

Job agreed to teach Kevin how to play chess. Bobby hung around the living room, staring out the window, a morose scowl on his face.

"I'll help with the baking." Dinah tottered into the kitchen behind the girls. "We should use my recipe for sugar-free apple-oatmeal bread too."

"Good idea. Your friend Lottie is coming and she can't have sugar either." Cassie always tried to have at least one treat for the folks who were diabetics. "You know she'll bring those pumpkin snickerdoodles you like so much."

"They both sound yummy." Kathy scooted a chair closer to the wood-burning stove. She took her grandmother's hand and tugged her toward it. "You can sit here and supervise. Your hand is cold. You need to warm up."

The little girl was so perceptive. She had taken on the role of mothering Dinah as well as her younger siblings. She even bossed Kevin around when the situation called for it. Cassie recalled Principal Patterson's words: *"She's holding it all in. Don't be surprised if one day it all pours out at once in a major meltdown."*

"I'm fine, *kind*. You don't need to fuss over me." Dinah plopped onto the chair. She tightened the shawl around her shoulders and leaned closer to the stove. "I could use a cup of chamomile tea."

Kathy scampered to the shelf and selected the canister that held the tea bags. "I'll make it, okay, Cassie? I know how to do it."

Indeed she did. "You're such a gut helper. Just let me pour the hot water."

"Me too. Me too." Jennie grabbed the canister of flour and toted it to the counter. It was almost too heavy for her to lift. "I'll break the eggs. I like breaking the eggs."

The time passed quickly. Having little ones to teach how to bake bordered on dreamlike. This was what Cassie's life would be like when she had her own girls. What a gift. Teaching Kathy and Jennie to cook was like a practice run. *Danki, Gott, danki.*

She slipped the mini loaf pans into the oven, closed the door, and straightened. The bread would be ready just in time for their guests.

"Mammi, are you sleeping?"

Cassie turned at Kathy's question followed by a giggle. Sure enough, Dinah had nodded off. Her empty tea mug teetered precariously on her lap. Cassie gently disengaged it from her fingers. "Dinah. Dinah, wake up."

Dinah opened her eyes. Confusion clouded them. "What? Is it time to get up?"

"You drifted off while we made bread for the frolic. Are you feeling all right?"

"Of course I'm fine. I just rested my eyes for a minute." She sounded more peevish than fine. "It's this dreary weather. It makes me tired. I'd better go check to make sure all the sewing goods are laid out."

"I already did that. Why don't you go take a little nap?" That she was tired so early in the day was worrisome. Her blood sugar had been within the acceptable range at breakfast. She seemed to tire easily these days. "I'll wake you when we're ready to sew."

"I don't need a nap."

Even so, she rose, knees cracking, hand on her hip, and left the kitchen for parts unknown.

Cassie sighed and went to help the girls clean up their mess. Kathy washed and Jennie stood on a step stool, drying. More water seemed to end up on the floor than on the dishes. Suds flew. Soap bubbles floated on the air.

It was perfect, simply perfect. Soon, the heavenly scent of sweet bread fresh from the oven wafted through the kitchen.

"Mmm." Jennie danced around Kathy. Laughing, the older girl took her hand and twirled her. "That smells so good. It's making my mouth water. Can we have some now?"

"I'm with her." Bobby ambled into the kitchen and slouched onto the bench, his back to the table. "Just not the one with zucchini in it. I don't do vegetables."

"It doesn't taste like vegetables, I promise." Cassie turned back to the oven and removed the cranberry bread. "You won't even know it's in there. But we should let it sit for a little bit before we cut it. Kathy, can you get the butter from the refrigerator? We need to let it soften."

"Shouldn't we save the bread for the guests?" Frowning, Kathy did as she was told. "We didn't make it for us."

"They won't miss a few slices."

"I could eat a whole loaf by myself." Bobby stretched his long black-jeans-clad legs in front of him. His feet were bare, a fact that had escaped Cassie's notice earlier. He had clean socks. She did his laundry, so she knew. He leaned back, his elbows on the table. "How did you learn to be such a good cook, Cassie?"

"I don't know how good I am. I'm average, really. My mom taught me to cook. All Amish mothers teach their daughters to cook. That's what we do. It's one of our jobs. Most Amish girls start learning to cook when they're Jennie's age. Just like she'll start learning to sew today."

"I'm glad I get to eat your cooking." Bobby grinned. "That sausage-and-rice casserole you made last night hit the spot."

"I'm glad you liked it. We'll be eating leftovers for supper."

"I bet it'll be even better the second time around."

Cassie sought another topic of conversation. All these compliments were disconcerting. Amish folks didn't talk like that. No one wanted to get a big head. Or act like they were better than others. "Did you play chess with Job? He's hard to beat. My father has tried and he hasn't won once."

"I'm not into board games. I really miss getting together with my friends and skateboarding. Now that's fun. Or dirt biking. Or the mud races." He rocked so hard the chair squeaked. "A bunch of us, we get together on days like this to go to the movies. We had popcorn fights and ate candy until we wanted to puke. Sometimes we even skipped school—"

"Bobby!" Kathy's dismay was appropriate, but her horror made Cassie want to laugh.

"Oops." Bobby rolled his eyes. "Don't tell Mason. He'll have a cow. He's such an old man sometimes."

Being the mature one must've been hard some days. "On days like today I like to read or sew. And bake and clean house." Like any other day. Fun was what a person made it.

If Bobby was Amish and starting out on his rumspringa, he might do all those same activities. Only they would be new and different and might change the course of his life. He might still decide to return to his old life. That would be hard on his siblings.

One step at a time. One day at a time.

"How come a cute girl like you don't have a boyfriend? Or do you?"

This time Bobby changed the subject. To one that left Cassie with her mouth hanging open. "What? I mean . . ."

Rapping at the back door accompanied by a chorus of "hellos" saved the day. Cassie grabbed the dish towel, wiped her hands, and hustled to open the door. A platter of cookies wrapped in plastic wrap in her arms, Nadine traipsed through the door, followed by her mother, sister, cousin, and an assortment of other ladies from the district.

"Let the fun begin." Nadine thrust the platter at Cassie. "Mudder brought some extra dress material she doesn't need, and Lottie has denim she can donate to the cause."

"Wunderbarr. Come in, come in."

Cassie settled the sweets on the kitchen table as the women handed them off to her. She took hugs, made introductions, and managed to remember to take the last loaf of bread from the oven.

Bobby rose to his feet and took a bow when she introduced him. He smiled, nodded, and even said a word or two in

Deutsch. He *had* been listening to her lessons with the younger kids.

"I'll leave you ladies to your frolic." He grinned at Cassie. "I don't want to be underfoot."

Nadine's thick eyebrows were getting a workout. "You didn't tell me how cute he is."

That was because Cassie hadn't given it any thought. And she hadn't given it any thought because her sight had been fixed on his older brother. Mason was cuter and her age. Bobby was far too young to even cross her mind. Besides, both of them were English. A big fat no-no.

"Why is your face so red?"

"We've been baking. It's warm in here. We made four kinds of bread."

"Yum. My dresses are already getting too small." Nadine was skinny as a rake. "Bobby would be a gut match for my little sister."

Nadine's little sister, Serena, had turned sixteen the previous week and had gone to her first singing on Sunday. She was a sweet but timid girl who liked to read and draw sketches of flowers. Matchmaking those two would be like trying to mix molasses and gasoline.

Cassie didn't bother to say all that. She simply shook her head and rolled her eyes. "The sewing machine is that way."

Giggling, Nadine lifted her skirt and skipped from the kitchen. She was a silly goose.

An hour later Cassie's mother joined the festivities. She was late because she'd gone to Hutchinson to shop for a new mattress for their bed. Her cheeks turned pink when she mentioned it, which made Cassie laugh. "How long has it been since you've had a new mattress?"

"Fifteen years."

"You're due."

Her mother slid off her sweater and took a seat at the work-station Cassie had set up in the living room. "I picked up some pretty lilac material for the dresses." She opened the plastic bag and pulled it out. "Do you have the pattern ready?"

"I do."

"Is this for my dresses?" Jennie slipped beside the chair and ran her plump hand over the cotton material. "I like purple."

"Me too." Mother pointed to her own dress, which was a darker shade of purple. "You must be Jennie. I'm Connie, Cassie's mother."

Jennie cocked her head and studied Mother. Finally, she nodded. "You look like Cassie. You're nice like her too. Can you help me thread my needle?"

"I would be happy to." Mother patted her lap. "Would you like to sit with me while I help you get started?"

Jennie climbed onto her lap. Mother patted the girl's head. Her smile held bittersweetness. "I can see why you're so smitten."

"I told you. Love at first sight."

Mother went to work demonstrating for Jennie how to thread her needle. Cassie paused to simply enjoy the moment, to en-grave the memory on her heart. There must've been a time when Mother did this for her. She didn't remember it, but it felt famil-iar and warm and sweet. The gentle buzz of conversation was reminiscent of the soft buzz of bees among the flowers outside the kitchen window on a summer afternoon. The foot pedal on the treadle sewing machine gently *click-clacked* as Nadine pumped it up and down. Lottie and Dinah leaned their heads close together as they chuckled over something Kathy said.

Life was sweet and full. "I'll get the snacks and the lemonade."

Still smiling, she headed into the kitchen where she sliced bread and added it to the cookie trays with a stack of napkins. She'd need a second trip for the lemonade and glasses.

Another rap sounded on the door. Mentally Cassie counted heads. All the women were here.

She opened the door. Mason stood on the rug.

Cassie's hand went to her *kapp*. She hadn't been expecting him. She had flour on her dress and egg on her apron.

What did that matter? He hadn't come to see her.

"Hey." He peered over her shoulder. "Have I come at a bad time? I saw a bunch of buggies in the yard. I can come back some other time—"

"No, no. I'm sorry. You're always welcome here." Flustered, Cassie backed away from the door. "Come in, please come in. We're having a sewing frolic to make clothes for the kids."

"Oh. Okay. I went into Hutchinson yesterday to get materials for my boss. I stopped at the store and bought socks and underwear for the kids. I don't want Job and Dinah to think they have to carry the whole load."

Cassie took the plastic bag he offered and peeked in. "You didn't have to do that. Job and Dinah have help. The whole community jumps in when unexpected expenses come up. That's why all these women showed up today to sew. They brought material too. That's how we are. God first, family second, community third, all woven together in a tight, warm fabric."

"That's what Bryan said. I've never really seen it before." Mason lifted his baseball cap, scratched his forehead, and re-settled the cap. "You don't really have any idea how lucky you are. The world out there isn't like this. We hardly knew our neighbors in Wichita, and we lived next door to some of them for eight years."

Cassie moved to the counter. She set the bag down. "It's not luck and I do know a little of the world out there. I'm not that naive. At least I don't think I am."

"It's not a criticism, believe me." Mason had followed her to the counter. He smelled like sawdust and pine. "I wish I could be like you and live in this cocoon of goodness. It's nice. I like it."

An unexplainable warmth started in the vicinity of Cassie's heart and spread. Sadness came with it. Mason's innocence had been taken from him by circumstances beyond his control. He deserved better.

She picked up a knife and sliced the last remaining loaf of bread. "Would you like some banana bread or cranberry? There's apple-oatmeal-cinnamon. It's sugarless, but it's still good. It's all still warm." She was nattering in her nervousness. "I have lemonade. I like milk with the bread, though."

"Can I have one of each?" Smiling, Mason leaned against the counter. He was so close Cassie could've reached out and touched his face. She didn't. "Milk would be nice."

She busied herself loading slices onto a platter. For some reason she couldn't face him.

"Did I say something wrong?"

"No, why?"

"You seem nervous all of a sudden."

Cassie forced herself to respond. "No, but I should probably get back out there and get to work. My mother's there."

"Of course. Right." He straightened. "Maybe I should go."

"Don't go." She held out the saucer. "You haven't had your treat. You have to stay. The kids would never forgive you if you left without seeing them."

"Okay, if you're sure."

"Very sure."

He laid the saucer on the table. "I just have to do one thing first. It's driving me nuts."

"What?"

"You have flour, something white, on your cheek. And your forehead, as a matter of fact." Amusement crinkled his face, and Mason wiped away whatever it was with his forefinger. "There, much better."

"You probably have lots of practice at that with the kids." Heat rushed through Cassie. He had a gentle touch.

"I do, but with them, I use a little spit to clean them up. Mom always did that. I figured you wouldn't appreciate it."

His laugh had an easy sound about it. Cassie laughed with him.

"Well, isn't this cozy." Nadine trotted into the kitchen. "We wondered what was taking so long with the treats. Who do we have here?"

More heat, this time from head to toe. Cassie made the introductions. She handed Nadine the platter of bread and cookies. "Let's get back to work. Mason wants to see the children."

Nadine gave Cassie the look. The one that said *We have to talk*.

Once they were safely out of earshot, she grabbed Cassie's arm and squeezed. "You didn't tell me he was such a handsome man."

"An English man."

"Son of a Plain woman, grandson of Job and Dinah."

"Still English."

"We'll see about that." Smiling like a woman with a brand-new wash machine, Nadine skipped ahead of Cassie. "We shall see about that."

CHAPTER 15

A month of working all day and driving to Haven in the evenings had taken its toll. Plus weekends. The Trailblazer coughed and complained. Twice it had stalled on the highway. Mason could baby it another few hundred miles, but the poor rust bucket would go to junkyard heaven soon. And then what? At least March was a little warmer—when the wind didn't blow from the north like it was today. He wasn't freezing his tail off on the drive.

Mason sat in his rust heap, parked in the driveway of the loneliest house on the block. To others this house in a blue-collar Wichita neighborhood probably screamed neglected dump, but Mason had called it home for eight years. Now it was time to say good-bye. He needed to be closer to the kids. He couldn't keep making the drive. Either he or the Blazer would keel over one day.

The fact that it was the last place Mason had lived with his family, his brothers and sisters, couldn't be allowed to matter. The rental lease would be up soon and he needed to move closer to Haven. To Yoder. Someplace where he could spend time with the kids without killing himself.

Despite his reluctance, Job, along with Bryan and a family law attorney who was a friend from Hutchinson, had attended a court hearing in which the judge had granted temporary custody of the kids to the Keims. Mrs. Blanchard had submitted a glowing report to the court. The attorney, who represented them pro bono, was working on finding Bobby and Kevin's father. The younger kids' father had hired a lawyer to help him explore his options. They were still waiting for his decision.

Mason took the time to grab the mail stuffed into the box at the street. It was mostly bills—bills he couldn't pay. He tucked them under his arm and doubled-timed it up the sagging porch steps. It was time to start packing. The landlord was happy. He could jack up the rent for the next family.

Inside, he strode into the living room, where he'd left a huge stack of moving boxes, a tape dispenser, and wrapping paper from the U-Haul. That stuff was expensive. He would borrow a truck to move what he kept. The rest would go to the Salvation Army.

He paused and stared at a sagging sofa covered with throw pillows with pithy sayings like Home Sweet Home. They covered up Kool-Aid stains, the place where Donny threw up the remnants of a pepperoni pizza and a root beer float, and stains that represented the many times Bobby plunked his muddy, grass-stained sneakers on the arm while he reclined and watched one of the Fast & Furious movies. It might not be a castle, but every room, every piece of furniture, held memories of his siblings. And of Mom.

Moving on to the particleboard shelves that lined the walls on either side of a cheap flat-screen TV, Mason surveyed a motley collection of dolls that needed face-lifts and new hair-dos. Cheap carnival glass won at the Sedgwick County Fair. A cuckoo clock purchased at a garage sale down the street. The owner said he bought it in Germany while stationed there in the army. Then Kathy had to have it. A smattering of books and magazines. Framed school photos of the kids from last year.

Not a single photo of Mom. She never wanted her picture taken. Not even on her wedding day—days.

A knot swelled in his throat. Not now. *Get over it, man.*

He swallowed hard. Finding a rental he could afford remained the biggest thorn in his behind. Rentals were cheaper in the rural areas than they were in Wichita. At least he had that going for him.

Suddenly so cold his bones ached, Mason tromped down the hallway to the thermostat. It read 76. Very funny. He might be a carpenter, but he knew little about HVAC systems. Maybe he had enough coffee left to make a pot to warm up. Rubbing his hands together, he strode into the kitchen. He needed warmth. The warmth of human touch. Not of a cup of coffee.

His mind conjured up a hot July summer night. Mom had sat in the swing, a tall glass of Long Island Iced Tea in her hand. She wore her hair in a ponytail like a kid. Her cotton capris were pink, her feet bare. She had them drawn up underneath her on the seat. The kids were playing in the sprinkler in their shorts and T-shirts. Their screams of laughter filled the night air. Mason sat on the step soaked in his own sweat. He swatted at mosquitoes, picked at a splinter in his finger, and contemplated joining the kids.

"Why so blue?" Mom lifted the glass to her lips. When she lowered it, pink lipstick ringed the glass. "Girl troubles?"

He snorted.

"Baby, at your age you should have girl troubles. Why don't you ever bring a girl around?"

To this dump? He didn't say the words aloud. She did her best. He was a carpenter. He could fix the place up, if he had the time and it actually belonged to them. Even with Clayton's income they didn't make enough money to qualify for a mortgage loan. She'd never owned her own house. She seemed content to rent and let the landlord worry about repairs. Mason managed to flash a smile in her direction. "I'm fine."

"I want you to be happy, Sonny. Really happy. Not just going through the motions."

"I'm fine, Mom."

"If something happens to me, don't try to be the hero, okay? You need to get out of here. Get a life."

"Nothing's going to happen to you. And if it does, I'd be the one to take the kids, not Clayton."

"My sins aren't yours, Mason. Don't ever forget that."

At the time he had no idea what she was talking about. Now, in hindsight, he could understand. The living will was dated only a few weeks after that conversation.

His phone rang.

Perry.

Mason had left a voice mail only a few days after his conversation with Cassie. He'd never received a response. Which hadn't surprised him. Cassie hadn't asked again. That didn't surprise Mason either. She wasn't a pushy girl. "Hello, Perry."

He couldn't bring himself to call the man Uncle anymore. He didn't deserve the title.

"Don't sound so surprised, Nephew." Perry did his usual jovial uncle schtick. A person wouldn't know he had never played the role in real life. "You rang. You said it was important. You sounded upset."

"A month ago. Which doesn't surprise me. You never step up in a crisis. You go into hiding. Like when you bailed out on us after your sister's funeral."

"I didn't bail out. I had to get back to work. I have responsibilities here."

A baby wailed in the background.

Maybe Mason was wrong. Maybe Perry did have a wife and kids. Why wouldn't he mention it? Or bring them with him to Mom's funeral? "Is that your baby?"

Perry's laugh filled the line. "Something like that. You said you had something to tell me. What's up?"

"Mom left a will. She wanted her parents—your parents—to have the kids."

Silence.

"Perry? Are you still there?"

"You're so full of it. Did someone tell you to tell me that?"

"No. She left a will. The kids are with your parents, Job and Dinah Keim, right now."

"Georgia would never do that. She hated that life. She wouldn't want her kids brought up like that."

"Come back here and I'll show you the paperwork."

More silence. Then Perry cleared his throat. "Good old Georgia. You never knew what she would do next. She'd get a bee in her bonnet . . ." He laughed, but the sound was raw and humorless. "Get it? A bee in her bonnet—?"

"I get it. I get that you both decided to blow off being Amish and left town years ago. But now my brothers and sisters are living in a house with no electricity and riding in a buggy to church on Sunday."

"Why are you calling me? What do you want me to do about it?"

"Nothing. Dinah wants to see you."

Perry made a coughing sound. More like a gagging sound. "Why?"

"Why does your mother want to see you? Because you're her son and now her only child."

"Who left twenty-three years ago and never called or wrote?" Perry mixed disbelief with a faint question, or maybe it was hope. "They're forgiving people, but that's a tall order, even for them."

"When she saw me the first time, she thought it was you and she fainted."

"Wow."

"Yeah, wow. She's in bad health too. She has diabetes, and she's losing her sight."

"You're really heaping it on."

"Hey, I'm just giving you the facts. You can find out for yourself by going to their house. It's on—"

"I know where it is. I grew up there. Remember?"

Mason tried to imagine Perry wearing Amish clothes, driving a buggy, and helping Job in the fields. Impossible. The guy drove a sleek black Infiniti. He belonged to a gym, favored black pants and button-down collared shirts, and always brought a couple of six-packs of microbrewery beer to the house when he visited. "Good, you know the way. If you don't go see her, you're a selfish coward."

"Buddy, I'm less Amish than you are."

"What's that supposed to mean?"

"Nothing. Nothing." Perry cleared his throat. "If Georgia wanted you to know, she would've told you."

"Told me what?"

"Ask your grandmother. Ask Dinah why your mother left."

"You can't just drop a bomb like that and not explain."

"I have to go."

"Yeah, do what you do best. Run and hide when the going gets rough."

Dead space greeted Mason's statement. He pocketed his

phone. "That went well," he told the refrigerator. "Good job, Mason. Why, thank you."

Good thing no one was around to hear him not only talking to himself but answering.

If Mason were a betting man, he'd bet that Perry would stay true to form and disappear into whatever hidey-hole he'd created for himself.

Leaving Mason to figure out why his mother left the Amish way of life and what it had to do with him. He thrummed his fingers on the kitchen counter. His mother left Haven twenty-three years ago. Mason was twenty-two. She refused to say one word about his father. Not even to make up a story to satisfy a little boy's longing for a small piece of who he was.

She'd simply walked away. He'd stopped asking.

Mason had only known his grandmother a short time. He couldn't pop over to her house and ask her personal questions. Could he? Especially when he'd failed to deliver Perry to her doorstep?

He would keep working on Perry for his grandmother's sake. In the meantime, he would take a few more of the kids' things to the farm. Any excuse to spend time with them.

CHAPTER 16

Everyone should have the chance to see life from a child's perspective. Cassie had helped plant vegetable gardens in March every year since she was Jennie's age, but she'd forgotten how much fun it had once been. Usually they planted earlier in March, but persistent rain this month had forced them to postpone. Not good for the produce stand, but for now, for today, she was planting a garden with two girls who'd only ever eaten produce from a grocery store. To them this was playing in the dirt and running around outside in the fresh spring air.

Smiling at the thought, Cassie planted herself in the grass next to Tater, who barely raised his head to take in her presence before he returned to his nap. She took off her sneakers and socks so she could enjoy the garden preparation the way the girls were. Every time Jennie stepped in the cool, wet dirt, she squealed with delight at the way the earth tickled her feet. Cassie wanted to feel that way too. Her feet sank into the cool dirt. It felt good between her toes. She couldn't contain a chuckle.

"We finished planting the peas." Kathy stood and brushed dirt from her hands. She looked like a Plain girl in her long, blue cotton dress. Cassie had braided her brown hair and covered her head with a white kerchief. Her cheeks were pink and the paleness she'd had when she arrived at the Keims' had long since disappeared. "What's next? Can we plant the potatoes? Will they be red potatoes or yellow? Mom liked to fry the baby red potatoes in butter and salt and pepper. They were so gut."

"These are red potatoes." Cassie picked up the basket of potato seeds she'd cut up a few days earlier. The girls had found it hilariously funny that the buds on the potatoes were called eyes. Now she did too. "I think I like all potatoes. Because potatoes become french fries and mashed potatoes and baked potatoes and scalloped potatoes and fried potatoes and potato salad. I think potatoes are my favorite vegetable. You can never have enough potatoes."

"I like tomatoes because tomatoes become pizza sauce and spaghetti sauce." Kathy wrinkled her nose. "But my teacher says tomatoes are a fruit. My favorite vegetable is broccoli."

"Eww. Broccoli stinks." Jennie squatted in the next row, playing in the dirt. "I like strawberries."

"They're not a vegetable." Kathy braced her hands on her hips. "You like carrots, don't you?"

"That's because Mason says if you eat carrots, you can see all the way to the beaches in Texas. I want to go to the beach."

Kathy sidled closer to Cassie. "Mason made that up to get her to try the cooked carrots," she whispered. "He told us broccoli was little trees and cauliflower was a flower. He was on a kick to get us to eat vegetables. It didn't last long because Bobby kept throwing them away when Mason left the room."

"At least he tried." It was easy to imagine Mason making up stories to get the children to eat their vegetables. He obviously tried hard to do the right thing. "We'll plant tomatoes and carrots in May. We can start the tomatoes in pots inside, and when it's warm enough we'll transplant them out here."

Cassie settled the basket on the ground next to the long

eight-inch-deep trenches she'd made with the hoe. "Okay, girls, are you ready to plant potatoes?"

"Me first, me first." Jennie hopped over the row of peas they'd planted earlier and landed on her knees next to Cassie. "What do I do?"

"You stick a seed potato piece in the ground every foot or so and cover it up with dirt." Cassie demonstrated. "Easy-peasy."

"Aww, how will the eyes see if we cover them up with dirt?" Kathy giggled and plopped down next to Jennie. "Do we put the eyes up or down?"

"Up, I guess."

"Can the potatoes breathe underground?" Jennie seemed genuinely concerned. "How does it know which way to grow?"

"It grows toward the light." Was that the right answer? Hopefully. Cassie had never given it much thought. They planted seeds, watered them, and they grew. Because God made things work that way. "Gott makes everything work together so we have food when we need it."

"Do we have to plant cabbage?" Jennie plopped another potato seed into the trench and covered it with more dirt than needed. That potato plant would have to be particularly industrious to make it out to the sun. "Cabbage makes me toot."

"Jennie!" Kathy elbowed her sister. "Who told you that? Kevin or Bobby?"

The little girl shrugged. "I think it was Mommy." She wrinkled her brow. "I don't 'member for sure."

Jennie didn't talk about Georgia much anymore, but Kathy did. All the time. Like she was afraid she might forget her. Little girls shouldn't have to hang on to their mommy memories so hard. They should all have a mommy. "Mom didn't like cabbage because it stank up the house. She was the same way about broccoli. I think she really didn't like vegetables much. We ate a lot of fruit, though, when she had the grocery money."

Occasionally Cassie got glimpses of what life had been like for the kids when their mother was alive. Fruit but not vegetables. When there was money. "I'm sure she wanted you to be healthy, so she fixed foods even if she didn't like them."

"I s'pose." Scratching a bug bite on her neck, Kathy squinted against the sun. "But Mason was the one who worried about that stuff the most. He even bought some awful green stuff called kale one time." She pretended to stick her finger in her mouth and made gagging noises. "We had a big mutiny. We told him no more kale or we would all run away together."

"What did he say?" Cassie froze, fascinated by this insight into Mason's approach to parenting. *Don't forget to plant the potatoes.* The garden would never be done at this rate. "Did he insist you eat it anyway?"

"He said anyone who ate all his kale salad got a DQ Blizzard for dessert." Kathy grinned. "I held my nose and gagged it down. So did everyone but Jennie."

"I still got a Blizzard." Jennie giggled. "'Cause I'm the littlest and I'm his favorite."

They both laughed at the memory. Cassie laughed with them. She'd never eaten kale, but she knew enough to realize Mason had worried so much about the kids getting nutritious meals that he bribed them with ice cream to get them to eat the vegetable. Whether he saw the contradiction in those two actions, she probably would never know.

A sputtering engine in the distance caught that thought and held on to it. Mason was about to make an appearance. His SUV had a unique—almost pitiful—sound. Jennie hopped to her feet. So did Kathy. "Mason's here, Mason's here."

That they loved their big brother would never be in doubt.

He pulled into the yard, stuck his head out the window, and waved. A second later the engine turned off.

"Mason, Mason, we planted peas and potatoes," Jennie yelled. "Potatoes have eyes."

Grinning, Mason slid from the SUV. "I know how much you love peas."

"I like the way Cassie cooks them." Kathy skipped out to meet him. "She's a better cook than you are."

Mason picked up Jennie and stuck her on his shoulders for a piggyback ride. She shrieked with delight. "But I give better rides."

"I'm sure you do." Cassie started toward him. Then she remembered her bare feet. Cheeks hot, she settled into the grass to put on her shoes. Dirt clung to her feet along with bits of grass and leaves. "You also follow vegetables with DQ ice cream, or so I'm told."

His grin broadened. "It's my own recipe. I'm happy to share it. Are you girls having fun playing in the dirt?"

"We're planting, not playing."

"You have dirt on your face."

"Ach." Cassie flipped her apron up and used it to wipe her face. Between the warm sun and her embarrassment, it was surely radish red. "That just means we had an extra helping of fun."

"Where's Dinah?"

"She wasn't feeling well this morning." That was happening a lot lately. "She went back inside to lie down for a bit."

"I hope it's nothing serious. Tell her I said hello." Mason frowned. "I saw Job and the boys down at the crossroads. They seemed hard at work too."

"He took them down to the produce stand to do some maintenance. It needed painting, some boards replaced, and a new sign."

"I could've helped with that." He raised his face to the sun and closed his eyes. Jennie grabbed his hat and slapped it on her head. It slid down over her eyes. "Hey, that's my baseball cap. Now I won't tell you what Kevin told me about the surprise."

"What? What did he tell you?" Jennie replaced the hat on her brother's head. "What surprise?"

"He said it's in the barn. He said you're really gonna like it."

"Let me down."

Mason knelt. Jennie and Kathy ran on ahead, alternating between skipping and a full-tilt hustle.

Grown women didn't sprint ahead. Her faithful hound at her side, Cassie walked sedately next to her guest. Especially since that guest was Mason. "Did he tell you what the surprise is?"

"He did not." Anticipation simmering on his face, Mason picked up speed. "What do you think it is?"

"It's hard to say."

The barn doors were wide open. Inside, the children huddled, giggling and whispering, in the farthest stall. "Don't let Tater in here," Kathy called. "He'll scare them."

Scare them? "Stay, Tater, stay."

Tater barked once, then quieted. He knew who was boss.

"Cassie, Cassie, come look, come quick." Jennie popped through the stall door. "Hurry, hurry."

"I'm hurrying."

What surprise couldn't be shared with Tater? Cassie rushed to the stall. Jennie grabbed her hand. "You have to see. They're the sweetest ever."

Coco, one of two cats who'd adopted the barn as their territory, lay in the corner on a thick bed of hay. She raised her head and meowed—a sound somewhere between a welcome and a warning. Cassie could see why the cat might be concerned with any newcomers. She had several of her own—five newborn kittens took turns eating and mewling.

"Oh, they're beautiful." Cassie dropped to her knees and squeezed between Jennie and Kathy. Neither child seemed to register her presence. "Coco, you did a gut job. Your boplin are beautiful."

"Wow. I've never seen kittens so tiny." Cocking his head to one side, Mason squatted next to Cassie. "They're like miniatures."

"It's springtime. All the mommies and daddies are having babies." Cassie loved this time of year. In a city like Wichita they probably didn't see much of it. "The cardinals have a nest in the poplar tree in the front yard. The cattle are having calves. Horses are foaling."

"The cycle of life."

Exactly. "Daddy must've been black or a dark-striped gray." Cassie tucked Jennie in her lap and tried to see better. Coco was so named because she was a deep, rich brown color, like cocoa. Her kittens were black, dark gray, black with a hint of gray stripes, and brown like herself. "They're so cute. They're adorable."

Even as newborns they already tumbled and swatted at each other in an attempt to play. Kittens were almost as much fun as puppies. If it wasn't for the need to get lunch started, Cassie could've sat here for hours just watching them.

"We always wanted a dog, but Mom said no 'cause they eat too much." Kathy leaned against Mason's shoulder and sighed. "Tater doesn't eat that much, does he?"

"He eats just the right amount." Cassie studied the three of them. Mason had a different father, but they still favored each other. They had Job's eyes, but the shape of Dinah's face, especially the chin. "But I understand why your mom said that. I love animals, but feeding you children comes first."

"That's what I always said." Mason's arm slid around Kathy. "Mom wasn't trying to be mean. She liked animals, but she couldn't feed one more mouth. And Clayton said dogs chew on everything and poop in the yard and bark at night."

Depended on the dog.

"Can I hold a kitty?" Jennie crawled forward. "What are their names? Can they come in the house? They'll be cold out here at night."

Cassie scooped the little girl back into her lap. "They're too tiny for you to hold. Their mommy won't like it if you touch them. These are outdoor cats. They earn their keep by hunting mice and keeping critters out of the barn. They're not like Tater, who's mostly a pet. As for their names, let's give it a few days. It's best to see their personalities before you name them."

"It must've been fun growing up on a farm, Cassie." With a wistful sigh, Kathy snuggled against Mason. "You probably played with kittens and planted potatoes and ate whoopie pies all the time. You rode horses and learned to make quilts and swam in the pond in the summer. It must've been fun."

The girl had summed up Cassie's childhood in a few sentences. To see it through a child's eyes sent a wave of repentance through Cassie. She would never again take for granted the sweet, carefree days of her childhood. Not everyone had such a blessed one. She knew that, but these children, so appreciative of each new experience, were teaching her to count her blessings. How dare she worry or fret about the future. No matter what happened next, she had been blessed.

Mason's eyes held deep sadness. Far too much sadness for such a young man. "You and your siblings are still young. You can still do all those things. You are doing them."

Kathy was only eight and thought life had passed her by. How must Mason feel? "You, too, Mason. It's never too late to be a part of Gott's natural world."

"I don't know. I'm so busy working, paying bills, and trying to do what's right with the kids, I don't have time to stop and smell the roses."

"Let us take some of that weight off your shoulders." Shyness suddenly gripped Cassie. Here she was in a barn talking to this English man like she knew him and he knew her. "You can smell all the flowers here at Job's farm. He won't mind."

She deposited Jennie on the straw and stood. "I had better go make lunch."

"Wait." Mason kissed the top of Kathy's head and rose. "I have some more of the kids' stuff in the Blazer. I'll carry in the boxes." He walked with her to the barn door where Tater sat patiently waiting.

"Good hund. You're a good, good hund." She gave the spot between his ears an extra scratch. "They'll still love you, I promise."

He didn't need to know he'd been replaced by a litter of kittens.

"This is what they need." Mason stood so close she could smell his scent of sawdust and mint toothpaste. He patted Tater, who smiled and panted with sheer joy. "All they've gone through, the loss of our mom, they can heal from it. They can still have the childhood you had."

"We know our lives are different. We try to keep ourselves separate from the world." Cassie sought to find the words to explain how much she appreciated the world in which she'd grown up. And how much she'd like for these English children who'd come into her life so suddenly to have those same experiences. "It doesn't seem like anything special. We don't try to be special, I guess is what I'm trying to say. But to them, it's all so new and nice. They didn't have it before. It makes me feel like I should go home and thank Mudder and Daed for giving me this life."

"You're doing a good job. I see a difference in them already. They're planting gardens and learning to bake and sew." Mason straightened. His smile held a bittersweet mix of happiness and resignation. "They're starting to heal. Maybe they'll forget a little how hard it was before."

"Don't worry. They won't forget your mother."

"Jennie will and Donny might. It might actually be better that they do."

"No, they learned from her. All of us are becoming the sum of our experiences, good and bad. That's what my mudder always tells me." Cassie surveyed the open fields beyond the corral where Job would plant corn, alfalfa, and milo. "I thought this was about me and Job and Dinah taking care of them and teaching them, but I'm learning from them every day."

"I learn from them too." Mason studied the ground in front of them. "I'm also learning from you. I like it."

She studied the sky, trying to ignore the question in his tentative smile. The answer had to be no.

How Cassie wished it could be yes.

CHAPTER 17

Recipe for disaster: Dump hot boiled potatoes into a big bowl. Add milk, butter, salt, and pepper. Attempt to mash potatoes while staring out the window to see if Job has returned with the children yet. He'd insisted on picking them up from school instead of Cassie. Sighing, Cassie knelt on the kitchen floor and scooped the hot potatoes back into the bowl using a washrag to protect her fingers. Now she would have to start over by peeling more potatoes and boiling them until soft. "Haste makes waste indeed. More like distraction makes a mess!"

"What was that noise?" Dinah tapped her way into the kitchen. "Did you break something?"

"Stop there before you step on the potatoes," Cassie called out. "Nothing's broken, but I dumped a whole bowl on the floor just now."

"Whoops. Who were you talking to?"

"Myself. And whoops is right." Cassie stood and dumped the mess into the trash can. She went to the laundry room and grabbed the mop and a bucket. When she returned, Dinah had settled into a chair at the table. Cassie went to the sink to fill the bucket with soapy water. "I'm sorry I wasted a good batch of potatoes. Now I have to start over. Can you wait, or do you need to check your sugar and take your shot?"

Supper couldn't be late. Dinah had to eat on schedule. Cassie had started early out of the need to keep busy. Mason knew to be on time. He'd gotten into the habit of coming for supper a few times a week. The kids seemed to need it. He was the constant from their old life. Cassie liked it too. Not that she would tell Dinah that. An English man coming to supper was no reason to act foolish. It wasn't as if she hadn't cooked for English friends many times.

Mason wasn't a friend. But something about him tugged at her. His diffident smile that tried to hide a world of hurt but couldn't. No, that made it sound like she felt sorry for him. She didn't. She respected how he anchored the world for his siblings. Plain folks valued family second only to God. So did many English people, but not all of them. Mason didn't turn away from hurt or pain. He slogged through it for the sake of those children.

Being around him felt comfortable. Like they'd known each other for years. Not that she could tell any of this to Dinah. Or anyone else. A Plain woman shouldn't be having these thoughts about him.

Gott, what is wrong with me?

"Cassie? Cassie!"

"Jah. Jah. I'm listening. Where's Jennie?"

"See, I knew you weren't listening. I said Jennie has decided she's too old to take a nap. Next thing I know, I find her sprawled out on the rug with Tater as a pillow sound asleep, the doll you gave her at church sleeping under the afghan next to her. Anyway, we're not in a rush. Leastways, I'm not."

"I guess all that housework tuckered her out."

"I guess so. She still objects to making the beds. She claims Georgia said there was no purpose to it because they were just going to sleep in them again the next night."

"So why do laundry? We're just going to get our clothes dirty again."

"That's what I told Jennie. Or why brush your teeth or take a bath? That one backfired on me, though. She liked the idea of not taking a bath. She says our house is too cold."

"She's a smart cookie."

"That she is. So tell me why you're starting supper so early."

Because she wanted to fix her chicken and dumplings and they took a while. All the kids liked her cooking. So did Mason. Her repertoire was limited, but she planned to check out a cookbook at the library the next time she went into Hutchinson.

"Hello?" Dinah's walking stick thumped the floor. "Earth to Cassie. What's got you in such a tizzy?"

"Nothing. I'm not in a tizzy." What was the question? "I'm fixing chicken and dumplings. It takes a while."

"You're in a tizzy and you're cranky." A tiny bit of asperity tinted Dinah's words. "That's definitely not like you."

"I'm sorry, Dinah." Cassie leaned the mop against the wall next to the back door and went to the table. She squeezed onto the bench next to the woman who was more friend than employer. "Jennie is still having nightmares. Kathy has a cold that won't go away. And Bobby hates working outdoors. How much more will he dislike it when it gets hot?"

"They're kinner. They'll have ups and downs. No one day will be perfect when you have this many kinner. Each one is different. They're doing fine. They're happy."

Dinah sounded so sure. She also sounded happy.

"You're right. I'm silly to worry." Cassie rearranged the salt and pepper shakers. "It seems strange to me that I can be so attached to kinner I've only known five weeks. How is that possible?"

"You have a mother's heart." Dinah's hand scooted across the table and found Cassie's without fumbling. "The first time you hold your own baby, you'll love him or her more than anything in the world. You won't be able to contain it. You'll do anything to keep him safe. You'll lose sleep at night. You'll worry even when you know worrying is a sin. You'll make mistakes and hate yourself for them. You'll wish you could go back in time and change things you've said or done. You'll cry when you realize you can't. Be careful, Cassie. Loving like that can come at a terrible cost."

"On their first day of school, Principal Patterson told me to be careful of their hearts. She didn't say anything about my heart."

"She's a wise woman who's loved many children in her life—none her own. She's watched them grow up and leave her behind without a second thought. That doesn't stop her from loving the next batch that comes through the doors for a new school year."

"There's no way to control it, is there?" Cassie squeezed Dinah's hand. Her fingers were cold. "You can't love in half measure. It isn't possible, is it?"

"Nee. We need to pray and leave it in Gott's hands. Gott knows what He's doing." Her sentiment was familiar, but no one had ever said it to Cassie with so much determination, so much certainty. "I remind myself of that morning, noon, and night. Now go on, make your mashed potatoes. Or just toss some potatoes in the oven and bake them. Easy-peasy."

"True. Or I could cut them up and deep fry them like french fries. The kinner would like that." Even if they didn't really go with the chicken and dumplings. The kids had hollow legs. It took a lot to fill them up. Cassie gave Dinah's hand a final squeeze and let go. She stood. "But first I'm getting your sweater and serving you some hot tea. You're chilled."

"I'm fine."

The sound of the front door banging against the wall and children all talking at once drowned out the rest of Dinah's words.

"Cassie, Mammi, where are you?"

Dinah rose and grabbed her cane. "They'll wake up Jennie."

Cassie let her go first. "She needs to get up anyway, or she won't want to go to bed tonight."

Before they could get to the door, the kids descended on the kitchen.

"Grandma. I made a picture of our family." Donny held up his artwork featuring a group of stick figures. It was obvious which one was Job because of the black hat and suspenders. Donny had drawn Dinah with her walking stick. "It's everybody. Even Mason, because he's my brother even if he doesn't live here."

"It's beautiful, Donny. We'll hang it on the refrigerator."

"Kathy made a family picture today too." Job traipsed in behind the mass of kids. "Apparently how families are different but are still families was the topic of the day."

"So school was good." Cassie bustled forward. "Take off your coats and hang them on the hooks. I've got cocoa. You must be worn out and cold."

"I have homework," Kathy announced as she unwound a knitted scarf from around her neck. "A lot of homework."

"I have sight words and a reading assignment." Donny sounded rather chipper at the idea. "Tomorrow I get to lead the line to the cafeteria for lunch. I fed Clyde and Beatrice twice today. Tomorrow it's someone else's turn. We have to take turns at everything."

He never stopped talking, even while tossing his coat at the hook and missing, clambering onto the bench at the table, and dumping the contents of his backpack all over it.

"That will be fun." All the tension flowed from Cassie, making her bones and muscles feel like icicles that suddenly melted into a gush of water. "Start on your homework while I finish making supper."

Despite the groans that greeted her instructions, the kids settled at the table and went to work. The chatter abated. Cassie concentrated on making the dumplings and shredding the chicken for her favorite dish. She'd just dropped the last dumpling into the savory chicken and vegetable concoction when Jennie skipped into the kitchen to announce Mason's arrival. "He brought apple cider. I love apple cider."

Sure enough, Mason followed, a huge glass jug of apple cider in one arm. "Sorry. I know I'm early. It was the boss's birthday, so he let us all go a little early this afternoon."

"You're right on time." Cassie took the jug from him. "You didn't need to bring anything."

"It sounded good and I feel bad always showing up here for free meals and never contributing anything."

"Just your presence is enough."

The words popped from Cassie's mouth before she had a chance to consider how they might sound. "I mean—"

"Thank you. It's nice to sit down to a home-cooked meal. At home, I mostly get takeout or make a sandwich."

"No sandwiches here. On the menu we have homemade chicken and dumplings." The heat in her cheeks was the result of the wood-burning stove and not her big mouth. "There's always room at the table, isn't there, Dinah?"

"Always. How was work?" Dinah took the conversation and

ran with it, leaving Cassie to direct Kathy and Jennie to set the table while she checked on the food and regained her composure. Why did she always feel slightly off balance around Mason? She was never good with boys. Which probably explained why she was still single.

Mason was different from the Amish men she'd known. Old beyond his years. Wearied by the world. Yet kind and careful with his words. He wore his responsibilities like an old suit that fit perfectly.

Why spend so much time analyzing this English man? Cassie mentally rolled her eyes. Nothing good could come of such mental meanderings. Instead, she focused on finishing up the food and getting it on the table.

The kids attacked the food as if they hadn't eaten in weeks. Kevin practically inhaled his dumplings. So did Bobby and Kathy, who cleaned their plates in record time.

Donny wasn't as enthusiastic. He pushed his food around his plate with his fork. "I didn't eat the peas or the carrots. They're gross."

"The carrots will help you see all the way to Wichita." Mason was working his way through his second big helping of dumplings. Cassie grinned to herself. He liked her cooking. Or maybe he was starved for any home cooking. Mason flexed his biceps. "Vegetables turn you into the Incredible Hulk."

"I already ate my peas. I held my nose, but I ate them." Jennie sat next to Mason, which she considered the place of honor. "I ate my carrots too."

"You'll be a better baseball player than your brother, for sure." Mason and Jennie exchanged high fives and bumped elbows. "Before you know it, you'll be hitting home runs in Kauffman Stadium in Kansas City."

"Girls don't play for the Royals," Bobby objected.

"Then I guess you can't either, 'cause you throw like a girl." Kathy stuck her tongue out at him. "And that's a compliment because I throw really good."

"That's enough, kinner." Job pushed aside the bowl that held a few remaining canned peaches. "Finish eating. You have chores to do."

Conversations at the Keims' table had surely changed since the kids came to live with them. They were funnier. Even if they shouldn't be. Cassie stood and picked up the empty pot that had held the chicken and dumplings. "If you're done eating, you can start clearing the table, Kathy."

"Me too, me too." Jennie scrambled down from the bench. At four she was more of a hindrance than a help, but she was learning fast. Her enthusiasm for the small jobs Cassie gave her made up for the mishaps with dropped bowls and odd table settings. "Can I wash this time?"

"You're too short to stand at the sink and wash." Cassie patted her shoulder. "But you can help Kathy dry. She'll dry and give the dish to you to put away. How does that sound?"

"Gut."

Cassie grinned. "You're doing gut with the Deutsch."

"Wunderbarr!"

Everyone laughed.

"I'll follow along and keep you company." Dinah picked up her walking stick from its spot leaning against the wall next to her. "We can work on your Deutsch vocabulary some more."

"Jah, jah, jah!" Jennie sang as she skipped away. "Nee, nee, nee."

"So much energy. She's like the Energizer Bunny." Mason

chuckled. "When she stops moving for a few seconds, she'll pass out and sleep."

Job stood and headed to the coatrack. He pulled on his coat. Bobby followed without his usual smirk. He knew the routine. Feed the animals and whatever other chores Job gave them. The kids were to help and then do their homework.

If they had time they played games and had story time with Dinah, if she wasn't too tired. Then bed. At first it had been a contest of wills to get them to bed at an hour suitable for people who arose at dawn, but with no TV or video games to fill the space and early breakfast time, they'd stopped fighting it.

Mason frowned. "Aren't the boys going to help?"

"Menfolk don't do dishes. They have their own chores."

"Tell me they at least make their own beds."

He was so funny in his English ways. Cassie shrugged. "Sorry."

"Division of labor, I guess. We always rotated. They used to argue over whose turn it was, so I had to make a chart. 'Course cleanup was mostly sticking dishes in the dishwasher. We didn't cook from scratch like you do. Fish sticks and bagel bites for five were more my style." He picked up his plate and handed it to her. "Which is why I really appreciate a good home-cooked meal. I did everything but lick it clean."

Cassie wanted to say so many things. That he'd done the best he could. That the kids were good kids. Nice, considerate, kindhearted. The important attributes. "You sure you don't want some peaches?"

"I'm stuffed to the gills." Mason patted his flat belly. "I'll need someone to cart me to the living room in a wheelbarrow."

Cassie shifted the pot to her hip and picked up the water pitcher with her free hand. "More to drink?"

"Thanks, but no. I'll explode. Let me help with the dishes. It's the least I can do."

"The girls will get them. It's good for them to have chores."

"That's true." Mason cleared his throat. He drummed one index finger on the table. "I talked to Perry. A while back, actually."

"Is he coming to see Dinah? She'll be so excited."

"No, I'm sorry. I know he's my uncle, but he's not a very nice person. She's better off not knowing that."

"His refusal to see her after Georgia's death will tell that story." Cassie could already see Dinah's determined resignation. *"Gott's will be done,"* she would say. But her attempt to hide the pain would be futile. It would show in her sagging shoulders and the way she clutched her hankie until she was forced to dab at the tears on her cheeks. "How did the son of two such sweet people turn out like that? I don't understand. I want to be a mother, but I sometimes wonder what I'd do if my children turned out like Job and Dinah's—no offense."

She cringed inwardly. One minute she was offering him more food and the next she managed to insult his mother.

"None taken." Mason studied the floor, his boots, the table, as if seeking something lost long ago. "I don't know much about good parenting—I haven't seen a lot of it. I do know my mother loved me and all her kids. Sometimes people do the best they can. They're not perfect, but neither are we."

Mason studied the table some more. "Do you think maybe we could talk later . . . outside? It'll be chilly—"

What a terrible idea. Yet every bone in Cassie's body wanted her to say yes. There was no harm in a quick chat on the front porch once the kinner were in bed. Except Plain women didn't step out for late-night chats alone with English men.

"Cassie, Jennie dropped a glass and broke it." Kathy stuck her hands on her hips and paused in the kitchen doorway. "Mammi doesn't want me to clean it up. She's afraid I'll cut myself. I won't. I'm eight."

Cassie backed away from the table. "I have to go."

"You all are doing a good job with them."

"You gave them a good start."

"Not really." Intense emotion blazed in his eyes. He wanted something from her. But what? She wanted something from him too. A taste of the immense love he lavished on his brothers and sisters. He was all in. Heart and soul. Cassie tried to pick up her feet, but they wouldn't move. "You'll be a good father one day."

A good husband.

A soul mate.

For some blessed English woman. How could she have let this happen? All she ever wanted was a man to love and a big family to raise with him. Now this man came along. This English man. She couldn't have feelings for him. She simply could not.

She should say no. No talking later. No talking ever. "I'll probably be putting the kids to bed and you'll need to get back. It's a long drive."

The emotion fled, replaced with a neutral mask that slid into place. "Sure. Right."

There was nothing right about it.

. . .

How could five weeks make such a difference? Mason leaned forward and studied the checkerboard on a cedar chest between Donny and him. Mason hadn't played checkers since he was seven and in day care after school. Or Connect 4. Donny, who used to sprawl on the floor, engrossed in cartoons on TV, had become a fiend at both games. Kevin, who had spent every waking second after school playing *Mario Bros.* and war games, now chewed on the end of a pencil, forehead furled, trying to write a story for his English homework at Job's desk. Jennie lay on the floor, propped up on Tater, half asleep but determined to stay awake until the "big" kids went to bed.

Only Bobby didn't participate. After finishing his chores, he'd gone upstairs without saying good night.

And then there was Cassie. Mason needed to steer clear of her. She played by a different set of rules, one he couldn't begin to fathom. She was sweet, kind, pretty, smart, and loving. And Amish. She didn't even want to stand on the porch and talk with him. Didn't want to or couldn't? Did it matter which?

"Woo-hoo, I win!" Donny jumped his red checker over two of Mason's black ones and landed in the last row. He grabbed the checkers from the board, crowed, and punched the air. "I win."

"And you're a gracious winner too." That's what Mason got for thinking about Cassie instead of paying attention to the game. Mason stacked another checker on top of Donny's. "That's three games now. I know when I'm outmatched."

Kathy giggled. She sat on the couch next to Cassie, who was teaching her to embroider cute sayings on pot holders she'd sewn earlier. Her demonstration on the Singer treadle sewing machine had been impressive. "Don't feel bad, Mason. Donny beats everyone."

"What can we do now?" Donny scooped up the checkers and put them back in their box. "I know, I'll teach you to speak Dutch, how about that?"

"Nee, your accent is bad." Kathy shook her head. "Let me."

"Or all of us." Cassie set the socks she was darning in a basket and stretched. "Donny, you start."

"Okay. *Dumkupp.*"

"Nee, nee." Cassie shook her finger at the boy. "Nice words. Not name-calling."

"What does it mean?" Mason was afraid to ask. "Why do kids always learn the bad words first?"

"It's not nice to call someone dumb." Jennie rolled over on her side and snuggled against Tater. "But Donny is a *bobblemoul.*"

"Hey!"

"Okay, that can't be good or gut." Mason knew a few words like *gut, nee, jah*—all the one-syllable words.

"She called me a blabbermouth." Donny stuck his tongue out at Jennie. "Takes one to know one."

"That's enough. Why don't I go next?" Cassie scooted around on the sofa so she faced Mason. "How are you? *Wie bischt du?*"

Mason groaned.

"Just try."

"Wie bischt du?"

"Not bad. See, you can do it." She glowed with pleasure. Mason liked that glow on her. He wanted to please her.

She cocked her head and smiled. "The answer can be *Ich bin gut* or *Ich bin schlescht.* I hope it's the first one, which is 'I am good.' The second one is 'I am bad.'"

Right now Mason was learning a new language from a pretty girl. "How do I say I'm doing very well?"

"*Ich bin zimmlich gut* is 'I'm doing pretty gut.'"

"That's me. Ich bin zimmlich gut." He couldn't contain his grin. "Ich bin zimmlich gut."

Cassie's cheeks turned a dusty rose. "Your pronunciation

is gut. Spending time with Amish men at work is helping, I reckon. That's all the time for lessons tonight. It's bedtime for the kinner—the children. You have schul in the morning."

A chorus of "awws" followed. Mason took the box of checkers from Donny. "Beat it, kid. It's bedtime."

"But we haven't heard a story from Mammi yet." Kathy added her pot holder to the basket, slid from the couch, and went to the hickory rocking chair where Dinah sat. Their grandmother had been quiet most of the evening. She and Job, who sat in the matching rocking chair across from her, seemed content to listen to their grandchildren's good-natured chatter. "Mammi, we can't go to bed without a story."

Except Dinah's eyes were closed. Once again she'd drifted off to sleep without them noticing. "Mammi?"

The multitude of wrinkles on her face moved. She opened her eyes and shook her head. "What? What is it, child?"

"We want a story."

"Not tonight. I'm too tuckered out."

Cassie rose and went to the older woman. "Let me help you up."

"I should be going." Mason placed the lid on the checkers box and stood. "I have to be at the work site early tomorrow."

"You work too much." Kathy sounded like an old woman, as usual. "You seem tired."

Tired from juggling two lives—one in Wichita and one here, but he couldn't tell his little sister that. "I'm fine. I'm young. I can take it. Good night, all."

His hope that Cassie would reconsider and at least walk him to the door died when she headed instead for the stairs with Dinah. She did nod as she passed, but that was it.

Her demeanor had shifted so suddenly during that conversation at the supper table. Had he said something to offend her? He reran the conversation in his head a dozen times on the drive back into Wichita. Nothing popped. Maybe Amish women weren't supposed to spend time alone with men. They were both adults over twenty-one. Could that be it?

The answer suited him better than the more obvious one. How did the saying go? *She's just not that into you, dude.*

CHAPTER 18

"Be careful. Your face will freeze that way."

Cassie halted at the barn door. Job's sarcasm told her everything she needed to know. He and Bobby still hadn't found a way to bridge the generation gap. Or whatever it was that kept them picking at each other. Clutching a jar of lemonade, plastic cups, and a baggie filled with peanut butter cookies, she peeked into the cavernous barn. Job stood near the long row of stalls that held his draft horses and the Morgans that he used to pull the buggies. He held out a pitchfork as if to give it to Bobby. The boy made no move to take it.

"Muck the stalls and then we'll groom the horses."

"No thanks." Bobby crossed his arms and thrust out his chin. "That's all I've done for the last two months. Muck is another word for scoop sh—"

"Hey, you two, I come bearing lemonade and cookies." Cassie shot into the barn before the conversation could escalate into a full-fledged argument. "It feels like spring out there. The breeze is downright balmy."

Weather was always a good conversation starter with farmers.

No response.

Bobby's face darkened and the scowl he'd worn since his siblings left for school earlier in the day—in fact, he wore it every day—remained firmly fixed on his face. He and Mason had some similarities, but their personalities were far from alike. His hair was brown instead of black, but he still had the blue eyes. He was stockier and broader through the shoulders. He didn't have Mason's sweetness either. Or Job's sense of humor. Or maybe Cassie just hadn't seen it yet.

Dinah said sixteen was a difficult age. Not quite an adult but no longer a child. Ready for more freedom but not always good with responsibility. Lots of raging hormones. Whatever that meant. Cassie's experience with sixteen-year-old boys was mostly from attending singings. The boys showed off for the girls, sang too loud, and chickened out when it came to asking a girl to ride home in their buggies. In Plain communities, boys Bobby's age were on the cusp of being adults. They were given the freedom to explore other ways of living. They started thinking about having a special friend and about baptism into the faith.

Big life issues and responsibilities.

Bobby already knew about big life issues. He knew about pain and loss. He didn't seem much interested in religion. Girls, on the other hand, definitely interested him. He'd made that abundantly clear.

"Watch your language." Job's tone had an edge that Bobby shouldn't ignore—not if he was smart. "This is what is required when you have livestock. You're responsible for feeding and caring for them. You said you liked horses."

"I do. I want to ride them, not clean up after them." Bobby edged toward Cassie as if to say, *Help me out here.* "I'm not your hired hand. You don't even pay me to do this."

"I'm your grandfather. I'm family. Families work together." Job took the thermos from Cassie. His fingers tightened around it until his knuckles turned white. "Everyone pitches in. I'm not asking you to do anything that I don't do."

"All we do is work. Chopping wood, fixing fences, cleaning the barn, cleaning out the chicken coop, oiling tack. It's like the chores are never ending. It's the most boring life in the world. It's like watching paint dry. It's like trying to count grains of sand." Bobby grabbed the stall railing with both hands and shook his head. "Don't you ever want to have fun?"

"Work is fun when we do it together with a willing attitude." Job turned his back on Bobby. He poured himself some lemonade with deliberate movements. "Danki, Cassie."

"No problem. I'm making chicken fried steak with mashed potatoes, gravy, corn, rolls, and pickled beets for supper." She was running at the mouth. All this tension was bad—bad for Job, bad for Bobby. *Please, Gott, help Job find a way to reach Bobby. They need each other.* "Dinah's lobbying for banana pudding and 'nilla wafers for dessert. Jennie thinks it's a gut idea too."

"Sounds gut. We still have work to do here, though."

He set the thermos on his workbench and nodded at Bobby. "It's here if you want it."

Bobby shrugged.

Carrying the plastic cup in one hand, Job walked with Cassie back to the barn door. He stopped and took a sip. "I can't reach him."

"I reckon it takes time."

"He reminds me of my suh, Perry. He's so much like him, it . . ." White lines tightened around Job's mouth. His breathing had a hiccup in it. "Perry was a sweet, happy-go-lucky kid who wanted to do everything I did. We worked together sunup to sundown when he wasn't in school. Hunted, fished, farmed. Then he turned thirteen and he became a stranger. Once I caught him coming up the stairs at three in the morning, smelling like cigarettes and beer. He was fifteen."

"Dinah says it takes time. Bobby will outgrow it."

"That's what she said about Perry. He never outgrew his rebellious, sinful ways. He left instead."

"I can't imagine how hard that must've been."

Job ducked his head. He took another sip of lemonade. "I aim to do better with our kinnskinner. It's probably too late for Mason, but not for Bobby and the other kinner."

Not too late for Mason. Mason sought something. He needed something. Cassie could feel it in every bone in her body every time he cast that wary, wondering glance her way. She chewed her lower lip to keep from speaking out of turn. That Job spoke to her at all about such important things was special. "Gott's will be done."

Surely it was God's will that all His children come to Him.

"I pray for them and for Perry every night."

"I will too."

"You should go."

"Maybe I could talk to him." Embarrassment made her voice squeak. Job would think she saw herself as better than him at handling a teenage boy. Her statement hung out there in the cold wind.

Job grunted and finished off the lemonade. He handed Cassie the cup. "I'll check on the hogs and the chickens. I've seen a fox poking around the last couple of days. The coyotes have been howling at night too. Besides, I need some fresh air."

"I know I'm not—"

"I'll be back."

Cassie watched him stride away for a few seconds. She squared her shoulders and returned to the fray. Bobby sat on a bale of hay, his back against the wall, drinking his lemonade. He seemed half asleep. At the sound of her footsteps, he straightened up and grinned. He was a completely different person when he smiled. "Hey, you're back."

Cassie went to the workbench and grabbed the bag of cookies. "I used chunky peanut butter because it makes the cookies crunchier. Do you want one?"

"Sure. Your cookies are the best."

Bobby had nothing but kind words for Cassie's cooking. He carried his dishes to the sink after meals, even though Cassie told him to let the girls do it. He brought in wood for the stove without being asked. He always smiled at her. Why couldn't he channel some of that kindness toward Job? Because Job told him what to do and she didn't?

Cassie handed him two cookies and then took one for herself. She plopped onto the stool next to Job's workbench. "It must be like living in a foreign country, being here. We talk a different language. We wear different clothes. We don't have electricity."

"They call that a third world country." Bobby chortled. "A really poor country. One of those socialist countries where all they do is work and never get rich."

Cassie wouldn't go that far. Socialist countries frowned on organized religion, if she remembered any of her social studies lessons. "Working is how we have fun. We talk and laugh and tell jokes while we work. Parents work. Children work. Everyone works. That's what we do."

"Job's not my parent."

"No. He's your grandfather. Your mother wanted you to live with him and Dinah. We don't claim to know why, but the fact remains she had a reason and your grandparents respect her wishes. So does Mason. We all have to do what our parents want, whether we like it or not."

"Mom was nuts. That's all I can figure. She didn't want to live here—why make us do it? Especially me. I'm practically an adult." Bobby stuck half a cookie in his mouth, chewed, and swallowed. "These cookies are great. Mom never baked. All our cookies came from the store. I'm a city kid. I've never been on a farm, let alone cleaned up cr—stuff."

"You said you liked horses. When were you around them?"

"Just at the county fair." He dusted his hands off, stood, and trudged over to the pitchfork. He tapped the pitchfork on the dirt floor in a nervous one-two-three rhythm. "The ag barns were cool, I guess. They stank, though. The fair is in the summer when it's hot, and all that animal manure made it smell really bad."

"Did you get to pet a horse or ride one?"

Bobby tried for a nonchalant shrug, but it had more of a disappointed kid feel to it. "Naw. They don't do rides. Mom helped the girls pet the horses while I took Donny to the bathroom. She didn't want nothing to do with the porta johns, so we got the dirty work. And then Kathy talked about the horses we didn't get to see for weeks after that. She wanted her own horse. She wanted to learn to ride. She wanted to keep one in the backyard. Finally, Clayton told her to shut up about it already. Mom didn't like that much. She told him *he* should shut up already. Then they yelled and slammed doors like they always did."

Kathy liked horses. What little girl didn't want one? Cassie rose and went to the first stall. She stroked Casper's soft muzzle. The horse whinnied as if to say, *It's about time.* Casper loved attention and anyone who gave it to him. "Casper's waiting for you to say hello to him."

"That's okay."

"Why don't you brush him? He'd love that."

Bobby sauntered to the first stall where Casper peeked over the gate, all ears at the conversation. Casper was the oldest of their three horses and the most laid back. He also was the most likely to beg for a treat—even from a stranger. "I'm a city boy. I want a hot rod, a hot girlfriend, and unlimited bandwidth so I can play video games twenty-four seven."

He would get none of those things here. "You're hurting Casper's feelings. You said you liked horses."

Bobby rolled his eyes. "Hey, Casper, what's up?"

Casper tossed his regal head and snorted. Even horses knew when someone was being insincere.

"Get the brushes over there on that rack on the wall. You can show me what you've learned."

"I'd rather you show me how to do it. You're a prettier teacher than Job." Bobby hustled to exchange the pitchfork for the brushes. Maybe he thought he was getting out of removing the dirty hay from the stalls. Not a chance. Job would never allow that. His pace slowed as he approached the stall. "How much do you think he weighs?"

"About a thousand pounds. Which is small for a horse."

"Doesn't seem small to me."

"Maybe you should give him a pat."

Tentatively at first and then with more confidence, Bobby did as directed. Casper stretched his head closer and nudged his hand for more. The horse neighed softly. Bobby smiled. "You're okay, Casper. You're what Mom called a gentle giant. She said horses were special because they work hard and never complain. They work in the snow and the heat. They never complain about the food you feed them."

"Your mom was right. She must've loved horses too. Did she tell you that?"

"Nope. She never said nothing about dumping us in a cult when she kicked the bucket either."

Cassie counted to twenty silently, then held out the curry-comb. "We're not a cult."

"Are too." Bobby took the brush. His fingers trailed across her hand. He grinned. "You have to swear allegiance to one God and get water poured over your head so you can spend the rest of your life mucking stalls and picking potatoes."

Cassie took a step back. He was trying to get a rise out of her. She wouldn't give him the satisfaction. She faced Casper. The horse neighed and ducked his head so his warm breath touched her cheek. "You start near his head and you brush in a circular motion. Apply some pressure. That gets the encrusted dirt, sweat, and dandruff loosened up. He likes it too. It's good for his circulation."

Cassie demonstrated the proper technique for a few seconds just the way her father had shown her. Casper's head bobbed again. He whinnied. "See, he's thanking me for getting that spot that itched right there on his neck."

Bobby slid closer, so close Cassie could smell his scent of soap and a spicy aftershave. There wasn't a single whisker on his chin yet. He took the brush and mimicked Cassie's actions perfectly.

"Take your time. Work your way toward his haunches. When you've done that side, you'll pat him on the rump and make a wide arc around him to the other side."

"This is fun. Just you and me and the horses. You're a good teacher."

"Thank you."

"Maybe you can teach me to ride too."

"Job will want to do that."

"I'd rather you did it."

The statement had an odd undertone that made Cassie turn to study Bobby's face. His glance skittered away but not before she saw something there. Something soft. A yearning. A longing she recognized. It wasn't the countenance of a young boy. In that moment Bobby became all man. She jerked her gaze back to Casper. Maybe this wasn't the best idea after all. "I should get back. I need to start supper."

"I haven't done the other side yet." His hand touched her arm, then withdrew. "Why do I have to pat him and do the wide arc?"

Cassie edged away. He was a teenager, stuck between child and man. An awkward place to be during a time of such pain and upheaval. He surely had no idea how to handle his emotions. He needed someone to talk to. Like Mason.

Cassie took a breath. "That's your way of telling him you're there, you're moving around him. And so he doesn't kick you in the teeth." *Treat him like an adult. Like a family member. Like a brother.* "You really think your mother would leave you with your grandparents if she thought we were a cult?"

"I don't know what she thought. She never said anything to us." Bobby patted Casper and made such a wide arc around his backside, he brushed against the stall's far wall. "But I heard her talking to Clayton in the living room. I started to walk past, but I heard her say something about her dad. I'd never heard her talk about family. When we asked, she said she'd lost touch with them a long time ago and it was none of our business. So I stayed in the hallway, listening. She was telling him about wearing that thingamajig on her head like you—"

"A prayer covering. We call them kapps."

"Yeah, that. And long dresses and aprons and stuff. He was laughing and saying he'd like to see her in such a frumpy getup. She said it wasn't frumpy, but it symbolized—that's the word she used—how prudish and repressive the Amish way of thinking was. I googled the Amish later so I could figure out what she meant. She said she couldn't stay and be brainwashed into thinking the only thing a woman is good for is having babies, cooking, and cleaning."

Yet she had six kids and worked in a store. As good an occupation as any, but she could've worked in a Plain store in Yoder if that's what she wanted. At least until she married and had children of her own. Instead, she thought life would be better out there—somewhere.

"We don't brainwash anyone. We share with our children what we believe. They have a time when they check out what's going on in the world. Then they decide if they want to be a part of the world or be Amish. It's their choice."

Only Georgia decided to be baptized and then chose the world. She gave them no choice but to shun her.

"I don't know about that, but she made it sound like she was the one who didn't have a choice." Bobby stopped currying for a second. The brush remained suspended over Casper's back. "She said she had to leave because she'd done something to shame Grandma and Grandpa. Something that couldn't be forgiven."

"There's nothing that can't be forgiven." The words came automatically. What had Georgia done that she thought couldn't be forgiven? Did Dinah and Job know? "Forgiveness is the Christian thing to do in all circumstances. What did she say she'd done?"

"I don't know. I sneezed. I couldn't hold it in. Clayton got up from the couch and walked into the hallway. He knocked the cr—stuffing out of me for eavesdropping. Broke my nose. Then Mom and him got into it about that. Screaming and slamming doors followed. And it was all my fault."

No wonder Bobby had such a hard time with authority. The man in his life had abused it and him. "Time to use the stiff brush. Some people call it the dandy brush." Cassie picked up the next brush from the trough's edge. "Start at the neck and work toward the rump using a flicking motion. That'll get rid of the dirt and hair you've grubbed up currying."

A multitude of emotions rolled across Bobby's face as he took the brush. "You're such a nice person. You really believe everything can be forgiven. You've probably never had a bad day in your life. That's what makes you so sweet. Sweet and pretty."

"Bobby, it's nice that you think well of me, but—"

"I know. You think I'm just a kid."

"I think you've been through a terrible time. You lost your mother and now you're living in a strange new place with some strange people with strange customs. You need a friend."

"Don't give me the friend speech. Guys and girls can't be friends."

He was probably right about that, but neither could he and Cassie be more than that. He was far too young and English. "I hope we're going to be more like family."

With a smirk, Bobby went back to brushing Casper. "Like I'd know what that's like."

"What I'd like to see is you giving Job and Dinah a chance. Give this way of life a chance."

"If it'll make you happy, I'll try."

"You can't do it for me—"

"Sure I can. I like you, Cassie."

"I'm twenty-two. I'm Plain. You're sixteen. You're English."

"If you don't like me, just say so. Don't give me excuses."

"Cassie, you'd better get back to the house. It'll be time to start supper."

Cassie whirled. Job stood in the doorway, a dark figure silhouetted against the sunlight behind him. Embarrassment blew through her. "I was just showing Bobby how to groom Casper."

"I've shown him half a dozen times. I think he has it by now. It's time for him to do his other chores." Job glowered at them both. "Bobby, grab the pitchfork and start removing the dirty hay. Replace it with clean hay. Don't leave the barn until you've done all three stalls."

"Sure thing. Whatever you want."

He was as good as his word, but he was doing it to impress her, not Job. This was not the idea. Cassie picked up her pace to match Job's long stride. "He's had a hard time. He's lost his mother. His life has been so different up to this point. It's no wonder he's having a hard time adjusting."

"I shouldn't have let you talk to him alone. He's not a child. He's not Plain. He's his mother's son." Job's stride quickened. Cassie had to skip to keep up with his long legs. He was somewhere else, far away in time. "I caught Georgia once. She was sneaking out the back door dressed in jeans, sandals, and a tank top on a summer night. She wore lipstick. Baubles hung from her ears and around her neck. I'd heard a car idling in the driveway well after eleven o'clock. I caught her just as she opened the door. I pulled her back inside. She was so angry. So disappointed. She told me I had no right to stop her. She was seventeen. It was her rumspringa."

Georgia was right, but the unwritten rule demanded that teenagers not rub their parents' noses in their rumspringa shenanigans. The memory had festered in the back of Job's mind all these years. Was it Georgia he couldn't forgive or himself?

"I wanted her to want to do the right thing. That wasn't her nature. I could never understand why."

According to the rules, he should've let her go. Rumspringa was a necessary rite of passage. Without it they had no way of comparing the lives they could choose. Not all teenagers threw themselves into parties, English clothes, and alcohol. Cassie hadn't. But many kids did.

"Two years later, she was baptized. She acted happy. Two more years and she left. She took Perry with her. I never understood why she bothered to be baptized if she was so unhappy."

That last sentence carried an even deeper hurt. "It is hard to understand. So many things in this world are." The urge to comfort Job was powerful, but what could a woman of scant years and little experience say that would help? "But they have a way of working themselves out if we stand back and let Gott take control."

Her mother's words came in handy at times like these. They would never know why Georgia did what she did. Only God knew.

"I only wanted what was best for her. And now for Bobby. It would be best if you keep your distance from him."

He pushed through the door and left Cassie to come in and close it. He didn't answer Dinah's query. He stalked through the kitchen and down the hallway.

Heat seared Cassie's cheeks. Had she done or said something that made Bobby think of her as more than a friend?

She scoured her memories for the past six weeks. She tried to be kind, comforting, encouraging, like a big sister. Nothing more. Nothing less.

Bobby's expression when he took the brush from Cassie had not been brotherly.

CHAPTER 19

Job's stony face said it all. Mason halted on the foyer rug inside the front door. "What's wrong? Who's hurt?"

"Nobody is hurt." Despite the statement, Job's demeanor didn't lighten. "I was just leaving for Bryan's house to call you. We can't find Bobby. I thought maybe he went home—to your home."

"You can't find Bobby?" How was it possible to lose a teenager? Thankfully Mason didn't pose that question aloud, given Bobby's track record for running away. "What happened? Was there an argument?"

Mason followed Job into the living room where he squeezed onto the couch next to Kathy, who was playing with her collection of Polly Pockets. "I need to know what happened and how long he's been gone. He's run away before. I may know where to search for him."

In the past Bobby had run away for good reason, but the Keims didn't need to know what a poor mother their daughter had been at times. Not always, but often enough for a kid like Bobby. He tried to come off all macho, but inside was a sensitive guy who wanted the family every kid wanted—and deserved.

"He's mad at me." A flush crept across Job's face. "I keep pushing him to do chores, like every other boy around these parts. He usually does them. Halfheartedly and not very well, but he does them. Today he refused. Cassie tried to talk to him.

He said some things to Cassie that were . . . out of line. I left him in the barn to finish his chores. When I went back out there to check on him, he was gone. We've searched all over the farm. He's not here."

Out of line? His brother had done nothing but compliment Cassie at every turn whenever Mason was at the house. "What kind of things?"

Cassie stood, one foot in the living room, one in the hallway, as if she, too, might flee any second. "It was nothing, really. I think he has a crush." Her face went crimson. She ducked her head and studied her white sneakers. "I think his feelings were hurt . . ."

Her words felt like a punch in the gut. How had Mason not seen that coming? The compliments at the supper table. Chopping wood and bringing it into the kitchen for the stove. Being all smiles. These weren't the self-centered actions of the teenage boy Mason knew.

And now he was embarrassed. He probably thought he had to leave. He was too embarrassed to stay and constantly be reminded of her rejection. How awkward for Cassie. Knowing Cassie, she'd been kind and tried to let him down easy. She probably gave him the friends speech. Nobody liked that speech.

Mason knew exactly how Bobby felt. Cassie hadn't wanted to hang out on the porch with Mason either. It didn't feel great at twenty-two. At sixteen it would be just as bad, maybe worse. He would feel stupid and embarrassed and like he couldn't face Cassie ever again.

"He just needs time to get over it." Mason sought to sound positive. "He'll come back when he's had time to think about it."

Maybe.

"Poor Bobby." Jennie's plaintive cry matched the tears that trickled down her face. "He'll be cold. Where will he sleep?"

"He's big. He knows what to do." Donny put his arm around her. "He's almost as old as Mason."

The perspective of babies.

"Kathy and Kevin, why don't you take the little ones upstairs to play." Dinah leaned forward in the rocking chair, her walking stick clasped between both hands. "Supper will be a little late tonight, but if they get hungry you can make PB and J sandwiches."

"I like PB and J." Jennie's tears dried up almost instantly. "I'm hungry now."

"You just had cookies and cocoa, Sissy. They're just trying to get rid of us so they can talk about Bobby without us. I don't want to go. I want to stay." Kathy shot a rare scowl at Cassie. "I'm not a baby. I want to help."

"Me too." Kevin stood, legs spread, arms crossed, the spitting image of the man Mason saw in the mirror every morning. "I want to search for Bobby."

"Guys, Donny's right. Bobby knows how to take care of himself. More than most kids his age." Mason picked his words carefully. Last thing he wanted to do was glamorize running away for three impressionable, world-weary kids. "He shouldn't leave and make us worry and wonder and wait up for him. He made a stupid choice, but he'll be okay. In fact, he'll probably come back on his own."

Maybe. Doubtful. "Right now, I need you to listen to Dinah. Let us grown-ups decide what to do next. Kathy, I think the PB and J idea is a good one. Pick out some fruit and some more cookies. You and Kevin can make sandwiches and take a picnic supper upstairs."

He glanced at Cassie for the okay. Would they be appalled at the idea of taking food from the kitchen? She nodded and smiled encouragingly. "You know where everything is, Kathy." She gave the girl a hand up. "But if you need anything, call and I'll come running."

"I don't need help to make sandwiches." Kathy sniffed and crossed her arms, her chin up. "I've done it a million times."

"Me too," Kevin chimed in.

"Me too." Donny beat Jennie to the words by a millisecond.

Mason waited until they traipsed from the room and turned back to Job. He stood and tugged his phone from his back pocket. "It'll be dark soon. I'll drive the route to the highway and to the gas station. He's probably out there right now trying to thumb a ride. If I don't find him, I'll call the Reno County Sheriff's Department to report a runaway. If they're like the police in Wichita, they'll have people who work runaways specifically."

Some worked harder at it than others. Mason knew that from experience too. The Wichita PD detective had put Bobby's information and photo in a database for runaways. He'd talked to family and friends and gone to places Bobby liked to hang out. After a couple of days, he even put the information on social media. Finally, a patrol officer picked Bobby up at a homeless shelter soup kitchen. Mom had been furious. She said he took food from the mouths of homeless people when he could've come home to eat.

More recently, Clayton objected to contacting the police in Wichita and Mom went along, probably because she didn't want CFS getting involved after the police learned why Bobby ran.

"Maybe he'll call you." Cassie moved to stand next to Dinah, who still hadn't said anything about the situation. "He could go to your house."

"I doubt it. He knows I'll be forced to bring him back here. It's the first place CFS will search for him."

CFS. Wait until Mrs. Blanchard found out. There would be recriminations all around.

"We don't usually ask for help from the sheriff, not unless a crime has been committed." Job's face turned a deeper crimson. "I should tell our bishop. He'll want to be involved in that decision."

"Do what you have to do, and I'll do what I need to do." Mason strode to the door.

"Wait."

He turned. Cassie had returned to the living room. "I'd like to go with Mason. I think I could help convince Bobby to come back."

"It should be me." Job lifted his wool hat from his head and ran his fingers through his already unruly silver-streaked hair until it stood on end. "I set this in motion. Bobby and I need to have a meeting of the minds."

"You were right about talking to Bryan. I know it's unusual, but this is an unusual situation. We need to get Bobby home." She paused as if searching for the right words. "Before we have to tell Mrs. Blanchard."

She was right. The specter of CFS descended and hovered over the room. It grew darker. Or maybe that was Mason's imagination. "I wouldn't mind the help." Why they didn't want Cassie going with him wasn't clear, but it didn't matter at this point. Only finding Bobby mattered. "She'll be safe with me. I'm a good driver. No citations on my record. I never speed—not much anyway."

"It's not that." Job closed his mouth. His thin lips pursed over his bushy black-and-silver beard. He stood and paced between the couch and the hallway for five or six strides. He stopped in midstride. "It's not that. Fine. Go. Stop at your daed's, Cassie, and ask him to call Bryan. Ask him to come over, too, in case Bryan thinks we need to organize a search party. If he has a problem with you . . . being involved in the search, stay there."

A search party comprised of a bunch of buggies and tractors driving fifteen miles an hour on dark country roads. Mason started to object, but Cassie's frown stopped him. He nodded. "Fine. Let's go."

Cassie grabbed a sweater from a row of hooks by the door and followed him out before she put it on.

Embarrassment suddenly pulsed through him, and he opened the passenger-side door and tossed empty fast-food wrappers into the backseat. The Blazer stank. With work and all the trips to Haven, he hadn't had time to clean it out or wash it. Dirty napkins papered the footwell. "Sorry about this. I'm not usually such a slob. It's just been a crazy time." He brushed crumbs from the seat and backed away so Cassie could get in. "What was that all about?"

"You need a wife to clean up after you." Cassie's cheeks turned pink, but maybe that was from the cold. She gave him a sheepish smile. "Plain women don't take rides alone with English men. I've never been anywhere alone with an English man in a car. Or anywhere with a Plain man who's not part of my family."

Mason chewed on that piece of information while he ran around to the driver's side and hopped in. Key in the ignition, he paused. "You're kidding me."

"Nee. No."

Such a different view of the world. *Quaint.* Mom had used that word the time she'd driven through Yoder. It was a quaint town. The Amish had quaint customs. How could she have hidden so much of her past from everyone, but especially from him, her oldest son? "Well, I hate to disappoint you. I won't sprout horns or fangs or whatever they're worried about. I'm a pretty average guy when I'm not trying to be father, brother, and mother to a bunch of kids. And I promise, your virtue is safe with me."

Even if she was pretty and sweet.

"I never thought it wasn't." She sounded as if she were strangling on the words. "But you might have to convince my father."

Meeting the parents and they hadn't even had a date.

Where did that thought come from?

Stop it. She's Amish, for crying out loud.

Perry's words wafted through his brain. *"You're more Amish than I am."*

What did that mean? He needed to find out, and soon.

CHAPTER 20

Her virtue was safe with him. What a funny way of putting it. Even so, the butterflies in Cassie's stomach settled. She adjusted her seat belt and leaned against the seat. The SUV smelled like the forest—thanks to a little green tree hanging from the rearview mirror—stale french fries, and sweaty boy socks. The realization made her relax even more. In some respects Mason was no different from her male cousins or uncles. He was just a man. A man driving through the gathering dusk, searching for his younger brother and needing her help.

Cassie allowed herself a sideswipe glance. Not just like them, of course. He drove an SUV with an engine that sputtered and squealed when he started it. Country songs blared from the speakers at first. He'd apologized and turned down the radio to a mere whisper that harmonized with the air whooshing by outside the SUV.

Now it felt like they were flying through the darkness, just the two of them, no one to see them, no one to hear them.

Such a silly thought. Cassie banished it. At least she tried.

All this talk of virtue had allowed thoughts of romance to pop up in her brain, right next to the ones that reminded her that his mother might have been Amish, but he was English. The intense blue eyes that reminded her of a hot Kansas summer afternoon didn't matter. The wavy black hair allowed to grow a little too long around his neck and ears didn't matter. Neither did the broad shoulders, solid biceps, and long legs. Or the calluses on his hands that said he worked hard for a living. Or the intensity with which he loved and cared for his half siblings.

Stop it. This was why the community didn't want young men and women who weren't courting to fraternize alone outside the watchful gazes of their elders. Father would not be happy when he saw her with Mason. He would probably make her stay at the house. She was only trying to help. "I'm sorry. I know our ways are different. We're just careful, that's all. But I love being around your brothers and sisters. I want to help them. And it's good practice. I want lots of kids, a big family. I just know not everyone gets that."

Cassie put her hand to her mouth. This time she didn't try to hide the cringe. How could she share such an intimate detail of her life with Mason? "Just ignore me. It's been a long day. I'm babbling."

"No, you're not." Mason halted at a stop sign and took a right to the dirt road that marked the beginning of her parents' property. They'd gotten here in less than ten minutes. "Why would you worry about, you know, having kids? All you Amish women have tons of kids."

"Not my mom. Not Dinah."

"Dinah had two. That's usually what regular families want. I mean, English families. I guess that's what you call it. How many brothers and sisters do you have?"

"None. I'm it."

"I see."

From the way his eyebrows furrowed and nose wrinkled, he didn't really see a thing.

"My mother lost babies before me and after me. I was the only one she carried to term. That doesn't mean I won't have tons of children—if I get the chance."

"Why wouldn't you?"

"First I have to find the right person, the right man."

She just kept digging the hole deeper. She couldn't seem to help herself.

"Ah." Mason fiddled with the radio station. The music changed from country to rap. Then he changed it back. He adjusted the rearview mirror. "You don't believe in . . . relations before marriage either, do you?"

Despite only tepid air from the SUV's heater, sweat formed under Cassie's arms. Heat billowed through her. Words disappeared. Her mind went blank. "Wh-aa-t? I mean . . ."

"I'm sorry to be so blunt." His face was as ruddy as an overripe tomato. "Perry said something weird when we talked on the phone. It made me think maybe there was another reason my mom left Haven when she did."

His cheeks turned a deep scarlet that eventually engulfed his neck and his ears. "Do you know what I'm saying?"

"You think she was in a family way?"

"With me. Yes."

"What did your uncle say?"

"He said I was more Amish than I know. I always assumed my father was a regular guy and that's why she left. If he was Amish, she could've stayed and they could've gotten married. Mom wouldn't talk about it at all. The other kids know who their dads are. I'm the only one who doesn't."

Mason had a reason for telling her this family secret. "Perry didn't say who it was?"

"No. He hit me with that zinger and hung up."

Twenty-three years was a long time. Georgia's beau could be any one of dozens of men, now married, moved away, or even dead like Georgia. "Why are you telling me this?"

"You wanted me to get Perry to come here, and I'm willing to keep trying." Mason wiggled in his seat as if he was trying to get comfortable. "But I need something from you. I need you to see if Dinah knows who my dad is. Or someone else. You folks all know each other. I bet the gossip was hot and heavy back then. Your mom might even know."

If she did, she wouldn't want to talk about it. Not with Cassie, anyway. "It's true there's a grapevine, but this was a long time ago. Before I was even born. We truly try not to gossip. Your mom may have left before anyone had a chance to know."

"Don't you think she told the father?"

"Not if she planned to leave instead of marrying him." Cassie could only guess how scared and trapped Georgia must have felt. She and her beau—if he was Plain, as Perry had suggested—could've gone to the bishop and confessed their sin of fornication, done a kneeling confession, and suffered a period of shunning before being forgiven. Then they would've been allowed to have a small, quiet wedding and move on with their lives. Georgia hadn't wanted that. "Maybe Perry's wrong and he was English."

"I need to know." Mason's voice turned husky. "Can you understand that? If my dad is still around, I want to know him."

"I can understand that." But could she help him? Cassie grasped for bits of hope she could offer Mason. "I'm willing to ask Dinah, but I can't ask my mother. She'd be horrified that I had this conversation with you."

"It's worth a try, don't you think?" He smoothed the wheel with both hands. "Every kid should at the very least know who his dad is or was. It might be too late to have him in my life, but at least I can know who he is, what kind of man he is."

"I'll try."

"Thank you."

"I haven't done anything yet."

"I'll stay after Perry."

Cassie leaned her head against the window's cool glass. She was tempted to open it and stick her head out until the conversation blew away.

"Are you all right?"

She straightened. "What will you say to Bobby when you find him?"

"I get it. Changing the subject." Mason adjusted the rearview mirror. Then he fiddled with a knob on the dashboard. "Bobby should be living with me. He's practically an adult, but he's still a kid too. With lots of hormones thrown in. I can see how he might get his wires crossed, you know, misunderstand signals."

"There were no signals." Cassie longed to shove open the door and escape. "None. I would never—"

"I'm not saying you would." He took one hand from the wheel and rubbed the stubble on his red face. "In fact, I know you wouldn't. You're not like that. Plus there's the whole religion thing."

"A deeper faith in God might help him get through this difficult season in his life. You, too, if you let it." Cassie touched the cool window glass as she sought the right words. She wasn't saying them for herself. But for a mixed-up teenager and his older brother. *Gott, You are my witness.*

"You should come to one of our services. You could stay after and eat with other folks from Haven. Give us a chance. Get to know us."

Bryan would allow Mason to attend. Cassie was sure of it. He was Job's grandson. His mother was Plain. Whether it would help was an entirely different pit of quicksand. The church elders conducted portions of the service in High German and the rest in Pennsylvania Dutch. Neither of which Mason would understand. The service lasted three hours, long enough to wear even a Plain person down.

Mason tapped on the wheel for several seconds, but he finally nodded. "It's not right for me to form an opinion about something I really don't know anything about."

A church service was only the beginning, but Cassie would take it. "I'll tell Job you're interested. He'll talk to Bryan and the other elders about it."

"Changing my mind won't help with Bobby. He's old enough to have his own opinions."

"But he's influenced by you. He wants your approval."

Mason nodded again, but his smile was tight. "I'm the closest thing he's ever had to a father."

"That's a lot of pressure." It also said a lot about who Mason was. He didn't flinch from the burden. He would be a good father to his own children one day. The thought pressed into Cassie's heart, seeking entry. She closed the door hard. He might have an Amish mother, even an Amish father, but he was English. She didn't dare risk her heart.

Her heart seemed to have other ideas. *Gott, help me.* "They all love you. They want to please you. You've done a good job."

"Maybe. Bobby's been a runner for years. Kevin is stuck in the middle. He doesn't know which way to go or who to trust. Kathy has never been a little girl. Donny is scared of his own shadow. Jennie loves anyone who pays attention to her more than two seconds." Mason's face filled with regret laced with sadness. "There's still a chance for the younger ones to have a real childhood. But Bobby has one foot out the door all the time. He wants to be a cop. To do that he needs to go to college. I want that for him. I never wanted to go myself, but if that's what he wants, I want him to have his dream."

They'd arrived at Cassie's parents' home. Cassie undid her seat belt, but she couldn't bring herself to open the door. Not with the sound of Mason's voice—his sad, sad voice—ringing in her ears. The children would have a chance at a real childhood with Job and Dinah, but saying so now might only add to Mason's sense of failure. He was too hard on himself. He never had a childhood either. Her heart wanted her to touch his hand, give him a hug, tell him he'd done well. Her brain scrambled to throw up roadblocks to that dangerous path. *Think about something else!* "What's your dream?"

"Book learning was never my thing. I couldn't wait to get out of school. I'm good with my hands." He ducked his head and smiled. "I want to own my own construction and rehab business. I want to buy old houses, renovate them, and flip them."

"Flip them?"

"Sell them. It's hard work, but it's honest work. I like the idea of taking something that's falling apart and making it whole again instead of tearing it down and starting over. A lot of the old houses around here have solid bones; they just need TLC."

His enthusiasm tickled her. It also made her hope that he would achieve his dream. Who did Mason rely on? Who made sure he had his chance at happiness? Instead he'd been father to five kids. Mason had made sacrifices. Had he sacrificed love? Did he want children of his own?

Ignoring the painful ache in the vicinity of her heart, Cassie held her tongue. *"Mind your p's and q's, child."* That would be her mother's voice. Cassie's father opened the front door and stared out at them. "We'd better get in there. It'll be dark soon and that much harder to search."

"After I talk to your dad, I'm calling the sheriff's department."

That wouldn't go over well with the bishop, but Mason had no reason to abide by the bishop's wishes. Especially with CFS's intervention on the horizon. "You have to do what you think is right."

"Darn straight."

As soon as Cassie hopped from the SUV, Father moved to the porch and let the door shut behind him. He nodded now and then during Cassie's recitation regarding the day's events. He lifted his wool hat from his head, ran one calloused hand over his bald pate, and resettled the hat. "I'll head to the phone shack and make the call. Then I'll go to Job's. Cassie, you go on inside."

His edict wasn't unexpected, but Cassie had held on to hope the entire drive. "Daed, I want to go with Mason—"

"Go inside, Cassie."

"If I can't go with Mason, at least let me go back to Job's with you."

"Tomorrow. Stay in your own room tonight."

Banished, just like that. "Dinah will need me."

"You'll go back tomorrow. After I talk to Job."

"It was my idea—"

"Go."

She went.

CHAPTER 21

The Amish were like throwbacks to the Puritans or maybe even the Victorians. Like Mason knew much about either group. History hadn't been his best subject. Cassie's cheeks were scarlet and her head down, but she went. Had his mother been in a similar situation many moons ago with Job and decided to bail rather than put up with being smothered?

Mason shifted from one work boot to the other. He would have to wrap his brain around this one later. The sun was setting. He needed to get moving. "I'm sorry. I didn't mean to get Cassie in trouble. I think she's right. Bobby might respond better to her than one of us. She has a soft touch—I mean, not literally. Figuratively, I mean—"

"I know what you mean." Leroy Weaver eased toward the steps. "I'd better make that call and get over to Job's. I'll tell him you're planning to drive the route back to Yoder to search for Bobby. Stores will be closing soon—it's a little town. Not much nightlife."

In other words, move along quickly. "If I don't find him, I'm calling 911. They'll treat it as a missing person. They won't waste any time coming out to Job's."

"I'll let Bryan—the bishop—and your grandfather know." Leroy stalked down the steps. "We'll help you find your brother safe and sound."

In other words, no need to involve law enforcement. "Thank you. I hope I didn't offend you."

Leroy waved one hand and kept walking. "You didn't."

"Good."

With a shrug Mason strode back to the Blazer. He got in and started it. The engine sputtered and died. *Come on, stay with me. I can't afford to replace you right now. Come on.* Two tries later, the engine caught and putted but didn't die. *Thank you.*

He took South Haven Road to Lake Cable Road to South Kent Road, scanning the landscape, hoping to see Bobby standing on the side of the road waiting for a ride. God willing, no one had given him one. It didn't seem likely a child predator roamed these Kansas back roads, but then, no one ever thought he'd be the victim of a crime of opportunity.

Mason had seen too many teen horror flicks. *Stop freaking yourself out, dude.* Trying to ferret out shapes in the shadows, he scanned from one side of the road to the other in the gathering dusk.

Nothing.

No skinny kid in holey jeans, cowboy boots, and an oversized, fleece-lined jean jacket hung around the intersection of South Kent Road and Highway 96.

At the Quick Stop, the gangly attendant with the biggest Adam's apple Mason had ever seen cocked his head and shrugged after listening to the description. "I don't think so, dude, but I just came on duty about an hour ago."

"If you see him, tell him his brother said to get his sorry behind back to the Keims'."

"Will do, brother."

In Yoder, population 777, some of the businesses, which mostly catered to the Amish tourism trade, had closed for the day, as Leroy had said. The most happening place seemed to be the Carriage House Restaurant and Bakery. Even there, cars parked outside were few and far between. Mason picked a spot in between a minivan and a buggy and went inside.

A hostess in Amish clothes seemed delighted to see him and offered him a menu. Mason shook his head. "Thanks, but I'm searching for my brother." He went through the same spiel with her as he had the clerk. "It's a long shot, I know. He probably doesn't have a dime in his pocket to eat at a place like this."

No spark of recognition flared when he showed her the photo. "Sorry, sir. We get lots of folks in here. I don't remember him."

Lots of English folks, she meant.

"Thanks anyway."

"I hope you find him."

Mason murmured his thanks and strode back to the Blazer. This was a stupid waste of time. Regardless of what he'd told the Keims, Mason needed to call 911. He made the call and told the dispatcher he would meet the sheriff's deputy on patrol at the Keims'.

Twenty minutes later he was back at their doorstep. Two buggies and a tractor were parked in the Keims' wide gravel driveway. Mason took a spot behind the tractor. A minute later a dark-blue SUV with *Reno County Sheriff's Patrol Division* displayed on the driver's door pulled in next to him.

A sheriff's deputy in a blue uniform slid out immediately. Mason went to meet him.

"How long has the minor been missing?" The deputy, who identified himself as Doug Waters, had the grizzled face of a man closing in on retirement. He barely allowed for introductions before he cut to the chase. "Are you his guardian?"

Mason checked the time on his phone. "We don't know exactly, but somewhere in the range of four to five hours. I'm his oldest brother—half brother."

Waters started toward the front door. "Where are your parents? Inside?"

"Wait. It's a complicated situation."

The deputy halted and pointed to the buggies. "If Amish folks are involved, I assume it will be, but the sooner we have all the facts, the sooner we find your brother."

Mason explained as succinctly as possible. Waters had the poker face down. "The Amish are reluctant to get law enforcement involved." He moved once again toward the house. "But CFS isn't. Call the caseworker. She needs to know ASAP. I'll talk to the grandparents."

Mason didn't want to call Mrs. Blanchard. Not yet. If she decided to yank the kids out of the Keims' house, she might decide he couldn't have them back either. Especially since he still hadn't found a house nearby that he could afford to rent.

Mason followed the deputy inside. Half a dozen men in black wool coats and black hats, including Bryan, milled around in the living room. Job sat with Dinah on the couch. The rest of the kids were nowhere in sight. Bryan stepped forward. "We didn't call the sheriff's department. We're organizing our own search party, Deputy." It was a statement, not open to discussion. He expected the deputy to listen to him. "We appreciate you coming here, but I have no doubt we'll find him. If we don't, we'll ask for your help."

"Who are you?" Deputy Waters seemed unfazed by the peremptory dismissal. If he dealt with the Amish much, he was likely used to it. He consulted his notebook. "I need to speak to the grandparents. Job and Dinah Keim."

"Here." Job stood and came forward. "That's Bryan Miller, our bishop. Bobby is our grandson."

"In the case of missing minors, we like to move immediately, Mr. Keim." Deputy Waters tapped his pen on his notebook. "First I'd like to know the circumstances of his decision to leave home. I also need what he was wearing, any friends he might go to, anything you can tell me that will help us track him down."

"It's my fault." Job hesitated. He rolled his shoulders and pulled at his collar. "I needed to school him in obedience—"

"Did you hit him?"

"No." Job pressed his lips together. His eyes went cold. "We do use corporal punishment when needed, but I wouldn't do that with a boy his age. I told him he had to stay in the barn until he cleaned it to my satisfaction."

"That's all well and good, but I understand this is a teenager brought up by non-Amish parents, Mr. Keim."

"Job."

"Job. So I'm just trying to understand what went down."

"It may be that Bobby left because he felt . . . rejected. He seemed to have developed feelings for Cassie, our housekeeper. She's twenty-two and unmarried." The discomfort on Job's face deepened. "Of course that's not something that could be encouraged. His feelings might have been hurt."

Everyone in the room seemed to be chewing on this new piece of information, except the deputy. "Teenage boys have tender egos. I raised three myself, so I know. Where do you think he would go?"

Job's attention, along with everyone else's, shifted to Mason. He put up both hands like stop signs. "He usually—"

"He's done this before?"

"Many times, but this is the first time for the Keims. Before, he was in Wichita, in familiar surroundings." Mason forced himself to stand still. No fidgeting like a kid in the principal's office. Before, verbal abuse and hitting had been involved. Bobby had reason to run. "But it's a pattern, still, I guess you could say."

"Where do you think he'll go?"

The wind whistled through the eaves of the old house while Mason grappled with the question. Bobby had a few friends at his old school, but Mason had no idea who they were. His brother didn't bring them to the house. None of the kids did. It was too embarrassing. He hung out at a diner down the street or the closest skateboarding park. He and his friends went to the dollar movies when the weather was bad. "I don't know the names of his friends, but I can give you a list of places he used to go. He's been here for the last two months, so it's been a while. What about an Amber Alert? Can we do that?"

"Your brother wasn't abducted. Amber Alerts don't apply to runaways. Sorry."

"Me too."

"Where are the other children?" Waters studied his notebook. "Mason, you said there are four more, ages four, six, eight, and ten. Where were they when this was going on?"

"They're upstairs doing their homework and getting ready for bed." Tension reverberated in Job's stance like a guitar string strung too tight. "They were at school. They don't know anything about their brother leaving."

"I'd like to ask them for myself."

"That's not necessary." Bryan sidled closer. "Job has said they don't know anything. You can take his word for it."

Mason's chest hurt. He'd been holding his breath. He forced himself to suck in air. "I'd like to say good night to them too."

"They'll be scared with all these men down here." Dinah spoke up. "They're worn out and worried about their brother."

"Where's Cassie?" The kids would feel better if Cassie was with them. Mason sought out Leroy. His face stony, Cassie's father stood by the fireplace. "Didn't she come back with you?"

"No."

No explanation. None needed. The reason was obvious in Leroy's scowl.

"I'll do it." Dinah started to rise. Job shook his head. She sank back down. Job's measured tread on the stairs said he was in no hurry to acquiesce to the deputy's demand.

"In the meantime, do you have a picture of him?" Waters knew enough about the Amish to direct that question to Mason. "Something recent?"

Mason dug out the photo he kept in his wallet. Bobby showing off the new skateboard Mason had given him for his fifteenth birthday. It was a garage sale find, but Bobby's open-mouthed pleasure had been priceless. He didn't seem to notice the gouges of missing paint on it. "It's a year old, but it's the best I can do. His hair is longer and he's a few inches taller now, but otherwise, he's pretty much the same."

"I'll get it back to you."

The kids coming down the stairs in flannel nightgowns and pj's kept Mason from telling the deputy he would make sure of it. Job carried Jennie. She had her head on his shoulder and her arms around his neck. Kevin, his face red and angry, led the parade, followed by Kathy, who'd put on her down jacket over her nightgown. Donny paused on every step to rub his eyes. Job had to nudge him along.

"I don't want to go. I like it here." Donny ran to Mason and threw his arms around one leg. "Can't we stay? Just because

Bobby left doesn't mean we want to. Please don't let the police-man take us."

His brokenhearted sobs filled the room. The lump in his throat painful, Mason disengaged Donny's wiry arms and knelt next to him. "It's okay, buddy. He's not here to take you—"

"It's okay, Donny." Kathy trotted over behind her little brother. She patted his shoulder and smiled at Mason. Her eyes belonged to an old woman. "We have to be strong, remember? We'll say our prayers just like Dinah and Cassie told us to. Mason will take care of us. I know how to make pancakes now and oatmeal and banana bread. I'll cook like Cassie does. We'll still see them, won't we, Mason?"

Mason wrapped his arms around both of them. Kevin plopped down on the stairs out of reach. His mouth turned up in a twisted smirk—a sure sign he was trying not to cry. "That's not what this is about. You're not going anywhere. Deputy Waters just wants to ask you some questions. I promise."

Kathy tugged free and faced the deputy. "Bobby wants to be a policeman like you. He wants to drive a car with lights and sirens. He likes having a phone and a TV. Me and Donny and Jennie don't mind not having TV. Do we?"

She tugged on Donny's shirt. The little boy raised his head from Mason's shoulder. "I like *Paw Patrol . . .*"

"Donny!"

"But it's okay. I like Cassie's gingerbread cookies more. And this weekend Daadi is going to teach us to ride horses."

Waters squatted next to the kids. "I know there are a lot of adults here, so if you need to tell me something, we can go in the other room and talk. I promise no one will be mad. You can tell the truth. I'll make sure no one hurts you."

"No one is hurting them." Job stomped over to the sofa and sat, Jennie in his lap. "We're not that kind of people."

"I'm talking to the kids, Mr. Keim."

"I'm tired." Jennie yawned and stretched like a baby kitten. "Can I go to bed now, Daadi?"

"Soon, little one."

"I want Mammi."

Job handed the little girl to Dinah, who curled her arms around Jennie and began to rock. It was hard to say who was being comforted.

"This is really important." Wincing, Waters leaned forward so his squat turned into a kneel. "I'm getting too old for this. Did Bobby say anything about leaving? Did he tell any of you where he was going?"

"If he did, I wouldn't tell you." Kevin slowly cracked his knuckles, one after the other. "He's my brother. But he didn't say a word."

"He's ADHD." Kathy pulled her coat tighter around her skinny body. "Mommy said he was worse than a popcorn kernel in a skillet of hot oil."

"I understand your loyalty to your brother, but don't you want to make sure he's safe? Lots of bad people are out there, just waiting to take advantage of a teenager alone."

"Bobby can take care of himself. He always said he graduated top of his class from the school of hard knocks." Again Kathy volunteered this unhelpful tidbit. "He's probably at a truck stop where a waitress is feeling sorry for him so she's giving him free chili and cherry pie."

It did sound like Bobby. He could turn on that puppy dog sweetness that women—especially young ones—couldn't deny. But it also required that he hitchhike to the truck stop. That's where the fantasy acquired dark edges.

"He said not to worry," Donny piped up. "He said he'd come back for us someday and we'd all live in a nice house together with a pool in the backyard and we could eat all the ice cream we wanted. He said he would get us a puppy and two or three kitties."

"Bobby says to wait here," Jennie added. "He says he loves us. He'll come get us a long time from now."

Their faces somber, the children fell silent, apparently in agreement with Jennie's pronouncement.

Waters frowned. He took the time to size up each child individually. "Are you sure he said nothing specific about where he'd go first?"

"Nope. Can we go now?" Kevin stood and grabbed the railing. "It's stupid making us sit around here in our pj's in front of a bunch of old men."

Mason agreed, although he would've tried to be more tactful than a ten-year-old.

"Go."

Mason gave the three younger kids tight hugs before they scurried up the stairs. With Kevin he simply nodded and tried to silently convey his feelings. *You did good, kid.* Kevin's skinny shoulders slumped, and he trudged up the stairs like a man on the way to the electric chair.

Waters waited until they were out of sight to speak. He tapped his pen on the notebook. "I'll file the missing person's report. We'll canvass businesses on the highway and in Yoder and Hutchinson. We'll notify Wichita PD as well. If we don't find him right away, we'll get the juvenile detective involved."

A plan of action. At least that was a start. "What can he do?"

"He'll put out a press release and then work social media. They've had decent luck recently using social media to track down runaways. Either the kid gets on social media or his friends do."

Again everyone turned to Mason. Unlike most of his friends, Mason wasn't much for social media. He didn't have time, plus who wanted to spend all that time talking to strangers? He barely had time to talk to people he actually knew. "Bobby spent a lot of time on his phone. I don't know if he was into that stuff, but it's possible."

"Most kids his age are. Did he have a girlfriend? Could he have run to her?"

"He's been away from Wichita for almost two months. If he had a girlfriend there, he kept it to himself."

Waters took his time, studying each person around the room. "I don't see much purpose in having a search party with buggies. This isn't a young Amish child we're talking about. Bobby likely thumbed a ride the second he reached the highway. It takes you too long to cover the territory. Let the sheriff's department handle this."

Bryan nodded, but he didn't appear happy. "I assume you'll let Job know how your search progresses." He turned to Job. "We'll be back tomorrow to check in with you."

The lines around Job's eyes and mouth deepened. Dinah dabbed her face with a hankie. Neither spoke. Mason sought words to console them. Nothing came. "I'll head home, in case he shows up there." Bobby wouldn't. He was too stubborn. He'd rather starve. Mason slid on his coat.

"You called CFS, right?" Deputy Waters's eyes were hard as stone. "What did the caseworker say?"

"I haven't called yet. I wanted to get everyone's take on the situation first." Mason let his fingers curl around his cell phone in his pocket. "It's late. She's not going to come out here tonight."

"I agree." Dinah spoke for the first time. Her wrinkled hands flew to her face to wipe away tears. "Please wait until tomorrow. That will give Deputy Waters time to search for Bobby."

She was afraid too. "I—"

"If he doesn't call her, I will." Deputy Waters frowned. "It's protocol in these cases, ma'am, where CFS is involved. They get pretty persnickety if we don't notify them ASAP. Especially if one of their charges is in danger."

Dinah's face crumpled. She covered it with her hankie. Job stood. "Do what you have to do. When you find him, bring him home." His arm swept in a wide arc. "This is his home. This is what our daughter wanted. We're his blood relatives. Mrs. Blanchard knows that."

Job turned to his wife and spoke to her in Pennsylvania Dutch. Her weeping stopped, but her pain followed Mason from the house and into the dark night.

CHAPTER 22

Clouds stifled the moonlight. Darkness blanketed the house. The porch light was out again. Mason fumbled with the keys, finally unlocked the door, and stepped inside, glad to be out of the cold. Only the air was no warmer inside than it had been outside. He flipped the switch in the hallway. A tepid light bathed the decrepit area rug but not much beyond it.

"Welcome home, Mason," he murmured and laughed. The sound reverberated in the empty hallway. More talking to himself. At least this time he hadn't answered. He'd spent the last few hours driving around Wichita to Bobby's favorite haunts. The skateboard park. The diner where he and his friends gathered after school for Cokes, fries, and clowning around, trying to impress the girls. The movie theater where he went to dollar matinees with his first girlfriend.

Nothing. He didn't know Bobby's friends. Had Bobby even stayed in touch with them after they were sent to live with Job and Dinah? He probably felt like he'd never see them again.

Mason walked through the house, turning on lights. It wouldn't really make a difference. The little time Mason had spent in the Keims' house had shown him the difference between a house and a home. The warmth and the light in their home had nothing to do with the propane lamp, the flames in the fireplace, or the cookstove in the kitchen. Love made it a home.

Family made it a home. Having someone to yell out, "Hey, I'm glad you're here, glad you made it home." The aroma of food cooking and the sound of dishes clinking and women chattering made it a home. Did all Plain folks have homes like the Keims', or was it just them?

Mason would lay odds most Amish homes were like that. They had a way about them. A serenity, a calm, a peace that a person didn't see every day.

At least he hadn't. *So get over it.* With a groan Mason tromped through the dining room to the kitchen.

An empty cheese wrapper had been left on the counter next to a dirty skillet. Mason always cleaned up after himself after he cooked. Otherwise the cockroaches took over.

Bobby.

He hadn't bothered to return the fake butter to the refrigerator. Or tie off the bag that held what was left of a loaf of white sandwich bread. The kid liked his grilled cheese sandwich, but he was in a hurry.

Bobby didn't have a key. How had he entered the house? Mason strode to the back door. Cold air wafted through its single, now broken, window. Anger blew through Mason, warming him. "Just wait until I get my hands on you."

He might have some old wood in the garage he could use to patch the hole. But first, what else needed fixing? What else had Bobby done while in the house? Mason made the rounds to the living room and then the bedrooms. They were already bare. Mason had taken most of their stuff to the Keims' already.

Then it hit Mason. Picking up speed, he raced to the kitchen. To the ceramic cookie jar they never used to store cookies in because they turned stale in a day's time. It was shaped like a chubby kid in a chef's hat. Mason turned it upside down. Not a dime fell out. Mom's emergency fund was gone. He'd made a point not to touch it, but he knew exactly how much was there. Her emergency fund had become his: $487.79.

Mom used to call it her walking-around money, but Mason knew better. She stashed a portion of every check in that cookie jar in case she needed to take the kids and get out. In case one of Clayton's funks got out of control. It didn't make sense to Mason. The house belonged to them. Clayton should be the one to go. Mason could make him go. He wanted to make him go.

Now Bobby was the one who was gone. And he had nearly five hundred dollars to get him wherever he wanted to go. Knowing Bobby, he was figuring all the angles. How could he turn the cash into more cash? Now that the weather was warming up, he could buy a bike and use it to get around. Especially if he got a job.

Where would he go? The homeless shelter? Even though he was no more homeless than Mason was.

Truth be told, it was a relief to know Bobby had the money even if it was wrong of him to run away. Wrong of him to worry everyone, especially Dinah. Wrong of him to break into the house instead of simply staying. But at least Bobby wasn't wandering the streets penniless. He could get out of the cold. He could buy a hot meal.

If he didn't flash a wad of cash and get himself rolled by thugs in a dark alley.

So much could go wrong. So many ways a kid could get hurt on the streets.

Bobby, come home, please come home. You stupid jerk.

It stank to love people who did stupid stuff.

Mason closed his eyes and rested his head on the table. He was so tired. He was tired of not having someone he could talk to about all of this stuff. Someone who could tell him what he should do. Someone who could tell him he was doing okay.

The doorbell rang. He jumped and raised his head.

Maybe it was Bobby. Maybe he came back.

Mason sprinted to the door and jerked it open.

"Howdy, Nephew." Perry grinned at him. Somebody should tell him he used too much product on his jet-black hair. "Well, don't just stand there. It's cold out here. Let me in." He held up a six-pack of microbrewery beer. "I brought us some brewskis."

Mason started to answer but coughed instead. Perry also wore too much aftershave. Mason coughed into his elbow, breathed, and tried again. "What are you doing here?"

"You said my mother wanted to see me. I decided the decent thing to do would be to grant her wish."

What was he, some kind of fairy godson? This had nothing to do with being decent. "You said no on the phone."

"I was hasty." Perry brushed past him. "Whoa, turn on the heat, why don't you? It's colder in here than it is outside. Don't stand there with the door open—you're letting in more cold air."

He always was good at giving orders. Maybe if Mason left it open, Perry would get the hint and leave. "Were you hasty when you said you couldn't take in the kids? Did you change your mind about that too?"

Not in this lifetime. Mason knew better.

"Hey, you're not still holding a grudge about that, are you?"

"A grudge? A grudge!" Mason grappled with anger that threatened to spill over into a full-blown fist in the face for his uncle. "The kids were scared and lonely and sick with grief because they just lost their mom. They needed as much family as they could get. You're their uncle. I could've used your help with them."

Perry traipsed down the hallway toward the dining room. "I couldn't take them. I told you. I had no place to put them. I live in an apartment. With my girlfriend and her two kids."

"You could've come here, lived here with us. Or at least come to visit on a regular basis."

"Sheila's not down for dealing with five more kids on top of the two she's already got. And I'm here to tell you she can hardly handle the two. They're holy terrors. But you're right, I could've spent some time here. I'm thinking I might do it now." He set the six-pack on the table and surveyed his surroundings. "Love what you've done with the place. You need a housekeeper."

Mason stood with the table between them. That way if he was tempted to take a swing at Perry, he'd be too far away to hit him. *This wasn't what I had in mind, God, when I asked for someone to talk to.*

He tightened his hands on the back of the chair in front of him. Had he just talked to God? The power of Cassie's suggestion? People who believed in God were never alone. They always had someone to talk to. Was it any different than him talking to himself?

"Mason, dude, where's the bottle opener?" Perry had wandered into the kitchen where he opened and shut drawers. "This place is a pit. You know that margarine will go bad sitting out like that, right?"

"When are you planning to see Dinah—your mother?"

"What? You don't call her Mammi?" Perry held up the bottle opener in one hand and pumped his fist with the other. He proceeded to open two beers and slide one across the counter that separated the kitchen and dining room. "Come and get it. If you need help translating, let me know. Hard as I try, I can't erase all that *Deutsch* from my memory bank."

"How can you be so cavalier about them? You haven't seen your parents in more than twenty years, and you act like it's no big deal." Mason stayed where he was. After a few keggers, after which he ended up puking his brains out in an empty cornfield before walking back into town, he'd sworn off alcohol. That and years of watching his mother and her boyfriends pickle their brains with it and act stupid. "My mom did some crazy, mixed-up stuff, stuff that hurt her kids, but I'd give my right arm to talk to her again."

He could ask her one more time who his father was. Perry denied knowing. Maybe Perry had lied. "So, Perry, who's my father?"

"I told you, I don't know."

"I don't believe you. You said I was more Amish than you are."

"It's speculation, based on the rumors floating around at the time and the fact that I never saw her with an English guy. But she never said who it was, and I never asked."

"It's selfish. I have a right to know. Every kid does. I don't get it."

"You have to get your mother. She didn't have a traditional view of marriage or parenting or what a family should be. I would think that would be obvious to you. Georgia never tried to keep you from being who you are. She might not have been much for cooking and cleaning and doing mom stuff, but she made sure you had minds of your own. You could be whoever you want and do whatever you want in life. That's something."

Some parents showed they cared by coming to parent-teacher conferences, buying winter coats, and sitting down with their kids for supper every night. "She had her moments."

"She had her moments as a sister too." The good humor drained from Perry's face for a few seconds, then reappeared. "But the last thing Georgia would've wanted was for us to be down about her demise. She was all about living in the moment. She loved living it up. Have a beer. I'll order some food to be delivered. You don't mind if I camp out here for a while, do you? Sheila would just as soon spit on me as take me back right now."

Unlike Perry, Mason didn't have it in him to turn away family. "No, I don't mind. Why aren't you staying with Job and Dinah? They're your parents. I know Dinah will welcome you with open arms."

"It would be too weird for all of us. I was never baptized, so I'm not technically shunned, but I bailed without saying goodbye." Perry sauntered into the dining room. "Plus, I'm not planning to stay, and I don't want them to get the wrong idea."

"They're decent people. They're good with the kids. What was so bad about them that you had to leave like that?"

"It really wasn't them. Even Georgia said that. She wanted to be the daughter they needed her to be. She even went so far as to be baptized, thinking it would force her to buckle down. But she was miserable."

"That was Georgia. What about you?"

"I had a really good rumspringa. The people keeping track say that about 85 percent of Amish kids decide to stay and be baptized. That means 15 percent don't. I'm one of them."

"So it was nothing Job and Dinah did?"

"Nope."

"You should tell them that."

"Maybe. Someday. First I need to get my act together."

At least he recognized that. "I can't guarantee the sheets are clean on any of the beds, but you can take your pick of rooms." At least Mason wouldn't be alone here. Was bad company better than no company at all? "Don't worry about ordering food for me. My stomach is ripped."

"Why? What do you have to be stressed about now? The kids are in a decent home—weird but decent. What is it? Bills? I can't help you with those, but I'm here if you just want to vent."

"It's not money." The bills worried Mason, but they didn't compare to the stress of not knowing whether Bobby was out there somewhere in the city in trouble. Wichita was the largest city in Kansas. With its size came the usual crime stats. Bobby might consider himself street savvy, but he was fooling himself. He had nothing on the gangbangers who cut their teeth on drug deals and street fights. "Bobby ran away again."

"I bet that went over well with my parents." Perry took a swig of beer. He swallowed and began to tear the label from the bottle. "It probably felt like déjà vu to them. Poor things."

"There's a lot that's good about the situation. They're good people. Horses, cows, pigs, chickens, good food, a pond to swim in." If Bobby felt that way, why was he so determined to have custody of the kids? Because he didn't want to be alone? Because he was afraid Job and Dinah would die and leave the kids alone all over again? "They get three regular meals a day that don't come out of the microwave. Church on Sunday. Kevin and Kathy and Donny like their new school. Jennie's not stuck all day with a woman who spanks her all the time. They like Cassie—"

"Who's Cassie?"

Mason allowed himself a grin. "She's a real sweet girl and she loves the kids already."

"Sounds like she won you over too." Perry downed the last of his beer and pulled his phone from his jeans pocket. "Don't stress about Bobby. He'll come running back with his tail between his legs when he gets hungry enough."

No sense in telling Perry about the stolen money. Normal people kept their money in banks and used debit cards. Explaining Mom's emergency fund to his uncle meant delving into her relationship with Clayton. Not going there. Not tonight or any other night. "I hope you're right. Job and Dinah are beside themselves. They're afraid CFS will take it as a sign and remove the kids from their house. That's the last thing they need."

"Did you call CFS?"

"In the morning. I wanted time to search for him first. If I don't do it then, the sheriff's deputy will."

"You involved the law. My parents must've loved that." Perry grimaced.

"Mom wanted them with her parents. They're in a good place now. Job and Dinah will do right by them."

"Like I said, they've sure won you over. Are you thinking of converting?"

"I respect them . . . their values. They're good people. The kids have never had family like that before. It seems selfish for me to try to take that from them. I'm figuring it out as I go."

His head down, Perry thumbed something—presumably a food order. He'd mastered the art of multitasking. "All that clean living is great if you don't mind not being allowed to have an original thought. And woe to the person who decides to live a little on Saturday night."

Partying on Saturday night wasn't all it was cracked up to be. It gave Mason a headache and an empty wallet. "Whatever. I'm going to bed. I have to be up early in the morning to give my two-week notice."

Perry's eyebrows popped up. He was the spitting image of Job in the face, but he had inherited Dinah's slight stature. Which was weird because Mom had been tall like Job and had

Dinah's eyes. A sardonic grin spread across Perry's face. "You're quitting your job. That's kind of extreme, don't you think?"

"I'm planning to get on with one of the Amish crews that work out of Haven or Yoder."

"That's a long drive. Why would you do that?"

"I won't be driving. I'm moving up there so I can be close to the kids. I've been working on it for a while, but I've been having trouble finding a big enough rental that I can afford."

"That's definitely extreme." Perry belted out a laugh. "I'm trying to imagine you in a straw hat and suspenders. Are you ready to exchange your Blazer for a buggy?"

"I didn't say that."

Mason stopped. Unexpected emotion wrapped itself around his throat. Maybe it was the long day. Or Bobby's disappearance. Or residual emotion from the funeral. Whatever the case, his throat hurt with the effort to keep tears from falling.

Man up. Don't be a big baby. Don't be a baby. Man up. He swallowed hard and cleared his throat. "Just because *you* don't need family doesn't mean I don't. They're all I've got."

"I get it, man, I do." Perry swallowed the last of his beer and set the bottle on the table with a hard clink. "I just hope you don't get your feelings hurt. The Amish district, including my parents, will expect you to toe the line, to follow the rules. Don't expect to have an original thought and get away with it. Don't expect to have your own life. They're all about controlling you."

Perry's words rang in Mason's ears as he fled the dining room. It was all about perspective. They cared. They loved. They weren't afraid to show it. They wanted respect and clean living in return. That didn't seem like too much to ask.

He had nothing to lose and everything to gain.

CHAPTER 23

No one chattered. No lights were on. A good sign no one was up yet at Job and Dinah's house. Cassie gently nudged the back door shut and turned to survey the kitchen. Her plan to arrive at the Keims' before Dinah had to fix breakfast for the kids seemed to have worked. She had knocked on her parents' bedroom door well before dawn with the plea that her father take her to Job's while Mother made breakfast rather than afterward.

Father didn't ask for an explanation, so Cassie offered none. Nor did he seem inclined to rehash their discussion of the previous evening. She was an adult. She knew better than to get into the SUV alone with an English man. His disappointment still lay heavy on her shoulders.

"You don't want to have a conversation with Bryan about this, do you?"

No, she did not. Embarrassment raced through her at the thought.

Cassie shucked off her coat and hung it on a hook. She would do her job and stay out of trouble. Even if that meant avoiding Mason.

The English man with the blue eyes, calloused hands, and bruised heart. The hardworking, loving man who put his brothers and sisters before his own needs.

Stop it.

The scent of coffee brewing registered. Cassie pivoted and went to the stove. Sure enough, the old tin pot Job preferred sat on the stove, percolating.

"Guder mariye."

Cassie whirled. Job stood in the doorway scratching his cheek above his beard. Tater trotted past him and made a bee-line for Cassie. The dog's tail wagged so hard it made a *whap-whap* sound as he passed the chairs. "You scared me. I didn't think anyone was up yet."

"Just me. I didn't know you were here."

Job's faded blue shirt was wrinkled. So were his black pants. His suspenders hung down around his thighs. His silver-streaked black hair stuck out in all directions. His eyes were bloodshot, his face gray with fatigue.

"You waited up for Bobby, didn't you?" Cassie patted Tater, who grinned and settled at her feet—squarely in her path of travel. She stepped over him and went to the refrigerator to extract a container of eggs and a slab of bacon. "No sign of him, then?"

"Jah. Nee." He rubbed his bloodshot eyes and tried to smooth his unruly hair. "I thought I would, but I ended up falling asleep on the couch. He's not coming back. Not voluntarily."

"I'm praying the sheriff's deputy will find him. Or Mason." She laid the eggs and bacon on the counter and picked up the skillet. "I'll have breakfast ready in a jiffy. I can take the kinner to schul."

"Your daed spoke with me last night after everyone left."

Cassie stiffened despite herself. Her back to Job, she went to the stove. "He told me."

"I made an error in judgment—both in letting you go with

Mason and letting you talk alone with Bobby. It never occurred to me that he would think of you in . . . a different light. I've been out of touch with teenage boys for a long time. I'm sorry."

"And I have little experience with them. But I'm not sorry. I'm here, helping to take care of these kinner. I'm not sorry I went with Mason either. Even if it didn't help find Bobby. Mason is a gut man. He loves his bruder. His mind was on finding him, nothing else."

Almost nothing else.

"And you are a gut *maedel*, but I told your daed I would be more careful in the future. Otherwise, he won't let you stay." Job went to the wood-burning stove and held his hands over it. "That would be hard on Dinah. I don't want that."

"Me either. We'll do better." Enough—more than enough— on that topic. Cassie counted eggs. She would need at least fourteen to feed this mob. "The kinner need to get up. They'll be late for schul."

"I'll go roust them."

"Let me do it." Cassie grabbed a pot holder and poured a cup of coffee for him. He took it strong and black. "Drink your coffee and then you can go change."

She sounded like a wife, not an employee. "If you want, that is."

He took her offering and eased into a chair. "That would be gut." Sadness blanketed his words.

Cassie twisted the pot holder in her hands. "I'm sorry. It's my fault. I didn't know Bobby had feelings . . ."

"It's not your fault. I should've realized . . . He's at that age. I may be old, but I haven't forgotten what it feels like." He cupped his hands around the mug and leaned into its warmth.

"I was blessed. I saw Dinah at a school picnic and I knew immediately that I would marry her. We were both sixteen, though. Both young. It took four years to convince her, but I knew. "

Would Bobby cling to his feelings or let them go? "He's been through so much. He's seeking something that he can hang on to." The thought made her heart hurt. It couldn't be her. She couldn't give him what he needed. "I should've seen it."

"His heart will mend. I just hope he stays safe in the meantime. The kinner should be awake by now. Go on, get them up. I'll change later."

He couldn't make any guarantees and he knew it. No one could. Cassie scurried up the stairs and down the hallway to Dinah and Job's room. "Dinah?" She halted in the open doorway.

Dinah raised her head. "You're back." She burst into tears. "I'm so glad you're back."

"Of course I'm back."

"Is Bobby?"

"Nee, but he will be, if it's Gott's will," Cassie answered automatically. Did God's will cover a nonbeliever like Bobby? Did God's plan involve letting him wander alone in the wilderness until he came home like the prodigal son? The questions were far too big for a simple woman such as herself. *Gott, I humbly ask that You keep him safe. He's just a bu.*

And Mason, Job, Dinah, and all the children had suffered so much already. *It's not my place to tell You what to do, I know that. I'm asking, not telling, please don't let there be more suffering, Gott.*

"It's my fault Georgia died a lost soul. If I had convinced her to stay, she would never have left her faith." Dinah sobbed even louder. "It's all my fault. Now Bobby is gone too. We'll never see him again."

Cassie trudged to the bed. She settled on the edge and put her arm around Dinah. "Nee, Bobby will come back. Mason will find him. What happened with Georgia was her fault. She made her choice."

Did it have something to do with Mason and his father? Now was as good a time as any to ask. "Do you know why she left?"

"Georgia left because she was in a family way. She didn't want to marry the bopli's father." Dinah used her sheet to dry her eyes. "She said he was a nice, kind man, but she didn't want to live this life. She knew Job would insist. So would the bishop."

"Why didn't you insist?"

"I tried. Georgia didn't cry. She didn't apologize. She blurted it out over a tub of dirty breakfast dishes. She was determined to go. Nothing I said made a difference."

"Maybe she was right." Cassie's parents wouldn't agree. Neither would Job. Or the bishop. "To be yoked to a man she didn't love because of a single sinful act."

"If I had convinced her to stay, she wouldn't have died a lost soul."

"You don't know anything about the state of her soul."

"She left the church." Tears ran down Dinah's wrinkled face. The lines around her mouth and eyes deepened until they seemed cavernous. "She didn't raise her children in our faith. Or any faith at all, as far as I can tell."

"Did you know she was taking Perry with her?"

"Nee. I didn't know. I would've tried to stop him."

"Did Job know Georgia was expecting?"

"Not until after they left." Dinah caught her long white hair into a ponytail and wrapped it around her gnarled fingers. Her dim eyes focused somewhere far beyond the bedroom. "I was afraid to tell him. I knew Job would want to confront her and make her go to see the bishop. I knew Georgia would not change. She did not belong in this Plain world. Job would never have accepted this truth. That day Georgia paraded her worldly nature around the kitchen in front of me.

"She said she wasn't ashamed. She liked him. He liked her. They made a bopli. Boplin are gifts from Gott. She spit my words back in my face. I wanted lots of boplin. She thought she could give them to me. To fill up the house with kinnskinner. If things were different, but she knew they'd never be different."

"Did she say who the daed was?"

"Nee. I asked. I begged her to go with him to the bishop and make a free will confession. They would be forgiven. The wedding would be small, but they could start a life together for their bopli's sake. She unpinned her kapp and removed the bobby pins from her hair. She let it swing loose. Then she told me she was leaving Haven and leaving her faith. She took off her apron, hugged me, told me she loved me, and walked away. Her last words to me were, 'I've been gone a long time, and you know it.'"

"I'm so sorry. Mason would like to know who his father is too. He's wanted to know his entire life. Georgia refused to talk about it with him."

Dinah plucked at loose threads on the Wedding Ring quilt. "She didn't tell me, but you know how the grapevine is."

"What are you saying?"

"At one of the quilting frolics, Millie Mast told me she thought Georgia and her son Caleb were courting. After

Georgia left, Millie stopped talking to me. She's been giving me the cold shoulder for more than twenty years."

Caleb Mast. A master carpenter and furniture builder who owned the furniture store in downtown Yoder. He was tall and had curly black hair and blue eyes.

Mason, tall, with wavy black hair and blue eyes, a carpenter, was the son of an Amish couple.

"Did you ever ask Caleb?"

"Nee, and he never came to us. It would've served no purpose. She was gone."

Dinah blotted her face again and threw back the covers. "We need to get the kinner up. I'm lying here feeling sorry for myself, and they're going to be late to schul."

"I'll get them. You get dressed."

"I'll come with you and then get dressed."

The girls' door was closed. Cassie opened it and peeked in. The girls were a picture of peaceful slumber. Dinah slipped in beside her. "They're so sweet. I hate to wake them."

"I know." Cassie tickled Kathy's rosy cheek. The girl opened one eye. She grinned and threw her arms around Cassie's neck. "You came back."

Warmth flooded Cassie. She returned the hug twofold. "Of course I did. You don't want to miss school, do you?"

Kathy sat straight up. "No, I mean nee. I like school." She threw back the covers and slid from the bed to give Dinah a hug. "I'm hungry, Mammi. Let's eat. I don't want to be late for school."

"Everyone should be so chipper in the morning." Dinah turned to Jennie. "Rise and shine, little one."

Jennie rolled up into a ball. She pulled the quilt up over her head.

"Ach, not everyone is, however." Dinah squeezed the quilt where Jennie lay underneath. Giggling and squealing ensued. After a few seconds, Jennie's head popped out. Her hair was a mess and her face red from laughing. Dinah laughed too. "Who wants pancakes with chocolate chips for breakfast?"

"I don't know if we have time—"

"Me, me!" Jennie slid off the bed, landed on her behind, picked herself up, and trotted toward the door. "Me first."

"Get dressed first." Cassie followed after her. "Shoes and socks too."

"Spoilsport!" Still smiling, Dinah stood more slowly and groped for her walking stick. "Go ahead and get the batter started and the grill hot. I'll shepherd them downstairs after I'm dressed."

"Dinah, wait."

Dinah stopped at her door.

"Will you tell Mason about Caleb Mast?"

"Nee, I can't. I can't talk about such things with my grandson. And you shouldn't either. It's not seemly." Her head lowered as she seemed to study the walking stick. "I understand why he wants to know. He has a right to know, but I don't know anything for sure."

"He brought it up, not me, but you're right. I should've told him I couldn't say. He doesn't know our ways. I know better."

"It's not your fault. My dochder did something years ago that brought shame upon our family. It's not Mason's fault. He was an innocent bopli, now a grown man who's never had a real father. I pray Gott's forgiveness on my dochder and on me."

"I will also. I need to get breakfast going."

"Tell Mason that his mudder courted Caleb Mast the summer before she left. Leave it at that. He can draw his own conclusions."

Did a young man simply walk up to an older man and ask him if he was his father? Like the dog in the children's book *Are You My Mother?* "I'll tell him."

"Don't linger in that conversation."

"I won't."

Cassie quickly descended the stairs. In the kitchen she measured, mixed, and poured as the kitchen rapidly filled with children who claimed to be starving. In no time breakfast was served, lunches packed, and they were on their way to school.

No time to think. No time to ponder the whereabouts of one ornery teenager or the choices made by Georgia Keim that left a boy without a father. At the school she waved good-bye from the buggy and turned toward the grocery store. They couldn't seem to keep up with the amount of food consumed by this horde of children.

Maybe she should pick up some of Jane Mast's pretty pot holders at the Mast Furniture Store.

Just to get a peek at Caleb Mast.

Did that amount to meddling? How could she tell Mason that this man might be his father based on twenty-three-year-old gossip and their similar features? It was none of her business.

"Cassie, you don't have nine lives like a cat. Curiosity killed the cat, remember?" Mother's voice sounded loud and clear in Cassie's head.

CHAPTER 24

A gray SUV parked in front of the Carriage House Restaurant stood out like a pit bull in a herd of tabby cats among the buggies and tractors. What was Mason doing in Yoder so early in the morning? *None of your business, nosy.*

Cassie focused on the grocery store ahead. She'd been thinking of him, and there he was nearby. So often life was like that. Did it mean something? That remained to be seen.

"Cassie. Cassie! Wait."

Should she ignore Mason's entreaty? Probably, but she couldn't. Cassie pulled up on the reins and halted just outside the restaurant's parking lot. He strode toward her, his long, jean-clad legs eating up the distance. "I thought that was you. Sorry about last night." He laid one hand on the buggy seat and stared up at her with a tired smile. "Any sign of Bobby this morning?"

Hadn't she just told Job she would steer clear of this man? Job couldn't have known Mason would seek her out the very same day. "No. I'm sorry."

"He was at the house last night—before I got home." Dark circles ringed Mason's bloodshot eyes. Pain mingled with irritation in every word. "He broke in and took some money."

"Ach. That's terrible." Cassie's heart twisted in sympathy for the older brother who doubled as father to Bobby. So hard to do when he had no father of his own to act as an example. She needed to tell him about Caleb Mast. But not now. Not in the middle of the street. "What is going through his head?"

"Sometimes I think he was born that way; other times I blame my mom." Mason lifted his ball cap and smoothed down his hair. He needed a haircut. "I guess I owe you an apology about last night. I didn't mean to get you in trouble. I had no idea it was such a big deal."

"It was fine. I was able to return to Job's this morning." Cassie studied a spot of bacon grease on her apron. She rubbed it with her thumb. "It just can't happen again."

"You were helping me. It was harmless. I can't see how us spending time together hurts anyone."

"We don't do that unless we're courting." The words came out of their own accord. *Gott, strike me down now.* Mason was sweet and kind and a good brother and pleasing to the eye.

Stop it. English. In big, fat letters. ENGLISH.

She drew a breath. "Anyway, it can't happen again."

"Okay, I get it. I guess." A muscle in Mason's jaw twitched. "It's just weird. I like your company. You're easy to talk to. I haven't done much dating—"

"I was just helping you out. That was all." Father would be proud. The words were the opposite of what she wanted to say. "We can talk. Just not alone in your SUV."

"Got it." He seemed to take an undue interest in the dirty slush on the street. "I'm meeting someone you may know here to talk about a job. Obadiah Hostetler."

"I know Obie. You're giving up your job in Wichita?"

Mason studied the ground some more. "Maybe you could come in with me. I could buy you breakfast and tell you my plan. See what you think. It's a public place. A bunch of people will be there. Nobody would object to that."

Like a date. Like two people getting to know each other better. How lovely. Job's admonitions marched side by side with her father's. "A Plain woman doesn't do that either. I'm sorry. I shouldn't be sitting here talking to you now."

Mason shifted his work boots. His gaze ricocheted off hers and shot back to the ground. "Sorry. I don't mean to put you in an awkward position, yet I keep doing it."

Awkward because she wanted to walk into the Carriage House with him. She wanted to sit across the table from him. All this time she'd never felt a tug like this and now it was happening with an English man. Her heart's desire for a husband and a mob of children seemed to move further away than ever. She only wanted what every Amish woman wanted. A family.

How could this be God's plan for her? To fall in love with an English man?

Love was the scariest word in the dictionary—English, German, or otherwise.

People always wanted what they couldn't have. Father's voice whispered in her ears. "*Watch yourself, Cassie.*" She took a long breath and let it out. "You want to work here because it's closer to the kids?"

"Yeah. Exactly. They'll be staying with Job and Dinah. So I need to rearrange my life to stay in theirs."

He was willing to make every sacrifice for them. Which made him all the more desirable. The more time he spent with the kids, the more often she would see him.

This was not good. Yes, it was. The two voices in her head were like blue jays arguing over territory. The noise was deafening. "It's important for them to know you're always going to be around for them. The more stability they have, the better.

And you need family too. You need them as much as they need you."

"You're right about that. I see them with you and my grand-parents and I see everything they've missed. Everything I've missed." Mason unbuttoned his coat as if somehow he was too warm. "I'd like to have it, if it's not too late."

The yearning on his face matched the longing in her heart. Cassie swallowed a sudden lump in her throat. "It's not too late," she whispered.

She should tell him about Caleb Mast. He had an Amish father. He needed to know that. "Dinah says—"

"Cassie!"

Cassie turned. Her father approached them on his tractor. A frown darkened his stony face. She fixed a smile on her face, waved, and turned back toward Mason. "Dinah thinks your father might be a man named Caleb Mast, but she's not sure. He owns the furniture store here in Yoder."

She ran the words together in her haste to get them out before her father descended upon them, but it was obvious Mason got the gist of it. Pure excitement lit up his face. "An Amish man?"

Cassie nodded.

"Thank you," he whispered as he tipped his ball cap and smiled at her father. "Hey, Mr. Weaver."

"Leroy."

"I was just asking your daughter if there was anything new about Bobby."

Something like that.

Father didn't seem convinced, but he nodded. "And?"

"Nothing." Cassie spoke in English for Mason's benefit. "I just need to get a few things at the store, and I'll be getting back."

"I'm meeting Mrs. Blanchard at Job's at eleven thirty," Mason offered. "She was hot under the collar that I didn't call her sooner."

"I'd better get back and let Job know." Cassie picked up the reins. "Good luck with your job interview."

"Thank you." Mason nodded at her father. He started to turn away, then hesitated. "You might also tell Job and Dinah that Perry might show up at some point. He's at my house now. I'm not sure when, but at least they'll be prepared. I don't want Dinah fainting again."

"Perry's back!" Cassie clapped. The reins fell into her lap. She grabbed them up. A silver lining. The return of Job and Dinah's prodigal son. "I can't wait to tell Dinah."

"There's a good chance he won't stay." The grimace on Mason's face penetrated Cassie's glee. "Prepare her for that. All things considered, they might not want him to stay."

Nothing could make them want Perry to leave again. Helping him to return to the faith would always be their first priority—at whatever cost to their comfort and happiness. What could he possibly say or do worse than leaving without saying good-bye? Being gone for more than twenty years without a single letter to let his parents know he was alive and well? "You should be the one to tell Dinah about Perry. You can explain better than I can."

"I can try. We'll see what Mrs. Blanchard has to say about Bobby. There's a lot going on. I also want to talk to Job about houses for rent in that area. I'm searching for something with at least three or four bedrooms. You wouldn't happen to know of any, would you, Mr. Weaver?"

"It's Leroy." The lines around Father's mouth deepened as he frowned. "There are a couple of houses in Haven that are empty. I don't know if they're for rent or sale. One's on East Fourth and the other's on West Second Street."

"Thanks for the tip. I'll check them out." He nodded at her father and touched the bill of his baseball cap in Cassie's direction. "See you all later."

He turned on his heel and strode toward the restaurant.

Cassie watched him go.

Father cleared his throat. She whipped her gaze to Job's roan. "Watch yourself, Dochder. Watch yourself."

Cassie forced herself to stare him square in the face. "I am, Daed, I promise. The kinner need him."

"And you need to be careful. He's moving up here, lock, stock, and barrel. He doesn't know what's what. You do." He tapped his temple with one stubby index finger. "Use the noggin Gott gave you. Go on, get your groceries and get back to Job's."

He had a right to be concerned. Cassie couldn't lie to herself about that. Mason was a special man—kind, generous, compassionate, a hard worker, honest, a family man. She'd learned all this about him in the last few months. It seemed likely that list only scratched the surface.

He was English.

But he was the son of two Plain people.

"I see your brain churning, Dochder. You're setting yourself up for heartache." Father shook his head. "Not just you, but everyone who cares about you."

"I would never do anything to shame you and Mudder." She swallowed back sudden tears. No matter what happened, those words were true. She had been baptized, taken vows, and chosen her life. She would never abandon it, not even if that meant she couldn't have her heart's desire—the love of a good man and a big family. "Don't worry. There's no need. I promise."

Though he didn't seem mollified, he started up the tractor, put it in gear, and drove away without even a *See you later*.

He'd never spoken to her like that before. He sounded . . . afraid for her.

CHAPTER 25

Plenty of frowns to go around. Sucking in a deep breath, Mason moved into the living room. Mrs. Blanchard perched on the edge of the sofa next to Dinah. Deputy Waters had taken a seat in the rocking chair by the fireplace. Job stood. No Cassie. Maybe that was better. After their conversation in town, it was obvious he needed to back off. The first time he truly felt something for a girl and it had to be her. An Amish woman. A good, kind, decent, beautiful Amish woman. The last thing he wanted to do was make her life harder. Somehow he had to stay clear of her while staying close to the kids.

A tricky tightrope to walk. He could start by focusing on the problem in front of him. Now wasn't the time to think about the bomb Cassie had dropped on him in Yoder. His father was—or might be, she'd said—an Amish man. *Later. Think about it later.*

He had been late getting to Job's. The meeting with Obie Hostetler had taken longer than Mason expected. He snagged the job, but only after a long conversation about his work habits, ethics, and experience.

Now all he had to do was find a house to rent near Yoder.

"We're so glad you could join us." Mrs. Blanchard shot him a glare dripping with ice. She hadn't been happy when he called her cell phone while drinking his first cup of coffee at the crack of dawn. "Surely Bobby has contacted you by now."

"I'm sorry. I got here as quick as I could." All the chairs were taken, so he remained standing by the front door. "Bobby hasn't texted or called. I tried doing both with him, but he didn't answer. He has to be in Wichita, though."

Mason went on to tell them about the break-in at the house and the missing money. He didn't mention Perry. His presence was neither here nor there. Cassie would tell Dinah.

The creases on Deputy Waters's forehead deepened. He wrinkled his nose. "You should've reported the situation to me last night. Our juvenile detective will want to get in contact with his counterparts in Sedgwick County and the Wichita PD to be on the lookout for your half brother."

"I figured he has money so he has the ability to get out of the cold and get a hot meal. It was wrong of him to break in and steal the money, but at least he's not wandering the streets penniless. If we drag him back here, he'll just leave again."

"So you want to leave a sixteen-year-old out on the street on his own?" Mrs. Blanchard's double chin quivered in her indignation. "You should've called me immediately. And you should've called Deputy Waters the minute you realized Bobby was in Wichita."

"I want to be able to tell him that he can live with me." Mason tried to communicate a silent apology to Dinah. She likely couldn't see his expression or much else about him. He took another breath. "Bobby may be better off with me. I can handle him. He may be too old to fit into this situation. Let me find him and bring him home—to our home."

"Maybe you give up after you stumble over your first obstacle, but we don't." Job went to the sofa and squeezed in next to Dinah. "We knew it would be a bumpy road and it would take time for all the children to adjust. We're not giving up that easily."

"It's not a matter of giving up," Mason rushed to explain. The words stumbled over each other.

Calm. Be calm. Be an adult. Show them you can do this.

"I got a job with an Amish crew in Yoder. Now all I have to do is rent a house in the same area. You can visit the kids whenever you want. You can be grandparents to them. They need grandparents."

"Or they could continue to live here, and you can visit them here." The set of Job's jaw was firm. He exuded calm. "This is what your mother wanted. We had our differences. Things didn't turn out as we had hoped, but this is something we can do for her now, something she wanted from us."

How could Mason argue with that?

"That's a conversation for another time." Deputy Waters stood. "My concern now, and I'm sure Mrs. Blanchard's as well, is getting Bobby back safe and sound. You were going to provide me with a list of hangouts and friends. Do you have it?"

Mason handed over the list. "I went to all these places last night. I didn't see any familiar faces. I worked a lot, so I never really met Bobby's friends. I only know first names of a few."

"We'll check with the school, talk to his teachers. They often know who's hanging out with whom." Deputy Waters scratched the whiskers on his chin as he reviewed the list. "I took a gander on social media. I didn't find him on Instagram, but he does have an Instagram account. We'll keep an eye on it to see if he posts anything. Crazy as it sounds, kids sometimes post stuff that tells us where they're hiding out."

The deputy tucked the list in his pocket and headed to the door. He brushed past Mason. "If you find out anything or hear anything from him, I should be your first call."

"Understood."

"And I'm next." Mrs. Blanchard remained at her post on the sofa. She waited until Deputy Waters shut the door to continue. Her arms folded over her ample stomach, she fixed a stern frown on Job. "You, sir, should have called me yourself. It's not Mason's job to do that now. It's yours. I know you don't have a phone here, but you assured me you had access to one in emergencies. I assure you the disappearance of one of your charges is an emergency."

Job shrugged and spread both hands wide. "We're used to handling such situations ourselves—"

"Be that as it may, the welfare of these children falls in my bailiwick. Regardless of what you may have heard about CFS, I take my duties very seriously. I stay on top of the circumstances of every child to whom I'm assigned."

"We understand. It won't happen again." Dinah spoke when Job didn't.

"What my wife means to say is we also have our grand-children's best interests at heart." Job crossed his arms. His chin came up. "You know that Bobby is a rebellious teenager. It's been hard for him and for us to help him make the right choices."

Mrs. Blanchard huffed. She pulled a clipboard from her worn satchel. "There's a lot of paperwork involved when a child goes missing. We might as well get started."

"I have to go to work." Mason moved toward the door. "I'll go back to all Bobby's old hangouts after I get off at five. I'll call Mrs. Blanchard and Deputy Waters if I find out anything. They can get word to you."

"You should stay for lunch. It's ready." A dish towel in one hand, Cassie trotted into the living room. "Everyone should stay and eat. I made a big pot of spaghetti and there are two loaves of garlic bread."

Whatever tension had flowed between them in town, it was gone now. Her smile was sunny.

"That sounds lovely." Mrs. Blanchard stood. "I hate to impose, but I can't leave until I speak with each of the children when they return from school. I'm going to be here for a while."

"We'd love to have you eat with us." Dinah stood as well. "You can talk to Jennie afterward."

"I have to go." Mason couldn't face a meal with Mrs. Blanchard on one side of the table and Dinah and Job on the other, mending fences and bonding. Besides, he needed to give his two weeks' notice. He couldn't leave his boss in the lurch. He'd been too good to Mason. "I'll be in touch."

"Come back for supper then." Cassie clutched the dish towel in both hands. "There will be leftovers. There's a green salad and whoopie pies for dessert. Have you ever had a whoopie pie?"

"I don't think so."

"They're really good."

She worked so hard. And tried so hard. Mason's stomach rumbled. "It depends on how long I spend searching for Bobby, but we'll see."

Cassie smiled. "Gut. I'll set a place for you."

"I want a word with you before you go." Her satchel in hand, Mrs. Blanchard followed him out to the SUV. "So you're quitting your job and moving to Haven. That's a big step for you."

"I got a job with an Amish construction crew out of Yoder. I'd like to rent a house nearby."

"So that you can be closer to your grandparents and your siblings."

"Yes."

"Good. That's a step in the right direction. I'm glad to see you want to make this work." Her smile felt like a gold star. She pulled a book from the satchel and held it out. "Read this. This might help also."

The big, fat book had a picture on the cover of a barefoot boy wearing suspenders, his back to the camera, gazing at clouds in the distance. The title was *The Amish* by someone named Donald Kraybill and some other people. She was trying to be nice. Mason couldn't just reject it out of hand, could he? He took the book and thumbed through the pages. Lots of words. No pictures. "I don't read much."

That was an understatement. Car mechanic manuals, DIY projects, and assembly instructions were the only reading he'd done since graduating from high school.

"You might want to make the effort to read this. And then sit down and talk to Job. He's your grandfather. Get past the clothes and the beard and find out who he really is." Her double chin shaking, Mrs. Blanchard pushed her glasses up her nose with one finger. She reminded him of his high school English teacher who never tired of trying to tempt Mason to read novels—with no luck. "You're family, and from what I can tell, you could use some adult conversation. You need these people in your life, my friend."

Was she his friend?

"If you were my friend, you'd see this situation through my eyes." Mason struggled for words to explain to a woman who'd seen it all, much of it heartbreaking, how hard it was for him to trust that life would work out with his grandparents, that things wouldn't fall apart all over again. He had to be ready to pick up the pieces if they did. "You think I'm a kid. I'm not. I'm a very old twenty-two. I've been taking care of myself and those kids for years. Don't think of me as a college-age kid. See someone who's been a father and a mother to five kids for the better part of his life. Give me some credit."

"Believe me, I do." Mrs. Blanchard tapped the book's cover with a blunt fingernail. "That's why I went to the trouble to get this book for you. You've done a really good job raising those children. I respect you, Mason. You've adapted to some difficult situations. That's how I know you can adapt to this one. Read the book. Talk to Job. Find a compromise that puts the kids ahead of what you want and what the Keims want. Think only about what's best for them, no one else."

With that, she turned and waddled back toward the house.

Mason lifted the book like a dumbbell. It weighed at least five pounds. "It has five hundred pages. I don't even know where to start."

"Most people start at the beginning." She raised one hand and waved. "Then they read one page at a time. I guess you'd better get started."

Easy for her to say.

CHAPTER 26

Sputter, sputter.

"No, no, no, not now." Mason smacked his hand on the wheel, gritted his teeth, and growled. "Seriously? You've got to be kidding me."

Par for the course. "No, no, no."

Mason was alone in the Trailblazer, so no one heard his lament. He yanked the wheel to the right and guided the SUV to the shoulder of the road. At least the Blazer had waited until he turned off the highway onto the county road that led to Job's farm before it decided to do its death rattle, *put-put*, and die.

They were expecting him for supper. He'd started his new job in Yoder, but he still hadn't found a rental house. In fact, he couldn't even find an apartment in the area unless he moved to Hutchinson. It was closer, but it didn't give him a place to bring the kids for sleepovers. So he continued to drive back and forth from Wichita, putting more miles on the Blazer, which led to the death rattle.

And he continued to live with Perry.

He brushed the thought aside. The last thing he wanted to think about right now was the uncle who'd moved in and refused to move on.

Could he do that? Basically squatting in his dead sister's house for the last month.

Not thinking about it right now.

Mason popped the hood, shoved open his door, and went to investigate the Blazer's latest malady.

Smoke rolled from the engine.

Okay, so it got a little overheated. Again. Not a problem. Mason opened the hatch and pulled out the orange plastic container of water he kept there for just such occasions. He would have to let the engine cool off first, but a drink of water should help.

At least it was May and not August. At least it was Saturday and he didn't have to be at work. A soft breeze rolled off a field of winter wheat. The smell of dirt and the sound of someone mowing in the distance were nice after a week of paint and oil fumes mingling with pounding hammers, electric saws, and drills.

He could nap or he could take another run at the book Mrs. Blanchard had given him. It lounged on the front seat, mocking him. Who could understand all this stuff about twin pillars of faith, *Gelassenheit*—he couldn't even pronounce that word—and "a living hope"? Yet he kept at it just so he could tell the caseworker he'd tried.

Really tried.

He needed to understand. This was his heritage. Until he understood, he didn't have the guts to approach Caleb Mast, who might or might not be his father. He kept putting it off. Why? Fear of disappointment? Fear of rejection? Fear that Dinah was wrong?

Or maybe you're just a coward, an irritating inner voice taunted him. The voice that kept him awake at night in a house haunted by eight years of the good, bad, and ugly times that would never be again.

Read the book. Anything was better than sitting here contemplating his situation.

"Okay, okay." The book practically jumped into his hands. Mason slid in on the passenger side and turned to the next page. "'Be not conformed to this world.'" What did that mean? Romans 12:2. He had never read the Bible. Ever. In fact, there had never been a Bible in the house.

No wonder he couldn't understand this stuff. If he was going to read this book, he needed a Bible. His own Bible. Now there was a thought.

"Grrrrr." Growling like an old bear. That's what Mom would've said. He shoved his KC Royals cap back. An engine rumbled behind him. He turned. A bright-green John Deere tractor pulled in behind him.

A tractor driven by none other than Leroy Weaver, Cassie's dad.

"Lord, have mercy," he muttered to himself. Did that count as a prayer? Mason had no way of knowing. "Amen."

Just in case.

The book still in his hand, Mason slid from the Blazer and walked back to say hello.

"I thought that was you." Leroy hopped from the tractor and met Mason halfway. "I'm guessing you have yourself some car trouble."

"It overheated. I was waiting for it to cool off."

"Care for some company while you wait?"

Mason would've sworn Leroy didn't like him. But then again, Amish folks didn't hold grudges. They forgave. He'd learned that much from reading the book. "Sure. That would be great. Where are you coming from?"

"I went into town to pick up some fertilizer and seeds." He

pushed back his straw hat and surveyed the Blazer. "Your car's been rode hard and put up wet."

"The Blazer has been a true friend and companion for five years. I traded the old Ford pickup truck Mom helped me get when I turned sixteen for it so I could cart the kids around to stuff." Mason leaned against the bumper and propped one boot against it. "It feels wrong to abandon it. Besides, it's paid for and I really can't afford a car payment right now."

The understatement of the year. Car repairs or deposit and first month's rent on a house?

Decisions, decisions.

Leroy joined Mason on the bumper. "I reckon I understand that."

The silence stretched between them.

"Anything new in the search for your brother? Last time I talked to Cassie, she said the police hadn't found hide nor hair of him."

"The juvenile detective called me yesterday. They had a sighting on Instagram. Some guy tagged Bobby in a picture. They were at a skateboard park in Wichita." Adrenaline surged through Mason just as it had when the detective first shared this new development. Bobby was alive. He was okay. He was skateboarding. "He said they were hanging out after work at the grocery store. Apparently they're coworkers."

"So the detective will go there and find him."

If only it were that easy. Kids came and went from that busy skate park. Even if Bobby wasn't there, they might have seen him or know him, even know where he was staying. "They contacted Wichita PD. They're checking it out. Also the closest grocery store. It's a lead."

A good lead. More than they had before.

"That's gut. Very gut. This Instagram, what is it?"

Mason explained as best he could to a man who had a rudimentary grasp of computers and the internet. Leroy nodded once or twice, but mostly he appeared perplexed. Mason understood that. He wasn't a big fan of social media, unlike so many of his peers. "It's a big time suck and strangers know way more about you than they should. I don't get it."

"People seeking connection with strangers is hard to understand." Leroy shrugged massive shoulders. "I want my family and friends close, where I can see them face-to-face."

Mason too. Which was why he was stuck out on this road that led to Job's house. "Can I ask you a question?"

Leroy jerked his chin toward Mason. "Does it have something to do with that book you're clutching like a life preserver?"

An observant man. "Yeah. Mrs. Blanchard thought I should read it, but I can't make heads or tails out of it. And how come you're driving a tractor when it says most Amish people don't use farm equipment or cars that go on the road? You have buggies like other Amish people, but then you show up in Yoder on a tractor. It's confusing."

Chuckling, Leroy took off his straw hat and fanned his leathery face. "It's hard to understand why someone would bother writing a whole book about us. It's even harder to fathom why people spend their hard-earned dollars to buy the book and read it. Don't they have anything better to do? Why do people care how Plain folks live? They even read made-up romance stories about us. We're just trying to live our lives in a way that pleases God."

All very good questions. None of which Mason could answer. He hadn't given a rat's behind until his siblings ended up living with Amish grandparents they never knew they had.

"And driving a tractor or a buggy pleases Him? How do you know that?"

"I'm no bishop, but I'll explain as best I can." Still fanning, Leroy wiped droplets of sweat from his forehead with his sleeve. "First thing is there's no central church. Every Amish district has its own set of rules. The members vote on them. We consider every single issue individually. The colors of our clothes. The kapps our women wear. Whether we have phones and such. This district decided we needed tractors to make a living. So we changed our rules, our *Ordnung*, to allow it."

"Just like that?"

"Not just like that. It was a hard decision made with much discussion and prayer. We consider how it will change our lives. Will we remain apart from the world? That is our goal. So that we don't get sucked into the wicked ways of that world."

"A tractor could do all that?"

"It's a slow slide. A little bit at a time. Tractors, cars, electricity, TVs, radios, computers. Pretty soon we've abandoned our values and beliefs and we're leading sinful lives."

This was way better than reading a book. Just go straight to the source. Cassie's dad was a fountain of information. Mason handed the book to Leroy, tugged an old rag from his back pocket, and turned to the SUV's engine. *Please don't let hot fluids spray my face, God.*

How was that for a prayer? He was getting the hang of it. Mason twisted off the radiator cap using the rag. No fluid spewed out.

"Fill her up." Leroy handed him the water container. "Have you had this problem before?"

"Sure. It also has an oil leak. I keep extra cans of oil in the back too." The water gurgled. Steam burbled from the radiator. "Hopefully that'll do the trick."

He returned the radiator cap to its rightful place and wiped his hands on the rag. "So if you do everything right, the way God wants you to, you'll go to heaven?"

"You sure have a lot of questions. Good questions. You should have a sit-down with Bishop Bryan. He's better at this than an old farmer like me." Leroy walked with Mason back to the driver's-side door and handed him the book. "That's our hope, but the best I can tell you is we're humble folks. We figure we don't know what God's will is. We don't know what His plan for us is. We only know that He has a plan. His will be done. We hope for eternal salvation, but it's God's will, not ours."

"Okay. So you do good stuff and earn points and hope it's enough?"

"You can't earn salvation with good works. But you try to live life according to Holy Scripture. Following Jesus, doing what He tells you to do in the Holy Bible."

It sounded like a lot of rules. Which wasn't necessarily a bad thing. Mason had grown up without rules, and it hadn't been all that great.

He slid into the Blazer and dropped the book on the seat next to him. More food for thought. He turned the key. "Here goes nothing."

A whirring sound. *Chug-chug-a-chug.*

Silence. He turned the engine off and on again.

Nothing this time.

Nada.

Zip.

Only Leroy's presence kept Mason from smacking the wheel again. He closed his eyes and opened them. "That's not good."

"I figured as much." Leroy patted the door. "I tinker some with engines that we run with propane. I know enough to do maintenance on the tractor. But this here car is beyond me."

"I've been babying it for years." Mason drummed a one-two-three beat on the wheel. "But I think I may have hit the point of no return. I just replaced the battery, so it's not that. It sounds like something in the electrical system."

It sounded like big bucks.

"Do you have roadside assistance?"

Mason snorted. "Nope."

"I reckon you were headed to Job's."

"I was."

"Why don't I give you a ride over there? You can get some grub and they won't worry about you. When you're ready, you can call a tow truck to tow it to your mechanic."

"Thanks. That sounds like a plan. I appreciate your help." Mason got out of the Blazer and locked it up. Together they walked to the tractor. Leroy didn't need to know Mason didn't have a mechanic and couldn't afford one right now. Also, he'd never ridden on any farm equipment. "Towing it all the way to Wichita will cost an arm and a leg, but a guy's gotta do what a guy's gotta do."

"What will you do to get around in the meantime?"

The million-dollar question. Rental cars were expensive. "I don't know. My stepdad's car was destroyed in the accident. They hauled it to the junkyard after the accident investigation was over. I sold my mom's car to pay bills." Not that he got much for a purple Buick on its last leg. It was less reliable than the Blazer. He stared up at the bright-green tractor with yellow wheel coverings. "How fast does this baby go?"

"Faster than a buggy, but we don't care about speed." Leroy

climbed into the cab. "This one goes about twenty-five miles an hour. There are others that go faster. I don't have the need. You'll have to stand next to me. You can hire a driver like we do."

"Maybe. For work I can probably take the van that brings the Amish guys to the work site."

"There you go." Leroy turned on the engine, put the tractor in gear, checked his mirrors, and pulled onto the road. "Just so you know, Amish don't marry outside their faith."

The change in topic hit Mason between the eyes. "S-sorry?"

Leroy changed gears and the tractor picked up speed. Its engine sounded much smoother than the Blazer's. "You were asking questions about us. I thought that might be something you needed to know. We don't marry Englischers."

"Knowing what my mom did, I figured as much." Heat seared his face despite the cool breeze created by the tractor's brisk movement toward Job's. "But Job and Dinah keep talking about the kids getting baptized when they get older. Like they can become Amish."

He was no kid, but he was their grandson, so that gave him the same option, didn't it? Was he really considering it? This had nothing to do with Cassie. It had everything to do with belonging somewhere. It had to do with feeling right in his gut.

Would anyone believe that?

"They're young enough that they might find it in their hearts to join our faith." Leroy didn't sound convinced. "Adults very rarely make the leap. Some try, but it doesn't stick. I reckon you can figure out why. If they do, it's not because there's a girl."

"This isn't about Cassie. It's about the kids. I'm trying to learn all this for them. To help them make a decision."

For the most part. If they became Amish, what would happen to him? Would their lives veer off on a separate path that had no room for their so-called English relative? Would he become like Perry? An outcast from his own family?

"You can't join because of her or to be close to your half brothers and sisters. It won't work." Leroy might be a mind reader. "We're baptized into the faith because we believe in Jesus Christ our Savior and we're willing to follow the Ordnung—the rules. We don't want anything to do with the world. Like driving cars or using electricity or having cell phones. But even more, because we want to be humble and obedient before God."

Mason's head throbbed. Sleepless nights. Perry in the kitchen every morning, wearing boxer shorts and scratching his armpits. A broken-down SUV. A lecture from a worried father. The certain knowledge that he would never be good enough to be baptized into the Amish faith—or any faith.

This had been a day. *God, I could use some good news for a change. Something. Anything.*

His cell phone rang. Maybe he should let it go to voice mail. Leroy obviously didn't think much of phones.

"Go on, answer it. We'll be at Job's in ten minutes or less."

The real estate company. They'd found a house that had just become available for rent. A two-story, four-bedroom, two-and-a-half-bathroom house with a garage and a fenced yard. Unfurnished. The monthly rent was actually less than the house in Wichita. "When can you come out and view it?"

Good question. "Actually my car broke down this afternoon. Can we do it on Monday? That'll give me time to figure out something regarding transportation."

"That's fine. Just don't mess around too long. These rentals don't come along very often. Someone will snap it up right out from under you."

"Will do."

Whoa, God, You mean business. Thank You. Thank You so much.

Mason stuck the phone in his pocket and leaned against the cab's wall. A small step forward.

"Good news?"

"Finally."

"Did you have any more questions for me?"

"I think you've given me enough to chew on for now, but I might have more questions later."

"Talk to Job. Or Bryan. They know way more than I do."

Mason wasn't so sure about that. Leroy knew a lot. In fact, Leroy seemed to know too much. But he didn't know Mason. People had been underestimating him his whole life. From the fourth-grade teacher who wanted to put him in special ed because he had trouble reading to the high school algebra instructor who said he would never amount to anything if he didn't take geometry. To the counselor who told him he would end up on welfare if he didn't go to college. To Mrs. Blanchard who didn't believe he could be father and mother to five younger brothers and sisters.

He would show them all.

CHAPTER 27

The kids welcomed Mason like a conquering hero. He leaned through the tractor cab's window and waved. They didn't know he was just a guy with a broken-down car left on the side of the road. Leroy drove into Job's backyard, pulled in near the corral, and turned off the engine.

Grinning, Kathy took one hand off the saddle horn and returned the wave. Donny screamed, executed a perfect somersault, landed on his bare feet, and raced toward the tractor. Jennie pirouetted, did her version of a handstand despite her long dress, and skipped after Donny. Kevin hung on to the corral fence, but his grin stretched across his face.

Mason's own welcoming committee. Even Job, who kept one hand on Kathy's horse, smiled and waved. It felt good. So different from going home to a dark, cold house in Wichita every night. Mason hopped down from the tractor. "Thanks, Leroy."

"No thanks necessary. If you need a ride back to your SUV, let me know."

The intricacies of communicating with Amish folks had become routine for Mason. Leroy would eventually check the recorded messages in the phone shack, but the tow truck driver would probably give Mason a ride and it would be faster. "You've done enough already, but thanks."

"You know where to find me." Leroy climbed down and

headed for the house. "I need to talk to Cassie. Enjoy your visit."

And stay away from my daughter.

The unspoken words hung in the air. Leroy might as well have trumpeted them.

If only it were that simple. Mason dragged his focus back to the kids. Nothing could be more important than them.

"Mason, Mason, over here!" Kathy waved wildly with one hand, the other gripping the saddle horn. "I'm riding a horse."

"You sure are." She was so proud. Mason suddenly felt proud too. God could take four city kids, plop them down on a farm, and turn them into country kids. With the help of grand-parents who wanted nothing more than to teach them how to live simply. How could he argue with that? "I'm proud of you. You're a regular cowgirl."

"You have to see the kittens. They've grown so much." Jennie grabbed his leg. Her face was tanned. Someone had caught her hair back in two braids and covered her head with a white handkerchief tied in the back. In her long, pale-blue dress, she could've been a little Amish girl. "I can count to twenty-five now. Cassie taught me."

"That's good. That's really good." Mason knelt and envel-oped her in a hug that quickly included Donny. Kevin hung back until Mason fixed him with a stare. "What are you wait-ing for, dude? Group hug."

Kevin obliged.

It felt good. Really good. A guy couldn't get enough kid hugs. They smelled of dirt and sweat and sheer happiness. After several seconds, he forced himself to let go, but Jennie and Donny still clung to his legs as if staking their territory. "You know it's only been a few days since we've seen each other."

"Daadi says I can play baseball on a team in Yoder when they start up next week." Kevin's skin had turned golden brown. He'd grown at least two inches in the last month. Cassie would need to sew new pants soon. "He's teaching me to drive a tractor."

"I'd rather play volleyball." Kathy wore a larger version of Jennie's dress. She'd hitched it up to sit in the saddle, revealing a pair of leggings under it. "All the kids play after church on Sunday now that the weather's warmed up. Cassie is teaching me to sew my own dresses. I made cornbread from scratch yesterday."

"I set the table and I make my bed." Jennie let go of Mason's leg and danced around him. "I know how to put clothes through the wringer too."

"That's great, really great." They liked their new life. They exuded contentment. It was all good. "That's what I like to hear. I really mean that. Next thing I know, you'll be all grown up and taking care of yourselves."

Mason settled his ball cap's visor farther down on his forehead, but his gaze still collided with Job's. The other man shrugged and offered a smile.

"Kathy, why don't you get down so you and your brothers and Jennie can check to see how the kittens are doing." Job patted her leg. "I reckon the mama cat will let you hold one now."

Kathy slid willingly from the horse. The kids ran ahead to the barn while Mason fell in step next to Job. Neither of them spoke for a few seconds. Casper nickered and shook his head.

He sounded as weary as Mason felt.

"So I guess your car broke down."

No sense in belaboring the point. "Yep."

"I guess you don't want to talk about it."

"Nope."

"Any word on Bobby?"

Mason repeated his report. Job's face lit up. "They'll go there and find him."

The same conclusion as Leroy. Job also had no clue about Instagram, and he had even less understanding than Leroy when it came to computers. Finally he shrugged. "Do you like horses?"

Changing the subject was a good idea. Without breaking stride, Mason patted Casper's long neck. It was the closest he'd been to a horse since they went to the county fair the last time. He'd been sixteen and sure he was too old to be seen with his mom and kid brothers and sisters. He'd wanted to hit the carnival rides with a bunch of friends. Mom wanted him to help her ride herd on the kid pack. He should've hung on to those moments instead of chomping at the bit to get away. Hindsight. "He's a beautiful animal."

"That he is. The best kind of beautiful. Good-natured and useful." Job was an animal lover. That was obvious from the way he leaned into the horse. "He's a hard worker, and he has a nice disposition."

Animals could be easier to love than people. "When I was a kid I wanted a horse."

"What did Georgia—your mother—have to say about that?"

"She laughed, but she got this faraway look on her face." Mason slowed, snared by the memory of how she would throw her head back in a belly laugh like he was the funniest comedian ever. "She said she loved horses, but they didn't belong in the city. They should be out where they can run around. She said horses were good friends. She said it like she knew what she was talking about."

"She loved to ride horses. It's not something we do for fun. Horses are work animals, but she liked to saddle up a horse and ride over to her friends' houses instead of taking a buggy."

"She never did anything the regular way, did she?"

"She did not. She was a force to be reckoned with." Job's Adam's apple bobbed. "Something I didn't figure out until she was gone. Until it was too late."

"I don't know if it helps, but she seemed happy. She liked her life. She even seemed to like all the drama with her husbands. Like it kept things interesting, as weird as that sounds."

And with no thought to how hard it was for her kids. For all her good qualities, his mother had been the center of her own universe.

"It doesn't sound weird. It sounds like my daughter."

"I'm sorry she wasn't what you wanted her to be."

They had reached the barn doors. The kids' laughter and excited chatter floated on the air. Jennie wanted to hold a kitten. Donny thought she would hurt it. Kathy mediated as usual. Job halted. He squinted against the sun. "I never said I was sorry about what happened with Bobby. I should've. I *am* sorry."

What could he say to that? Mason didn't want to have this conversation. He'd rather eat octopus or watch a rom-com in French with subtitles. "Bobby took the brunt of abuse from Clayton. Bobby just rubbed him the wrong way. So Bobby started running. It became a habit."

"I wish I had known more. Maybe I could've handled him differently."

Mason leaned his forehead against Casper's long neck and entwined his fingers with the horse's mane. It was easier than going eye to eye with Job. The man exuded guilt. "I tried to tell Mrs. Blanchard this wouldn't work. Not for Bobby. Maybe for the little kids but not him. She wouldn't listen. CFS has one way of handling these things. Step one, step two, step three. There's no room for variation. No room for humanness."

Anger and sadness stomped around in Mason's gut. He sucked in air. This stuff made him want to puke. Job's hand touched Mason's. He swallowed hard and forced out the words. "I don't think he's coming back this time. I think he's gone forever."

"We have to rely on God's provision for him."

Mason withdrew his hand. He cleared his throat. "I don't know how to do that."

"You say your prayers and leave the rest to God. He has a plan for Bobby and for you and for me. His will be done."

The desire to believe was so intense Mason fought the urge to double over. "I know—"

"Hey, Mason, come on, come see the kitties!" Donny stood at the door and yelled. "What's taking you so long?"

"We're old. We don't move as fast as you little whipper-snappers. Hold your horses." Job saved Mason from having to answer. "The kittens aren't going anywhere. What's the hurry?"

Donny whirled and ran back into the barn, but his excited words carried on the breeze. "Daadi says to hold our horses. He says they're old."

Mason laughed. Job joined him. The relieved laugh of two men who hardly knew each other but had shared something unexpected.

Inside, the steadying smell of hay, horses, dirt, and manure greeted Mason. He sniffed and wiped at his face with the back of his hand. "Stupid allergies."

With a wry smile Job nodded. "They're bad this time of year. Go see the kittens while I unsaddle the horse. They've doubled in size since the last time you saw them. Mom can hardly keep track of them."

The horse tossed his head and whinnied. Ignoring Donny's insistent shouts, Mason lingered by the stall door.

Job's bushy eyebrows lifted. "Whatever you want to ask, ask it."

"Do you think you could teach me to ride a horse?"

His grandfather's perplexed stare gave way to a wide grin. "I sure can. Whenever you have time." Job uncinched the saddle and lifted it from Casper's back. "Are you still staying for supper?"

"I'd like to." Mason considered his options. The Blazer wouldn't go anywhere without him. What was the big hurry to have it towed with money he couldn't afford to spend? "I don't actually have a way home right now. The Blazer is dead on the side of the road, and I haven't even called for a tow."

"Why don't you spend the night? Come to church with us tomorrow? We'll worry about the car after that."

A gnarly feeling like the one he got when he was six and the doctor said he needed his tonsils out gripped Mason. "I don't know. I've only been a few times in my life, mostly at Christmas and Easter. Are you sure you want me in your church?"

"Everyone should be in church somewhere on Sunday morning. Come see what it's all about. Kevin will fill you in on what's happening." His movements unhurried, Job dumped oats in Casper's bucket. He dusted off his hands and faced Mason. "He's gotten used to it. So have the others. I think they may even like it."

"I like it." Jennie slipped up behind Mason, took his hand, and tugged. "Cassie brings me snacks and I sleep on Mammi's lap."

Who wouldn't like that? Mason smiled at Job over the little girl's head. "I'll give it a shot."

"Good. You can bed down with the boys. They can make up a bed on the floor. Those two can sleep anywhere. Church starts early. A good night's sleep is important."

Mason let Jennie drag him over to see the kittens. Five rough-and-tumble acrobats who alternated between bugging their mom to eat and trying to find their way out of the stall. Like kids. He'd come here for a quick visit and ended up staying.

An unfamiliar light feeling floated in the air.

It felt like hope.

CHAPTER 28

Moving the table into the open space that served as a combination dining room and living room meant carrying the dishes farther, but it also gave them a lot more room. Cassie surveyed the leftovers on the table with a satisfied smile. The hamburger-vegetable casserole had been reduced to a few lonely peas and carrots. Only crumbs remained of the rolls, and the kids had finished off the last piece of raisin cream pie by dividing it into bites served on a single spoon passed around from child to child. Thank goodness they already had each other's germs.

Mason had seemed suitably impressed with the way Job had added a leaf to the table and built two new benches so it easily sat nine people—more if they had company. He ate supper with them so often now he was by no means considered company. Now he was spending the night and tomorrow he would attend church.

So much for keeping Mason at arm's length. Her resolve crumbled a bit more every time he said something as simple as "Pass the butter, please."

How could it not?

Grow up.

Cassie picked up the casserole dish and carried it into the kitchen where Kathy and Jennie sang "This Little Light of Mine" at the top of their lungs. Their enthusiastic rendition had Dinah in stitches. "Join us," she yelled. "They want to make sure Gott hears them."

"I have no doubt He does," Cassie called back. "They give new meaning to 'make a joyful noise.'"

Still smiling, she grabbed a washrag and returned to the front room to wipe down the table. The front door opened and Mason tramped in with Job and the boys. "You are such a cheerful worker." Mason paused by the table while the others ambled toward the living room. "Today you worked at the produce stand, you cleaned house, and you cooked three meals from scratch for seven or eight people—you have to be tired. Yet you're still smiling."

"I love my life." Cassie peeked over his shoulder. Job headed straight for his rocking chair. He was the one who was tired. He would read for a while or play chess with Kevin. By nine thirty, he'd be nodding off in his chair. "I enjoy cooking and sewing. And I get satisfaction from seeing a clean house."

Mason swiveled. He moved a few steps closer. "I really need to talk to you. Just for a few minutes. Later." His shy smile melted any resistance Cassie tried to muster. "Please don't say no. Just talk. Nothing more."

She nodded. "For a few minutes."

"Just talk. Nothing more." Those words followed Cassie around for the remainder of the evening. It seemed as if bedtime would never come, even though the kids went to bed early to be ready for church in the morning. Dinah followed almost immediately. Job hung on for a while but soon nodded off. Mason tiptoed out first. Cassie followed a few minutes later.

"Did he hear you?" Mason sat in a lawn chair on the porch. He leaned forward so she could see him better in the feeble porch light. "He seemed dead to the world when I passed by."

"He didn't move." Cassie adjusted the empty lawn chair so she could face Mason—and so they weren't so close together. "He's tuckered out. He's been planting spring oats and preparing the fields for alfalfa all this past week. He does both a fall and a spring planting of alfalfa."

"I thought he didn't farm anymore."

"Just what he can use as feed or to sell around here to other farmers who need it for their livestock."

"How are things going at the produce stand?"

"Gut. We're selling a ton of canned vegetables and fruit we put up last summer." Surely he hadn't wanted to talk about the produce stand. They could've done that in the house. "Plus the sewing goods. Sometimes I do baked goods, if I have time."

With the children she had less time for everything, but she didn't mind.

"How do people know how to find you?"

"The Yoder Chamber of Commerce put together a little map of the area for tourists."

"You don't mind if they come by to gawk and take pictures?"

"I try to be neighborly and treat them nicely." Truth be told, she liked talking to them. Seeing her world through their eyes. New perspectives were good for keeping a person grounded. "Job says that's how we witness for Jesus, by our actions and our words."

Like she was doing with Mason now. Cassie wiggled in her chair. "Father said you asked him some questions about our faith. He said you're reading a book about us. Can I ask you why?"

"I'm trying to understand." He took off his baseball cap and laid it on the bushel basket turned upside down between them. It served as a table of sorts. His shaggy hair was matted to his head. Cassie itched to give him a haircut. Touching his hair, being that close to him—the thought sent a shiver through her. He smiled a soft, diffident smile—which didn't help. "I want to understand a faith that works so well for all of you. I like the idea of not feeling like I'm in this fight alone. And . . . I want to understand . . . you."

"Me?" The single syllable came out in a croak. The shiver turned warm. Cassie contemplated the moonlit sky. "Why me?"

"You're not like any girl I've ever known." He laughed, the sound a mixture of humor and nerves. "Not that I've known many. I've been too busy taking care of those rug rats."

The full moon was so bright he would surely see the blush on her face. Despite the night breeze, she felt warm. The ice under her feet thinned. Any minute she would fall into the deep, icy water. "I'm not that interesting."

"You are. You're sweet and kind and smart and you know how to do so much. You don't have to show off skin or paint your face to be beautiful. You take care of the kids way better than I did. You're a natural."

His kind sentiments washed over Cassie. He sounded almost bewildered by his own emotions. She certainly was. The urge to crawl under the chair or flee to her room overwhelmed her. Yet she wanted to stay. To stay with him. So many compliments heaped on her by a man who had done hard things in his life. He'd never known his own father. He'd lived through his mother's multiple romances. He'd taken care of his siblings. He'd buried his mother. He was the kind and smart one. And yes, pleasing to the eye.

Gott, help me. "That's nice of you to say."

"I want to know you better, but your father says I can't. That it's not done." He fiddled with the frayed hem of his T-shirt.

"What do you say about it? Do you want to know me better? Or is it all in my head?"

"My daed is right." The words didn't come out nearly as firm as they should. They sounded as if she wanted to argue with her father. Cassie went back to studying the moon. It lit up the night so she could see the barn and the corral and the elm tree branches dipping and swaying in the May breeze.

She folded her hands in her lap to still them. "I'm Amish. You're not. Leastways, you don't practice the faith. I wish you did. That's the truth. I wish it more than anything."

"I'm trying to figure it all out." Tilting his head to one side, he spread his hands wide. "Help me. Help me understand. I want to have faith. I need it. I see what you have, and I think it must be so nice to let someone else make the plan."

The desire for faith was a start, but it couldn't be about her. Or about them. To think otherwise was selfish and ungodly. "Tomorrow after church, talk to Bryan. Tell him what you're thinking."

"He'll think I'm crazy."

"He might be skeptical, but he won't reject your questions out of hand. You're the son of an Amish woman who belonged to this district and maybe an Amish man too." Cassie tore her gaze from the night sky. "Have you talked to Caleb?"

"No, I can't. I don't know why, but I can't." He drew in a long breath. "Yes, I do know why."

"You're afraid." Maybe she should've phrased that differently. No man wanted to be called scared. "I mean, I would be scared, not knowing how he'll act or if he's even the one."

"I can't sit still. Walk with me." He brushed past her and bounded down the steps without waiting to see if she agreed. "I've waited so long to know my father. I've always wanted to know who he is. It seems stupid that I can't bring myself to go see this guy, find out if he is really the one."

His words faded away. Cassie pelted down the steps and scurried to catch up. "That's understandable. Really, it is. Dinah doesn't know for sure. Your mom never actually said."

Mason turned and walked backward instead of waiting for Cassie. "I keep thinking about how different my life would've been if she'd stayed. I'd be Amish. I would've grown up with all this." He waved toward the corral and the barn. "With Job and Dinah as my grandparents. Church. With family the way it should be. With you."

He plowed to a stop. "I'd be able to know you better."

Cassie slowed, but Mason came to her. He grabbed her hand. "Did you think about that? Do you think about me at all?"

"I try not to," she whispered. His hand was big, warm, and calloused. It enveloped hers. She should tug free, but she didn't. *Gott, please, help me do the right thing.* "But I can't help it."

"Me neither." His hands slid up her arms, across her shoulders, to her face. He traced her jawline with his thumb. "What are we going to do?"

A heat wave worse than any August afternoon in Kansas engulfed Cassie. She took a breath, then another. "We're going to do the right thing." She backed away from his touch. A lonely cold replaced the heat. "Just imagine—if your mother had married your father, your brothers and sisters wouldn't be here. Maybe things happened the way they were supposed to for some reason that we can't see. All we can do is work from here. And that means whatever you decide from here on out cannot be based on feelings for me. This is about you—who you are and who you want to be."

"You're right. I know you're right. I'm sorry, I shouldn't push you." Mason turned around and started walking again, slower this time, his shoulders hunched. He stuck his fists in his jeans pockets as if to keep them out of trouble. "But it's hard to understand. I've never felt this way about a girl, ever. It's not fair."

Life wasn't fair. If anyone knew that, Mason did. Cassie took solace in the fact that he was open to learning more. There was hope for him. And for Cassie. She would pray for his faith to grow. For him, not her.

Gott, I'm sorry. I'm only human. Thy will be done. I know it's not about me.

"If Dinah suspected it was this Caleb Mast, why didn't she ask him? Why didn't they get together and search for her?"

"They never asked him, and he never came forward to talk to them. I wondered myself if Caleb tried to find her. Maybe he did. Maybe he couldn't find her either. If Georgia had stayed, there would've been conversations among the parents and the bishop and the couple. But with her gone, there was no reason to talk about it. She made her choice and they abided by it."

Mason stopped at the corral fence. He slapped his hands on the top rail. His knuckles turned white. "He's a furniture builder. A carpenter. Like me."

Cassie chose a spot farther down the fence line. Every muscle in her body wanted to comfort him. Her instinct was to rub his back, squeeze his hand, and tell him things would turn out. She had no right to do any of those things. "I thought it was strange too. Sort of serendipitous." She liked that word. She'd read it in a book once and held it close in her head. Hoping for serendipity in her life.

"He's a nice man too. He married. He and his wife, Elizabeth, have six children. The oldest one, Rachel, was two years behind me in school. She has dark hair and blue eyes."

"His life went on."

Had Caleb's heart been broken? Would he welcome a son he'd never known? It would turn his life upside down—and his wife and children's. "Life has a way of doing that."

"I don't know which is worse, not knowing or knowing and not being sure of how he'll react."

"The only way to know for sure is to talk to him. If he's not the one, he'll say so. If he is, he'll let you know how he feels about it. You'll feel better. I know you will. Knowing and having it done, one way or another."

"You're right. I can't go on like this, that's for sure. It's driving me crazy." Wincing, he pinched the bridge of his nose with two fingers. "Tomorrow I'll go to church. I'll talk to Bryan. Then I'll get the SUV towed into Wichita. On Monday I'll ask Obie if I can take a long lunch, and I'll go to see Caleb Mast at the store. Not his house. That way he can tell his wife himself, if he wants to. If he really is my dad."

His hand came out as if he might reach for her. Cassie edged away. He crossed his arms instead. "I wish you could come with me."

"It's not a conversation he'll want to have in front of a woman." Nor could Cassie be seen in town keeping company with Mason. Her job was here—doing laundry, cooking, and sewing for the children. They weren't her children, but they might be the closest she'd ever be to Mason. "You don't need me there. You'll do fine."

"What if he's at church?"

"He lives in the east district."

"What does that mean?"

"We keep our church districts small so we can fit everyone in the barn or house for church and we all know each other.

There are three districts in Haven. Caleb Mast lives in a different one on the east side. We're on the west side."

"I couldn't hijack him in front of his family anyway. It's not the kind of thing you tell a guy at church."

It spoke well of Mason that he recognized this fact. "I know waiting is hard, but you can do it on Monday."

"I finally found a house I can afford to rent in Haven."

Cassie tried to follow Mason's meandering thoughts. He'd be moving to Haven. He'd be close. To his siblings, his grandparents, maybe his father. He'd be around even more often. How could she maintain her distance if he was always here? "That's good. The kids will love that."

"Will you love it?"

She would learn to deal with it. "How is Perry doing? Any chance he'll change his mind and come out to see Dinah and Job?"

"He sits around in his underwear and watches TV. He doesn't know what to do next." Mason's expression was a mixture of confusion and irritation. "I don't know what his deal is. I don't think he does either."

"Does he talk about coming to see them?"

"Nope. He's a big talker, but he doesn't want to talk about them." Mason rubbed his face with both hands. His eyes were red. "Now that I'm moving to Haven, maybe that'll force his hand."

Haven. Just down the road. It would be nice having him close. So close, yet so far. "I'd better go in. It's late and we have church in the morning. You don't want to doze off." Cassie managed a chuckle. Did it sound as forced to Mason as it did to her? She turned and headed for the house. "Good night."

"Cassie, wait."

She kept walking. She had no choice. She raced up the porch steps. At the door, she paused. "I'm sorry. It's just so much upheaval. It's hard."

Mason paused at the bottom of the steps. "I agree. I feel like every day is something new. If my life were a road, it would be littered with potholes."

His smile held pain. The urge to smooth it away chased Cassie into the house, Mason right behind her.

"What have you two been up to?"

Startled, Cassie jumped. "Job! You scared me."

The hickory rocker creaked under Job's weight. He stood and strode toward them. "You should go upstairs now. I'll have a word with Mason."

"We were only talking—"

"Guder nacht."

Cassie fled up the stairs, but she stopped at the top. Like a naughty child sent to her room, she felt her ears and cheeks burn. Job's deep voice carried. So did Mason's.

Mason would spend the night in the barn. As long as Cassie worked for the Keims, he would not be able to stay in the house. Any more forays alone into the dark and Job would send her home.

Mason was Job's grandson. He should sleep in the house. She should not, could not, come between them.

Dinah and Job needed her help.

Gott, help me. Help me do the right thing. Even if it hurts. I'm weak. Thy will be done.

Even if that meant she would never be more than a housekeeper.

CHAPTER 29

Jennie's squeal of delight and Kevin's pleased grin were enough to make Mason glad he'd agreed to stay for the church service. He almost changed his mind after a night spent tossing and turning on a bed of hay in the barn. Instead of sleeping, he'd spent far too much time thinking about Cassie and then about his Amish father and then about Perry and then the kids. Round and round until he was dizzy. He couldn't solve any of his dilemmas, but his brain insisted on trying until the sun came up. His back hurt, he had straw in his hair, and he was still tired. The chances of him surviving a three-hour service without falling asleep would fit on the head of a nail.

Cassie's refusal to lay eyes on him during breakfast hadn't helped. She barely said good morning. Even Dinah noticed, and she couldn't see Cassie's gloomy frown. Cassie had brushed off her inquiries, saying she didn't want to be late for worship. As soon as they arrived at the minister's house, she and Dinah had taken the younger kids and veered over to the cluster of women headed into the barn. That left Mason with Kevin.

"We sit on this side." Kevin jerked his head toward the rows of backless wooden benches on the left side of the Bylers' barn. "All the guys sit on one side and the girls on the other."

Mason inhaled the now-familiar scent of hay, manure, and

motor oil. Somehow the combination didn't seem strange. He tried to get the lay of the land. The men all wore black pants, blue shirts, suspenders, and black hats. Dinah had presented Mason with one of Job's clean shirts, but he'd had to make do with the blue jeans he'd worn the previous day, grease stains and all. Did God care what he wore? "Why don't families sit together?"

"I dunno." Kevin scooted into the first empty row behind the older men who'd come in first. Job stood up front where he seemed to be in deep conversation with Bryan and Samuel Zimmerman, the deacon. "I like it better this way. Kathy says Dinah thumps Donny on the head with her finger if he gets too loud." He demonstrated in the air with his thumb and index finger. "I don't want no one thumping me on the head."

Neither did Mason. He rubbed his eyes and stifled a yawn. "So how does this go?"

"They sing two songs, a preacher preaches, there's some praying on our knees, a Bible reading, another sermon, more praying, and more singing." Kevin's grin said he liked knowing something his big brother didn't. "It's all in German or Pennsylvania Dutch. I've been learning the Dutch, but I still don't understand much. Kathy's the one who speaks it like she was born here. It's so boring. It's more boring than watching paint dry. Or watching golf on TV."

How could they be expected to learn anything if they didn't understand the language?

"Hey." Kevin waved at a kid in the next row over. He pointed to Mason. "This is my big brother."

The boy nodded his approval. Kevin was proud of Mason. It felt good. No one had ever been proud of him before.

Kevin turned to Mason. "That's Micah. He's Nadine's

brother. She's a friend of Cassie's. Micah and Bobby got into it the first Sunday we went to a service. Bobby called him a hick from the sticks."

Nice. Vintage Bobby. Where was he now? Still hanging out at skate parks, knowing full well how worried Job and Dinah were? The kid needed a swift kick in the seat of the pants, and Mason was just the person to give it to him.

"Micah's okay. I see him at school. We're friends."

"It's good that you're making friends."

"School is stupid sometimes, but I figure I'd better learn something." Kevin sank onto the bench. Mason joined him. "I've only got until eighth grade."

"If that's what you want. The decision is yours." Mason leaned closer and whispered, "You don't have to be Amish. Are they pressuring you to be?"

How could Kevin even know what it meant if he couldn't understand sermons delivered in Pennsylvania Dutch?

"Nah. Job says the same thing. He says it'll be my choice. He sits next to me during the service and explains what they're saying. The bishop gave him special permission."

Kevin felt special. Job made him feel special. Mason leaned away from his brother. He put his elbows on his knees and clasped his hands, his head down. His behind already ached from sitting on the hard bench, and it had only been five minutes. At least with the doors open, a breeze wafted through the barn. These old buildings didn't have much ventilation. Summer services would be hotter than Hades.

Mason leaned forward. "But you're thinking about becoming Amish?"

"I'm learning to farm. I know how to plant vegetables. I can ride a horse. I can hook up a horse to a buggy and drive it. I'm ten. Job says I can learn to drive a tractor when I turn twelve. Cassie is a good cook too. I like eating three square meals a day." Kevin sounded as surprised at his accomplishments as Mason was at his brother's delight in them. "I don't even miss TV. Or video games. Hanging out with Job is a lot more fun. There's a bunch of rules, but I don't mind. It's weird. I kind of like it when Job and Dinah tell me what to do. I don't have to figure it out myself."

Was this the same kid who lived for video games and waited until the girls went to bed to blow up firecrackers outside their bedroom window? Kevin had delighted in torturing his sisters. He needled Kathy endlessly about being an egghead. He refused to play with Donny. He hid Jennie's Barbies or popped their heads off and left them on her pillow to find when she went to bed.

Who are you and what have you done with Kevin?

"But what about the church thing and believing in God?"

"No biggie." Kevin shrugged. "When I'm sixteen, I get my rumspringa. After that it's up to me to decide if I want to be baptized and join the church. That's years from now. I've got time. That's what Job says."

"What about school?"

"I can read, write, and do arithmetic. What else do I need?" He sounded content with his lot.

"They're about ready to start." Job loomed over them. "Let me sit between you two. That way you can both hear me. It'll be much more beneficial if you know what's being said."

Mason obliged and Job folded his long, skinny body onto the bench. "Bryan wants you to sit with him after church, Mason. He wants to continue the conversation you started back when you first met."

That should be a fun chat. *Not.* Had Job mentioned Mason's walk with Cassie the previous evening? What was the big deal? All they did was talk. Even though the desire to do more was almost unbearable. Maybe it was the full moon. Whatever it was, he needed to stow those feelings before they got both of them in trouble. Dinah needed Cassie. The kids needed Mason. "Sounds like a plan."

The first song started. One long note followed by another even longer note. Mason surveyed the people around him. Many of them held the hymnal, but they all seemed to know the song. Job had a deep bass. He sang off-key, but it didn't seem to bother him. He pointed at the words written in a fancy serif script in the hymnal like Mason could pronounce them. Kevin gave it his best shot, but it didn't sound anything like what anyone else was singing. It went on and on.

Finally, the song ended and the first sermon began. Minister Delbert Byler walked up and down in front of the congregation. He had no notes, no microphone, no sound system, and no podium. He started by apologizing that he wasn't more learned. The people hung on his every word. A blue jay jabbered outside the barn's open doors. The wind whispered in the eaves. Delbert's singsong cadence was reminiscent of the late-night televangelists who promised healing in exchange for a sizable recurring donation to their church.

Job put his arm around Kevin and drew him closer. "He's preaching from Isaiah 43:2," he whispered. "'When thou passest through the waters, I will be with thee; and through the rivers, they shall not overflow thee: when thou walkest through the fire, thou shalt not be burned; neither shall the flame kindle upon thee.'"

So God was with people in the bad times. Why make people

go through bad stuff? Why didn't God stop the floods and the fire to start with?

"Psalm 119:171 says, 'My lips shall utter praise, when thou hast taught me thy statutes,'" Job murmured. "Psalm 34:19 says, 'Many are the afflictions of the righteous: but the Lord delivereth him out of them all.'

"James 1:2–4 says, 'My brethren, count it all joy when ye fall into divers temptations; knowing this, that the trying of your faith worketh patience. But let patience have her perfect work, that ye may be perfect and entire, wanting nothing.'"

Ask and an answer will be given. Or so it seemed. How could it be good for Mason to have gone through so much horrible stuff in his life? How could it be good for Bobby, Kevin, Kathy, Donny, and Jennie? They were only kids.

"When we come out of a season of suffering, our character has been honed. We're stronger. We can help others when it's their turn to suffer." Job's soft whisper had the same singsong cadence. "God is the God of comfort. As He comforts us, we are to comfort others."

That made sense. Mason rubbed his forehead. Trying to follow Job's whispered commentary was giving him a headache. No wonder Kevin wasn't a fan. His brother's head lolled against Job's shoulder. His eyes were closed.

Mason smiled. Job smiled too. Then he elbowed Kevin. The boy's eyes popped open. He straightened and rubbed his eyes. "Sorry."

The boys behind him tittered.

Job swiveled and shot them a glare. Rather like the one Mason had experienced the night before. Quiet prevailed.

Giving meaning to suffering held promise. A spark of hope. Mason could've had a different life if his mother had stayed in

Haven and married his father. But then he would be a different person. He might still be a carpenter, but he would've been brought up to believe in something. Parents should give their children a foundation. If he ever had kids, he would. But first he had to figure out what he believed.

Everyone knelt. A few seconds late, Mason joined them. The minister spoke some words. Everyone stood and began to sing in that slow, methodical way that sounded more like a chant.

A person didn't have to know what the words meant. The joy on their faces and the joyous way they sang told the story. They were a community worshipping a good God. They truly believed.

Mason closed his eyes and let the sound envelop him. Voices of the young and old mingled. No musical instruments were needed.

The words died away. For a few seconds silence reigned. Sweet silence.

A soft murmur swelled. Mason opened his eyes. His bushy eyebrows raised, Job cocked his head. "Are you all right?"

"Yes. It was pretty."

"I've heard our singing called many things, but pretty is not one of them." Job chuckled. "Come, let's go find a seat outside. The women will bring the food. Bryan will find us."

Kevin shot ahead of them. He joined the other children who trotted toward the barn doors. Then they broke into a run once they cleared the doors.

Job's chuckle turned into a belly laugh. "One minute they're falling asleep, the next they're racing out the door, full of energy."

"What's the rush?"

"Volleyball, baseball, a trampoline, games, you name it." Job moved into the flow of adults exiting the barn at a much more sedate pace. "They'll play while the men get fed. After a while they'll start drifting back to the tables to eat."

"Sounds like fun."

"The singles get involved too. The girls help serve first, but they'll play later. So will the boys."

People like Cassie. "I'm not much of an athlete. I played baseball and basketball as a kid, but once I got to high school, I got a job and that was the end of that."

"That's what happens around here, but there's still time for fun now and again."

He led Mason to a card table set up near a volleyball net. "Take a load off. I see Bryan headed this way. I'll be back in a bit."

Job offered no excuse for abandoning Mason. He nodded at Bryan as the two crossed paths. The bishop slid into a folding chair across from Mason and let out an exaggerated sigh. "I love Sundays, don't you? Worship, family, visiting, food. This is the day the Lord has made."

Mason used to like Sundays, too, when he could sleep in, work on his car, and hang out with the kids. Now he couldn't wait to get out of the house and away from the other lone occupant, Perry. "This is nice."

"What did you think of the worship service?"

"I've always wondered why bad things happen to people. If God is everything He says He is, why doesn't He stop tornadoes from hitting churches filled with praying people or little kids from being abused or people from dying of cancer?"

Why didn't He stop the accident that killed my mother? Why didn't He stop Clayton from beating on Bobby?

Mason studied the vinyl tablecloth's checkered pattern.

Talking about this stuff to a stranger felt weird. "I didn't understand everything that was said today, but I got the gist of it. Going through trials is supposed to make us better people."

"That's the crux of what Scripture tells us. Jesus says, 'In this world, there will be trouble. Have no fear. I have overcome the world.'"

"I don't like it much."

"Most people don't."

Mason shifted in his chair. Too much sitting. Too much thinking. His brain hurt as much as his backside did. His throat felt parched. His stomach rumbled. Hoping to cover the sound, he cleared his throat. "I figure it's easier to get through the bad stuff with God than alone."

"That's a good start."

"It would be nice to know God has a handle on stuff like my mom dying and my brother Bobby running away."

"He has a plan and He works everything for our good. You can hold on to that." Bryan's brow furrowed. "No word on Bobby then?"

"The juvenile detective really is trying." Once again Mason shared the information about the Instagram sighting. Would Bryan understand this better than Job and Leroy? He was younger and he had a business. "The police in Wichita have been to a skate park several times where Bobby likes to go. Some of the kids know him, but no one knows where he's living. The detective says it's a matter of time. At least I know he's alive and he's okay. He's skateboarding, for Pete's sake."

While his family worried about him. Mason had gone to that skate park himself—twice—hoping for a miracle. Bobby would be there. He'd ream him up one side and down the other. Bobby would agree to come home. But he hadn't been there and not one of the scraggly bunch of kids had seen him. Or knew where to find him.

"As you say, he's alive. He's skateboarding. Pray that God continues to keep him safe, that He works in Bobby's life, that He brings him home safely. Then you can chew him out for making you worry while he's out playing."

Bryan paused. Cassie approached with plates mounded with food in both hands. Kathy followed her, carrying two cups of coffee. Cassie settled the plates on the table, complete with silverware wrapped in paper napkins. "I wasn't sure what you would like, Mason, so I put some of everything on your plate. Bryan, Esther fixed your plate."

"Danki." Bryan's smile encompassed both Cassie and Kathy, who handed Mason's coffee directly to him. "You two read my mind. I think Mason's hungry. At least his stomach is."

He laughed. Mason laughed with him. Cassie smiled and took Kathy's hand. "If you need anything else, send one of the kids in and we'll fix you up."

Hand in hand, they walked away. Kathy began to skip. Cassie joined in. Mason couldn't contain his smile. Cassie was a special lady. She would be a good mother. A good wife. A good friend.

A soul mate.

"Cassie is a sweet girl."

Bryan's dry tone brought Mason back to earth. "She is. She's good with my brothers and sisters. I appreciate how she's made them feel at home at Job and Dinah's. It could've been a much harder transition. They seem to love living there."

"Which worries you."

Mason took a long sip of water. Taking his time, he un-wrapped the silverware. "It's not worry exactly. It turns out that the transition has been harder for me than for them. I miss them. I miss being a family. I want what's best for them."

The moment of truth had arrived. "I've done a lot of soul searching in the last few weeks. I work with Obie Hostetler and his crew. I see how they are, their strong faith, their good moral values, their commitment to family." His appetite shriveling, Mason stared at the sandwiches, beets, pickles, pretzels, and cookies on his plate. "I've never seen it in action before. I admire it. I'd like to have it. I just don't know how."

"It takes a big man to admit that." Bryan took a big bite of his sandwich and chewed. He motioned toward Mason's plate. "Eat. You'll feel better."

Mason nibbled at the sandwich. Peanut butter, but not like any peanut butter he'd ever tasted. Incredibly sweet and creamy. No wonder the kids clamored for peanut butter sandwiches. "What is this?"

"*Schmeir.*" Bryan grinned. "Like eating dessert first, isn't it? It's peanut butter, corn syrup, and marshmallow fluff."

"It might be the best invention since s'mores." Mason gobbled down half a sandwich and took a sip of black coffee strong enough to take the enamel off his teeth. Fortified with a megadose of sugar topped off with caffeine, he regrouped. "My mother was Amish. My father was probably Amish too. I know that doesn't make me Amish, but I believe I deserve a chance to figure out who I am, the same way Kevin and Kathy and the little ones will."

Bryan choked on his coffee and coughed. He settled his glass on the table. Still coughing, he patted his chest. Finally, he took a long breath. "Sorry, you caught me by surprise. It is very rare for someone to join our faith as an adult and make it work. Your mother may have been Amish once, but she left the faith before you were born. I thought your father was unknown."

Maybe Job hadn't told the bishop about Dinah's suspicions. Knowing the Amish people's aversion to gossip—or maybe it was simply shame—he probably hadn't. How did Mason backtrack now? "Nothing is for sure, but I aim to find out if I can."

"It's not a decision made for love of another person but rather for love of our God."

"I'm aware. It's been a long haul." He struggled for words to describe something even he didn't understand. "I keep thinking it shouldn't be so hard. I understand life is full of struggles. But it must be easier knowing you're not alone. That God is in charge and you don't have to be. My mother was always searching for something. She never found it. Maybe that's because she left it here. In Haven."

Bryan's nose wrinkled. He took a bite of a sugar cookie. After a few seconds of methodically chewing, he swallowed. "I will ask Samuel to meet with you to study the Articles of Faith. He will report back to Delbert and me regarding your progress." He brushed crumbs from his beard. His stern, penetrating stare pinned Mason to his chair. "I heard you plan to rent a house in Haven."

"Yes. As a matter of fact, I've found one." Mason explained which house it was. "I'm hoping to check it out tomorrow and sign the papers before someone else grabs it."

"That's the Fishers' house. They moved into Hutchinson when Marvin's fraa got MS. It has no electricity. Don't wire it."

"Okay."

"You work with Obie and his crew."

"Yes."

"Ask to have his van pick you up to take you to the work site from now on."

"Okay. That works well. My SUV broke down yesterday."

"Maybe you shouldn't get it fixed."

"How will I get around?"

"You're moving into a house in Haven. You'll be able to use Obie's van for work. Job has an extra horse and buggy for short rides. Try living like we do. See how it feels." Bryan rose and picked up his paper plate. "I must go now. My wife's family from Garnett is visiting this afternoon."

Pushing his black Sunday hat back on his forehead, he loomed over Mason. "One more thing. These small steps don't give you leave to pursue a Plain girl. You will find we are very different when it comes to questions of love. Don't overstep."

First Leroy, then Job, now Bryan. These guys stuck together. "I hear you loud and clear."

Bryan's frown melted away. He smiled. "Gut. You could also learn from your sisters and brothers. I hear Kathy's Deutsch is getting good. Have her teach you. It will make worship more interesting."

He walked away. Mason breathed a sigh of relief. His hands were sweaty. His shirt stuck to his back. The two sandwiches, pretzels, pickles, and three sugar cookies with orange cream cheese frosting and sprinkles he had snarfed down in a nervous frenzy threatened to come back up with the coffee.

Gut. It is all gut.

CHAPTER 30

Into the looking glass. Mason sneaked another peek. He moved between a beautiful pine china cabinet and an oak chest of drawers to get a better view of Caleb Mast. His might-be father stood behind the counter in the heart of Mast Furniture and Antique Store talking to a couple interested in buying one of the handmade quilts that hung from the second-story balcony. The woman didn't mind spending a bundle on a quilt, but her husband did—loudly. Caleb didn't seem the least bit perturbed. They were his only customers on this Monday morning in May. Caleb hadn't employed any of the classic moves of a salesman eager to move merchandise. He simply bided his time.

Staring at him was like peering in a mirror from the future. If Mason decided to grow a beard. Same height and build as Mason. Black hair, only Caleb's had silver highlights in it. Same blue eyes. Same nose. People said Mason was the spitting image of his mother. They'd never seen his father. Caleb Mast and Georgia Keim could've been brother and sister.

Mason needed to do this, and quickly. Obie had extended his lunch hour and even offered to call the van driver to take him to the store. It was too far to walk, so Mason had no choice but to accept. The driver had gone to lunch and would be back in an hour.

"Can I help you with something?"

Mason jumped and turned. A young man in a blue shirt, black pants, and suspenders stood on the other side of the chest of drawers. He pushed his straw hat back and smiled. "Do you see anything you like?"

"I really like this chest of drawers. The workmanship is excellent." Both statements were true, but Mason couldn't in his wildest dreams afford to buy this furniture. Most of his family's furniture came from big-box discount stores. Someday he'd construct his own. "Whose handiwork is it?"

"My dad's, my uncles', mine, and my brothers'. We all work on pieces."

On second thought the man was likely a teenager. Maybe seventeen or eighteen. He also was Caleb's mini-me. Same black hair and blue eyes, but not as tall and thicker through the chest. He was trying not to show his pride in the work, but it peeked through. Mason realized he was staring. "So you're one of the Masts who own this store?"

"Yes. I'm Joel Mast. My father is Caleb." He motioned toward the counter. "If you decide you'd like to buy it, let one of us know. We can help you load it in your vehicle, or we offer delivery for a fee if you're in the Reno County area."

"Good to know."

Joel cocked his head and frowned. "Have we met before?"

No, but you could be my half brother. Mason shook his head. "I don't think so." He held out his hand. "I'm Mason Keim."

"Nice to meet you." Joel's forehead wrinkled. He offered a tentative smile. "Are you related to Job and Dinah?"

No way to extricate himself from the conversation now. Mason summoned his own smile. "They're my grandparents."

Let Joel chew on why Mason was not Amish and had his

grandparents' last name. *Because my mother never married your father and none of her husbands bothered to adopt me.*

Joel's shrug was almost imperceptible. "Okay, well, if we can help you with anything, let me know. My dad has been known to offer discounts to local families."

As a Keim, Mason might qualify. "Thanks."

Joel ambled to the counter. The man had won the argument. The couple marched away, the disappointed woman jawing at her husband as they went. Their heads bent together, Caleb and his son spoke quietly. They were so alike, father and son, so in sync.

Mason took a step back, then another. Thrusting himself into Caleb Mast's world could set off an avalanche of hurtful consequences. How much had Caleb told his wife about his past when they married?

Maybe Mason was being selfish. Maybe he should leave well enough alone. Why torpedo a family over a mistake Caleb Mast had made more than twenty years ago? Mason trudged to the door.

"Hey. Wait. Please."

Hand on the lever, Mason stopped. He swiveled. Caleb came straight at him. "My son says you're Job and Dinah's grandson."

"That's right."

"I heard they had grandchildren staying with them." A deep blush burned its way up Caleb's neck and across his face. He slowed and stopped a few steps from Mason. "I thought they were all younger. I didn't realize one was . . . an adult."

Mason's heart hammered against his rib cage. He sucked in air and tried to breathe. He'd dreamed of this moment since he was old enough to understand that other kids had both moms and dads.

Yeah, my dad's an Army Ranger. He's fighting in Iraq. My dad's a surgeon. He saves lives. My parents are divorced. My dad lives in California. He makes movies. My dad is a cop in Houston. My dad's a smoke jumper in Montana.

Mason had made up all sorts of stories. His dad never came to his baseball games. He never played one-on-one basketball with Mason. He never taught him to drive or explained how the whole boy-meets-girl thing worked.

Never had Mason imagined his father to be an Amish man who worked with his hands in a little town in Kansas. "I'm Georgia Keim's son. I think you might have known her."

Recognition flashed in Caleb's eyes. Emotions ran pell-mell across his face. He cleared his throat and spoke to his son in Deutsch.

His son waved in response.

Caleb turned back to Mason. "Could we talk outside for a minute?"

"Sure. I'm on my lunch break. I don't have much time, but sure."

Mason pushed through to the long, narrow porch that ran the length of the storefront. Bright sunshine blinded him momentarily. He blinked and shaded his eyes with his hand. His nerves jangled like he'd touched a live wire. His breaths came in short spurts. Despite the breeze, sweat dampened his armpits. *Breathe . . . breathe.*

Wooden benches with sale price tags on them lined the porch. He took the one at the far end. Caleb leaned against the railing so he faced Mason. He didn't say anything. His jaw worked and his eyes reddened. "You've got her smile."

Easy. Easy. Breathe. "You knew my mother?"

"I did." Caleb's Adam's apple bobbed. "A long time ago."

"Twenty-three years ago, more or less."

"More or less."

He wasn't going to make it easy. Mason stared at the parking lot. His heart thumped so hard it felt as if it would jump out of his chest and do a kamikaze dive into the flower boxes crowded with pansies, petunias, and marigolds.

Breathe. Breathe. Just breathe.

He sucked in the flowers' sweet scent and exhaled. "How well did you know her?"

"Is it true she's dead?"

"Yes."

Caleb straightened. He crossed his arms over his chest. The lines around his mouth tightened and turned white. Nodding, he cleared his throat again and blew out air. "I always thought I'd see her again."

His lips thinned as if he held back a sob. Or a scream.

"Which brings me back to my question. How well did you know her?"

"I've been married for twenty years to a good woman. We have children. Six of them."

"I'm not here to cause you trouble." Mason clutched his hands together. Sweat dampened his palms. His chest hurt. He leaned forward. "She never wanted to talk about her past. She would never tell me who my father was. I need to know."

"I reckon that would be me."

Finally. Raw emotions roiled inside Mason. Relief. Pain at so much missed and denied. Bewilderment. Hurt. An aching for more. Such a mess of stuff a person couldn't begin to know how to say it. "Did you know . . . about me?"

Caleb's hands went to his face. He wiped at his eyes. He

straightened and moved to sit next to Mason. "I knew. She told me and then, in the next breath, she said she didn't want to marry me. She said she cared for me, but she couldn't abide this life. Georgia could always be counted on to speak her mind. I thought I liked that about her."

"So you said okay, whatever?"

"When your mother made up her mind, there was no stopping her. You had twenty-two years with her. I reckon you know that."

Mason did. "Did she tell you she was leaving?"

"Not in so many words. I figured I'd keep trying to convince her. If she didn't marry me, she would be shamed. There would be a kneeling confession and a period of meidung. I went to the restaurant where she worked. They told me she didn't show up for work, quit without notice. One of the other waitresses took me aside and told me Georgia and Perry were gone. No one knew where."

"And that was it."

"That was it. You know more about what happened to Georgia after that than I do."

"Your life just went on without her."

"It took me two years to move on. Every night I prayed Georgia would return. It wasn't God's will. I met my wife. I learned to be happy again." Caleb heaved a sigh. "Did your mother have a happy life?"

How did Mason even begin to answer that question? He watched the cars zoom by on Switzer Road. Images of his mother kneeling in the dirt, planting roses and tulips, spun like a home movie in his head. Or playing in the sprinkler with the kids, her red hair plastered to her head, her blue eyes dancing with laughter. Her delight when they surprised her with a cake Mason made from a box mix for her birthday. Those memories came first.

Then the others. The hurled insults, the slamming doors, the near fistfights, with one husband or another. Mason had stopped keeping track of who did what or said what. He couldn't even be sure how the arguments started. All he could do was keep the kids out of harm's way. He tried telling them stories, playing music, and singing songs. Anything to drown out the insanity.

As Bobby got older, he simply left the house and roamed the streets. Kevin shoved earphones on his head and played war video games. Kathy took over the role of keeping Donny and Jennie occupied with pretend games. Once Mason found them stuffed in the closet, pretending to hide from a fierce dragon that could burn them alive with his breath.

Or a man who could pummel them black and blue with his fists.

"Mason?"

"She married three times and had six kids. She was always searching for something, but she couldn't find it. She never found it."

Because she'd left it behind in Haven?

Caleb's somber nod held understanding and sadness. "It must've been a hard way to live. To grow up."

"I was in school before I realized how messed up things were. I always knew her husband wasn't my dad. It always came up when they argued. Besides, I didn't have their last name. Then he left and the next one came along. She would be happy for a while. Over the moon. Giddy. Then it would be like a popped balloon. All the air would whoosh out and it would fizzle."

"How did she die?"

Mason told the story yet again. He explained about the will and the Keims.

Caleb clasped his hands in his lap, but his whole body seemed poised to leap up and somehow save the day. No one could save the day. "What now?"

"I'll be around. I'm working for Obie Hostetler. I'm planning to rent the Fisher house on East Trail Road. We might run into each other. But I'm not here to cause you any trouble. I just needed to know."

"It's a hard row to hoe—"

The store door opened. Joel stuck his head out. He said something in Pennsylvania Dutch. Caleb replied. Joel withdrew.

"I have to go in." Caleb stood. He faced Mason. "There's a phone call from a store in Kansas City that sells some of our furniture."

"I understand. Thanks for talking to me." Mason rose as well. "I won't bother you again."

"It's no bother." Caleb took a step closer. He held out his hand. Mason shook it. His father's hand was hard and calloused, his grip firm. "My wife knows. I couldn't marry her without telling her of my past. My sins are forgiven. I have a clear conscience. It's the children who don't know."

Being categorized as a sin that had to be forgiven rankled. Mason let his hand drop. "Don't worry about it. I'll make myself scarce."

"That's not what I'm saying." Caleb rubbed his whiskered cheeks with both hands. "I only ask for time so my wife and I can talk. She has a say in what we tell the children and when. I want to do right by everyone. It's not easy opening up an old wound."

"I'm not a sin. I'm not an old wound." Mason swallowed

back anger and frustration. Caleb offered far more than he'd expected. Yet he still disappointed somehow. "I'm your son."

"You are your mother's son. You have her backbone." Caleb smiled for the first time. "Just know that I'm so glad to meet you. I've always wondered about you. If you were anything like me and who you became. I'm glad to know you, Son."

The throb of the wound where Mason's heart should've been ceased to ache. He was the son of an honest, hardworking Plain man. For now it was enough. "I'm glad to know you too."

He couldn't say it. Not yet. Maybe one day he would call Caleb dad. But not today.

Caleb strode to the door. He grabbed the knob and paused. "Talk to you soon." He went in and the door closed behind him.

It sounded like a promise. So many promises broken in the past made it hard to hope. *God? Bryan says Your promise is one I can count on. I need to count on somebody. Can I count on You?*

Time to go see the house. Then go back to work with his Amish crew. He had an Amish father. Amish grandparents. Amish coworkers. He would soon live in an Amish community. How much more would it take to make him Amish?

CHAPTER 31

Cassie stuck the first aid kit on the shelf over the kitchen counter. A few feet from where Dinah stood. Just in case. They didn't need a repeat of the cocoa scalding scene. By the same token, this was still Dinah's kitchen and it was good that she wanted to bake. Lately, she'd been lethargic. She napped in the afternoons, something she'd never dreamed of doing before. Job chalked it up to the demands of four grandchildren, but Cassie wasn't so sure. She'd lost weight and her appetite was off. Making a cake would deplete what little energy she had. "Why not let me make the carrot cake?"

"It's my recipe. I have it in my head." Dinah groped for the mixing bowl sitting on the counter. She insisted she could make cake with Jennie's help. "Go work on the pants you're making for Donny. Even I can see the ones you made last month are already too short, and I'm blind. The bu is growing like a weed."

"I can help Mammi." Jennie climbed onto the chair she'd pushed to the kitchen counter. She grabbed a plastic measuring spoon and held it out. "See? Carrot cake is Bobby's favorite. If we make carrot cake, he'll come back."

The sweet optimism of a child. If only it were that easy. Bobby had been gone three months. Spring had given way to summer. The kids were out of school. They loved life on the farm—fishing, swimming, riding horses. Jennie followed Dinah around the house, chattering nonstop. She soaked up Dinah's attention like a water-starved flower suddenly blooming after a spring rain.

Tomorrow they would spend the night at Mason's new house—their first sleepover away from Job and Dinah's since arriving in February. It would be far too quiet around the Keim house for that one day and night. Mason would bring them back in time to attend church on Sunday morning. It had seemed like a good idea at the time.

"Which measuring spoon is this?" Dinah held it up for Cassie to see. "I need the half teaspoon."

"That's the teaspoon." Cassie picked up the correct one and handed it to Jennie. "Give this to your mammi. Then you can get the baking soda and sugar from the shelf by the stove."

Singing a made-up song about kittens and baby horses, Jennie did as she was told.

"You know I've been cooking, baking, and canning for more than forty years. I made three meals a day seven days a week. You name it, I've cooked it." Dinah's words came faster and faster. "Not once have I started a fire. I don't need a babysitter."

"I know that. So does Job. He just worries about you—"

Pounding at the back door drowned out Cassie's words. Tater raised his head from his resting spot by the potbelly stove and barked.

"Hush, Tater, I'll get it."

A tall, lean, older version of Mason stood at the door. Or a younger version of Job. "You must be Cassie."

"I am. Who are you?"

Before he could respond, Jennie shoved past Cassie shrieking in delight. "Hi, Uncle Perry. What are you doing here? Are Job and Dinah your grandparents too?"

Perry.

"Perry?" The two syllables held incredulity mingled with

the same delight that had colored Jennie's greeting. Dinah clapped. "Is that you?"

Tater barked again, this time louder. He uncurled his thick body and trotted to Cassie's side, still barking.

"It's okay, Tater, it's Perry. He's family." Cassie grabbed Tater's collar and held on. He had passed judgment on Perry very quickly. Tater liked most people on sight, but not this man. "Hush. Sit. Sit!"

Tater obeyed, but a low growl hummed in his throat. Nor did he seem convinced that this was a good course of action. Cassie moved aside to allow Perry to enter, but he stood motionless. Cassie patted Tater's head. "He's harmless, really he is. Come on in."

His hands up, Perry eyed the dog and stayed on the welcome mat.

Dinah clutched a dish towel to her chest. She took a tottering step forward and stopped, but she didn't faint this time. "I knew you'd come home. Praise Gott, you came home."

"In the flesh." He had Job's deep voice. "It's good to see you, Mudder. Can I come in?"

Tears trickled down Dinah's cheeks. "Of course. Come in, come in. Let him in, Cassie."

Cassie tightened her hold on Tater's collar. "As I said before, please do come in."

This time Perry moved. He left the scent of spicy aftershave and hair spray in his wake. Cassie stifled the urge to sneeze. "I can't believe you're here. Mason said—"

"Never mind what someone said. I'm here, in the flesh." Perry took the towel from Dinah's hands and tossed it on the counter. He drew her close. "Let me eyeball you. I can't believe it either. You're still a pretty spring chicken."

"You shouldn't lie. It's a sin."

His arms closed around Dinah. She leaned against her son's chest and closed her eyes. Despite Perry's words, she appeared as ancient as the prairie lands of Kansas.

"I want a hug." Jennie tugged at her uncle's sleeve. "My turn."

Dinah let go. Perry took Jennie's outstretched hand and let her drag him to the worktable Job had built to replace the supper table. "We're making carrot cake. Bobby likes carrot cake. Do you?" She climbed onto the bench and pointed at it. "You can sit next to me. Would you rather have vanilla or strawberry ice cream? I like chocolate, but Mammi says it doesn't go with carrot cake."

Perry slid his hand down the girl's silky brown hair. "I like coffee-flavored ice cream. Besides, all ice cream goes with cake. Where's Dad?"

"Yuck." Jennie made a sour face. "I don't like coffee. It tastes nasty."

"Just wait until you get up at the crack of dawn after dealing with a colicky baby all night." Perry chuckled. "So. Someone say something. Is Dad here?"

"I'll make kaffi." Cassie nudged Tater toward the rug in front of the stove. He whined but took the hint. "Behave yourself, hund."

Her face wet with tears, Dinah settled on the bench across from Perry. "Job went to town to fetch something he needed from the hardware store. He took the other kinner with him."

"I'm back."

Cassie had been so busy staring at Perry and trying to absorb his unexpected appearance, she hadn't heard Job come in the door. The children spilled in after him. There were only three of them, but they could make an entrance.

"Uncle Perry, Uncle Perry, where have you been?" Donny

threw himself at his uncle. "We thought we would never see you again. Mason said you were gone forever."

"Mason is a drama king." Perry handed out hugs left and right. He high-fived and fist-bumped and elbow-bumped like a champ. "I had to take care of some business at home, but now I'm ready for a good visit."

Funny how he failed to mention he'd been living at Mason's house for months. And refusing to visit them or Dinah and Job all that time. Should she mention that? No, it would only hurt Dinah and Job, not Perry.

"Kinner, go pack up your stuff for your trip to your brother's."

"We have all evening. We don't leave until in the morning." With that tart observation, Kathy squeezed onto the bench next to Dinah. "I want to know where you went, Uncle Perry, after Mom's funeral."

"Yeah, and why didn't you come check on us?" Kevin didn't bother to remove his backpack. He went on attack. "You just left and never came back."

"I want a snack." Donny seemed oblivious to the tension in the room. "My stomach is all rumbly."

"Go pack. We'll talk about all that later." Job pointed to the door. "Now."

His no-nonsense tone communicated itself to the kids. They dashed from the room, pushing and shoving to be first out.

"Mammi already packed my bag." Jennie climbed into Dinah's lap. She grabbed a fat crayon and went to work on a picture she'd been drawing on a brown paper bag. "Mammi loves me best."

Job's wince made Cassie smile. Jennie had both of her grandparents wrapped around her little finger. It happened even in Plain families.

"I'll get the kaffi." She turned off the flame under the aluminum pot and set out the cups. She had chocolate chip cookies left over from church on Sunday and some of the sugar-free lemon sandwich cookies that Dinah loved. "Don't mind me. I'll start supper."

"Where have you been, Suh?" Job posed the question in Deutsch. "All these years and not a single word from you. We didn't know if you were dead or alive until these kinner showed up at our doorstep."

"Let's go with English for now, why don't we?" Perry sounded as cool as watermelon on ice on an early July day. How could he after twenty-three years of being gone? Just gone. Gone, gone, gone.

"Where have you been?"

"Here and there." If Perry's blithe assumption that all was well irritated Job and Dinah as much as it did Cassie, things would not go well for him. "I know I should've come back sooner, but I couldn't. I had family responsibilities—"

"We're your family." Job's voice thundered. It bounced off the walls and the floor and the ceiling.

Jennie peered up from her picture of a horse. Her eyes widened and her sweet rosebud lips formed an O. "Daadi, you're supposed to use your inside voice. That's what Mammi told the boys."

"I'm sorry, little one. Maybe you should go play with your dolls in the living room while your mammi and I talk to Perry."

Jennie's nose wrinkled. "It's been forever since I've seen Uncle Perry—"

"Jennie, do what your daadi says." Dinah lifted her from the bench and set her on her bare feet. "That's what good little maedels do. You can see your *onkel* later."

"Okay." A pout forming on her chubby face, she trotted from the room. "But I want carrot cake. And ice cream. And Uncle Perry sits next to me. Not Donny."

"We'll see about the ice cream," Dinah called after her. "Be sure to pick up after yourself."

"Things have definitely changed if you're serving up cake on demand for a four-year-old." Perry cocked one index finger at Dinah. "Mason tells me you've had health problems. I'm sorry to hear that. It must be rough."

"Why didn't you come find us when Georgia died?" Job moved to stand next to Dinah. His pain and bewilderment hurt Cassie's heart. She took a swallow of lemonade to force down her own tears. Job put his hand on Dinah's shoulder. "We had a right to know. We had a right to be at the funeral."

"I didn't think Georgia would want it." Finally, a single speck of repentance showed itself in the way Perry studied his hands. "I had no idea she had decided to leave the kids with you. We never talked about it. We never talked about you. I'm not being mean. It's just that once we made it to Wichita, we found work, settled into a dumpy apartment, and put all our energy into scraping by in the real world."

"Gott bless whoever helped you." Dinah sopped her face with a handkerchief. "Someone had to have given you money to make a start."

"Nobody gave us anything. Georgia had saved up her money from working at the restaurant. I saved my money from the hardware store. Things were tough for a long time, but we had each other, and we were determined to make it."

"Things were so horrible here?" Dinah tucked her arms around her middle and rocked. Couldn't Perry see what he was doing to her? "We were so horrible?"

Cassie carried the coffee and cookies to the table. She laid three of them on a napkin for Perry. Maybe that would sweeten him up. Dinah didn't deserve to hurt like this. Cassie nudged the sugar bowl toward him. "Do you need milk?"

Perry shook his head. His insincere, happy-go-lucky facade fell away. He leaned over the table toward Dinah. "Not horrible. I probably would've made the best of it if Georgia hadn't decided to leave. I'm not saying it was her fault I left. She had the guts to do it, even knowing what she knew. Which gave me the guts."

Knowing what she knew.

Cassie added an extra cookie to Job's napkin. His face turned a deep shade of magenta. Almost purple. *Ach, Gott, help him guard his words. Don't let him say something he'll regret.*

Dinah jumped in before he could explode. "I can't imagine how she did it. She raised a bopli . . . Mason . . . on her own."

Job jumped up and paced between the stove and the door. He opened his mouth. Closed it.

Perry didn't seem to notice. Or he didn't care. "You'd be surprised at the services available to poor single moms. She took a job waitressing and the owner, a really okay lady, turned her on to social services, free diapers, formula, free health clinic, food stamps." Pride shone on Perry's face, as if he'd had something to do with it. "She wasn't proud. She was determined. She did whatever she had to do to get what she needed for that baby. I helped. I babysat whenever I could. Whenever she needed it."

Everything a baby needed except a father.

"What do you do to make money?"

"The only thing a guy with an eighth-grade education could do. I got a job working the night shift on the loading docks of a big discount store. You make more when you work nights, but it's still peanuts." He rubbed his bicep and frowned. "It was backbreaking work, but I was better at it than most of those English guys. I was used to hard work. Even so, it encouraged me to get my GED. During the day I took classes at the community college until I had enough credits for an associate degree in information services. You probably don't even know what that is."

He was right about that. Cassie took a whole chicken from the refrigerator. She plopped it on a cutting board and picked up her sharpest knife. Cutting up a chicken would be good therapy in the midst of this painful walk down memory lane.

"It doesn't matter. You went on with your life right down the road from us." Job crowded Cassie at the counter. He poured himself a glass of water and drank deeply. He should've eaten the cookies. He, too, needed sweetening. Anger hummed in his every move. "You said yourself you never talked about us. You never came back. You didn't care about how we were doing."

"We moved on. I can't say I'm sorry I did. I am sorry we made you worry. I'm sorry we made you sad."

The sound of a muffled sob made both Job and Cassie swivel. Dinah was crying into her hankie. Perry had moved to sit beside her. He put his arm around her.

Cassie whacked off both of the chicken's wings. *Whap. Whap.* Perry had made Dinah cry. What was wrong with him? If Job didn't straighten him out, Cassie would.

"Thank you for saying that. Even if you don't mean it. Is that why you came here today? To say you're sorry? Apology accepted. You can go about your business with a clear conscience." Job stomped back and forth between the counter and the table. "I forgive you. I forgive Georgia too. It's the right thing to do. That doesn't mean I want to sit around and act like this is a happy reunion."

"You sure have a funny way of showing forgiveness. Is this

your version of 'I forgive but I don't forget'?" A muscle twitched in Perry's jaw. His hard eyes glinted. "I don't think that's how the Scripture goes."

Whack, whack. Cassie removed the drumsticks and thighs. *Come on, Job, give him your two cents' worth.*

"Are you saying you haven't forgotten what the Holy Bible says? Do you remember it says, 'Children, obey your parents in the Lord: for this is right. Honour thy father and mother; which is the first commandment with promise; that it may be well with thee, and thou mayest live long on the earth.'"

Cassie sliced down the middle of the chicken, separating the breast meat from the back.

"Ephesians 6:1–3. I believe it also says parents shouldn't provoke their children." Perry's sardonic smile had a gotcha quality that he surely knew would aggravate his father. "'And, ye fathers, provoke not your children to wrath: but bring them up in the nurture and admonition of the Lord.' Ephesians 6:4."

"So you have kept up on your Scripture. That's gut."

"It's not a matter of keeping up with anything. It was hammered into our heads."

"Are you sitting here now because you're ready to come home?" A wisp of hope wrapped itself around Job's words. Cassie heard it and felt it. Dinah and Perry surely did too. He moved toward the door. "I'll go with you to talk to the bishop. He'll counsel you. You can work toward baptism."

"I don't know what I want. I'm sure Mason told you I'm at loose ends right now." Perry pulled away from Dinah's touch. "I need time to figure it out."

"Let us know when you do." Job let the door slam shut behind him.

No one spoke for several seconds.

"He's hurt. He's nurtured that hurt for more than twenty years. He's fed it and warmed it by the fire." Dinah was the one person who could truly know how Job felt. She felt it herself. "He doesn't know how to let it go and let something better, something sweet and lovely, replace it. He wants to. I know he does. I want to. If only you'd come sooner, before Georgia died. Even so, we can move forward. We can heal." Dinah offered a healing balm there for the taking.

"Georgia died to you and Father the day she left home." Perry's shoulders slumped. All his earlier jocularity had disappeared. He squeezed Dinah's hand. "I should go."

"Stay for supper." Butcher knife in one hand, a chicken breast in the other, Cassie stepped into his path. This longed-for reunion couldn't end this way. The past could be overcome and forgotten. *Please, Gott, heal their hurting hearts.* "You haven't talked with the kids yet. They have questions."

"They won't understand the answers. I threw them under the bus, plain and simple."

Why would a man let his family, his flesh and blood, be separated from him? "You can explain your reasons to them. Children forgive more easily than adults."

"Tell them my girlfriend said it was them or her? I don't think they'll be overcome with affection for me when I tell them I chose her over them."

Dinah grabbed her walking stick. She banged it on the floor. "What happened to you out there, Perry? How could you be so cold to your family?"

"You have no idea what it's like out in the world. You have to take care of yourself first."

"Then stay here. Stay. Work things out with your daed. With the kinner."

"I don't know." Still, he sat. "The truth is, I came here because I have nowhere else to go. My girlfriend threw me out. IT is so boring it sucks you dry. I'm living on my savings. Mason is moving to Haven. He says I can stay at the new house, but I know he's just being nice, because despite everything he's been through, he's a nice kid."

Cassie breathed again. Perry didn't want to leave. He felt obligated to act like he should leave. "If Mason said you could stay with him, you can. He wouldn't say otherwise."

"Now that he's into being Amish, he has no choice. He has to act forgiving."

"It's not an act." *Please, Gott, don't let it be an act.* Mason's determination to join the Amish faith was unwavering. If he truly believed, he would have a new life. Someday that life might include Cassie. "And even if he didn't intend to join our faith, he would still forgive you. He's that kind of man."

"You know him so well." Perry shot her a half smile. "He speaks highly of you, too, just so you know. He's smitten."

"He's not. He's being nice."

"Still, he's moving and it's obvious he doesn't want me to come with him. So here I am."

"Here you are. You're wanted." Dinah reached for his hand. "Everyone deserves a second chance. You. Job. Me. Your daed and I had a hand in your leaving. Give us a chance to make amends."

"It's gut to know you can see that." Perry spoke in Deutsch. He grabbed Dinah's hand and hung on. "I'm sorry I didn't come to tell you when Georgia died. I'm so sorry."

Finally, the shell broke and the true Perry emerged. The prodigal son had returned.

CHAPTER 32

The silence boomed. Not even the hum of an AC unit or the *tick-tock* of a clock punctured the quiet. Mason wiggled in his chair at the breakfast table—a table he made himself from pine he bought and stained. The kitchen window was wide open to allow nature's sounds to enter. Nothing. Not even a fly or a bee buzzed. Where were the chatty birds when a guy needed them? A breathless humid July morning offered not even a warm breeze to rustle the cottonwood and sycamore trees' leaves. No cicadas. No bullfrogs. They'd all deserted him.

He shredded a piece of burnt toast, tossing the pieces onto the remains of a cold, congealed egg. He added another tablespoon of sugar to his coffee and took a tentative sip. Sweet and thick enough to pass for syrup. The bacon was overdone, the eggs hard, the toast burnt. Still, the food was edible and getting better. Obie's wife had given him her recipe for pancakes. He had all the ingredients. He just had to get up early enough to make them before the kids had to be back at Job and Dinah's for church tomorrow.

They would arrive for a sleepover soon. If Job came through. Dinah wasn't partial to the idea of the kids spending the night. Not that she didn't trust Mason, according to Cassie. More that she was afraid they would visit and want to stay.

That didn't seem likely. He didn't even have bedding yet. They would be using sleeping bags.

Maybe he should get a dog. Two dogs to keep each other company when he was at work. And a cat. A bunch of cats that could live in the barn. The kids would like that.

The icing on the cake would be a horse. The kids would be over the moon.

For now he had the use of Job's old backup buggy and one of his Morgans. He could always go out to the barn and talk to his trusty steed Barnabas.

Someday soon Mason would need to buy his own horse and buggy.

All in good time. That's what Bryan and Delbert would say. They took turns schooling him in the basic tenets of their faith. Obedience. Humility. The twin pillars. The latter was easy for him. The former a little more difficult. He'd been in charge of himself for most of his life. Giving up control to an unseen God tested his commitment every day.

One day at a time like an addict. Only Mason was addicted to control.

He groaned, glad no one was there to hear him.

Might as well wash dishes. Cooking from scratch meant so much more time preparing meals and cleaning up. No wonder Mom preferred toaster waffles.

It didn't matter. He would get the hang of it, God willing.

God seemed very willing so far. Mason had this house and a good job. He liked his coworkers.

He liked everything except living alone in this house. Knowing Cassie was only ten miles away. Knowing his father lived only fifteen miles in the other direction.

Cassie had to keep her distance. So did he. Otherwise he'd

undo everything he'd done so far. He had one chance to get this right. Allowing his feelings for a woman to get in the way would destroy his future.

It stank.

His father, on the other hand, was family. Why didn't he reach out? He had to know where his newly discovered son lived. Maybe his wife rejected the idea of introducing a long-lost son to their other children. Maybe Caleb couldn't see how Mason would fit into his family.

Maybe it was too complicated.

"Get over it." He took his dishes to the sink and added them to the tub of soapy water that already held the skillet. "Be content."

Bryan's commands. *"Be content. Rely on Gott. Humble yourself. Give up control. Do not conform to this world. Bend to Gott's will. Wait on His plan."*

Be content.

Mason let his plate slide into the water. Tiny, iridescent soap bubbles floated around him. One popped on his cheek. That would've tickled Jennie. Little kids found joy in small, simple things adults took for granted. He closed his eyes, inhaled, and let the air out. The clean scent of Palmolive calmed him. A mourning dove cooed. *There you are.* Another answered. *Chatter away, guys, please.*

A horse neighed.

A horse?

A sharp rap on the door broke the spell. Startled, Mason opened his eyes.

Noise. Woo-hoo. Another human being. The kids. They were early. No complaints here. He wiped his hands on his pants and strode through the house to the front door.

Caleb Mast stood on the porch.

Simple words evaded Mason. He opened his mouth, then closed it.

Caleb cleared his throat. He shuffled his boots and stuck his hands on his hips. "Hey."

"Hey."

"Can I come in?"

Two weeks in the new house and boxes, packing paper, and junk still littered the living room. A full day's work left Mason too tuckered out to do much unpacking in the evenings. "It's a mess."

"I won't judge." Caleb smiled and shrugged. "That's expected when a person moves."

Mason stepped aside. Caleb wiped his boots on the welcome mat and came in. His curiosity apparent, he surveyed the room. "Gas lamps and lanterns. No electricity then."

"I'm keeping things simple." It was too soon to share his efforts to embrace his Amish heritage. "It's cheaper, that's for sure."

Mason grabbed boxes from the sofa and set them on the floor. "Where are my manners? Have a seat. Have a seat."

Caleb sat on the edge of the sofa. Mason took the over-stuffed chair that had once been Clayton's preferred real estate. Neither spoke for several seconds.

"It's a nice house," Caleb said finally. "Good piece of land too."

"I like being able to walk down to the creek and fish." He would like it as soon as he bought poles and lures. Or night crawlers. The kids would love it too. Especially Donny. "I'd like to have horses, eventually."

And a buggy. If he made it that far.

"I'm sorry I didn't come by sooner."

"You weren't obligated to come by at all."

"A man who's any kind of man is obligated to be a father." Caleb's somber gaze didn't waver. "I didn't get that chance with you before. I want to take it now. If you do, that is."

He did. In the worst way. "What does your wife say about that?"

"She sees it as God's will. She'll not stand in His way." Caleb gripped his hands together, his elbows on his knees. "She is a good woman. A good wife."

"What did you tell your children?"

"The truth." He ducked his head and shook it. "It wasn't easy. The older ones understand the nature of my sin. The younger ones think having another big brother is a good thing. They want to know when you're coming to live with us." His chuckle didn't hide his embarrassment.

Mason forced a smile. How different his life would've been had his mother made better choices. It did no good to walk that road. Or to heap his bitterness on a woman who'd wanted a life free of constraints.

"Instead of coming to live with us, I thought maybe you could come by for supper one night . . ." Pain flittered across Caleb's face. He pointed at a framed photo lying on top of a box of knickknacks and books. "Is that her? Is that Georgia?"

Mason tugged the dusty photo in a cheap fake wood frame from the box. His mother smiled at him from the front porch swing. Luckily she hadn't noticed when Clayton snapped the photo. She hated having her photo taken. Mason now understood why. He could smell the kids' suntan lotion and sweat on that August day. Was it two or three years ago? The memory of Donny's high-pitched whoops as he dashed through the sprinkler and Jennie's giggles as she slid belly-first on the Slip

'N Slide returned. There *had* been good times. "Yes, that's her a few years ago."

He handed the frame to Caleb. He took it as if it were a fragile artifact and studied her image for several seconds. His fingers smoothed the edges. "She didn't age, did she?"

Hair color from a box helped, but the man was right. "She kept moving for the most part. I think she'd say that was her secret."

"It took me a long time to understand why she went." Caleb continued to study the photo. He murmured, as if he were talking to himself. "I thought a better man would've been able to make her stay. With time I realized no one could've held her back. It would've been like capturing a butterfly in a jar. She would've fluttered to the ground and wasted away."

"Maybe." Or maybe they would've loved fiercely and forever. "I keep wondering what it would've been like if she'd stayed and married you and made a family."

"Seems like God had another plan." Caleb's head came up. "I love my fraa. We have made a family. I'm content."

High-pitched laughter and a sound like a herd of cattle on the porch brought Mason to his feet. And it allowed him to swallow his first response. "It sounds like the family my mother made is here."

Kathy threw open the door, and the mess of kids—only four of them, but it sounded like thirty or forty—tumbled into the living room carrying backpacks. "We're here, we're here. Daadi brought us. Cassie sent supper. Can we go down to the creek—?"

"Whoa, whoa!" Mason swooped Jennie into his arms and settled her on his hip. He tucked his arm around Donny and grinned at Kathy and Kevin. "Easy, one at a time. Welcome to our new house."

A large foil-covered skillet in his hands, Job filled the doorway. He cast a long shadow on the living room floor. "Caleb? I didn't expect to see you here." His gray eyebrows rose and fell. "It's been a while. Delivering furniture?"

"Nee."

If Caleb wasn't going to fill in the blanks, neither would Mason. He introduced the kids. They were all smiles and hellos. Not a shy one in the bunch. "These are my brothers and sisters."

Georgia's kids.

His expression solemn, Caleb accepted Donny's proffer of a handshake. What Donny did, Jennie had to do as well. Caleb shook her tiny, plump hand. The little girl pumped hard. "Hi."

Tears trickled down his tanned, sun-damaged face. "I should get out of your way."

"Why are you crying?" Jennie's face scrunched up with concern. Her lower lip protruded. "You can stay for supper if you want. It's okay."

"Some other time." Caleb smiled through his tears. "I'd like that, though."

Mason settled Jennie on the couch. "I'll be right back, Sissy."

He followed Caleb out to the front porch. His father churned down the steps. At his buggy he turned back. "I can see a little of her in each of them. Not as much as I see in you, but she's there."

"I see it too."

"Come for supper Monday night. Elizabeth would like to meet you."

"If you're sure. And she's sure."

"We're both sure." Caleb drove away in a cloud of dust.

Mason heaved a long breath. *God, one thing at a time, please. That's all I can handle. If that.* He shoved open the screen door and found Job still standing in the foyer, the skillet in his hands.

"You didn't need to bring food." Mason took the skillet. Something smelled like fried hamburger and onion. "I bought the stuff to make pizza."

Job's doubtful smile made Kathy grin. Mason tried not to bristle. "The dough is in one of those cans you pop open and the sauce is in a jar, but I know how to shred cheese and spread around pepperoni."

"Cassie was afraid we would starve." Kathy plopped on the floor and sat cross-legged next to a box of books. She pulled out the top one, a Nancy Drew mystery, and clutched it to her chest, an ecstatic smile on her tanned, freckled face. "We made a meal in a skillet. It's got hamburger and potatoes and onions and carrots and cheese. I helped. It's yummy. All we have to do is warm it up in the oven."

"I'd rather have pizza." Kevin pretended to gag. He took off his straw hat and slouched on the couch. His tan was even deeper than Kathy's. "You can eat the carrots. I'll eat the pepperoni."

"It was nice of Cassie to send food." Even if it showed a lack of faith in Mason's ability to cook. "We can eat the casserole for lunch and have pizza for supper, how about that?"

"I can always pick out the carrots." Kevin shrugged, his grin philosophical. "Right, Jennie?"

"I like carrots." She flopped on the floor next to Donny, who was trying to take the plastic off the box of checkers. "Mason says carrots make you see all the way to the Gulf of Mexico."

"Good girl. You guys can take your backpacks into the bedrooms for now. You can tell which is which by the sleeping bags."

"Sleeping bags?" Kathy hopped up and cartwheeled across the room toward the hallway. "You got us sleeping bags?"

"We can have a sleepover in the living room tonight, if you want, or you can use the bags on the beds."

His words likely went unheard over the thundering elephant herd stampeding to the bedrooms.

Chuckling, he headed for the kitchen. Job followed.

"Caleb's the one, isn't he?"

Mason kept his back to his grandfather while he placed the skillet in the oven. It served no purpose to pretend he didn't understand. "Yes. He's my father. We didn't do any fancy blood tests, but he's the one."

Job sat heavily in a chair at the table. "It's strange to know for sure after all these years that it's a man I see all the time in Yoder."

"It's strange for me to know after years of wondering and making up stuff about who my father might be."

"To grow up without a daed is sad."

"Bryan would say God allowed it so that my character could be honed."

"He would be right." Job traced a knot in one of the table's pine slats. "It's easy to mouth such platitudes, but it's hard to live them."

No truer words had ever been spoken. "I'm taking the kids for a walk down to the creek after lunch. I saw a turtle, a rat snake, and some jackrabbits the last time I hiked in that direction."

"Why didn't Caleb insist Georgia stay?"

Job was still stuck in the past. It was human to want to go back and fix the past—even if it couldn't be done. "He tried. He couldn't, any more than Mammi or you could."

Mason held out the pot holders. Job took them. His features softened. "He's a good man."

"He wants me to have supper at their house."

"His family knows then."

"Yes."

"That's gut. Hiding these things only leads to more heart-ache."

Nobody needed more heartache resulting from what Mason's mother had done all those years ago. "I should go ride herd on those crazy kids. It sounds like they're having a party out there."

"Perry showed up at the house."

Finally. It had taken Perry long enough to get up the courage to face his parents. "I told him he could stay here if he decided he wanted to be close to you. He didn't seem taken with the idea."

Which was strange considering how long he freeloaded at the old house.

"I think Cassie and Dinah have him convinced to stay with us." Job didn't seem too thrilled with the idea. Forgiving could be easier than forgetting. "He seems lost."

Or he put on a good show. Mason kept that thought to himself. His grandparents would find out soon enough if Perry was sincere in his desire to know them again. He would never be Plain again. Of that Mason was sure. "He's far too old to be drifting along like he is."

Agreement flashed in Job's face, but he said nothing in response.

"I know it's wrong for me to judge. Forget I said that."

"Jennie is doing much better, but she still wets the bed once in a while."

They were done talking about Perry, which was just fine. "I'll deal with it."

"At least the nightmares have stopped."

"That's good. She feels safe with you." And she would feel safe with Mason. "You and Dinah and Cassie enjoy the quiet."

"The women won't know what to do with themselves."

Neither would Job.

"Come on, bro, we want to play in the creek." Kevin shot through the kitchen door. "You're wasting the day blabbing. Don't be a bobblemoul."

He was right. Their time together out from under Job's watchful eyes would be short. "Sorry. I'm all about the creek before it gets any hotter."

Job followed them into the living room. The girls had Barbie dolls lined up on the couch with Dentist Barbie working on Teacher Barbie's teeth. Donny had the checkerboard set up on the coffee table. He seemed to be playing himself.

"*Beheef dich.*" Job patted Kathy's head. She grinned up at him. "Don't burn the house down your first night here."

"I always behave, Daadi."

"They'll be fine." Mason moved toward the door. This long-drawn-out good-bye would be harder for Job than the kids. "I'll have them back in time for church."

"Seven thirty sharp."

"I promise."

"I'll hold you to that." Job shoved his straw hat back on his head and stomped through the door. "Cassie will come for them."

Would she come for Mason? He paused for a second to make sure he hadn't posed the question aloud. "Job, you don't have to worry. I promise."

Job sighed. He cleared his throat. Finally, he smiled. "You're a gut big bruder, Mason."

"Danki."

"*Gern gschehme.*"

CHAPTER 33

A person should be careful what she wished for. Cassie patted her damp face with her apron. Not a leaf stirred on the sycamore and walnut trees clustered near the produce stand. She leaned against the counter and scratched at the mosquito bites on her wrist and neck. She'd asked to work at the stand because she liked talking to the tourists. She liked being outdoors. It had nothing to do with keeping her distance from Mason on this hot August day.

Better to keep her distance than be constantly reminded that he was off-limits. No peeking at him when she thought he wouldn't notice. No memorizing his warm smile or the way his dark, wavy hair lay on his neck. No checking out his long-legged stride. No listening for his laugh from the kitchen when he was in the living room doing jigsaw puzzles with the kids.

No nothing.

He had to choose his own path with no thought for what it might mean for them. If there was a them. For the last few months Mason had been excruciatingly careful to keep his distance. Was it as hard for him as it was for her? All she ever dreamed of was the love of a good Plain man and a big family.

God had quite the sense of humor.

Have faith, child. Wait and have faith.

Easy for God to say. He knew what the plan was.

The *clip-clop* of hooves sounded on the hard-packed, sun-dried dirt road that led from the highway to the Keims' house. Cassie straightened, stretched her arms over her head, and yawned. It must be a neighbor. Maybe her mother or father. Company would be good before she rested her head on the counter and took a nap.

"Hello."

Not her mother's voice. Or her father's. Hands suddenly shaking, Cassie smoothed her apron and turned. Mason pulled up in a buggy and stopped. What did they say about the best-laid plans? Maybe this was God's way of answering her prayers. Or maybe that was wishful thinking. "Hi. What are you up to on this fine summer day?"

"I came for a visit." Grinning, Mason hopped from the buggy. He still wore his faded, holey jeans and white T-shirt, but he wore a straw hat instead of a baseball cap. "I'm supposed to practice driving on the highway, so I thought I'd practice coming over here."

"And going back."

"Eventually." He pulled a jug of lemonade from the buggy seat along with two plastic cups. "You must be parched in this heat."

"I like the heat. I want to store it up for when it's cold in the winter." Cassie opened the swinging half door and stepped out from inside the stand. *Talk about the weather. The weather is safe.* "I'd rather be warm than cold."

"I can see both sides. I wouldn't want a permanent diet of either one." He settled the cups on the counter and poured the lemonade. "Here's to Kansas seasons."

They clinked glasses and drank.

"That hits the spot. Danki." Cassie held the cup against her cheek, seeking what little cool it could offer. "It's been quiet out here. It's even too hot for the tourists."

"How is Dinah? Is she feeling better?"

"Still listless. Still not eating. I couldn't even tempt her with banana pudding and vanilla wafers last night." Diabetics had to eat whether they liked it or not. It seemed mean to force food on a woman who was nauseous, but it had to be done. "If she keeps losing weight, we'll have to take her back to the doctor, and she hates going."

"When I was over for supper on Friday, she seemed confused. She said she wanted a glass of water, but she didn't seem to know where to get it. Job had to help her."

"When she takes too much insulin and doesn't eat enough, she has episodes where she becomes confused and even combative. I hope Job can convince her to drink some juice or eat a granola bar. That usually helps."

Mason nodded, but he still seemed worried.

Worrying didn't help, but it was hard not to do it. "How are your Deutsch lessons coming?"

His command of the language had improved daily. He still filled in words and sentences with English when he didn't know the Deutsch word, but that was fine. His pronunciation was off frequently but improving too. The time he spent working with Obie's crew helped tremendously. He deserved an A for effort.

"Gut. Between work and Kathy pestering me sunup to sundown on the weekends, I should be a native speaker in another week." Grinning, he leaned on his elbows against the counter, back to the stand, and raised his face to the sun. "I understand a lot more of what's being said in church, which is the most important part."

"That is gut."

Mason eased closer to Cassie. His scent of clothes soap and aftershave was fresh and clean, despite the summer heat. A shiver scooted down Cassie's spine. *Think about something else.* "And the cooking?"

"Not so great. I miss my microwave." He slid another step closer. "I need a fraa."

Dangerous territory. Cassie snagged a bag of cookies from the counter and opened it. She held it out. "Do you like pecans? I do. Lots of them. They make the cookies crunchy."

"Cassie." He took the cookies and laid them aside. His fingers returned to wrap themselves around hers. "We have to talk. Leastways, I need to talk."

"There's no point in it." His hand was warm and his grip strong. Cassie tugged loose. "You should be focused on the Articles of Faith and your baptism."

"That's what I wanted to talk to you about." Mason drew her closer. "Just give me a chance. Please."

"A chance at what?"

"So you have no feelings for me?" He leaned into her space. He touched her cheek. A sweet emotion recognizable even by someone as inexperienced as Cassie flooded his face. "You don't feel about me the way I feel about you?"

Heat sizzled through Cassie. She raised her hand to cover his and let her cheek rest on his palm. "I never said that."

"I know I'm getting ahead of myself. I will focus on baptism. I just want to know if you'll wait for me. That you'll not let some other guy sweep you off your feet before I have a chance."

"Plain men don't sweep Plain girls off their feet." At least not Cassie. She let her hand drop and backed away from his touch. "You haven't spent any time with the other women in our district. You need to take your time. Get used to your new life. Get used to your new community. There's no rush. Gott will lead you to the right fraa."

"He already did."

"You can't know that."

"My heart is telling me you're the one. I've never felt like this about any other woman."

"You have so much experience, then?"

"Nee, that's not what I'm saying. I was always too busy taking care of the kinner to date much. Then when they went to live with Daadi and Mammi, I decided to remake myself into something new. I haven't dated in two years or more."

"I think you're lonely."

"I think you're all I think about."

The heat burst into a flame. He was all she thought about too. Especially in the middle of the night when it was impossible to sleep. "You need to take the time to get to know the other women in our district."

"You're the only one I want to know." Mason stuck his hands on her hips and drew her closer. He bent so his five o'clock shadow brushed against her cheeks. A shiver ran rampant from her head to her toes.

He smiled and tucked his arms around her waist. "My feelings for you will never change. I've spent most of my life taking care of my brothers and sisters. I know I'll keep taking care of them with Job and Dinah and then when they're gone. I need a fraa who won't resent that, who'll see them as her flesh and blood. I know you'll do that."

Cassie closed her eyes and leaned her head against his chest. *Just for one second, Gott. Please let me have this for one minute. Okay, that's sixty seconds, but in a lifetime, it's nothing.*

His lips brushed her lips. Warm, soft, full. Fleeting.

Her first kiss came and went so quickly, yet the aftermath exploded like fire in a drought-stricken forest. She stood perfectly still until the last remnants faded. Cassie opened her eyes.

His expression wary, Mason stared down at her. "I shouldn't have done that, I know."

Cassie's fingers went to her lips. "Ach, Mason." She pushed hard against his chest. "Go back. Go back now before I don't have the strength to send you away."

His hands sought her hips and tightened, holding her close. "Promise you'll wait for me and I'll go."

"I'm not going anywhere. That's a promise."

His gaze settled on her mouth. He shook his head. His hands dropped and he backed away. "To be continued." He turned and strode away.

"To be continued." Cassie whispered the words as she watched him turn the buggy around and disappear, leaving a cloud of dust behind. "To be continued."

Soon.

CHAPTER 34

D inah? Dinah! Are you all right?"

No answer. Cassie pushed open the bathroom door. Dinah knelt next to the toilet. The smell of vomit mixed with Lysol knocked Cassie back a step. Dinah swiveled. Her kapp was askew, her face white, and her nose running. "I'm fine."

"You're not fine. When did this start?"

"My stomach is upset, that's all."

"You didn't say anything at breakfast." Cassie helped Dinah to her feet. Her bony arm wasn't much bigger around than Kathy's. "You need to eat some toast with peanut butter."

"Nee. Don't talk to me about food." Dinah tried to tug free. She stumbled and grabbed the towel rack. "Just give me my walking stick. I'm tired. I need to lie down."

"We need to check your blood sugar again."

"Nee." She tugged harder. "I'm not a bopli. Don't treat me like one."

The diabetes did the talking, not Dinah. The episodes when Dinah's blood sugar was out of whack were firmly imprinted on Cassie's mind. Like the time Job had to force her to swallow orange juice. Awful would be an understatement. Dinah spewed angry words at her husband—words Cassie couldn't believe the sweet woman knew. Her frail body seemed to gain superhuman strength. She stumbled through the house and fell at the bottom of the stairs. Once she'd locked herself in the bathroom and Job had to knock the door down.

"Eat half a piece of toast. For me. *Sei so gut.*"

"I said I'm not hungry."

Despite her petulance, Dinah allowed Cassie to lead her into the kitchen. Cassie made quick work of toasting the bread on the wood-burning stove. She added sugar-free peanut butter and set a glass of orange juice on the table next to the saucer.

With a grimace Dinah grabbed the toast. Her hands were shaking. She took a big bite—too big—chewed, and swallowed. She immediately gagged. "I can't." She grabbed her walking stick and stood. "Just let me sleep for a little bit. I'm tired. I'll be nicer when I wake up. I promise."

Cassie walked a tightrope. Dinah was a grown woman and her elder, but she still needed to be convinced to eat. "How about a grilled cheese sandwich or a small bowl of oatmeal with cinnamon and bananas?"

Dinah grunted and kept walking.

"I'll come check on you in a while."

No answer. She banged the walking stick on the floor and kept walking.

Perry entered the kitchen as his mother left. She didn't acknowledge his greeting. His forehead furrowed, he turned to Cassie. "Is she okay?"

"She isn't feeling well. She's going to rest."

"It seems like she's been doing a lot of that."

"I know. Job will have to take her to the doctor." Cassie dumped chopped-up potatoes into a skillet filled with hot oil and adjusted the gas flame under it. "What are you doing back at the house?"

"The boys sent me to see what goodies are for lunch."

More likely, he ducked out from the fieldwork early, saying he needed a drink of water. He had a lot of excuses for not finishing a day's work. Sunburn. Bug bites. Headache. Blisters from his new work boots.

At least he was working. Job seemed pleased with his efforts. Who was Cassie to judge? "Ham and cheese sandwiches, fried potatoes, pickled beets, sliced tomatoes, and fruit and whipped cream salad."

"Wunderbarr. I'm starved."

He'd begun sprinkling his conversation with Deutsch words. Another good sign. Cassie smiled her approval. "When Job and the boys come in from cutting the alfalfa, I'll put food on the table."

Perry returned the smile with his own pleading one. "Aw, come on, Cassie girl, I could eat a horse."

Add another child to her brood. Cassie carried Dinah's uneaten toast to the counter. She would finish it herself. They couldn't afford to waste food. "You'll live. We all eat together. That's what families do."

"I guess I'm out of practice." His usual sardonic humor faded away. "A person forgets what real family is like."

"Maybe if you stick around, you'll get the hang of it. Job and Dinah would like that."

"You think? It seems like they've got what they've always wanted. A bunch of little kids to raise. They don't need me around."

Did he really think grandkids could replace children? "They have room in their hearts for all of you."

"You really think so?" He moved to the counter where he snagged a piece of cheese and popped it in his mouth. "Georgia and I broke their hearts. I don't know how they can forgive that."

"Have you forgotten everything you learned before you left home?" Cassie closed the plastic bag that held the chunk of cheddar. "There's nothing that can't be forgiven. Job and Dinah love you. They've prayed for years that you would return home and be baptized."

Perry winced. He shook his head. He'd stopped using so much hair spray and let his hair grow out. It actually moved. "That's hard to imagine. I like my car an awful lot."

"I guess it depends on what you value most—a car or eternal salvation."

"Well, when you put it that way."

Cassie laughed with him. But she was dead serious.

"So what's the deal between you and my nephew Mason?"

The change in topic gave her whiplash. "There is no deal. He's an English man, even if he is the son of two Plain people. He's studying our faith and making a decision about joining our church, but right now he's still not Plain."

"I see you peeking at him when you think he won't notice." Perry smiled and shook his finger at her. "He does the same thing to you. Why don't you just get over it and take the plunge?"

"Please go away." Cassie scooted toward the refrigerator. "Make yourself useful. Muck the stalls. Clean the chicken coop. Feed the pigs. Earn your keep."

"More reasons to consider whether I really want to return to this way of life." Despite his words, Perry moved toward the back door. "How long until lunch is ready?"

"About ten minutes."

"I'll let Daed know."

Lunch was the usual silliness brought on by Jennie and Donny. The only thing missing was Dinah's delighted laughter at their antics. Job tried to hide his concern at her absence, but the worry lines that deepened around his mouth and eyes gave him away.

Cassie gave Mason a wide berth. If her gaze crossed paths with Perry's, he wiggled his eyebrows and made eyes at Mason.

Like a grade-school boy.

"Are you going back to the fields after lunch, Job?" She pointedly ignored Perry. "Or are you done for the day?"

"Mason is going to practice driving the tractor and pulling the tedder to fluff the alfalfa so it can dry evenly," Kevin volunteered. "I'm gonna show him how, since I already know."

"We know you know. You don't have to keep telling us." Kathy rolled her eyes. "You get to practice all the time. Mason works on houses during the week."

"I know that." Kevin shoved a big bite of potatoes in his mouth, chewed, and swallowed. "I don't see you working in the fields."

"I don't see you baking an apple pie."

"Okay, you two, you're both superstars." Mason laughed as he snatched another cookie from the plate in the center of the table. "It's gut to know I'll have lots of teachers."

"Turning into an Amish guy is a lot of work." Perry threw out the comment like a challenge. "Are you sure you're up for it?"

"I'm working on it. What would you know about it? You obviously weren't up for it."

Perry shrugged and smiled. "Never say never."

That almost sounded like a door had opened. The surprise and pleasure on Job's face said he heard it too. Cassie navigated around the table, picking up dirty plates. "To each in his own time."

"And right now it's dish-washing time." Kathy hopped up from the bench and stacked Donny's plate on top of hers. "I'll wash. Jennie will dry."

Jennie's housekeeping skills had improved greatly in the last few months. "Just make sure the plates are clean before you put them on the shelf."

Jennie giggled. "They'll just get dirty again."

It was her favorite line. Cassie smiled. "No one wants to eat on dirty plates, little maedel. I'll check on Dinah, and then we can go open the stand. We have tomatoes, corn, cucumbers, and bell peppers we need to sell."

"We might go fishing after a while." Mason tipped his head in the general direction of the pond. "You should come. It's so hot, we'll probably jump in the creek to cool off."

"We'll see." She managed another smile. The idea was to put space between Mason and her. "There's work to be done first."

The August heat had nothing to do with the warmth that flooded her entire body. She hustled from the kitchen. Every day it seemed harder to keep her distance. The memory of that kiss surfaced every time she saw Mason. It accompanied her while she washed clothes, baked bread, and mopped the floors. It kept her awake at night.

Soon Mason would be baptized. Until then she had to keep these feelings tightly bundled, locked up in a chest in the corner of her mind. *Gott, help me.*

Her face damp with perspiration, Cassie climbed the stairs and entered Dinah's bedroom. "Dinah, are you awake?"

No answer. Dinah lay on her side, her back to the door. She'd pulled the sheets up around her shoulders as if cold. "Dinah?" Cassie whispered. She tiptoed closer. "I just wanted to see if you're feeling better. Do you feel well enough to eat something?"

No answer. Cassie slid around to the other side of the bed so she could see Dinah's face better. It had turned a sickly grayish blue. Her mouth was slack. "Dinah?"

A knot formed in the pit of Cassie's stomach. Her heartbeat took off like a dog after a jackrabbit. With great care she touched Dinah's cheek. Her skin felt cold and clammy. Cassie took her hand. "Dinah, wake up. You need to eat something. Let's check your blood sugar again."

Dinah didn't move. Not even her chest moved in that natural rhythm of breathing.

Cassie gently shook her. "Wake up, Dinah. You need to eat."

Dinah's head lolled to one side. Cassie's stomach clenched. *Gott, help me.* "Dinah!" Cassie shook harder. "Open your eyes."

Nothing.

"Job, Job. Come quick!" Cassie thought she had screamed his name, but it barely came out. She had no breath. She shot through the door and ran to the top of the stairs. "Job, Job, come, please."

His heavy steps sounded and then he was there at the bottom of the staircase. "What is it? What's the matter?"

"I can't wake her. I don't think she's breathing."

Everything seemed to move in slow motion then, no matter how hard Cassie tried to rush. Job was in the bedroom and then Perry and Mason behind him. Job picked up Dinah's limp body. Her head fell back. Her eyes never opened.

Perry raced ahead to bring his car around to the front door.

Their faces scared, Kathy, Kevin, Donny, and Jennie huddled in the hallway. Jennie cried. Kathy picked her up and shushed her.

Mason stopped long enough to hug them. "We'll get Mammi help. She'll be fine."

He rose and headed for the door. Cassie rushed after him. "I want to go."

"Someone has to stay with the kinner."

He was right. They would need her. He shot down the front steps and jerked the door open. "She'll be fine."

Then they were gone.

Please, Gott, let her be fine.

CHAPTER 35

The doctor didn't have to speak. His aggrieved frown spoke for him. Mason stumbled to his feet. Perry remained in the hospital waiting room chair, rocking, his face so white he looked like he might pass out. Job, his hands loose at his sides, moved toward this man who would deliver news none of them wanted to hear.

"I'm sorry, Mr. Keim. She's gone." The doctor's eyes reddened behind frameless glasses. "We did everything we could. But she was already in a diabetic coma when you got her here. We were unable to bring her out of it."

"I know you did your best." Job's face remained stoic, as it had during the drive into Hutchinson Regional Medical Center. His soft, tender murmurings in Dinah's ear had filled the car during the entire drive. "Her days were numbered. She's gone on ahead."

The doctor nodded. His Adam's apple bobbed. "I don't know much about your faith, Mr. Keim, but I wondered if you would like to see her before you make arrangements with a funeral home. We have someone here who can help you with that when you're ready."

"That's kind of you. I would like to have a moment with her."

Mason eased back into the chair next to Perry. "Me, too, when you're finished, Daadi."

"Perry?"

Perry shook his head. Tears streaked his face.

Job followed the doctor from the room, leaving the two of them to their thoughts.

"I can't believe it." Perry slumped back in his chair. "I can't believe it. I just got her back."

"And I just found her."

Neither spoke for a while. A flat-screen TV on the far wall droned CNN news. A little boy cried. An old man coughed.

"I should've come home a long time ago." Perry hiccupped a sob. He didn't seem to be aware of the tears coursing down his face. "All those wasted years."

"You came home when you were ready. It seems like we have to go through stuff until we grow up enough to figure out where we need to be." Mason struggled for words. His heart hurt so badly with a pain that no medicine could fix. A pain he'd felt when his mother died. A pain he never wanted to feel again. Yet it had to be. Loving someone, having family, meant risking this kind of pain over and over again.

He tried to swallow the aching lump, but it wouldn't budge. "Bryan talks about being honed by the fire. He says that's what happened to me and the kinner. We were honed by the fire of our circumstances. That means we're becoming the people Gott wants us to be through these experiences."

"With all you've been through, you're on track to be super-human beings then." Perry snatched a tissue from one of the boxes strategically placed throughout the enormous waiting room. He blew his nose hard. "Me and Georgia played a role in your life. Not a good one either. We took off and left home. We rejected our upbringing. Georgia had you kids and never gave you an inkling about your background. Then she died and I ran out on you. I'm sorry, Mason, so sorry."

"You don't have to be sorry. I loved my mom. She was who she was. She couldn't change. I accepted that." Mason drew a shaky breath. "I'm just glad I got a chance to know Mammi. I'm so glad."

"I never said I was sorry. I never told her I loved her."

"She knew. Mammi was a smart lady."

Was. Past tense. The jagged shard of pain made Mason want to keel over. How would they tell the kids?

They just lost their mother. Now their grandmother. More honing with the fire. It seemed like so much for little children. So much hurt. So much loss.

"Job will be there for them." Perry must've read Mason's mind. "So will you and Cassie. And me."

"You're staying, then?"

"I'm not sure doing what exactly, but I'll be around."

"Job's going to need you."

"It would be nice to think that, but he is a strong man of faith." Perry leaned back in his chair. Grief made him seem much older than he had only minutes earlier. "This isn't the way I imagined us coming closer."

"Me neither." Mason closed his eyes and tried to see past the pain. For now he couldn't. But one day he would. If he'd learned anything from his mother's death, it was that cold, hard fact. Life went on. He straightened and swallowed his grief. "Me neither."

Job, his shoulders stooped, eyes red, waved from the doorway. Mason stood. "Are you sure you don't want to take a moment with her?"

"Nee."

Job showed Mason to the exam room, then left him. A tiny smile, so peaceful, adorned Dinah's face. Someone had arranged the sheets neatly. Her long white hair fanned out on the pillow. In their haste they hadn't brought her kapp. She would've been embarrassed. Mason stared at her placid features. His mother had Dinah's high cheekbones, her nose and chin. Everything else had been Job's.

"I'm so glad I got to meet you." Mason took her hand, wrinkled, covered with age spots and signs of a long life lived well. "I'm so glad my mudder decided to give us kinner the chance to know you. My life has been so different since the day I met you and Job. You gave me something I never had before. Hope. That sounds crazy, I know, but I thought I was stuck in a life and there was no changing it.

"Then I met you. I found out I could have a whole different life. That's pretty amazing. It's actually awesome. So danki for that."

The pain in his chest became more bearable. He kissed her cheek and leaned close to her ear. "And just so you know, I'm going to marry Cassie. So danki for that too."

He gently laid her hand back on her chest, kissed her cheek again, and turned to go. "Sweet rest, Mammi."

CHAPTER 36

The urge to rip the clock shaped like a gray barn from the wall and throw it across the kitchen grew with each revolution of the hour hand. This was one of those times when a phone would've been a godsend. Job, Perry, and Mason had taken Dinah to the hospital hours earlier. The waiting was like pacing barefoot on a floor covered with shards of glass.

Cassie plunked a bowl of goulash on the table. Kathy added a basket of rolls and a salad. Cassie had tried to make conversation, but the little girl hadn't responded.

"Do you want to put the pitcher of water on the table?" Cassie picked up a stack of plastic glasses. "I'll get the butter in a second."

"I don't see how we can sit down and eat like nothing is wrong." Kathy grabbed the pitcher and marched it over to the table. She smacked it down so hard water slopped over the side. "You're acting like Mammi isn't sick. Like everything is fine. Everything is *not* fine." She burst into tears.

Cassie rushed to her. "I'm not. It's just there's nothing we can do, so we have to keep doing what we always do."

"I don't want Mammi to die." Kathy turned her back on Cassie and covered her face. "I'm sorry. I'm sorry. I don't mean to make things worse."

Cassie squeezed the girl's shoulders and gently turned her back around. She peeled Kathy's fingers from her face. "Don't be sorry. You're not making things worse. You're worried and that's understandable. You have a right to be upset."

Wailing, Kathy threw herself into Cassie's arms. Her whole body shook with sobs. "Mommy died. Mammi can't die too. I can't do it. I can't take care of everybody."

Cassie rocked her. She stroked her long hair. "I know, I know. It's hard. It's so hard."

Jennie skipped into the kitchen. *"I'm hungry. I'm hungry. What's for supper?"* she sang.

Kathy jerked free from Cassie's arms. She wiped her face with both hands. "Goulash."

"Are you crying?" Jennie's smile melted away. Her forehead wrinkled. "Why are you crying?"

"I'm not crying."

"You don't have to hide your feelings either." Cassie handed Kathy a napkin. "We can tell each other how we feel. We're all scared about Dinah and worried. It's okay to say so."

"I'm the big sister. If I worry, Jennie will worry. It's my job to take care of her."

"Sometimes your job is just to be you. To be a little maedel. And that's okay. You have the rest of your life to be the big schweschder."

"I try not to worry, but I can't help it."

"It's hard, but we have to turn our worry over to Gott. He's in charge, not us."

"Worry about what?" Jennie climbed onto the bench and grabbed a roll. "Job is taking care of Mammi. She'll be back in a while."

"Gott willing." Kathy snatched the roll from her sister. "Wait for supper. You can have a roll when we all sit down to eat."

"Come here." Cassie sat on the bench and gathered both

girls into her arms. "No matter what happens, we have each other. Remember that."

Tater unwound his body from the rug in front of the pot-belly stove, stood, and barked. Her breath gone, throat tight, Cassie hugged harder.

The back door opened.

Job's gray, gaunt face as he walked in, Mason and Perry close on his heels, said it all. Cassie hugged the girls again. Jennie escaped her clutches and ran to Job. "Daadi, yay, you're home. Where's Mammi? Is she all better now? Did you get her some medicine?"

Kathy stood. Cassie did the same. She grasped the girl's hand in hers.

Job picked Jennie up. He hugged her close. "She's gone." His Adam's apple bobbed. He patted Jennie's back.

Kathy whirled and ran from the room.

"I'll go after her." His face lined with misery, Mason slipped past Cassie. "I'll tell Kevin and Donny too."

Cassie went to the stove and picked up a dirty skillet. She should wash it. Her arms were too weak to hold it. She carefully set it down. A dish towel slipped to the floor. She couldn't seem to bend over to pick it up. She swallowed her tears. Job needed her. The children would need her. Even Perry, scoundrel that he was, would need her. She couldn't be the one in need of comfort.

Mason had just found his grandparents. Now his grand-mother was gone. God, in His infinite wisdom, had a plan, and this was it.

How dare she question Him? *Gott, help me understand.* She turned. "I'm so sorry."

"We had many gut years together." Job murmured the words as if reciting them to himself. He carried Jennie to the table and sat down. The little girl laid her head on his shoulder. He smoothed her hair. "Her body was ravaged by that disease for so many years, she couldn't do it anymore. We can be thankful that she no longer suffers."

Jennie's lower lip trembled. She frowned. "Mammi's not coming home?"

"Nee."

"Where is she?"

Pain running rampant across his lined face, Job shot an SOS over her head at Cassie. He shook his head as if to say, *Help me.*

"She's in heaven with your mom, Jennie." Cassie managed to get the words out without crying. "She's telling your mommy all about what you kids have been doing here on the farm and the fun she had with you and how much she loves you."

Bryan wouldn't approve, but he wasn't here and this little girl who'd lost so much needed a sweet picture of her mother and grandmother together that she could hang on to.

Cassie couldn't catch her breath. Her chest was hard and hollow and empty. "I should've made her eat the toast."

"No one is to blame. You took very gut care of my mudder. You helped my daed take care of her." Perry spoke in Deutsch. "She wanted for nothing. She loved you both. You have nothing to feel guilty about." His gaze swung toward Job. "Daed hasn't eaten. Can you fix him something?"

"I don't want food."

Cassie went to the table and picked up the bowl of goulash. That was something she knew how to do. Comforting a man who'd just lost his wife was beyond her.

"I don't suppose you have a bottle of Jack Daniel's around here." Perry rubbed red eyes. "I could use a belt about now."

"Nee, sorry." Job stroked Jennie's hair. He sighed. "Gott is gut. She no longer suffers. We can draw comfort from that."

Her days were numbered. Cassie drew in a long breath. Soon others would come. The women would bring food. The men would do chores. Arrangements would be made. But now, in this moment, she had to carry the load. She filled glasses with cold peppermint tea and dumped the goulash back in the skillet to warm it. Whether he liked it or not, Job needed to eat. So did Perry and Mason.

Mason returned to the kitchen with Donny on his hip. Kevin and Kathy followed. "They say they're not hungry, but I think it would be good for us to sit down and eat together." Mason deposited Donny at the table. He smoothed the boy's tousled black hair and planted a kiss on his head. "It's important for us to stick together. That's what Mom always said. No matter what, we have to stick together."

Donny's face was red and tearstained. Kevin needed to wipe his nose. Kathy scurried toward the counter. "I'll help, Cassie. Let's have some of that banana pudding and vanilla wafers for dessert. Mammi would like that."

Her throat tight, Cassie nodded. "Good idea."

After a while, they sat at the table. Job took Kathy's hand, she took Cassie's, and around the table it went until they all held hands. They bowed their heads and prayed silently.

The meal was a quiet one. Kathy wiped away an occasional tear. Jennie cried because Dinah wasn't there to butter her roll. Kevin dried her tears and did it for her. Donny asked for seconds of "Mammi's pudding."

When the kitchen was clean and the dishes put away, Cassie didn't know what to do with herself. The kids went to bed early without argument. Job said good night to each one of them, administering kisses and hugs as needed. Then he disappeared into the room he'd shared with Dinah for forty-five years.

The house felt perversely empty, even though only one person was missing.

Cassie needed air. She needed answers. She went out on the porch and sat in a lawn chair. The night sky was clear. The stars sparkled in abundance. "Oh, Dinah."

The Bible said believers received new bodies in heaven. Dinah would be able to see again. She'd be able to walk freely. The stars must shine so brilliantly in heaven. Yes, her days were numbered. Yes, her time in this world was done. That didn't mean Cassie couldn't mourn her absence. Her friendship. Her loving-kindness. Her enthusiasm for life.

The pain was unbearable. Not even when her grandmother passed away at the ripe old age of ninety had Cassie felt such pain.

"There you are." Mason peeked from behind the screen door.

"Here I am."

"Are you okay?" He let the screen door close behind him. "Stupid question, I know."

"Are they asleep?"

"Everyone but Kathy. She asked if she could read for a while. Job said for as long as she wanted."

"He's so strong."

"He is. I would like to be that strong." Mason eased into the chair next to her. He leaned forward and clasped his hands. He cleared his throat. "It feels just like it did when Mom died. She went too soon. She was still young. The kids needed her. Now Dinah. We just met her. We were just getting to know her. Perry just came back. I've already learned this lesson. Now I'm learning it again."

"I don't know how you survived it." Tears clogged her throat. "I can't believe she's gone. I can't believe I'll never talk to her again."

Mason held out his hand. Without hesitation Cassie took it. She needed him. God knew. He saw. He understood. Mason scooted closer and put his arm around her. The tears came un-abated. She shouldn't cry. Dinah was home. "I don't know why I can't stop crying."

"Because you loved her. You took care of her. She was family in the best sense of the word." Mason rubbed her back. "Take it from me. I know. Family is a peculiar thing. You don't get to pick your blood relatives, but sometimes people become family by being everything that is good in that word. I only knew my grandma less than six months, but it was like I'd known her my whole life."

He brushed tears from Cassie's cheek. His gentle touch held such sweet concern and understanding. "I know how much it hurts now, but it will get better. When I think of Mom now, I remember the fun stuff. The good memories. I hang on to them and let the bad stuff go."

Like Dinah's animated gestures when she told the children stories from her childhood. The way she tickled Jennie awake in the morning. Her love of onion and butter sandwiches. Her zeal for mopping. Her joy at Sunday morning services.

They sat like that for a long time. No more words were needed.

Tomorrow they would go back to the place where they care-fully guarded the boundaries of their faith and community. For tonight, they needed each other in a way that could not be denied.

CHAPTER 37

The humid August air smelled like a county fair. The mouthwatering scents of cotton candy, kettle corn, and slow-smoked turkey legs called Mason's name. His stomach rumbled. He closed his eyes and inhaled. Mom would've loved this. She probably did love Yoder's annual Heritage Day. Maybe that's why she liked the Sedgwick County Fair so much. A bluegrass band entertained the crowd with an old Bill Monroe song, "Little Maggie," on the small stage set up in front of the post office. Jennie and Donny improvised a two-step, hip-hop dance while Kathy and Kevin egged them on with hooting and hollering interspersed with howls of laughter.

It felt good. In the weeks since Dinah's death, Kevin and Kathy had retreated into silent wariness. A sort of hands-off approach. They wanted everyone to think they were fine. They could take care of themselves. Kevin tried to act tough. Kathy was all about being brave. She wanted to take care of Job like the little mother she was. Jennie and Donny went in spurts. Playing and laughing one minute, sobbing and asking for Mammi the next.

Job insisted God worked everything for the good of those who loved Him. Everything. Even Dinah's death so soon after their mother's.

They still had each other.

Which was why Mason had insisted on bringing them to Heritage Day. Dinah wouldn't want them sitting around being gloomy.

Life was short. So very short.

"They're having fun, aren't they?"

Mason turned at the sound of Cassie's voice. She approached with her friend Nadine from the secondhand store. They could've been twins in their burgundy dresses. Except Cassie was much prettier. Both carried large Styrofoam cups of vanilla ice cream topped with caramel syrup, toasted miniature marshmallows, and whipped cream. Cassie's cheeks were pink and her face damp with perspiration. She was beautiful, as usual. Mason studied her black sneakers covered with dust and bits of dried brown grass. "Is it okay if they dance? I don't want to offend . . . the elders."

"It's good to see them laughing and playing again. Kids play. We understand that. It's a spontaneous act of joy." Cassie sounded almost wistful. "We try not to discourage joy. It can be so hard to come by."

Cassie had been quiet, too, since the funeral. She'd carefully distanced herself. Rightly so. They'd driven to the edge of the precipice. Then backed away until the right moment.

She needed time to find her balance after Dinah's sudden death. Mrs. Blanchard had attended the funeral and dropped in at the house more frequently now. Just to make sure everyone was handling the change, as she called it, well. The idea of an elderly widower raising small children seemed to concern her, but Cassie's steadying presence had reassured her.

Perry, surprisingly, hadn't run away. After the funeral he stayed a few weeks and then returned to Wichita "to tie up some loose ends." He showed up regularly on weekends.

The court hearing to finalize custody loomed in October. The younger kids' father, now remarried with a baby on the way, had decided to sign away his parental rights as "best for them." Bobby and Kevin's dad, now a successful, married new-car dealership owner in Kansas City, had no interest in resuming a relationship with his sons either. Job and Mason had agreed to wait until they were older to try to explain this to all of them.

For now they only needed to know they were wanted by their grandfather, by their big brother, and if all went well, by Cassie. "I'm surprised you came."

"You have the kids, so I have the day off." Cassie took a bite of her ice cream. Her voice softened, forcing Mason to stoop to hear her words. "It's too quiet around the house when they're not around. I miss Dinah so much. Having her to talk to made chores fun. Job works outside most of the day and goes to bed early. Still, it's hard to come here like nothing happened. Dinah loved Heritage Day. Nadine practically dragged me out of the house."

"She just needed an extra tug." Nadine grinned. "I see Carrie from the store over there. I'll be right back."

Still grinning, she strolled away.

Could she be more obvious?

"I thought she was your chaperone," Mason teased. Even so, his observation likely was true. Cassie had to be careful about being seen talking to him alone, even on a crowded street. "She sure took off."

"Since her dad is the bishop, she knows all about your plan to join the church." Cassie seemed absorbed in watching the kids' silly dance. "I think she's matchmaking—even though that's frowned upon. Especially before your baptism."

Nadine had the right idea. Mason didn't dare say that out loud. The song ended. The band immediately dove into another one. The crowd of farmers, housewives, and oversugared, sweaty kids clapped and cheered. Mason clapped with them. Maybe that's what Bryan had meant when he talked about how much more he would appreciate good times because of the dark times. *"Hang on to your joy,"* he said.

Did that include the joy of loving a girl and having her love you back? Wasn't love a spontaneous act of joy? At least it started that way. Sustaining it took work. If Mason had learned anything from his mother's failed marriages, it was that. Love was like a fire that started with a spark. Even a raging fire had to be maintained or it died down to embers and went out. Spend time with it, nurture it, add sustenance, and it would keep a person warm forever.

Now, before it was too late. Squeeze every last ounce of joy from it.

Mason eased away from the crowd, putting distance between himself and the loud music.

"Where are you going?" Cassie trailed after him. "You were thinking so hard it must've hurt."

"I take it Job didn't come."

"Nee." She sighed, a sound so soft he almost missed it. "He's working himself hard. It's as if filling every minute of every day keeps him from thinking."

"And the exhaustion makes it possible for him to sleep." A strategy Mason used as well. "What about Perry?"

"He's actually good with the kids and with Job. It's like he's made it his mission to make them laugh. He plays the clown. I know he's hurting, too, but he doesn't let it show."

"It's hard for me to believe, but I feel for him. He finally came back after all those years, and she's gone. He missed all that time with her."

"He'll have to forgive himself, and that will take time."

"I'll pray that he's able to do it."

Cassie smiled. "I like hearing you say that. I like the clothes too. Does it seem weird to dress that way, our way?"

Bryan and Delbert had decided it was time for Mason to adopt the Plain way of dressing. Delbert's wife kindly sewed a pile of clothes for him. All he had to do was pay for the material. His coworkers had elbowed each other and smiled the first time he climbed into the van dressed in a blue shirt, black denim pants, and suspenders, but they hadn't said a word. "It's okay. It's like I don't have to think about what I wear anymore." Not that he was one to think about it much anyway. "Every day it's the same and that's fine with me. I do kind of miss my belt, though. Suspenders are harder to put on."

"You'll get used to it."

He already had. Especially since he removed the mirrors from the house. He spent all his time with Plain folks—except the one he wanted most to spend time with.

Think about something else.

Mason eyed her ice cream. "Good choice. It must be ninety degrees in the shade with ninety percent humidity."

Lame. Talking about the weather was totally lame.

"You know how I feel about the heat. I love that autumn comes next. When it's icy cold this winter, we'll wish for summer. That's the way we are." She held out the cup. "Would you like a bite? I don't have cooties, I promise."

"Don't mind if I do." Mason wouldn't mind her cooties a bit. *Stop it.* He took the spoon and dug into the ice cream. Soft-serve vanilla. It had never tasted so good. "Danki."

"You have whipped cream on your upper lip." She tugged the cup back. Mason didn't let go. Her fingers wrapped around his. "Hey, let go." Cassie chuckled. "One bite is all you get. This one's mine. Get your own."

Mason let go. Her fingers slipped away. He wanted to grab them back. Bryan's stern words echoed in his head. *Faith first, family second, and community third . . . You must decide what you believe. If you wish to join the faith.*

Mason dabbed at the ice cream on his lip with his sleeve. "Here I thought you were so kind and generous, sharing your ice cream."

"I am. To a point. You're just like the kids. Use a napkin." Grinning, Cassie held out hers. He took it. Cassie's head bobbed. She waved the spoon around and droplets of melted ice cream landed on her apron. "I like this music. Do you?"

"I do. Mom liked bluegrass, country music, gospel, and the blues. Music played in our house all the time. She even bought a nice stereo system with a turntable so she could play old records." She'd said it was her one luxury. Mason had boxed up the system and the collection of records when he moved. It sat in the basement where it was cool and the records wouldn't warp. Someday he would give it to Bobby. Someday.

God willing. According to God's plan. Mason practiced saying those words each day. Along with the Lord's Prayer.

Cassie probably didn't know what records were. Or a turntable. She had no need to know. The simplicity of Plain life was one of its best qualities. Mason didn't mind giving up the sound system. He missed the washer and dryer. He also missed the AC, especially at night on breathless August nights, but he'd learned to cope. "Anyway, I grew up listening to this music."

"How are things going with your dad?"

Her train of thought made sense. From a mom who escaped from the Amish life and embraced all things worldly to a dad who lived a quiet, godly life with a contentment to which Mason could only aspire. "Going good. He's a nice man. He's teaching me woodworking. It comes natural to a carpenter. I'm building desks for the kids to use for their homework when they visit."

"It's good that you share a love of working with your hands."

Her gaze drifted to his hands. Her pink cheeks darkened to a rose red.

Her lips had been so soft. Her scent so sweet that day at the produce stand. Her hand on his that night on the front porch. What would her skin feel like if he touched her cheek? Her neck? Her hair would be silky to the touch.

Mason gritted his teeth and forced himself to watch Jennie's antics. The song ended. Donny pelted toward them. Jennie skipped. Kathy and Kevin walked more slowly, certain that they were older and not like "the kids."

"Can we get cotton candy?" Her cheeks red and her sweaty hair plastered to her forehead, Jennie hopped up and down. "And a pop. I want an orange pop."

"I'm so thirsty. So, so thirsty." Donny tugged on Mason's sleeve. "I think I'm gonna die, I'm so thirsty."

"You two are the drama king and queen." Mason laughed. "We've only been here an hour and you're dying already."

"You must think Mason is rich." Kathy shook her finger at them. "Stuff costs money."

"Hey, I told them I'd spring for treats. Don't rain on their parade." Mason shook his finger right back at her. Kathy's positive spin on life had ended up in a ditch when Dinah died. She worried far too much for an eight-year-old. "How about hot dogs and pops? I think cotton candy and pop are a recipe for bouncing off the walls. We'll get some ice cream later."

"I want to go to the petting zoo." Jennie stomped her bare feet. "You said I could pet the goat."

"One thing at a time, child."

"Whatever—just hurry." Kevin jerked his head toward Main Street. "The free throw contest starts in fifteen minutes."

Kevin didn't get excited about much these days, so his interest in the contest had been a welcome surprise. "You're signed up, but you can go ahead and head that direction. I'll bring your stuff to you."

"You're gonna watch me shoot, though, right?"

"I wouldn't miss it for the world."

Kevin trotted off in that direction.

"Gut job." Cassie smiled up at Mason. "You're so gut at this."

"At what?"

"Being their parent."

"Come with us. I'll buy you a hot dog."

She shook her head. "I have to stay with Nadine. Have fun."

Mason allowed himself to be dragged toward the concession stand by two determined children, but he called back to her, "We're staying for the fireworks tonight. Find us. Sit with us."

Sit with us. Stay with us.

Stay with me.

CHAPTER 38

Mosquitoes and flies. The inevitable companions that joined any crowd where kids spilled pop and scores of people ate hamburgers, turkey legs, and candied apples. Batting away a horsefly the size of her big toe, Cassie wove her way through the clusters of people already settled into their lawn chairs in front of the post office to await the fireworks display. Their faces sported new sunburns. Babies either cried or slept in their mamas' arms. Farmers discussed wheat and cattle prices while housewives exchanged gossip. Plain and English alike mingled on the temporary metal bleachers.

Small-town life. Who could ask for more? If only Job had come. Days like this, people like this, were a balm for even the most crushing grief. Life went on, little by little. Dinah wouldn't be forgotten, but the happy memories would be the first to bloom each day. A little bit, day by day. New, sweet memories would be made. Nadine had sneaked off with her beau. That left Cassie free to search for Mason.

Dinah's sudden death had changed everything. Cassie had been to her share of funerals before that. But watching Job's grief-ravaged face as his wife's casket was lowered into the ground had etched a lesson on Cassie's soul. No amount of time together would seem enough for two people who loved each other.

Job's words followed her through the house as she washed dishes, did laundry, cooked, and cleaned. *"Don't waste the days*

Gott gives you." God expected His children to use their time well. To lean into life.

He brought Mason into her life. He led Mason to his new faith. He placed Mason's half siblings in her care. Could the signs be clearer?

No, they couldn't. How did she tell Mason that? It wasn't her place to say anything or say it first.

"Cassie, over here. Cassie, Cassie."

She had no problem hearing four high, excited voices shouting her name. Nor did half a dozen people who stopped what they were doing to turn and stare. They all knew her. Smiling and nodding, heat spiraling through her, she ducked her head and wove between chairs, blankets, and kids sitting cross-legged in the sparse grass. A great way to go home with chigger bites. "Excuse me, excuse me, sorry, excuse me."

Finally she made it to the spot Mason and the kids had carved out for themselves. Mason opened a spindly lawn chair made of blue woven plastic. He set it behind the blanket where the kids had stretched out—within arm's reach of his own chair. They were sunburnt, exhausted, and happy. Mason bowed and swept his hand out in a flourish. "Your seat, mademoiselle. I was afraid you'd decided to go home."

"And miss the fireworks? No way. Danki." Glad to take a load off her weary feet, she sank into the chair. It squeaked. The kids giggled. Mason shushed them. Cassie laughed. "It's okay. I've eaten watermelon, ice cream, a Frito pie, a hamburger, and two snowballs today. I'm extra full at the moment."

"I ate three hot dogs," Donny announced with obvious pride. "Kathy only ate two, but I ate three and french fries and a snowball."

"I dropped my snowball." Jennie, who sat on Mason's knee,

her head leaning on his chest, sounded mournful. "But Mason got me another one. He's nice."

"Remember that when I tell you it's time to go to bed." Mason kissed the top of her head. "Don't be calling me mean anymore."

"You're not mean, Bruder." Jennie turned so she could curl against him. She sighed. Her eyelids drooped. "I can't wait to see the . . ."

"I think she fell asleep," Cassie whispered. "Poor bopli is tuckered out."

"It's past her bedtime. Once she stops moving, she passes out." Mason gently laid her on the blanket next to Donny, who would likely be next. "She'll wake up when the fireworks start."

"Can we get popcorn?" Kevin wiggled around on his knees to face Mason. "We need popcorn for the fireworks."

"How can you have room for anything else? You must have a hollow leg." Mason dug into the pocket formed by the flap on his denim pants and pulled out a crumpled bill. "Get enough for everyone. Kathy, you go with him and stay together. Come right back."

"It's right over there."

"I know where it is. I'll be able to see the line from here, but you know the drill."

The two took off.

Mason sank back in his chair and sighed. "I hope no one throws up tonight. Popcorn could be the tipping point. Anyway, now we can talk."

"I'd like that."

"The date has been set for my baptism."

Hallelujah. Cassie breathed for a few seconds. She hadn't said that out loud, had she? No. *Whew.* "You've made the decision, then?"

"I have. It was easy. Everything Bryan explained to me, everything I read, everything my daed told me—all made sense. For the first time in my life, I know Gott is in charge of my life. It feels gut not to have to worry anymore. It's not up to me. He's in control."

"I'm so happy for you." Cassie couldn't contain her smile. This decision was far more important than her feelings. It was about Mason's eternal salvation. She wanted to jump up and shout to all the people who crowded the lawn waiting for fireworks. *He believes. Mason believes that Jesus is his Savior. He has the living hope. He wants to live his life according to the Ordnung.* "That is the best news ever. Your daed must be so happy."

"He is. When I take the kinner to church on Sunday, I'll tell Job. He'll be happy, too, I know."

"Gott is gut."

"The fact that He loves me still blows my mind." Mason leaned closer. "I'm hoping you're as happy about it as I am."

"Happier."

"I don't think that's possible, but it's nice to know." His hand slid over her chair's armrest and reached for hers. Their fingers touched for a fraction of a second—a warm, breathless, heart-stopping moment. "I don't want to get you in trouble. I know nothing can happen yet. I just need to know if you will wait."

"I've been waiting almost since the day I saw you standing on the welcome mat at the front door." The words tumbled out, mixed up, upside down, inside out. "I'll wait as long as you need."

"Gut. That's gut."

"As long as you're not doing this for me. It can't be for me or for us." No matter how much it would hurt, the point had to be made. "This is about your eternal salvation."

"Believe me, I know."

"When will you be baptized?"

"The second Sunday in September."

Three weeks. *Danki, Gott.*

"Cassie!"

This time several dozen people perked up, it seemed, to see who called her name.

Her father, of course. He took a similar meandering path toward them, her mother trailing behind. Cassie stood. "I have to go."

"Jah, you do. I'll see you at church tomorrow." He grinned and winked. "Don't worry, I won't get too close."

Cassie winked back. It felt as if they'd sealed a vow.

She met her parents several yards from where Mason and the kids sat. It was better that way. "Where's Nadine? Job said you came with her." Her father didn't bother with a simple hello. "What were you doing sitting with Mason?"

"Nadine left earlier." No need to share all the details with him. "I was sitting with the kids so I didn't have to sit alone."

"You can sit with us." It was not a suggestion. Her father's glower made that clear. "You'll need a ride home. Since the kinner aren't at Job's, you can spend the night with us. Job can take you home from church."

Also not a suggestion.

Cassie had hoped to get a ride from Mason, but that was off the table now. "Mason's baptism is set for the second Sunday in September."

Her father sighed. Her mother waited until he passed in front of them to turn to Cassie.

She winked.

CHAPTER 39

"Can you confess: Jah, I believe that Jesus Christ is the Son of God?"

"Jah."

The single syllable joined in with the chorus of four other people who were to be baptized upon responding to Bryan's questions. It was amazing that the word came out at all, considering Mason's heart was in his throat. He and the others knelt on the hard-packed dirt floor in Job's barn in front of the entire Gmay—and Mason's father. The kids were there. And Cassie. If only Bobby were here, Mason's family would be complete. He breathed. His stomach rocked. *Sei so gut, Gott, don't let me hurl in front of all these people.*

Not the weirdest prayer he'd silently uttered this day.

"Do you also recognize this to be a Christian order, church, and fellowship under which you now submit yourselves?"

"Jah."

Forever and ever, amen. Despite the sweat born of nerves and the September humidity and the roller-coaster ride in his stomach, Mason could barely contain the urge to jump to his feet and dance down the aisle.

That would not be fitting for his first act as a Plain man. *Jesus, danki. Danki for having me. Danki for taking me in. For making me family.*

"Do you renounce the world, the devil with all his subtle ways, as well as your own flesh and blood, and desire to serve Jesus Christ alone, who died on the cross for you?"

"Jah!"

This time Mason shouted it. The word simply couldn't be contained. Heat burned his face. The faint sound of muffled laughter floated behind him.

A sliver of a smile flitted across Bryan's face, then disappeared. "Do you also promise before God and His church that you will support these teachings and the Ordnung with the Lord's help, faithfully attend the services of the church, help to counsel and work in it, and not to forsake it, whether it leads you to life or to death?"

Sudden emotion clogged Mason's throat. This was it. This was the biggie. He cleared his throat and managed a strong finish. "Jah."

Rustling told Mason everyone had risen. Bryan proceeded with the baptismal prayer from the prayer book. Such weighty words. They would be etched on Mason's heart forever. *They desire to live only for Jesus Christ . . .*

A pail of water and a cup in his hand, Delbert appeared at Bryan's side. Bryan's wife, Esther, followed along behind. She would bestow the holy kiss on the two women applicants. Bryan placed his cupped hands over Mason's head. The moment had arrived. Delbert scooped a cup of water from the pail and poured it onto Bryan's hands.

No going back. A new life in Christ. Mason closed his eyes.

"Welcome home, suh."

Lukewarm water streamed down Mason's forehead and wet his cheeks. Better that they not see his tears. His throat ached. His body trembled.

Home. God's house had many rooms. Enough rooms for everyone who called Him Father.

"I baptize you in the name of the Father, the Son, and the Holy Ghost."

Mason rose on shaking legs. Bryan took his hand and shook it. He then kissed Mason's cheek. "Welcome, my suh," he whispered close to Mason's ear.

Mason managed a nod.

The final words flew over him and out the open windows of Job's barn. "You are no longer guests and strangers but workers and members in this sacred and godly fellowship."

"Yeah, Mason!" Jennie whooped and yelled. "He's my bruder."

"He's my bruder too." That was Donny. "You can't hog 'im, Jennie."

"Shh."

Probably Kathy doing the shushing.

"On that note, you can go sit down."

A ripple of laughter floated through the barn. Bryan's kindly smile eased the acute embarrassment mingled with pride that raced through Mason. They were his family and they wanted everyone to know it.

On wobbly legs Mason made his way to his seat next to Job, who nodded his approval, and Kevin, who offered an enthusiastic fist bump. Mason allowed himself one peek in Cassie's direction. She sat two rows up and one row over next to her mother, who held Jennie on her lap. Donny sat on the other side. Cassie stared straight ahead, as she should.

Look back, look back. She didn't dare. Her mother leaned toward her and whispered something. Cassie glanced back.

He raised his eyebrows. She smiled and faced the front.

Two hours later the service ended. The kids stampeded out

of the barn. The adults might've wanted to do the same, but they restrained themselves for the most part. Smiling, Job clapped Mason on the back as they moved into the flow of men in the middle aisle. "I'm glad for you."

"Danki. Me too." The sentence stumbled around in his head. Nothing coherent surfaced. He ducked his head. "Me too."

"Dinah would've liked this. A lot."

She would've. "I wonder what my mother would've thought."

Job's smile lost some of its luster. "I never could figure her out. Your mudder had her own creed, it seemed. One the rest of us weren't privy to."

They stepped into the midday sun. Puffy clouds scudded across an electric-blue sky that seemed to stretch endlessly across the Kansas prairie. The details would forever be etched in Mason's memory. The scent of fresh-cut grass was so sweet, so familiar, Mason's throat ached for those not here to enjoy it with him. His mother. Dinah. Bobby.

"I think someone wants to say something to you." Job cocked his head toward Caleb, who stood under a massive sycamore tree, hands dangling at his sides, near the long line of buggies. "There's a strawberry-rhubarb pie calling my name."

"Danki, Job, for everything."

"I haven't done anything."

"You took in the kids—"

"My family."

The boulder in his throat prevented Mason from saying more. He strode across the yard to where his father waited. "You didn't have to come, but I'm glad you did."

Caleb stuck his hands under his armpits and studied his Sunday go-to-service shoes. "It does my heart gut to know you're part of the fellowship now. Coming from where you have been to this moment couldn't have been easy."

"It's been a long haul." But not as hard as he'd thought it would be. Simple. Quiet. Peaceful. Strangely, all the pressure had fallen away. Life no longer seemed complicated. "I could never figure anything out on my own. Now I don't have to."

"Praise Gott." Caleb's finely etched features were suffused with red. His hands dropped. He took one step forward and his muscled arms wrapped tightly around Mason's shoulders for a solitary second. "Praise Gott."

Before Mason could respond, Caleb stepped back. "I have to go. The kinner are chomping at the bit to fish for catfish at the river this afternoon. My fraa is hoping to fry up a mess of fish for supper."

He nattered on, which was good, because Mason couldn't have spoken if he tried.

"You're welcome to come by. Just know you're welcome anytime. Tonight. Any night." Caleb nodded vigorously. "There's always room at the table."

Mason cleared his throat, but he had to make do with a nod. His father backpedaled a few steps, then shot past Mason as if a pack of coyotes chased him.

Mason didn't answer. He couldn't. Instead he basked in the feel of those arms around him. A father's hug. Today he'd felt himself held in the arms of his heavenly Father, and for the first time, his earthly father.

Life couldn't get any better than that.

"Mason, over here."

Cassie's whisper floated on the warm breeze.

Or maybe it could.

• • •

The sight of Caleb embracing Mason had made Cassie's heart sing. *No waterworks,* her brain scolded her heart.

His expression when she called his name sent her heart into the heavens.

He hustled her direction. "There you are."

"Here I am."

He took her hand and tugged her behind the last row of buggies. "I'm so happy."

"I'm so happy for you." The joy bubbled up in Cassie and flowed out. "I think Dinah is smiling down on you right now."

Mason grabbed her around the waist, lifted her into the air, and whirled her around. "I believe you're right. Her sight is perfect now. No more shots. No more dizzy spells. No more weakness. No more tears."

"You're making me dizzy!" Cassie clapped her hands on his shoulders and laughed. "You'd better put me down before someone sees us."

"Where are the kinner?"

"The girls are helping Mudder serve food, and she's loving every minute of it. She wants to teach Kathy to crochet and Jennie to make fry pies. If she's not careful, she'll spoil them. The boys are playing baseball, of course."

"Take a walk with me."

"Aren't you hungry?"

"I can't eat. I'm too . . . full of everything that's happened today."

Together they strolled out to the dirt road that led to the highway. Mason's hand encompassed Cassie's. Deep contentment enveloped her. This day couldn't get any better.

Mason veered from the road. Cassie had no choice but to follow. Arms swinging, they meandered along the fence that separated the road from empty wheat fields until they reached the shade of a few enormous oak trees. "It's so quiet out. So beautiful." Cassie leaned against a tree and closed her eyes so she could listen to the rustle of the leaves. "I couldn't be happier."

"What if I did this?"

Mason's hands cupped her cheeks. His lips covered hers. This time he didn't stop. The kiss deepened until Cassie slid her hands around his waist and leaned into him. Her first real kiss.

Finally, he backed away. "How about now?"

"You're right. I could be happier. I am happier."

He grinned. "More?"

"More."

Time might have stood still. Or maybe it rushed by. Cassie was too busy to notice. Life tended to move on if a person didn't grab it and hang on.

"Will you be my girl?" Mason whispered the words as he nuzzled her neck. "Forever?"

"I think I've been your girl for a while now."

"You hid it well."

"I didn't want to influence your decision."

"I want you to be my fraa."

His words sent a wave of warmth crashing over Cassie. She'd waited for them for so long. Wanted them for so long. She sighed, opened her eyes, and leaned back so she could see his face. She put her hands over his. "I love you too."

"Why does it sound like there's a *but* coming?"

"But you took a huge step today. Let it sink in." Good advice for them both. The life she wanted was within reach. One step at a time. "Get comfortable in your new clothes."

"I've been wearing these clothes forever."

"You know what I mean."

"I do." He kissed first one eyelid, then another, then dropped a kiss on her nose. "Job and I have been talking. When we go back to court in October, he'll ask for permanent custody, but he also wants us to become the kids' legal guardians when he passes. The attorney ad litem has offered to help him with the paperwork. I hope that's many years from now, but he wants to get everything squared away so there's no hassle. We'll be a family, no matter what."

Cassie could see it. Kevin, Kathy, Donny, and Jennie. And Bobby. *Please, Gott, Bobby too.* "This is everything I've ever wanted. A mann to love and a big family. Being your fraa would make me so happy."

"And I would be honored to be your mann." He kissed her lips hard. "We'll walk through whatever comes next together."

"I trust Gott's plan. I hope and pray I can give you your heart's desire."

"My heart's desire is you."

How could a woman argue with that? Cassie didn't. Instead, she rewarded Mason with another kiss, slow and sweet. Then she backed away. "You know you still need time to adjust to life as a Plain man."

"Nee, I don't."

"Mason."

His kiss sent a shower of streaking lights like sparklers in the dark through her. He leaned back and smiled. "How long will you make me wait?"

Cassie drew a long breath. Waiting would be hard. "We'll know when it's right."

Mason nodded. "We'll talk to Bryan when the time is right."

Hand in hand, they walked back to the house that one day would be their home.

CHAPTER 40

Leftover wedding cake tasted every bit as good as it did the day it was cut. It was wedding cake, after all. It tasted like hope, love, and anticipation. Mason settled into the rocking chair by the fireplace. Job and Cassie shared the couch, Tater snoring on the piece rug at their feet. They were so busy eating, no one bothered to say much. Carrot spice cake with cream cheese frosting needed no discussion. The January wind whistled. The windows rattled. The smell of wood burning mingled with the mouthwatering scent of cinnamon rolls baking. The crackle and pop of the fire lulled Mason into a sleepy contentment.

"The kinner will be upset when they realize we ate cake without them." Job didn't seem too perturbed at the idea. "You might need another piece to fortify yourself before you brave the schnee to fetch them from schul. If this keeps up, they may get a schnee day tomorrow."

"A person really can't eat too much cake, can he?" Cassie licked frosting from her fork and held it up as if examining it for any remaining sweetness. "They won't care how much we ate once they realize we left enough for each of them to have a snack while they do their homework."

"To think you were sure one German chocolate and one red velvet cake would be enough. People around here do like their cake." Mason stood and stretched. "I reckon I'd better head out. Jennie always chews me out if I'm late."

Everything about the wedding the week before Christmas had been perfect. The Keim relatives from Garnett and Jamesport came. Caleb and his family attended. Cassie's family from Chetopa made the trek. Perry showed up with a woman he introduced as his wife and her two children. He seemed as happy as Mason had ever seen him. Even Mrs. Blanchard had attended. She sat between Kathy and Jennie and beamed with pride the entire time.

Only one more person was needed to make the day complete—Bobby.

But Mason's memories all centered around his bride in her homemade blue dress, her deep dimples on display, hand warm in his as they sat at the reception *eck* as man and wife after the ceremony.

"Now that Jennie's in kindergarten she thinks she rules the world." Cassie chuckled. "She's a smart one, that girl."

Tater unfurled his long body, stood, and barked.

"Settle down, you old coot." Only Job could get away with calling Tater an old coot since he was one too. "What is it?"

A *thunk, thunk* on the front door answered that question. They had company. "I'll get it." Mason rose, stretched, and went to welcome their guest. He opened the door and a gust of icy north wind blew through the house. Shivering, he focused on the man standing on the porch. *"Guder nammidaag."*

The man, who wore a dirty blue down jacket with the hood up, a gray scarf caked with icy snowflakes wrapped around his neck, black gloves, faded jeans, and a black ski cap pulled down on his forehead, said nothing.

An English man. "Can I help you?"

"It's me."

The voice, though low and hoarse, was familiar. Mason studied what little of the man's face was left uncovered. Blue eyes with dark lashes flecked with snow. A smattering of freckles across a blunt nose red from the cold. Chapped lips. A sharply drawn, baby-smooth chin.

"I didn't see your car. I didn't expect you to be here." The man's brittle laugh held disbelief. "I sure didn't think you'd be wearing those clothes."

Adrenaline blew through Mason. His whole body shook. His hand dropped from the door, too heavy for him to hold out. He cleared his throat and swallowed. "Bobby, is that you?"

"I wanted to come home, but when I went to the house, a lady with a baby answered the door." His hands fisted. He stuffed them in his pockets. "She said you didn't live there anymore."

"So you came home, here to this home." Mason fumbled for words. They ran in all directions, escaping him at every turn. "You came home."

"Who is it, Mason?" Job came up behind him. "Don't stand here with the door open. You're letting all the cold in and the heat out. Whoever it is, invite them in."

"It's Bobby."

A second later Job and Cassie both jostled Mason. Job tugged Mason aside. Cassie took Bobby's hand and led him into the living room.

"You're here, you're here!" Laughing and crying at the same time, she threw her arms around Bobby. "Welcome home!"

Bobby's arms came up and he returned the hug, but his gaze connected with Mason's over her shoulders. It was filled with uncertainty, with questions, with doubts. *Do you want me? Do you forgive me? Do I belong here? Will you love me? Will you even like me?*

"Praise Gott." An enormous smile plastered on his face, Job stood in the middle of the room as if he didn't know which way to go. "We prayed that you would come home and here you are."

"Where were you all this time—no, never mind, it doesn't matter." Mason edged closer. His heart beat again. His lungs filled with air. "You're here now. The kids will be so excited to see you. So much has happened."

He halted.

"Your grandma Dinah passed." Cassie finished Mason's thought. "Her diabetes was too much for her."

Bobby's shoulders hunched. He shook his head. "No, it can't be. I need to tell her I'm sorry I left. I'm sorry I didn't come back."

"She knows. Don't worry." His anguish tore at Mason's heart. "I know it's hard, but this is God's plan. We can't see how it's going to turn out, but it will turn out."

Wiping at his face, Bobby stepped closer to Mason. "When did you start talking about God?"

"I joined the faith."

"You're Amish?" Bobby squeaked. "A guy turns his back for six months and this happens."

Mason also found his father and more family. Found his faith. Found his true love. "I also got married."

"Good for you." Bobby pointed at Cassie. "It better have been you."

"It was. It is. We are." Cassie laughed. She laughed all the time now. "In December."

"Why are we standing in the middle of the room?" Job suddenly came to life. He flapped his arms. "Let the boy sit down.

Take his coat. Come on, Bobby, sit here by the fire. You must be frozen." Job grabbed a quilt from the back of the couch and held it out. "Cassie, get him some hot tea. He probably doesn't drink coffee."

"Coffee would be fine." Bobby took the quilt, but he laid it on the chair. Instead of sitting, he put his arms around Job's waist and hugged. "I'm sorry, Grandpa. I'm sorry I left. I'm sorry."

Job's hands hung in the air. His Adam's apple bobbed. The muscles in his jaw worked. He cleared his throat and returned the hug. "You're forgiven, Grandson. You're home now. All is forgotten."

Bobby backed away. He sniffed and wiped at his nose. "Coffee is good." He plopped into the chair and pulled the quilt up around his neck. "I walked from the highway. It feels like it's ten degrees with a wind chill of a hundred below. A truck driver gave me a ride from Wichita. He was a decent dude. He shared his two foot-long subs from the truck stop."

His grin stretching from ear to ear, Job grabbed his coat from the rack by the door. "I'll get the kinner. You stay here, Mason, and talk to your bruder."

Before Mason could respond, Job opened the door and disappeared into the blowing snow.

"Do you want to tell us where you've been?" Mason hesitated. "You don't have to. It doesn't matter."

"Here and there. I spent some nights in an abandoned house with a bunch of crack dudes. That was scary. And cold. I've never been so cold. They started a fire in a trash barrel, but somebody called the cops and we all had to scatter. But then a guy I knew from school let me sleep on his dad's couch. I got a job sacking groceries and stocking shelves."

"Sounds tough."

"I knew I wanted to come home almost right away, but I couldn't. I felt so stupid. I was too embarrassed."

"Don't be. But I can understand why you'd have those feelings, believe me."

"I'm sorry about the money I stole. I'll pay you back."

"We'll talk about it later."

"So you all live here now, together?" Bobby's gaze flitted around the room. "One big happy family."

"Jah. Yes." Mason waited for Cassie to hand Bobby the coffee. He cupped his hands around the mug and lifted it close to his lips but didn't drink, as if warming his face. Mason swallowed tears of happiness and unmitigated relief. His family was back together. "I was renting a house in Yoder, but when Cassie and I got married, I moved in here. Job needed taking care of, too, even though he doesn't admit it. We're a family. You're part of that family."

Bobby's face crumpled. He hiccupped a sob. "Good to know."

"Don't cry. You're home." Mason squeezed Cassie closer. Whether God decided they should have their own babies growing up in this house remained an unknown. Many more Keim children would be a godsend. Either way, the rooms in their home would be filled to the brim with love. "We all are."

Acknowledgments

When I sat down to write *Love's Dwelling*, my thoughts turned immediately to the research trip I took to Yoder, Kansas, a few years ago. That day my sister Debby Gfeller, ten months my senior, drove us from north central Kansas south to Yoder, between Hutchinson and Wichita. My mother, Janice Lyne, and my baby sister (nine years my junior), Pam Suneson, came along. It was the first time in years the Lyne women had all been together. We stopped in Salina at the Sam's to see a display that included one of my books. Then we drove into Yoder and ate at the Carriage Crossing Restaurant and Bakery. Afterward we browsed in the gift shop. We coveted beautiful quilts in the furniture store. We had a wonderful time because we were together. Those family ties are what the Amish Blessings series is about. Families blend together in many different ways. The recipe varies, but the result should always be the same—unconditional love.

My thanks to the Lyne women for coming on this journey with me.

I owe an enormous debt of gratitude to my HCCP editor Becky Monds. With the pandemic and the accompanying quarantine, I found myself floundering. The early drafts of *Love's Dwelling* were a hot mess. Becky, in her infinite kindness, described it as more of a lukewarm mess. But she didn't waver. I turned it in early and she jumped in to help me shape and smooth the rough diamond into a story I hope readers will find worthy of their time. Becky's patience, kindness, and stellar editing skills helped me move past my distracted dismay to a place where I could write again.

Not to sound like a broken record (for those of you who know what a record is!), I must again thank Julee Schwarzburg for nudging me to shape up and stop with the lazy word repetition. I promise to do better next time.

I couldn't do this without my husband, Tim. Thank you for taking care of me and putting up with me.

Readers, thank you for reading my books. This wouldn't be much fun if it weren't for you! I hope these stories continue to entertain and bless you.

Finally, I must thank my heavenly Father from whom all blessings flow. Thank You for giving me so much more than I deserve.

DISCUSSION QUESTIONS

1. Georgia chose to leave her Amish family and strike out for the big city with her brother rather than marrying the father of her unborn baby. What reasons might she have had for doing this? Do you think she made the right decision? Why or why not?

2. Job and Dinah felt responsible for Georgia's decision to leave the faith after she'd been baptized. Job particularly feels his actions led to her flight. Do you think he bears responsibility for her decision? Why or why not?

3. Caleb chose not to go after Georgia. He decided to honor her decision to leave. Did he make the right choice? If you were in his shoes, what would you do? Why?

4. Georgia chose not to tell her children about her roots in the Amish community and faith. Why do you think that is?

5. Even though she never shared her background with her children, Georgia decided they should be brought up by her Amish parents. Why do you think she made that decision? Do you think it was fair to the children? To Mason? Why or why not?

6. Mason wavers between wanting the children to stay with him and believing they would be better off with his grandparents. Which one do you think is the better option? Why?

7. If you found yourself in Bobby's or Kathy's shoes, how would you feel? Would you want to become Amish? Would

you give up the trappings of the mainstream world? Could you? Explain.

8. Cassie falls in love with Mason even though she knows she can never be with him unless he becomes Amish. She does her best not to influence his decision. Could you have done the same in her situation? Why or why not?

9. Mason and his siblings had just found their grandmother, and then she passed away only a short time after their mother died. Would such a hard loss affect your faith? How would you explain these trials to someone who isn't a Christian or is thinking of becoming a Christian?

10. How would you articulate the overarching theme of *Love's Dwelling*? What is this story really about? Explain.

About the Author

Kelly Irvin is a bestselling, award-winning author of almost thirty novels and stories. A retired public relations professional, Kelly lives with her husband, Tim, in San Antonio. They have two children, three grandchildren, and two ornery cats.

. . .

Visit her online at KellyIrvin.com
Instagram: @kelly_irvin
Facebook: @Kelly.Irvin.Author
Twitter: @Kelly_S_Irvin